Uncertain Battles

Kinship Covenant
Book Two

Robert Spitznagel

DEDICATION

*To Carolyn, Jeremy and Sharissa, Heather, Daniel
and Jordan, Elaine, David, and Terry
Then to my grandchildren: Shad, Paige, Mackenzie,
Skyra, River, Asher, Joselynn and Kyle.
Also to my great-grandchildren: Veyda, Nova, and Wesley.
And to those who desire God's possibilities.*

Acknowledgments

Thank you to my mother Elaine, my coworker Kathy, and my prayer warrior and friend Robin. You encouraged me to put my stories in writing.

Thank you to my wife and children, who are behind me in this endeavor, but think I am a little crazy. They could be right.

Special thanks to Skyra, who lovingly drew the Constellation on the back cover. It means the world to have my granddaughter's art on my book cover.

My editors Nadia and Tiffany are amazing. Their experience and knowledge have expanded my horizons in storytelling.

Most importantly, I want to thank God, who put the stories in my head.

No discipline seems pleasant at the time, but painful. Later on, however, it produces a harvest of righteousness and peace for those who have been trained by it.

—Hebrews 12:11

INTRODUCTION

On the island of Oahu, Hawaii, at an estate about thirty miles from Honolulu, two sets of friends were reunited. The men were once called Musketeers and the women were known as princesses. Benjamin Bickles, a six-foot, six-inch tall, well-fit man with straight brown hair, dominant brown hazel eyes, a patrician nose, and almost olive skin tone stood by Michael Roberts. He stood as tall and fit as Ben, with wavy blond hair and blue eyes. They were getting reacquainted, as were their wives.

Allison Bickles, maiden name of Ver Hoeven, was a woman who stood six feet tall. She had long wavy black hair and almost black eyes that hailed from her Vietnamese ancestry. She joined Carrie Roberts, as tall and statuesque as her friend, sporting a flaming red mane of long wavy hair, pale skin and green eyes. The woman sat next to their husbands, enjoying each other's company as well. Both women were quite pregnant. The topic of conversation turned to the reason why they had been separated these many years.

"Ben, my friend. What happened to you?" Michael asked, with a calming tone in his voice.

"That is a strange tale to tell," Ben said without looking away from the five children who called him father. "And you deserve to hear it."

"Should we wait to tell Derrick and Susan at the same time?" Michael replied. "Have you heard from them?"

"No, we haven't talked to them yet. And no, we won't wait to see them before we tell you what happened to us during the last sixteen years. I will get acquainted with my children I didn't know existed first. And then tell you everything. To be truthful, my brother, it has been a bit of hell."

Ben began to explain the circumstances from sixteen years ago that put Allison and him in the situation they were in at this time. "It began when we were on the cruise ship during our senior year of high school when we received the order to return to our rooms because of the typhoon that turned on us. You told Derrick, Susan, Allison and me to go on ahead. I thought you were going to recover Carrie before you returned to the room." A puzzled look came across his face. "By the way, what really happened to you two that night?"

The children belonging to the two couples gathered around to hear the story about their parents, some wondering how they are all connected.

Michael explained the situation. "Well, you see..."

MICHAEL AND CARRIE LOST

As he was scanning the room to help those struggling to leave, Michael noticed Marc Richards and Darrin Johnson behind the DJ's station. They seemed to be forcing Carrie Samuels through the door at the other side of the ballroom. Michael did not like the look of that and told his friends he would catch up with them. His friends, Derrick and Ben, who were concerned with helping Susan and Allison, agreed.

Michael took off running to try and catch up with Carrie. He came around a corner and saw the three of them at the stern[1] of the ship. Carrie was using all her defensive training and was making a good show of herself, but Michael noticed they were dangerously close to the rail.

Michael knew what was about to happen. He found an inflatable raft and, on the run, headed to the trio, constantly praying he would catch her before she hit the water.

Because of the noise of the storm and the blackness that surrounded the ship, Darrin and Marc did not notice him running at them. They had Carrie leaning over the rail so far, they couldn't stop her from going overboard. At that moment, something hit the two of them so hard

---

1 The stern is the rear of the ship.

that they hit the rail with their faces, causing them to lose a couple of teeth and start to bleed. They became a little dazed, but didn't see who or what it was that hit them.

Michael leaped past them as Carrie went over, smashed their heads against the rail as he used them for leverage and momentum. He caught her immediately with his right arm which was also carrying the raft, and maneuvered himself so that he would hit the water first. Immediately, with his left hand, he pulled the cord that inflated the raft without letting go of her. When they surfaced, they were in a seemingly calm area of the ship's wake and he was able to heave her into the raft. He soon followed. When she could breathe, she took some deep breaths. Then Michael tied both of them to the raft, knowing from experience that they were going to be tossed into the water quite a few times before this ride was over.

* * * *

On the ship, Musketeers Ben Bickles and Derrick Henderson, were helping Allison and Susan Schulte, the third Princess, back to their state rooms as per the order from the ship's captain. The girls had removed their four-inch-heeled pumps because the ship was rocking and rolling hard because of the typhoon.

They bounced around the hallway, helping other classmates to get to their rooms. Finally, they arrived at the doors of the boys' room, and next door, the girls' room.

"I think you would be safer with us," Ben said as they slammed into the wall. "At least I would be more at ease if I knew that you were actually safe."

"I agree." Derrick chimed in. "We can huddle together on the floor between the beds. When Michael and Carrie return, they can join us."

"You know, Ally, I am inclined to agree with them. We have always felt safest when we are around our Musketeers," Susan admitted.

Allison nodded as, once again, they were bounced off the wall. The ship rocked and rolled with the movement of the waves. "I think we are going to

sport some fancy bruises from the banging around
we are going through," she said.

Susan chuckled as she said, "I believe you hit the
nail on the head." Allison gave a short giggle
in response.

"Don't you mean on the thighs, butts, arms, backs,
and bellies?" said Susan as they were tossed again.

"Don't forget the shins," was all Allison could say
before they were all knocked to the floor.

After a few attempts, Ben was able to open the
door and all four dove into the room. They
crawled to a place between the beds and rested
for a few moments.

"Anybody hurt?" was always Allison's first response
when the opportunity to be injured occurred.

"I'm good," Ben said.

"Same here," Susan lied.

"I think my back is broken. I am going to die,"
Joked Derrick.

Allison slapped him on his knee. "You jerk. That's
Michael's line." She started laughing and the
other three joined her. "At least we are not getting
bounced around as bad here."

THE CALM THROUGH THE STORM

"Well, since we are in this position," Derrick said,
"how about Ben and I do what we always do when
we are this close to you—break out the combs and
comb your hair? Should be soothing time tonight
as the storm blows."

Susan looked at Allison and, together, they
shrugged their shoulders and agreed. Besides,
they loved having their Musketeers combing their
hair. Always made for a nice, intimate evening.

"Now is as good a time as any." Susan said as she turned herself around and sat between Derrick's legs. Allison turned to face Susan and Ben settled behind her, straddling his legs around her. The girls produced combs from their little shoulder bags and the boys commenced combing. Derrick dove onto Susan's blonde tresses and Ben started on Allison's black waves. Their hair was long and reached just below their waists.

The only sounds for several minutes were the creaking of the ship and the winds of the storm outside.

Finally, Derrick stopped and looked at the door. "One would think Michael and Carrie would be here by now." Ben and Allison noted the worry on Derrick and Susan's faces. Derrick and Susan couldn't miss the same on their friends. All looked at the door.

"Maybe he caught up with Darrin and Marc and got into a scuffle with them trying to retrieve her," thought Allison aloud.

"You know full well that those two wouldn't last two seconds against Michael. Especially if they tried to keep Carrie from him. No, I think he has rescued her, and they are hiding someplace safe until the storm passes." Susan stated. She was not as certain as her voice on the matter.

"We need to give them to God," Ben said as they all held hands and prayed for their friend's safety.

There was no more talking after they finished praying and returned to combing. Allison closed her eyes and was soon asleep, leaning her back against Ben, who was leaning sideways against the bed. Derrick and Susan were in a similar position. The rocking and pitching of the ship did not disturb their slumber. Through the night the storm passed on.

BANG, BANG, BANG came the sounds from the door. Ben tried to stand up, but a beautiful girl was leaning against him. Allison moved to let Ben get up and noticed the grimace he made as he tried to move.

"Maybe falling asleep in that position wasn't a good idea," he said as he stumbled, trying to get his body to waken up. Allison laughed. Ben struggled as he tried to get his numb legs and back to properly align. He stopped as he reached the chest of drawers and hung on until the blood and nerves started to flow. The tingling feeling that was moving up and down his legs told him he was still alive.

BANG, BANG, BANG. "ANYBODY IN HERE!" came a voice recognized to be the orchestra director turned chaperone, Mrs. Novotny.

"Yes," Ben called back. "On my way. Just a minute!" Derrick was trying to stand up and had the same issues as Ben. Susan and Allison were beside themselves to see their usually well balanced Musketeers stumble around as if they never learned to walk.

Ben opened the door and faced Mrs. Novotny and two others, Raphael Sanchez and Roseta Gonzalez, the bar tender and waitress from last night's ballroom dance.

Mrs. Novotny spoke first. "Who is there with you?"

"Derrick, Allison, and Susan."

"Michael and Carrie not with you?"

"No. We are hoping they found a safe place to hole up until the storm passed."

"Would they be in the girls' room?" she asked with a bit of an accusatory tone.

"I don't know."

"I will check, ma'am," Allison said as she hurriedly passed by to unlock the door to her room.

They all ran into the room calling Michael and Carrie's names. There was no response.

From down the hall some shouting could be heard.

"What the hell is all this racket?" The voice belonged to Darrin Johnson.

Ben and Derrick were the first to exit the room and face Darrin.

"Carrie with you?" Allison asked because she was right behind Derrick. The rest filed out right after.

Everyone instantly noticed the right side of Marc's face and the left side of Darrin's had collided with something. Each had a swollen eye and bruised lips along with a few missing teeth.

Must have been a rough night! Ben thought.

"No. Right after we left the ballroom, Michael grabbed Carrie and ran off in the opposite direction. To the rear of the ship." Then a bit offhandedly, he said, "Not very smart as they would have to go outside in this storm."

"That is a lie!" Roseta burst out. "The big blond man ran out the door right behind you. The rear door of the ballroom!"

"That is true. I saw the same thing," added Raphael.

Darrin saw the blood boil in Ben and Derrick's faces. "The main thing here is Michael grabbed Carrie from us. We were trying to get her to a safe place. And he wasn't very nice about it." Darrin said, pointing to the bruises around his eyes and nose and the cuts along his forehead. Marc was sporting the same injuries.

"If Michael had been forceful with protecting Carrie, you wouldn't be able to speak!" Derrick admitted.

"Yeah. Well. He did. And we don't know where they are." Darrin rubbed his forehead. "And now I don't care where they are. I hope they got washed overboard and drowned!"

Ben took a step before Allison intercepted him. "Ben. Stop. I want to kill him, too. But we have no proof one way or the other. Let's just find them and sort this out later." Ben glared at her and she just looked back at him. He should have known that she had never backed down from him when his anger was about to get the best of him.

"Alright," Ben said. He took a couple of breaths. "You are right." Then he looked at Darrin. "*We* will find them. And when *we* do," he pointed his finger straight at Darrin, "*we* will get to the bottom of this. And when *we* find your lies—"

"We will make everything right," Derrick interrupted. He, along with Allison, Susan, and Ben went back to the boys' room. Ben submitting to Allison trying to turn him around and away from the confrontation.

Mrs. Novotny scolded Darrin. "You had better not be lying. Either of you."

She turned to check on other students and didn't see the wink Darrin gave Roseta. It sent chills up Roseta's spine and she went running away in fear. Only Raphael, who remained standing in the hall, knew Roseta was right to run.

THE PORT INVESTIGATION

Raphael Sanchez contacted his supervisor, who informed the first officer, who informed the ship's captain that they had two passengers unaccounted for. The captain ordered a ship wide search, and when it was complete, he did not like the result he was given. He called the authorities in American Samoa with the news and was ordered to the dock in Pago Pago, where the inquiry would be held.

As the ship arrived, the pier crowded with law enforcement and military personnel. Upon docking, the personnel swarmed the ship. Chaperones and students were ushered into the ballroom where an interrogation began in earnest. Investigators from the revamped FBI found a small piece of orange cloth caught on the edge of the stern of the ship. Raphael recommended that Darrin and Marc be questioned, which they were, for a few hours. Unfortunately, because there was no proof of their falsehood, the interrogators let them go.

The Musketeers and Princesses were beyond themselves with anger at Darrin and Marc's release and sorrow at the possibility of Michael and Carrie's possible demise. Harry and Patrice Henderson, Derrick's parents and volunteer chaperones, sent word to the families back at home about the situation. Troy and Kristy, Michael's parents, and Brad and Petra, Carrie's parents, were immediately in shock and tried to console each other over the news. However, when they had calmed down, Kristy said something that made the others reflect.

"I have prayed for our children and God has given me peace that our children are not dead," she said. "It is not wishful thinking or false hope. I am at peace." The others admitted the same feelings of comfort. They held on to that impression on the lives of their children for sixteen years.

While this was happening, authorities launched a large search and rescue operation. They followed the path of the storm but found no traces of the missing teens. Their final determination was that Michael and Carrie were, somehow, lost at sea having, again somehow, fallen off the ship into the storm where there was no probability of survival.

"Probability, my butt," Derrick said. He was not being successful at being calm as they heard the 'final determination.' "You know what Michael would say about that?" Trying to mimic Michael's voice" he quoted, "'100 percent improbability equals 100 percent possibility.' God knows, if anyone can help Carrie survive the storm on the ocean, it would be Michael."

"You mean because he survived the hurricane in the Atlantic?" Susan asked

"Yes. It was after that incident that Michael solidified the equation. He figured things out on his first survival expedition in Alaska. I have no doubt whatsoever that Darrin and Marc are at the center of this. But I can't prove it, which is so frustrating!"

Ben closed the distance between him and Derrick and placed his hand on Derrick's shoulder. "I am as frustrated and angry as you," he told him. "But, we have yet to do the one thing we should have done first."

"Yeah, What's that?" Derrick replied, still highly agitated.

"Pray, brother," Ben said softly. "Pray."

Derrick was stunned as he realized Ben was right. Allison and Susan joined them in holding hands and kneeling as they started to pray. Individually, at first, then all at the same time. The door to the hotel room where they were staying during the investigation was still open and several classmates had stopped to listen to the discussion. Raphael and Mrs. Novotny also listened. All the observers knelt where they were when the prayers started.

Darrin and Marc went back to their room where Darrin started searching for information about one tiny waitress, Roseta Gonzalez.

Nobody got the feeling from God that their friends were dead.

"Someday, they will come to us," said Allison with more bravado than she really felt.

"Someday," they echoed.

Where's the Orchestra?

Classes had recommenced back at the school, and everybody went back to some semblance of normalcy, except those who had been on the cruise.

Those who went returned three weeks late because of the investigation. Ben, Allison and Susan's emotions caught up quickly when they were back on campus, whereas Derrick's emotions took longer to sort out, about an extra month. He struggled mightily with the loss of his friends. Michael and Carrie were in the back of their minds.

Susan made it her responsibility to console Derrick without being condescending, while Allison had her hands full with Ben. This was one time she could not get him to release his anger towards Darrin and Marc. Both girls kept each other posted on their progress with their respective Musketeer.

The tension in the school could be felt by everybody, from freshman to seniors, teachers, and even the administration. Opponents from other high schools' athletic activities felt something strange coming from the students at Washington High School, too.

Darrin and Marc did everything they could to avoid any contact with the remaining Musketeers and Princesses. Yet inwardly, Darrin was pleased with himself for starting to separate the

Musketeers and Princesses. *Michael and Carrie are gone for good*, he thought. *Ben, Derrick, Allison, or Susan will be next, not to forget Robert Jefferson, that big Black idiot.*

Three months later, there was still no word about the whereabouts of Michael and Carrie. The orchestra was preparing for their final concert, setting up the auditorium stage for the event. All the musicians were present. Ben and Robert were setting up the cello section. Allison made sure clarinets were positioned appropriately. The director, Mrs. Novotny, wanted to have one last rehearsal before she would let them go. Unfortunately, while everybody was warming up, she was called to the band room to solve an issue there. Robert was called to the principal's office for another matter.

"They caught you again, Robert, you bad boy," teased Ben as he put the last cello player's chair in place.

"You must have told on me," Robert joked back, mockingly wagging a finger at Ben. "I told you that it was a secret."

Quite some time later, Robert, as he left the principal's office, noticed Darrin Johnson and Marc Richards coming to the office. Robert stopped and turned to the principal and, dripping with sarcasm, said, "Itchy and scratchy are here." He turned, heading back to the auditorium. Upon entering the stage, he saw Mrs. Novotny as she entered from the side doorway at the same time.

They both saw an unbelievable sight.

Instruments were scattered on the floor with the chairs in disarray, and no musicians were present.

At first, they thought it was a practical joke. So, they searched the auditorium and found nobody. *Curious thing,* thought Robert. *The instruments are strewn about, all over the stage, on the floor, and in front of the first row of seats. They look like they were dropped or kicked. What happened?* He noticed a cello laying on its strings. When he got closer and looked it over, he found the bridge was broken.

"Mrs. Novotny," Robert called out. "Something is not right. This is Ben's cello and it's broken. He treats this cello with the utmost of respect." He pointed to the broken bridge. "Ben would never let this happen."

Mrs. Novotny walked over to where Robert was and inspected the cello. "You are right," she said as she scanned the rest of the room. "Something is not right indeed." She spun around, facing her student with the look of shock and fear. "Robert, go to the principal's office and let them know what has happened. I will check in the orchestra room. GO!"

They took off in opposite directions. Robert ran to the school's main office, getting called out by a couple of teachers for running in the halls. He paid them no mind, blasting past the secretary and into the principal's office. He interrupted what seemed to be cordial conversation between the principal, Darrin, and Marc. If he were a dog, his hackles would have been standing tall. *Have these two been here the whole time?* Robert immediately reported the situation pertaining to the missing students. He caught the quick glance Darrin and Marc made with each other, who seemed, for a second, to be pleased with the report. They immediately got up and left.

Robert felt in the pit of his stomach that those two were somehow involved. The principal seemed to be nonchalant about Robert's excitement. "Now let's calm down," he said. "They are more than likely playing a prank on you and Mrs. Novotny. I will make an announcement and get the pranksters back to the auditorium."

Robert couldn't believe his ears. *He's not taking this seriously at all!* He stormed out of the office and ran back down the halls, heading to where he knew Derrick was. He got called out by the same teachers as before. This time, he stopped and explained the situation to them. The teachers tore off to the auditorium, where they found Mrs. Novotny sitting in a chair crying despondently. They had also heard the message over the intercom from the principal and couldn't believe their ears because of what they were seeing at that moment.

Mrs. Novotny looked up when they neared her. "They are not playing a prank," she sobbed. "They are missing. And I believe they had no choice."

The teacher closest to her, Mr. Zephyr, a short, slender (bordering on skinny) English teacher who had been teaching for ten years, leaned over to hug Mrs. Novotny, who was beloved by most of the school. The other teacher, Mrs. McGillicuddy, whose body still showed her athletic background and average height, surveyed the stage and came to the same conclusion. "She's right," she said to Mr. Zephyr. "The students wouldn't do that to her. They love her. I will make sure the authorities are called." She ran out to tell the principal to call the police. Much to her surprise, the principal denied the need for such a call. A heated argument ensued between Ms. McGillicuddy, who had been teaching Dakota history for twenty-five years, and the principal. In the process, the principal fired the teacher for insubordination. Mrs. McGillicuddy was shocked that he was acting so stupid and looked to the secretary. As the secretary was about to make the call to the police, the principal hung up the phone and fired her as well.

The phone rang and the principal answered it instead of the secretary.

"This is the 911 call center. We saw that an emergency call originated from your position. Do you still have an emergency?"

The principal looked at the two people he just fired. "Yes," he said. "We have two people who are trespassing and refuse to leave. We could use your help in this matter." He scowled at the two ladies.

"Yes, sir. Units are on their way. Are they a potential violent hazard?"

"No. not at this time," he replied with a smirk. "Thank you."

SHERLOCK HOLMES WOULD BE PROUD

At the end of the principal's announcement about the orchestra, Derrick bolted from the classroom and ran smack into Robert. Such a collision would have sent less solid people to the hospital. Instead, these two only backed up a step. Like their friends, Derrick and Robert stood six feet, six inches tall and were solidly built, honed to perfection by the years of training their fathers put them through.

"What's the hurry, Musketeer?" Derrick asked as soon as he caught his breath.

"Everybody in the orchestra is gone," Robert said. "I was called to the office. When I got back, they were all gone." Robert waved a finger in front of Derrick's face. "It was not a prank! Something's wrong!"

At that they ran towards the auditorium with Robert giving a more complete report on the way. Unbeknownst to them, Susan was twenty yards behind them. She called for them to wait for her. They blasted their way through the doors and stopped immediately. Mrs. Novotny was still inconsolable, and Mr. Zephyr just looked around, still trying to calm the orchestra director.

As Susan entered, she noticed Derrick was already in tracking mode. So, she walked up to Robert. "What happened?" Robert told his story again. "Oh, no! Ben and Allison are in the orchestra!"

Derrick spun around and glared at Susan. "There is no call to worry yet. Let me see what I can find to tell the story here." Susan was astounded, having never seen Derrick in tracking mode.

Derrick silently prayed, *Lord, guide my eyes.* He pointed to the scuff marks that entered and exited through the doors. He went and stood where the conductor's podium would be and let his eyes take one slow sweep of the area. Instruments and chairs were scattered all over in a seemingly random manner. However, there were signs that not all was random. There seemed to be an isle made towards the percussion area. Derrick looked intently at the floor and the scuff marks that were barely visible and started to see a pattern. In the tuba section, He pointed to some scratches on the floor.

"Here," he said to anybody close by. "This is where it took four men to remove Tommy Dorsey. See? These four marks are the same but pointing in different directions." He walked over to the percussion section. "This is where he was taken."

Robert was the only one close to Derrick. "Four men?" he asked, then paused for a second. Derrick let him work it out. "Tommy was three hundred fifty pounds. No wonder it took four."

Derrick nodded. Then he spied something under one of the trombones. Using the back of his hand, He lifted the instrument just enough so he and Robert would see the item. "A tranquilizer dart." He thought he had said it quietly, but Mr. Zephyr heard and perked up.

"What?" he said with astonishment. "Did you say a tranquilizer dart? That would mean they were drugged and kidnapped. But where are they?"

"I have my suspicions, Mr. Zephyr. I believe we will have to look behind the drums." Derrick said. He stopped and sniffed the air. "Whatever chemical was used to knock them out caused someone to urinate or defecate." Looking at Robert with determination, Derrick said, "Ben had to be the first to be struck down. You know full well he would have fought something fierce otherwise." Robert could only nod in agreement. "This was well planned out and masterfully executed. Robert, we have someone worse than Judas in this school."

"How so?"

"Someone had to know about Ben. Someone had to know about the scheduling. I think it was a fluke that you were called out at that time. Otherwise, you would be gone as well." Once again, all Robert could do was nod.

Derrick immediately strode off behind the drums and the curtain, heading directly for the doors to the delivery dock. He studied the doorway and pointed out more scuffing that matched the four men carrying Tommy Dorsey. If Derrick hadn't pointed them out, it was more than likely those marks would not have been seen because they were so light and small.

"How can you see those marks?" Susan said, astonished at Derrick's ability.

"I utilize a common theme that is taught in the Sherlock Holmes stories. 'Observe what others only see.' Look closer." He pointed to the floor where both Robert and Susan saw only the floor. "This tiny scratch matches these over here." He pointed to an area a few feet from the first. They still didn't see anything. "Look closer."

Robert did and saw a tiny scratch. Then he looked at the other spots and finally saw what Derrick saw. "I see them!" He quietly exclaimed. "Why aren't they more pronounced and obvious?"

"Whoever did this had some kind of covering over their shoes to hide their markings." Derrick explained. Then quietly to himself, "This was well planned out."

Susan was too scared to ask the obvious question. *Were they kidnapped?*

Derrick turned around and walked right past Robert and Susan. He headed straight to the office, with Robert and Susan in lock step behind him. He reached the office at the same time the secretary and Mrs. McGillicuddy were being handcuffed and taken to the police cars.

Derrick called out to the officers and asked them why they were arresting those two and not looking for the students who had been kidnapped. The officers were confused about the question.

"The entire orchestra except for Robert and Mrs. Novotny have been kidnapped," Derrick told them. Then as he caught on to the situation, he glowered at the principal. "You had these two arrested instead of notifying the police of the missing students? You bastard!" He grabbed the principal by his shirt and shoved him into a chair.

The police were about to jump on Derrick when Robert intervened. "Officers!" he called out. I initially reported the situation to the principal. He simply denied everything and said it was a prank. You have been called for the wrong reason. Derrick can show the evidence to prove the situation."

Derrick led the officers to the stage and guided them along the scuffing to the place where he showed them how a truck could be seen to recently have been there. The police released the secretary and Mrs. McGillicuddy, then arrested the principal for filing a false report.

As they were escorting the principal to their
cruisers, Derrick just stood as though stunned.
"Ben and Allison." Susan said, moving up to him
as tears started to flood her eyes. She tried to wrap
her arms around his left arm, but he shrugged
her off. He glared at her and Robert and then ran
away. After that, he didn't talk to either of them
for over two years. Neither did he pray during
that time.

Susan and Robert were both stunned by Derrick's
actions. Susan's heart sank as her Musketeer, the
one she loved the most, bolted from her when she
needed his comfort. Robert was a good friend, but
the sting of Derrick's actions would hurt her for
several years.

A major search and blockade came up empty.
Once again, the school and the city were in shock.

Trucks and airports were investigated. One
Cargo plane left Sioux Falls about an hour
after the discovery by Robert and Mrs. Novotny.
Its flight plan was planned for arrival in San
Diego, California that evening. But the plane
never arrived.

The plane never arrived and it was determined that the transponder was turned off. Radar lost the aircraft somewhere over Colorado and an aerial search showed no crash site.

They were gone!

A Champion is Named

Most families and friends in Sioux Falls prayed constantly. Some cursed God. Others were totally numb. It would be a long time before any answers were understood.

The orchestra students woke up slowly and found themselves in the mezzanine of a large, arena-sized building, similar in nature to a large aircraft hangar. Ben was the first to awaken, largely because of the physical regimen which helped him metabolize the sleeping agent that hit him back at the school. As he wiped his forehead and face, he scanned his surroundings, noticing his classmates lying all over the floor. He stood up and immediately held his head when the headache worsened for a few seconds. As the headache slowly died away, he looked for Allison. She lay still several yards away from him, and Ben went over to verify that she was still breathing. She was, much to his relief. He heard a groan behind him and noticed Tommy Dorsey starting to wake up. *Because of his obesity, if all were given the same dosage, it would make sense he would wake up sooner than most,* Ben thought.

Tommy held his head as the waves of a headache washed over him. As he was able to open his eyes, he saw Ben walking towards him to check on him. He was relieved it was Ben.

"How are you feeling, Tommy?"

"I feel like you kicked me in the head and knocked me out," Tommy replied. He started to laugh at his own joke, but immediately regretted it when his head throbbed. "Ben? Don't do that again, Ok?"

Ben smiled, knowing Tommy was going to be ok since he was trying to joke about their situation,

then he laid his hand on his friend's chest. "Ok. I
will try." They both laughed and Tommy held his
head again while Ben helped him to his feet.

"Ben?" came a small voice to his right. He looked
over and saw Teresa Buchannon, junior clarinetist,
starting to move. Next to her was a smaller girl,
Roberta Salazar, freshman violinist.

Teresa started, "What happened—"

"—and where are we?" interrupted Roberta. Both
girls laid back down to let their heads settle down.

"At this point, I don't know is the only answer I
can give." Ben was just as puzzled as they were,
which set his anger mode in first gear.

"Ben?" a voice he knew the best called out to him.
Allison had finally awakened. She ignored her
headache and stood up, looking straight at Ben.
"How are the others?" she asked as more and more
of the group were waking up. Without waiting
for a response, she went around the other girls
to be sure they were doing good in spite of the
weakening headaches. Ben did the same with the

boys. After she verified that everybody was alive and well, all things considered, she ran to Ben, and they held on to each other tightly. They checked one another, asking if anyone knew where they were. Nobody knew a thing except they all had some kind of dart hit them before they passed out. Most of the students huddled around Ben, who was running his fingers through his straight brown hair. All of them knew Ben was the strongest and could be relied upon to protect them. He was looking around taking in their new surroundings. Unlike everyone else, Ben was not afraid. He was pissed! Allison's fear was not as strong as her other classmates,' mostly because she had Ben.

There was only one wall attached to their position, while the other three sides were bound by a ten-foot-high fence. This fence prevented the occupants from falling three stories to the main floor below. In the middle of the wall was a lone door. Beside the door, on the left, was one toilet and sink with a rusted faucet. Next to the sink was a long table with nothing on it. There was no other furniture in their area. The surrounding fence was horizontal for two feet and then straight up ten feet. This was to allow those in the higher position to look down, which most did. They saw directly into the top of what looked like a large apartment with a wide-open area that had viewing stands on the opposite wall. All available windows were painted over. The students had no clue as to where they were and some of them started to panic while others seemed frozen in fear.

Eventually, Roberta ran to Tommy and hugged him with her tiny arms. They couldn't wrap around more than half of his body. It was well known to the orchestra members that she and Tommy were more than friends. They were an odd couple, but everybody liked them. Tommy wrapped his arms around her, and she almost disappeared into his embrace.

Her flowered blouse and orange skirt accented her well and hid her early pubescent body. "Why did I have to wear a short skirt today?" Roberta moaned. She was feeling quite vulnerable and sought protection and comfort from her "teddy bear." Tommy wrapped his arms around her and she almost disappeared in his embrace. They were the odd couple but everybody loved them.

"I am not complaining about your skirt," he said, chuckling.

She smiled, grateful for his humor. "Pervert!"

After a couple of hours mingling around and finding no escape, five men entered the room and told everybody to separate. They wore black military cargo pants, black long-sleeved shirts, black berets, shiny black boots, Each man, three Asian and two South American, had pistols strapped to each leg. They also carried either an M-16 or AK-47 military rifle. The men pushed the boys to the left and the girls to the right. The weapons they brandished meant no disobedience. One of the men grabbed Allison and tried to remove her from Ben. He hit her in the ribs with his rifle and immediately pointed it at Ben. One of the other men grabbed her by her hair and dragged her to the other girls. Assured that Ben wouldn't do anything, they went over to the girls and started to grope them.

Ben wasn't having it!

He attacked them so quickly that the men had no chance to respond. The nearest man to Ben noticed the girls were looking past him and he turned around in time to have the heel of Ben's boot hit him across the bridge of his nose, causing the bone to stab into his brain. The next man had no time to respond as Ben's fist slammed into the man's throat, crushing his esophagus. Two down. The third man was about to bring his rifle to bear on Ben when his right knee was shattered by Ben's kick, tearing muscle, tendons, cartilage, and breaking both the femur and tibia. As the man was going down, Ben grabbed one of his pistols and shot the fourth man through the heart and the last man through the right eye. *All those years of combat arms training paid off.* His classmates were grateful and a little afraid of Ben because of the speed and ferocity of his attack.

As soon as the last man was killed, a strong, powerfully built, black-skinned man entered, dressed in a well fitted, black business suit with white shirt and red tie. He was accompanied by a large contingent of what looked like soldiers, who had their weapons all aimed at Ben. Ben took note of the short person shadowing the big guy. This short person, a middle-aged Japanese man that stood only five feet two inches, wore the outfit of a ninja.

Ben was always cautious with short people. *They can be too quick for a big man like me. Those eyes mean business.* Everybody was immediately separated again, and the man walked right up to Ben. The girls were left alone.

Ben guessed the well-dressed man was of Samoan decent. A couple of inches shorter than Ben but appeared to be built as strong. His black hair was long, straight, well combed and tied in a ponytail. The top of his head was showing a little thinning. His skin was as close to black as humanly possible. *Maybe not Samoan,* Ben thought. He had an air about him that said he was the ultimate authority here.

"I see we have found our champion," the man said. "Take him below." Then, pointing to fallen men, he quipped, "And dispose of these idiots."

Ben's mind was working a mile a minute, trying to figure out the situation as he was escorted to what looked like an apartment. With no ceiling.

He looked up and saw his orchestra mates staring down on him and his escorts.

What his friends saw about the apartment was that it had only one entryway with no door. That led to the main hangar area. There was a large room encompassing a kitchen, dining, and front room. Down a hall, the first door on the left was a smaller room small enough to be used as a bedroom or office. Across the hall was a simple bathroom with one sink, one toilet, and a shower. There were two larger bedrooms at the end of the hall. The floor was all concrete. In the kitchen a small stainless steel sink, refrigerator, and stove stood by a couple of metal cabinets. The countertop was stainless steel, but it was covered in grease and crud.

The well-dressed man entered the apartment with his ninja shadow and ordered Ben to strip off his clothes.

"What?" cried Ben.

"Let's get something quite clear. Disobedience means one of your friends will die. Obedience

means they will live. Now, since you questioned my
order, you will see I mean what I say." He pointed
to the open area and there stood a hundred
men in loin cloths. Two men dragged a girl in
front of the group of men. Ben saw that it was
Roberta Salazar.

"From here on out you will call me Master."

He turned to the group of men and signaled them.
They immediately set upon Roberta, beating
and raping her repeatedly. Her screams echoed
throughout the arena until she died. Most of her
classmates didn't want to watch, but they were
ordered to do so. Many were so upset at what they
saw that they vomited in response. Several just
sat down stunned with disbelief by what they just
saw. Some were dazed into inactivity. Roberta
was a tiny, young girl whose infectious laughter
was sometimes a disruption in class. She thought
everything was funny. After it was determined that
life had left her, a hole in the floor was opened
and her body was tossed in it. At the bottom were
several crocodiles waiting. The sound of bones
crunching, and flesh tearing echoed throughout
the hangar. As the crocodiles ate, the rest of

the class discharged whatever they had in their stomachs. All except Ben, who was very angry.

There was a loud wail from the mezzanine, a voice Ben knew well. Tommy was beside himself with horror and grief at what he saw. Ben knew Tommy's beloved little sweetheart had suffered the cruelest of deaths for a girl. Then Ben heard what sounded like someone being beaten. This set the wailing and cries to a higher intensity.

That was when he heard Allison's voice. "STOP BEATING HIM!" she yelled. "HE JUST WATCHED HIS GIRLFRIEND GET BRUTALLY MURDERED! LEAVE HIM ALONE!"

Out of the corner of his eye, Ben saw Master's face. It seemed as if he was in ecstasy. Ben called up to the folks in the mezzanine. "TOMMY! TOMMY! LISTEN TO ME!"

Through the haze of his grief, Tommy heard the voice of the one friend he would listen to. His wailing ceased, but his crying did not. "I HEAR YOU, BEN," Tommy blubbered. He tried to speak again but his sobs wouldn't let him.

Ben called back, "TOMMY! COME AND LOOK AT ME!" Tommy slowly rolled his obese body over and stood up among the soldiers that had paused their attack. He walked over to the edge and peered down to find Ben. When he did, they locked eyes. Tommy couldn't say anything. In his mind, he wanted to climb over the fence and crash to the floor below so he could join his beloved Roberta. But the look on Ben's face put a stop to those thoughts. He waited for Ben to speak.

With a strong voice without the previous shouting, Ben spoke, "Tommy, we all loved Roberta and we grieve with you. Please be careful to not let your emotions get away from you." Ben's jaw tightened before he said, "Don't give Master any cause to hurt any more of us than he already has. Tommy, I believe that Roberta belonged to Jesus before she died. Do you agree?"

Tommy nodded his head almost violently, "Yes, Ben, she loved Jesus more than she loved me or her family."

"Tommy, do you love Jesus as well and serve Him?"

With tears flowing freely, Tommy responded, "You know I do."

"Then she is with Jesus now. Roberta is waiting with the others for the rest of Jesus's followers to return home with her. She will rejoice when you are called home. Just make sure you are on God's time." Ben paused for a few seconds. "You will see her soon enough. However, you are still needed here." Then with emphasis, Ben stated, "*I* need you here. To help take care of everybody up there because I can't. You hear me?"

Tommy wiped his face and calmed down even more. His friend needed him. "Yes, Ben," he replied, "I hear you. I will help where I can. Thank you." A sob stuck him. "But it still hurts." He started crying again.

"I know, Tommy. I know." Ben turned to Master with a grim look of determination.

Master's facial expression did not change as he said, "If you don't do as I say now, another will be chosen."

"That won't be necessary." Ben said with a not-quite-subservient voice.

Benjamin took all his clothes off as previously instructed. As he did, Master continued his appraisal of Ben's body and fighting style. *Moves like a man who has been well-trained. Fluid and aware. Not a drop of fat with excellent muscle definition. Not body builder bulky but muscles are well packed. Most impressive for such a young man. Took care of the five idiots easy enough. Maybe I have found the one,* he surmised

"Now, you will live here," Master said. "Meals and water will be available to you and your friends. Showers and bathing rooms are down the hall. Medical services will be supplied, should you be in need. Now, you must fight when I tell you with whomever I tell you to. Don't worry. You won't be fighting your friends. You will be fighting my warriors." He pointed to the floor with added emphasis, "To the death. Am I clear?"

Not wanting to be the cause of another rape or death, Ben responded quickly. "Yes." *They had better be prepared for me,* he thought.

"Yes who?"

"Yes, Master," Ben said, with a very slight hint of rebellion.

"You learn quickly. The first battle will be in one hour. Get ready." Then the man left with his soldiers, leaving Ben by himself.

Ben tried to pray but the recent happenings fogged his mind. Soon enough, his training kicked in. He relied on that training he, Michael, and Derrick received from the time they were three years old. The four disciplines of martial arts and combat skills. He excelled at all levels of training, well surpassing the skills of his friends. More importantly, he leaned on what he learned in church, Sunday school, youth group, and witnessing his parents in their prayer life. He settled his mind and prayed. Ben wasn't sure what to pray for, but he trusted God to know what he and the others needed.

Allison gathered all who were willing and offered prayers for the situation and for Ben. All of the classmates surrounded her, even those who were not believers. They somehow understood the necessity.

ROUND ONE

With five minutes to go before the planned fight, Ben was escorted by the ninja to the center of the open area. It was an arena of sorts. There in the arena, another man stood. A soldier, Ben guessed.

"Remember, all fights are to the death," Master said nonchalantly. Now fight!"

The other man charged, and Ben avoided him easily. The next time, the man was a little more cautious in his approach and made a few wild punches.

Susan can beat this guy. Ben thought. He mentally confirmed that the guy was a soldier and had some fighting skills, but he telegraphed his moves too much. Ben side-stepped another swing and, with a quick swipe of his hand across the throat of his opponent, ended the other man's day, killing him.

As Ben realized what had happened that day, and that he had killed six men, the adrenaline finally left his body. His stomach contents came up and onto the floor.

Two men with poles pushed the dead fighter into the pit. The crocs were grateful for a second meal.

Ben was escorted back to his apartment where he found a full meal and water waiting for him. He couldn't even think about food at that time, but he was ordered to eat. He sat down and did his best to swallow the meal.

Hamburger steak sat on the plate, with sunny side eggs on top and a generous portion of ketchup, riced broccoli and cauliflower, and a glass of water. *My favorite meal*, Ben thought. *How did they know? But it seems so tasteless. Just give me the ingredients and I will show them how to make this, normally wonderful, meal great.*

Then he rested.

Up above, Allison Ver Hoeven watched him. *Oh, my Musketeer. Keep your cool and you will do well. Heavenly Father, cover him with your wisdom and strength. I think he is going to need you now more than ever.* She silently prayed for Ben as she ached from the pain in her side where the soldier hit her with his rifle. She focused on Ben and wasn't even interested in his nakedness at that moment. Her heart ached for her Musketeer. *He's my Musketeer,* she thought. *Yes. My Musketeer.* Her mind shifted, and her heart ached again, this time for the loss of Roberta. Allison's tears flowed as she prayed by herself.

Her classmates were still in a collective state of disbelief. Some cried by themselves, others in small huddles. After she finished praying, Allison went to check up on everybody, offering what comfort she could give. Most of the classmates were grateful for her and thanked her. They also prayed with her. After a time, an uneasy calm prevailed.

HAREM?

After a fitful night's sleep, Ben started a conditioning and training regimen. It carried him through the whole time he was in that situation, for lack of better terminology, imprisoned there.

A week passed before his next fight. His next opponent was better skilled, but Ben finished him quickly as well. I am sure the opponents will improve as the fights move along. How long do I have to wait until my skills will really be tested, Ben mused.

In the viewing area, standing behind Master, the ninja quietly observed Ben. *This man is dangerous. Master had better be prepared for the worst.*

As Ben entered his apartment, he was greeted by six naked women, all from his class. Among them was Allison. The others were two freshmen, one sophomore, one junior, and the last was a senior, Donna Schipper. He locked eyes with Allison, thereby letting everybody know that their nakedness was not a priority on his mind at this time. Still, all the girls blushed as they looked at him.

Master showed up and told Ben to choose a wife from these six.

"What? No harem!" Ben said. He was trying to push some buttons as he locked eyes with the ninja.

"You are Christian? Are you not?" Master asked almost rhetorically.

Ben answered without hesitation and stood tall when he replied, "Yes."

"Your god doesn't allow harems, does He?"

"No."

"Then choose one wife. Now!" He walked out while the body of Ben's opponent was pushed into the pit.

Ben looked into the faces of the girls. Even after finishing a fight and killing a man, Ben wanted to show as much sympathy as possible so as to not to scare or stare at them. "First," he said, "any of you who only feel compelled to marry me raise your hands." Four did. "Ok, you may go. I won't marry any girl under such compulsion."

They were surprised but grateful. The guards escorted them back to the mezzanine.

Ben walked up to the remaining two. Allison and Donna Schipper, the seniors. Donna really does look like a smaller version of Allison, Ben thought to himself. She must have some Vietnamese in her ancestry as well.

"So, are you really good with marrying me at this time?" He asked Allison, noticing the bruise on her side.

"I knew I would marry one of the Musketeers some time," she said. "Now is good time as any. I am ready. I have always prayed it would be you."

Ben turned to Donna, a petite, long haired brunette. She was commonly known as Little Allison, as she had the looks and physique that matched Allison, except she stood a foot shorter. "Donna, I am choosing Allison. Just know you would have been tops on my list otherwise." He hugged her.

Donna returned his embrace and didn't want to let him go. She felt a small rush of pleasure course through her. It was, however, short-lived as Ben had to, reluctantly, push her away before sending her back to the mezzanine.

"I really do love you, Ben," Donna told him. "I have always known you and Allison would be the couple. I just, I, held out some hope." Just as Donna was led away, a Catholic priest entered the room.

"Time for the marriage ceremony. Stand next to each other," The priest ordered. He did not seem all that happy to have to participate in the ceremony.

"Things happen fast around here." Allison observed. "Not quite the wedding I had planned, though."

"Planned?" Ben said, curious.

"Yes. *Planned*!" She said as if stating the obvious. "All girls dream about their future weddings."

"Oh. Really? Why?" Ben was completely oblivious of such important matters.

Even with the current circumstances, Allison was a little playful and tapped him on the nose. "That is why we girls dream."

"Enough chit chat!" barked the priest. "Let's get this over with."

In a few minutes, the vows were said. Ben and Allison signed the marriage license documents. Both noted how the locations on the papers were covered so they would have no idea where they were. They were officially married. "Officially." Master entered the room with his entourage and declared, "Now get to making babies." He turned to leave.

Ben stopped him. "One minute, Master. Since you have just made us a family, I am requesting a Christian Bible. New American Standard is my preference. If we are to be a family, then we need to have the tools to be a *proper* family."

The people around Master paled at the idea of anyone making demands of him, much less a high school kid. But Master faced Ben, then smiled and nodded to the priest before he walked out.

Even Allison was amazed Ben got away with the demand. She approached him with increased admiration, wrapped her arms around his neck and pulled her face closer to his. "Not quite the honeymoon I wanted," she said. "Not the most romantic of situations. Plus, we have an audience." They looked up and saw their classmates watching.

Donna called down. "We have been *ordered* to watch. This is getting just silly." She turned around to see several soldiers pointing weapons at the students.

"What is his game?" Ben asked.

FALSE HONEYMOON?

Allison put her hands on either side of his face and made him look directly into her eyes. "Ben, look at me." As always, it took little for her to gain his complete and undivided attention. "It is just you and me. Nobody else matters. You are my husband, I am your wife. Do not pay any attention to anybody or anything else but us. You now know which Musketeer marries which Princess."

She always had a way to soothe Ben's mind. He heeded her words and wrapped her in his arms. Ben kissed her for the first time, and that kiss lit a flame of desire in them both. Their lovemaking started off slowly but finished with an intensity they didn't realize they had. The students above watched with differing reactions. Most of the girls focused on Ben. Most of the boys focused on Allison. The majority didn't want to watch as they deemed it Ben and Allison's special time of intimacy. Donna looked on, daydreaming that she was Allison, but she still kept trying to turn away out of love for them both. The men standing

behind the students with the guns kept her
looking at the couple.

From the aftermath of their ecstasy, in which they
were fully sated, they finally caught their breath
and cuddled each other. As they did, they finally
got down to talking about their situation.

"Michael has Carrie," Allison said as she laid with
her head on his shoulder, fingering his chest hairs.
"You have me. That leaves Derrick with Susan. I
wonder how they are doing, losing all their best
friends in three months."

"I hope they are ok," Ben replied. "Although
I have my concerns about Derrick. Something
wasn't quite right with him when Michael and
Carrie went missing. I hope he takes good care
of Susan." Stroking her back, h looked up past
the students to the ceiling of the hangar, as there
was no ceiling for the apartment "I have so many
questions. Why do I have to fight? Why are we
naked? Why was our group chosen? Why are we
pressured to have babies? I pray they are not
for crocodile food." He turned his face to look
directly into hers. "One thing is for sure. You are

an excellent cook and nurse. I think I am going to need those services in the coming months."

"We must never neglect to pray for and with each other. Never, Ben. Hear me?" She plucked one of his chest hairs.

"OUCH!" he hollered. "Loud and clear. Now would be as good a time as any." They got up on their knees, held hands, and with their foreheads touching, they prayed aloud. The couple sought God's plan in all of the happenings, asking for God's wisdom for each day and complete protection of the classmates in the mezzanine. They asked for God to let their families know they were well and alive. They paused their prayer and thought of Roberta. After a moment, Ben said some special words to the Father about his friend.

Unbeknownst to them, a few in the mezzanine prayed with them. Through everything happening, they acknowledged God's sovereignty in all things and set their focus on that.

"Whatever we do, we must never lose our love and joy in Jesus. Never!" Allison declared. Again, she was straightening his mind. She looked at the room and made a notation. "Going to take a lot of work to clean this place for living. That countertop may take a month of scrubbing to make it clean enough to process meals. And just because you are fighting for us doesn't mean you are going to escape your part of the cleaning." She wrinkled her face at the offending situation. "Also, we need a comb. I want some normalcy in our lives. So, I need you to comb my hair. Please."

"Yes, dear. I will ask for one," Ben said as he adjusted his position behind her. "However, do you think my fingers will due until then?" He started combing through her tresses with his fingers.

"That's much better," she purred. As he worked, Allison felt tension releasing from her body. The tightness in her bones emanated from their circumstances and their lovemaking didn't release it all. "Can we please continue this every night like we used to. It is so calming."

He leaned forward and whispered in her ear, "It will be my pleasure."

"Also, I want music. Music so we can dance together."

"I will make that priority number two, behind the comb." He stood up and offered his hand to her. "But we don't need music to dance." She looked up to him. Then she took his hand, melted into his arms, and moved to the music he was humming into her ear.

He is right, she thought. *We don't need music.* Their movements were fluid, smooth, and slow. When they finally paused, their passions took over and lovemaking returned with a vengeance.

Once again, Donna admired them.

ALLISON'S PREGNANCY

A couple of months later, after a few more fights, Ben and Allison were resting after being intimate with each other in the morning. They heard a voice from the mezzanine.

"Don't you two ever rest?"

The couple giggled.

Allison then got a serious look on her face. "Ben, I think it is official. I have missed two periods. I am pretty sure I am pregnant."

That got Ben's attention and the intensity of his stare would have melted most men, but Allison was never afraid of him. "For real?" was all he could say.

"Yes."

Ben stood up and lifted her off the ground with his hug. After what seemed like a thousand kisses, he let her back down to the floor. Ben knelt in front of Allison and kissed her an inch below the navel, then he prayed for the little one whose life has just begun. "Father God," he said solemnly, "thank you for your rich blessing of this child. I don't care whether it's a boy or a girl. All I ask is that, in these circumstances, our child is healthy and Your hedge of protection would surround him or her. Thank you again, Jesus. I ask in your name, the name that has all power and authority. Amen."

Allison ran her hands through his hair as he prayed and followed it with her own "Amen."

The cheers from the mezzanine told the couple that there were many others who rejoiced with them. Unbeknownst to the couple, somebody else heard the news and immediately made a phone call.

An hour later, a person who looked like a nurse entered their apartment. Ben immediately stood in front of Allison. "Who are you and what do you want?" he stated.

The woman froze at the entrance of the doorway when she heard Ben's harsh question. "I am a nurse from the local hospital," she replied. "I am here to administer a pregnancy test on your wife."

"Hospital? What hospital? What town are we in?"

"I am sorry, sir. I have been ordered to never divulge where you are for fear of my life or the lives and safety of my family."

Ben then noticed she seemed a little nervous standing there as she frequently glanced outside the door. With her tiny stature, she would have reason to be on edge. He decided to be more gentile with his voice in an attempt to relieve her of some anxiety. He held his hands out with his palms facing her. "I am sorry for my gruff manner," he said. "Please, as long as my wife is willing, test her for pregnancy." He turned around to look Allison in the eyes. Without speaking, she nodded her agreement. Ben stepped aside and the nurse explained the test to Allison. Then we and Allison went into the bathroom to complete the procedure. When they came back out, the nurse placed the test on the table and stood by to let the test do its thing. She seemed greatly relieved, but she didn't say a word while the test was processing.

Allison stood by Ben, who reached around and pulled her close to him. She rested her head on his chest. The nurse saw and slightly blushed at the sight of the couple.

At the appointed time, the nurse checked the test and declared Allison was indeed pregnant. Then she placed a package on the table. Allison unwrapped it and found a Bible with the exact translation Ben asked for. Ben thanked the nurse generously for her assistance with the test and for gifting them with a Bible. She nodded and immediately left.

"Next time we should request some furniture," Allison said. Ben chuckled, but he knew he would. In spite of the circumstances, Ben and Allison were elated. They gave thanks in prayer and waved at the friends in the mezzanine.

FORCED ADULTERY

Two days later, Ben walked into the apartment after a hard fight. "Each opponent is getting tougher than the last," he said then froze at the door.

Allison was performing some enticing hip and pelvic movements. "If that is how you are going to greet your victorious husband, I am all for it!"

"Oh, hi," she said. "Now that I know I am pregnant, I am doing what Carrie's grandmother taught us. In order to keep our female parts in prime working condition before and after birthing a child, she had us practice Kegels."

"Practice what now?"

"Kegels. Doing them helps the uterus stay in place by strengthening the muscles around it. And since Master is going to have you keep me pregnant, I don't know how many children we are going to have. So, I need to stay in shape."

"You get no complaints from me."

"Also, since we believe Michael and Carrie are still alive somewhere, I am certain Carrie is doing the same thing as we speak. Susan is most likely doing something similar for Derrick, too."[2]

---

2 In fact, Susan and Derrick were not together at this time.

Allison glanced at Ben and noticed the glazed look on his face. "Are you thinking something naughty?"

"I am only thinking about you," he said lustfully, "in a *naughty* way."

"So, you are not thinking about Carrie? Or Susan?"

"That would be the most foolish thing I could do. It's *my wife* I see in front of me. Michael can have his own thoughts about his Princess. And Derrick can, too."

"Excellent. Keep that way. Oh," she said, looking at the door. "By the way, we have company." She pointed in the direction of the dining room table.

He looked up and saw Donna standing there. She was naked again. Ben blushed and Allison giggled at his embarrassment. He combed his hair with his hand as he looked sheepishly at Donna. "Hello again. Sorry, I didn't notice you standing there."

Winking at Allison, Donna replied, "I was actually enjoying your little tete-a-tete. Truth be known, we all do up in the mezzanine, and even back home. We have watched you and your friends for years and enjoy the fruits of your love for each other. However, forgive us for watching. We don't have a choice."

"Do you know what is up with all this nudity?"

Donna answered, "The girls have been ordered to be naked for the last two months but the boys were told to leave us alone. During today's fight, the boys were ushered out. I don't know where they are or why they were taken. Nothing makes sense. However," she straightened seeming to prepare herself to say something difficult, "today, us girls were told that each of us needs to be impregnated by you. Sorry."

"That is true," said Master as he walked through the door with the ninja behind him.

Ben spun around so quickly that Donna jumped a bit. His anger switched on. *Why is that ninja always shadowing Master?*

Allison stepped close to her husband and placed her hands on his left elbow and shoulder. Donna moved up to Ben also, placing her hands on the right side of Ben's back. When she touched the tightening muscles, butterflies began to dance in her stomach. She looked at Allison, who he yet to notice Donna's movement. *I envy you, Allison,* she thought. *You had better take great care of this man. This is a horrible situation, and I love this man. But I'll just love him from afar.*

Master continued, "In fact, I have a little demonstration for you. Watch!"

Through a door on the other side of the open area what appeared to be a young girl. But it was no young girl!

"ROSETA!" Ben yelled.

"Roseta?" echoed several classmates as they looked over the wall of the mezzanine.

"Oh. You know her?" Master had what looked like glee on his face.

"She was the waitress on the cruise ship we were on during the Christmas trip." Ben replied, his anger continued to rise.

"A well-serving subordinate of mine recommended her," Master said with a twinkle in his eye. "He's a countryman of yours. And he said she would be most excellent for this party." Master let that sink in.

Roseta recognized Ben and Allison. "Please, Musketeer and Amazon Princess, help me!" She struggled to be free from the iron grasp of the soldier holding her. A large man in uniform walked up to the tiny woman, grabbed her by her hair, and hit her across her jaw, stunning her.

"STOP THIS!" Ben demanded as he started toward her.

In response to his movement, ten more soldiers ran in and stood in front of Ben, aiming their rifles and pistols at him, Allison, and Donna. Behind them, people in suits entered the apartment and stood silently.

Ben stopped walking but didn't stop talking. He pointed directly one of the big men. "YOU!" he called out, "You are lower than swine. A rat has better dignity than you! You are worse than a filthy dog that eats its own excrement!" Ben's rage was at a fever pitch, but his taunting got the response he wanted from the soldier. Allison removed her hands and then noticed Donna standing right next to her, having removed her hands as well. The big man turned, charging at Ben.

Master just looked on, happy to see such sport. Ninja observed, too. Master's men in black business suits watched, no emotion on their faces. Allison could tell they didn't lack emotion, but knew better than to let anything show.

As the man charged, Ben stood still, looking like he didn't know what to do. The big man saw that as Ben's weakness. He couldn't have been more wrong as Ben tensed, his muscles coiling with power. Ben slammed his fist into the big man's throat, crushing his esophagus with a quickness and power the soldier had never seen before. The man grabbed his throat, trying to breathe, but Ben kicked him in the chest. He flew, landing on his back, still unable to breathe. Ben could have left it at that as the man would die in short order anyway. Instead, Ben walked up to the man and drove his right heel into the soldier's face at the bridge of the nose. The big man's head caved in and he died instantly.

Ben's actions froze the other soldiers as he walked back to Allison, who started checking his feet for cuts from the jagged bones. After wiping the remnants of the big man from Ben's foot, Allison declared there wasn't even a scratch. Donna stood by, her hands clasped in front of her chest, amazed and a little frightened by how close she was to such extreme violence.

Ninja was quite impressed although outwardly, nobody could tell. *Very impressive*, he mused. *He may just be the champion we have been looking for. He never fights the same way. Always changes. Never a pattern. Brilliant!*

Two of the soldiers that had previously leveled their weapons at Ben ran up and dragged their fallen comrade to the pit. They stripped him of his uniform and tossed him in. *The crocs will feast well today. Master thought.*

Up to this point, nobody noticed a pregnant woman had been brought in along with Roseta. The warriors that killed Roberta also came in.

Master pointed to Ben. Without skipping a beat, Master said calmly, "This is what will happen to your wife if you refuse." He signaled the warriors and they stripped the pregnant woman in front of everyone. Her screams echoed around the arena as they cut her belly open and extracted the unborn child. The warriors cut the umbilical cord and tossed the barely formed infant into the pit. Then the woman was tossed into the pit, still alive. Screams and crunching of bones were heard. Everyone was horror-stricken except Master and his warriors. Master seemed ecstatic.

"And you," he pointed to Donna. "This will happen to if you refuse."

THE OTHER WOMEN

All this time, Roseta was still holding out hope that she would be freed from her situation. She had been kidnapped two weeks ago and endured endless rapes. Seeing the Musketeer and Amazon, or was that Princess, filled her with a sense of the finality of her torment. She watched with a hazy glee, after being hit with the big fist, as the big brute was destroyed by the Musketeer. That glee went away as she witnessed the soldiers with their weapons trained on the Musketeer, Amazon, and that other girl. Since she realized she would not be freed anytime soon, she could endure things as long as she was just being raped. She felt heavy despair as the Amazon looked at his foot. Then the Amazon looked her way and Roseta recognized her own hopelessness. "Lord, Jesus, help me survive so I can be free again," she prayed silently.

Master signaled and the warriors attacked Roseta. Their assault was brutal. They didn't stop at just rape. In their lust-filled frenzy, they beat her, bit her, tore out chunks of flesh and clumps of hair from her scalp. Finally, Roseta knew her life was over. In her pain, she cried, "Jesus, as you said on the cross, I repeat to you. Into your hands I commend my spirit." Her soul left her at that point. It was a half hour later that the frenzy abated and the brutes realized she had long since been dead. They cheered the conquest, patted each other on their backs, and left to wash off the blood, sweat, urine, and fecal matter from their bodies. A cleanup crew came in to cleanse the apartment and toss her body into the pit.

When Allison had looked back at Roseta before the attack, she saw the despair in the tiny woman's face. It sickened her so much that she mentally prayed, "Jesus. If it is your will, please remove this moment from my memory and help me to never recall it as long as I live. Please, Lord Jesus."

God granted her prayer's request. From that moment, Allison never remembered what happened to Roseta and nobody tried to make her remember, especially Ben after she informed him of her prayer.

Ben's anger was at its peak and Donna shook with fear as the blood drained from her face throughout the ordeal. Allison moved over to steady her.

"What are you going to do?" Master asked Ben with a note of challenge in his attitude and face.

"You give us no real choice," Ben replied. He turned and talked to Allison for a few minutes. Using the technique she learned that worked best, she rubbed Ben's temples Whispering words of love and scripture that she knew, through years of practice, would have the greatest effect, she blessed her husband. She was able to help him release his rage as it was not needed at this time.

Ben submitted to her touch and whispered back to her, as he had done for most of their lives. Through it all, he knew that, at the moment, his wrath was not a positive thing. He knew he had to calm down and was so grateful to God that Allison was there for him. Especially now, if only for Donna's sake.

"Donna," Ben said, "go talk to Allison first." She and Allison walked over to a corner and started speaking quietly to one another.

"By the way," Master said as he left," you are not to have relations with your wife until that girl is pregnant."

"Anything else?" Ben said. He was pushing some buttons. Just a few. For now.

Allison had to come over and cool Ben down again. When he had settled, she went back to Donna, choking back tears. The two women looked intently into each other's eyes. Fear, anger, and sorrow crossed their faces before Donna could speak.

"Why?" Donna asked. "Allison, *why*? What did Roseta do to deserve that? What did we do to deserve this? What did Ben do to deserve the torment they are putting him through? WHY?!" Donna broke down and fell to her knees. Yes, she had seen the brutality Ben had to go through. Yes, all the girls had to go through the humiliation of being naked all the time and in front of the soldiers. It pushed her over the edge. Allison got down on the floor with her and held her tight, crying with her.

Ben came over and knelt, embracing both girls. "Job asked basically the same questions when things went bad for him," he told them. "Do you remember God's response?"

Through her sniffles Donna replied, "God didn't tell him why he suffered." She could say no more.

Ben continued. "He told Job to understand that, basically, no matter the situation, we need to live for Him and *trust Him*. We have no idea what is going to happen the next minute since we have not the power or knowledge of God. Come good or bad times, He is God, and we are not. He is Creator. We are not. As for me, I am making sure that, within my limited capacity, we all survive this horror. Also that we don't lose sight of who we are and, most importantly, who *He* is." Ben hung his head for a long moment. "And, to be truthful, I am not sure I'm doing it right. But I will trust in His best as we work through what we believe to be our worst."

Donna looked to Ben and Allison, smiled, and decided he was right. *I have decided to trust God, Ben, and Allison through this*, she thought. *Poor*

Ben. Forced to kill to protect us. Now forced to commit adultery to, again, protect us. Poor Allison for having to endure what her husband has to do. May we be doing this right, Lord. May this torture end.

"Thank you," Donna told them. "I still don't understand. But maybe I am not supposed to understand at this time." Looking Allison in the eyes, Donna said, "I am ready to hear what you have to say." Ben gave both of them a final squeeze and walked a short distance away.

Allison closed her eyes for a few moments before she spoke. *I can't believe I have to say this. But here it goes.* She sucked in a lungful of air and let it out. "Here is the situation. Ben will not be making love to you. It will only be impregnation. Making love is for me. There will be no kissing or fondling. That, again, is for me. He is not going to try to make you enjoy it. That is for me. Just impregnation. It sounds cruel, but that way we can get through this forced adultery. Ben is sacrificing himself to keep us alive. Do you understand?"

Donna nodded and hugged Allison. *This is not how I wanted my first time with a man, but I am grateful that through all this, it is with Ben.* Then she prepared herself. Allison refused to watch. So did the girls in the mezzanine. Nobody liked this situation except Master and some of his more lecherous soldiers, some of whom were in the mezzanine. They pointed their weapons on the girls and made them watch.

The intercourse between Ben and Donna was short compared to the lovemaking between Ben and Allison, but Donna didn't care. She enjoyed every minute because of her love for Ben. However, she did have a few pangs of sorrow. *Jesus, forgive me for enjoying this adultery. Ben and Allison, may the both of you forgive me as well because I love Ben so much that I cannot, even under these circumstances, deny my joy, as short in duration they are.*

Every time he finished with Donna, Ben went over to Allison and wept on her knees. Allison would place her hand on his head and weep with him. Standing alone, Donna was also shedding tears. She didn't want it be this way. She felt ashamed before Allison who reached out her arms and hugged the smaller woman. She whispered words of comfort to Donna, herself grieving as well.

Ben's fights were cut down to one a month. Still, no logical answer had been given for why things there happening.[3]

A month and a half after starting forced adultery, Donna was declared pregnant. She was immediately removed from the apartment when the pregnancy was confirmed. Ben and Allison felt a pang of fear for their friend. *What was going to happen to her?* Ben mused. *Where are they taking her? Would the child be ok and healthy? Would the child live with his or her mother or would there be a torturous end?* Ben was able to enjoy his wife again after receiving comfort from God in all those questions.

Two days later, Miriam Deng, a tall, shapely, athletic, very dark-skinned girl of Sudanese descent stood in the apartment after another fight. Allison had to attend to Ben's wounds. Then

---

3 The boys removed from the mezzanine were drugged, flown to the United States in crates, and delivered to twenty-two different cities around the country. This created a stir, especially in Sioux Falls when the boys trickled in. They told their stories but were unable to identify where they were held. Everybody was relieved to know their children and friends were still alive, except for Roberta Salazar's family and friends, whose grief was completely expected.

she prepared to have the same talk with Miriam that she had with Donna.

"Donna never came back to the mezzanine," Miriam said.

Ben and Allison looked at each with the same puzzled expression. Without saying anything, both knew what the other was thinking. *What on earth does that mean?*

Miriam was the first to speak after that. "Ben, I am sorry you have to go through this. Personally, I would rather have my husband on our wedding night be my first." Then to Allison she said, "I am sorry for you as well, Allison. I don't want to take any of your intimate times away from you. This situation is just horrid." Immediately she turned back to Ben and said defensively, "I don't mean you are horrid, Ben. Just all this." She waved her arms around, pointing to the whole arena.

Ben chuckled, "Relax, Miriam. We totally understand. And the more relaxed you are, the sooner you will become pregnant." Miriam blushed.

Allison was relieved to see a little red on her friend's dark face. She walked over to Miriam, hugged her, then took her by the hand to the other side of the room. There she gave Miriam the same lecture Donna received. Miriam nodded and walked over to Ben. Again, Allison would not watch. As stoic as she wanted to be, she couldn't help but let a tear fall down her cheek.

After Ben finished with Miriam that day, he called out to Master.

WINNER TAKES ALL

Master came to the apartment and Ben asked him the questions that were on his mind.

"First," Master said, "I will tell you that you are not the first to go through the fights. You are the only one to survive past the first month, and there have been twelve other groups before you. Every time a fighter fails and is killed, all the rest of the boys are tossed into the pit alive. After that, the girls are sorted. Some go into the fit and beautiful group and the rest are sold into slavery. The fit and beautiful are bred to provide babies for the Satanists and their sacrifices. Girls only. Boy babies are a snack for my pets," he said, indicating the alligators. "Then I have to hunt down a new group. I am looking for that one person who can replace me when I die. An heir, if you will." There was no hint of remorse in Master's voice as he said these words.

"Why do we have to be naked all the time?" Ben asked with a little annoyance in his tone.

"I have my own reasons that I am keeping to myself."

"Why do I have to impregnate the other girls?" Annoyance was still there but Ben tried to keep it under control.

"I don't want you to have it easy if you win," Master said a little bit smugly.

"What happened to the boys?"

"You will find that out if you win."

"What would I win?"

"My empire."

"What does that entail?"

"You find out if you win. Anything else?"

"Not at this time."

"Good." Master left.

"Well, that was informative." Allison snorted.

"At least I know what my job is. Enjoy my wife. Keep her pregnant. Raise our children. Protect our family. Impregnate whatever girl he sends. Be killed. Or win an empire. Have I missed anything?"

"All while being naked," Allison said with her hands splayed at her sides.

"Oh, yeah," Ben said dryly. "That too. Not exactly the life I was planning or expecting."

"Me neither."

"Me neither," Miriam retorted, adding her voice to the conversation. Ben forgot she was there.

"There are some other things that don't make sense," he said. "Our cupboards are full of food. We have proper place settings in plates, forks, knives, spoons, cups, glasses, priests, nurses, well-made beds, cleaning supplies. Just no clothes. Did I miss anything?"

"The babies' diapers."

"Oh, yeah. Someday I hope this all makes sense."

LIFE AMONGST DEATH

After two fights and one more impregnation, Allison gave birth to a baby girl. Medical personnel were on hand to assist her with the birth. By then, furniture was in place, and made things much easier. Ben was ordered to stay out of the bedroom where His wife was in labor.

"In America, fathers are allowed to be in attendance, if not fully helping their wives, while giving birth," he argued.

The doctor countered, "You are not in America. Get out!"

Ben wasn't going to let it go. "Try to stop me!"

Master was waiting just outside of the apartment and walked in at Ben's last outburst. "Do as the doctor says or the baby will become a croc snack." Ben glared at Master and walked out. "Don't you have something to say?" Master goaded him.

"What? You want me to say," Ben said, glaring, "'Yes Master'? That's not happening!"

Once again, Ben got away with sassing the master. It was a puzzlement to the underlings. Ninja paused a few seconds, staring at Ben. *What is the source of his strength and confidence? Surely, it's not the woman?* he pondered.

As soon as the baby was born and showed signs of living, the medical personnel left. Ben was finally able to see Allison and his daughter. Cherry, the next girl to be impregnated, was invited to come into the bedroom and view the baby. She put her hands on Allison and Ben's shoulders and kissed Allison's forehead. Cherry briefly blessed the family, then kissed Ben on his forehead and stepped back, letting the love between the true husband and wife flow.

A week later, she was declared pregnant and removed from the apartment.

With Allison a little weary after trying to nurse her baby the first time, mighty Ben held his daughter with a gentleness most people didn't conceive he had. Allison was fully aware of Ben's gentle nature. Growing up with him gave her a front row seat to his demeanor. Holding his daughter in his arms, the frustration of their current situation was put on hold. Tears of joy rolled down his cheeks as he loved on his little one.[4]

---

4 Without knowing it, they followed the same strategy as Michael and Carrie. Ben named the boys and Allison named the girls. Carrie was the name given to their firstborn.

Ben raised Carrie up and gave her a
blessing from God.

"What a little cherub," Ben said as tears continued
to roll down his face. "How perfect that our first
child would be a girl." Having been taught and
trained to fight, if necessary, Ben was unprepared
for the killing he was put through. Ben hated no
man, but being forced to kill, forced to commit
adultery to protect his wife and friends, forced
to expose his intimacy with his wife in front of
an unwilling audience, was wearing his emotions
down. This baby was a bright light in his world.
Now he had to protect her as well. He prayed
silently, *WHEN WILL IT END?*

Ben took care of cleaning the first bodily waste
from the little creature. With no diapers available
yet, the mess was not contained to Carrie's little
bottom. She left some on him, Allison, the bed,
and even the table; wherever she decided to
let it fly. By observing her, the parents would,
sometimes, get advance notice. When they did,
they would rush her to the toilet. Success was
about 50 percent.

One of the suits accompanying Master talked about the baby situation with him in his office. He said, in a hushed tone, "Sir, if you want them to have so many babies, should he continue to win the fights, they will have at least three children that are not toilet-trained at any one time. Sir," he said meekly, "that is not optimal."

Master responded without emotion. "What do you recommend?"

"That they are given diapers for the babies until they are toilet-trained," advised the suit. "Once they are toilet-trained, they can be naked like the rest of the family."

"You think he will last long enough to have lots of children?" Master asked.

"I think this one has already proven himself capable of lasting quite a while. Totally victorious? That is yet to be determined."

Master turned to look at his adviser for several moments. "You may be right," Master said. After a long pause, he nodded. "Diapers it is."

Much to the relief of Ben and Allison, Master sent diapers to keep the baby messes to a minimum. Master reiterated, "Let there be no mistake. Once they are toilet-trained, the diapers come off."

WINNING AND GROWING

Ben's requirements never changed, despite Carrie's birth. Within three months, Allison was declared pregnant again. Little Carrie had her first fever around the same time. The medical personnel helped the couple with the parenting until she was better. *Why is he going through all this to keep my family healthy?* Ben wondered. After four arena fights and the impregnations of three more women, Baby Susan was born.

Again, after five fights and three more impregnations, baby Whitney was born. And, so, a cycle of life had been worked out for the couple.

All of Ben and Allison's children were born in the same month of the following years.

Ben kept winning and killing. If one could call it winning. Allison watched her husband, beginning to see the mental beating Ben was taking.

The following few years added Roberta, Michael, Derrick, Robert, and Teresa.

One thing everyone in the apartment learned about baby boys. They were fully willing and able to baptize anybody changing their diapers. They did not discriminate, happily passing on the joy for all.

Schooling materials were soon added to the items on hand which helped keep the children active and not overly bored. Master only permitted reading, writing, and arithmetic. No history or social studies were allowed. Ben and Allison were happy with the items they received as it kept their minds sharp as well. Still, it was a puzzle to the growing family as to why these items were sent to their apartment.[5]

TERESA BUCHANNAN

The last girl sent to Ben from the mezzanine was Teresa Buchannan, a junior in their class. She was a small girl with a pear-shaped body, olive complexion, short brown hair and wide brown eyes. She stood before Ben and Allison as she calmly stated, "I cannot get pregnant. A doctor's visit showed something, I don't remember the official name, but it won't allow me to ovulate. I was scheduled for surgery a month after we were kidnapped. I will just go out there and let them have at me and die."

---

5 Unbeknownst to the Ben and Allison, the advisers in suits had a level of relationship with Master where they could, and did, convince him that the learning materials would make Ben a better fighter by keeping him from being overrun by small children with little to do.

Ben turned on his heels and went into the open area and called out to Master. In a couple of hours, he showed with his entourage.

Ben explained the situation. "Master, thank you for coming. I will be brief—"

"You had better be brief," Master interrupted, sounding annoyed. "I am not used to being summoned."

"I understand. The last girl you sent to me has an issue that needs to be acknowledged. She has a condition that needs surgery to repair. At this time, she is unable to become pregnant."

"Is that all?"

"I ask that mercy be granted to her as she is not in a position to rebel or comply with your orders. She is willing to comply but cannot." Ben was concerned about the response he was about to receive. *Lord, please soften Master's heart*, he prayed silently.

Master didn't answer immediately. The men in suits with him and his ninja shadow didn't show it, but they were interested in his response. Master didn't generally take kindly to being asked for mercy.

Without changing his expression, Master looked at Ben and stated, matter-of-factly, "Since you asked nicely, she will not be raped or tortured. Therefore, she will not be tossed into the pit."

Ben spun on his heels and went to tell the women what Master said. Allison thought something was amiss but held it to herself.

They hugged Teresa and prayed with her. When they were done, she said, "Thank you. Just so you know, everybody loves you both. Thank you. Win, Musketeer, win!" Then she walked out to meet Master.

As she walked, a huge man with a large sword quietly stepped up behind her. He brought the sword down on her and split her into two.

"WWHHHYYYYY?!" Ben roared. "SHE WAS INNOCENT!"

Master quietly said, "She wasn't raped or tortured. And she won't be tossed into the pit. I never promised not to kill her." He walked off with his team.

"YOU BEAST! YOU VILE BEAST!" was all Ben could say at that moment. What he didn't see was the smile that crossed Master's face. Ninja took note. *Master had better be aware. This man is not afraid.*

Ben's tailspin into insanity accelerated after that. His fights became much quicker and extremely brutal. His prayers decreased from infrequent to practically nonexistent. As a husband and father? Ben struggled there, too. He began alienating his family with his harshness. Even food was becoming flavorless to him during this time.

Allison prayed for wisdom as to how to get through to him. Soon enough, she received her answer.

LOVE YOUR ENEMIES?

Ben continued trying to be a loving husband and father, but sometimes his temper caused him to verbally lash out at his children. Over time they started to fear him. Eventually, Allison had had enough. She had thought long and hard about how to help Ben, laying out her need to Jesus in constant prayer. Now was the time. She got the children occupied with some craft to occupy their time while Mommy confronted Daddy.

"Ben, sweetheart, come sit in front of me," she asked. As she always did when Ben's anger was out of line, she quietly, but forcefully, called to him.

"Why?" He was feeling irritable. He thought to himself, *What now!*

"Please," she cooed, "just sit in front of me." She remained calm. On the outside.

"Oh, alright." He plopped himself in front of her. Looking annoyed and acting a little childish.

"Hold my hands." Ben did. Reluctantly.

She remained calm as she said, "Ben, do you love me?"

He was caught off guard. "Why ask such a question?"

Again, she asked, "Ben, do you love me?" Fear began creeping into his mind.

Tears started to well up in his eyes. "I love you with all my heart," He replied. *How could she ask such a question?*

"Ben, do you love our children?" Allison kept herself calm and quiet when speaking to him, especially when he was angered or being irrational. Otherwise, if she started to get angry with him, he would set his heels in and argue with her. She had to learn this the hard way when they were children.

"I love them with all my heart, as well." Tears streamed as the pent-up emotions were coming to a head.

"Ben, do you love Jesus?"

Sobbing, he replied, "I love Jesus with all
my heart."

"Ben, do you love Master?"

Ben stood up, his anger flaring instantly. "There is
no way I will ever love that monster!" He turned to
walk away.

"BENJAMIN MANFRED BICKLES! YOU COME
BACK HERE AND SIT DOWN!" He paused,
turned to face his wife. And after a couple of
minutes of mental battle, did as ordered. Allison
had never yelled at him before. He then knew he
had crossed a line that even she would not accept.
She knew this was one time that demanded she
stand firm.

"Did you hear that?" whispered Susan on the
other end of the apartment. "Mama said Daddy's
full name. He's in trouble now!" The other
children nodded, remembering how Mama used
their full names when they were in trouble.

"DO YOU REALIZE WHAT I HAVE HAD TO DO FOR THAT MONSTROSITY?" Ben screamed. He put his hands to his head. Trying to calm down he said, "I see Roberta brutalized every minute I am awake and, sometimes, when I sleep! I see every man I have killed! Their faces are always in front of me!" He started to pace. She let him, knowing he was starting to heal. "I can't seem to wipe out the memory of Teresa!" He fell to his knees, covering his face as tears flooded down his cheeks.

After a few moments of utter despair, he looked up to his wife. The woman who, as a little girl, knew how to calm him when he was on the verge of being out of control. Allison. She was still there, doing what she had always done. Loving him.

"And you," Ben blubbered, "I have dishonored you with my adulteries. I have dishonored our children by treating them harshly, when they did nothing to even deserve a scowl." He watched Allison as she waited patiently for him to process and verbalize his thoughts. "How can I ever redeem myself from all this to you?" He pointed to the children, who had formed a defensive huddle. "To them? And more importantly, to God?" He pointed to the fridge. "I can't taste food. It's all garbage to me. Even when I make it! I don't know if I have other children out there," He waved his arms around, pointing to nowhere particular. Then he placed his hands on the floor and with more tears and a few sobs he said, "How can you ask me to love the beast that has brought all this down on us? Do you realize what would happen to you and the children, possibly all of our families, if I fail? And you want me to love him?"

Allison's heart was at the breaking point, but she quietly asked God for more strength to help her husband. She felt God granting her the strength she needed. After a few seconds, she responded, "If you don't love Master, then you don't love the rest of us half as much as you say! Scripture is clear. Jesus himself said, 'But to you who are listening I say: Love your enemies, do good to those who hate you, bless those who curse you, pray for those who mistreat you... love your enemies, do good to them, and lend to them without expecting to get anything back. Then your reward will be great, and you will be children of the Most High, because He is kind to the ungrateful and wicked. Be merciful as your

Father is merciful.'" Allison knelt beside him
and placed her arms around him, kissing his
shoulder. "Master is evil," she said, "but God can
still restore his soul if he repents and turns his
life toward Jesus. Maybe, within this insanity, you
are like Esther. 'Born for such a time as this.'"
Then she moved around to face him and cupped
his face in her hands, raising his head so their
eyes would meet. "Preach to him," she told him.
"Fight when you have to. Talk to him about Jesus.
Give him a chance. Several chances if need be.
Love him as God loves him and then I will believe
how much you love us. And remember, 'The light
shines in the darkness, and the darkness has not
overcome it.'"

"Why am I the one to have to do this? What did
I do to deserve having to do this? When will
this hell end?" His earnestness was not missed
by Allison.

"Do you not yet know who you are? Not only are
you Esther but You are also Samson without the
complications of Delilah. You have been brought
here by God to destroy an empire of evil. Look at
your children." They both turned their heads to

look at their children, huddled together in fear and hopefulness. "All they see is terror from other men. Up until recently You have been the only light of love they see. Now they are beginning to fear you, too."

This last statement tore at his heart. He looked at his children and saw the truth. Ben was stunned. He remained silent for a long time. But then he turned, looking into Allison's eyes. That's when all the stress, bitterness, and anger began flooding out of him. Ben fell to the floor, sobbing. Allison went to the floor and hugged him. His children, seeing their mother, all came up and hugged him, too. He hugged them back, crying his apologies to them. "I am so sorry, my babies. So sorry. Please forgive me!" They forgave him and showered him with hugs and kisses. Ben cried the hardest he had ever cried in his life as they showered him with the love they'd been holding back for such a moment.

Carrie held his face, "Daddy, remember us! Don't forget us as you do battle. Please, Daddy!"

When his emotions settled down, Ben stood up. He pulled his wife to him and kissed her with a vigor she had not yet known. *God has given her the ability to be my voice of reason! He thought My missing rib!*

When he finally released her, he said in a calm voice, "I need to spend some alone time with God." Then he walked to his prayer place in the corner of their little bedroom. Ben was there for two hours, pouring his soul to God. Pleading with Him. Arguing with Him. Submitting to Him. The children huddled with their mother. And they waited. Finally, he returned to his family. Ben hugged each child and then Allison. Then, he sat down and gathered his family around him.

"I know what to do," Ben said. "God will speak through me. Everybody, please be in prayer. I am sorry, Allison. I am sorry, my children. I love you all with all my heart."

"*Thank you, Jesus,*" Allison silently prayed. They dusted off their Bible and read in earnest. When the next fight came, Ben looked at Allison and said, "I am ready." He kissed her and walked out.

BIGGER CHALLENGE

This time, however, he saw two men standing apart, facing him.

Ok. Bigger challenge. He wasn't fazed.

"Master, from here on I will have something to say before every fight."

"Dictating terms to me?" Master huffed.

"Call it higher orders from Higher Headquarters," Ben replied.

"Who is higher than me?"

"Jesus!" Ben said, matter-of-factly.

"Do you think I will bow down to that antiquated religious artifact?"

"Doesn't matter what you think. What matters is that I obey Him. I will still fight, but I will also speak." Ben's apparent act of defiance did not go unnoticed by the suited men and the ninja shadow.

"Go ahead," Master said. "Doesn't matter to me anyway."

Ben began, with a voice so all could hear, "In the beginning God created the heavens and the earth." Some of the Suits were stunned but inwardly rejoicing. The hadn't heard or read the Bible since their acquaintance with Master. Without showing any emotion, they listened intently with joy and anticipation.

Ben continued, keeping eye contact with everyone he was facing, noting their individual responses, if there were any. As he spoke, Ben flexed and unflexed his muscles to be prepared for a surprise attack, if there were any. "In the beginning was the Word, and the Word was with God, and the Word was God. He was with God in the beginning. Through Him all things were made that has been made."

While he was speaking, Allison and the children kneeled beside the bed, praying for their husband and father to preach well. They asked God to open the hearts, minds, eyes, and ears of the audience so the Word of God would soften a hard heart. They also listened from the open ceiling as they always did when Ben fought.

As she was praying, Allison thought, Lord Jesus, this is better for the children who have only heard the fighting and killing. May they remember and have only these words filling their minds. Please give them this.

They could hear him plain as if he was standing right next to them, "In Him was life, and that life was the light of the world. The light shines in the darkness, and the darkness has not overcome it. For He has rescued us from the dominion of darkness and brought us into the Kingdom of the Son He loves, in whom we have redemption, *the forgiveness of sins.*" Ben placed a little more emphasis the last four words which seemed to have an influence on the suits. The ninja was moved in his soul as well, although he didn't know why. Ben paused a couple of seconds and continued. "The Son is the image of the invisible God, the firstborn over all creation. For in Him all things were created: things in Heaven and on Earth, visible and invisible, whether thrones or powers or rulers or authorities; all things were created through Him and for Him. He is before all things, and in him all things hold together. And he is the head of the body, the church; He is the beginning and the firstborn from among the dead, so that in everything he might have the supremacy."

A small tear traveled down the cheek of one woman wearing a suit. She was grateful it was the cheek Master could not see from his position.

"For God was pleased to have all His fullness dwell in Him, and through Him to reconcile to Himself all things, whether on earth or in Heaven, by making peace through His blood, shed on the cross." As he spoke, Ben made sure to let the scriptures do the talking and convicting. "Once you were alienated from God and were enemies in your minds because of your evil behavior. But now He has reconciled you by Christ's physical body through death to present you holy in His sight, without blemish and free from accusation. Thus ends the Word for today."

There were men in suits, and the ninja, who were astonished by what they had just heard. The Bible was new to most of them, and hearing it in this setting was strange, to say the least.

"Good," Master said, seeming unmoved, although he was getting annoyed. "Now, fight." Ben noticed that some of the soldiers there listened and were puzzled. *Plant the seed, he thought.*

PLANTING THE SEED

The fight commenced with the two men. But because he often sparred with Michael, Derrick, and Robert at the same time, this was no contest. As his father and his father's friends had drilled into him, Ben never repeated a fight. In this case, he noticed that each man was well-trained, but one man seemed less confident than the other. He was fidgeting, which was barely noticeable to most people. At that, Ben formulated a plan of attack. He immediately charged toward the fidgeting soldier, which gave extreme false confidence to the other. A split second before the confident soldier was about to attack for the kill, Ben changed his attack to him, grabbing the soldier by the groin and squeezing with all his might. That soldier howled in pain at the assault and couldn't defend himself. Ben lifted him up and slammed him on the floor headfirst, breaking his skull and killing him instantly.

So quick and brutal was the attack that the fidgety soldier froze in place. He died when Ben's heal hit him across the side of his head, which broke his neck. The soldier dropped to the floor, limp as a rag. Some of the soldiers watching felt a shiver crawl up their spine while a few others started calculating what they would have done different. Once again, Ben had no marks on him.

The ninja pondered, *There could be something to this God of his.*

When he returned to the apartment, Ben resumed hugging and kissing his wife thoroughly. Then he got on the floor, hugged his children and began playing with them. He was renewed.

"Alright everyone," Ben said, "Daddy's is cooking supper tonight." The children cheered and Allison smiled with love.

"What are we having, Daddy?" Whitney asked. She was the most excited.

"Hamburger steak, baked sweet potatoes, veggies. And for you, Susan, all the ketchup you want."

More cheers erupted from the kids. The laughter and chatter at that meal was welcome noise to the guards on duty at that time. The family was restored. That evening, after the children were in bed, Ben combed Allison's hair, something he hadn't done for a few weeks. She posed a question that brought fond memories to them both.

"Do you remember the day Jesus became real for you?"

Memories flooded his mind that caused him to pause combing for a few minutes.

"I will never forget that day for as long as I live," Ben said.

"Tell me your side of that day. Please."

Ben put his hands at his sides, looked up, and took a couple of heavy breaths. Unknown to them, their children were still awake and listening.

"It was Michael that started it all. He was heavily affected by the pastor's sermon that day. Most especially the verse from Micah, chapter 6, verse 8, that says, 'He has shown you, O mortal, what is good. And what does the Lord require of you? To act justly and to love mercy and to walk with your God.' And then there were some verses from the New Testament that quoted Jesus. Matthew, chapter 7, verses 21-23—"

Allison interrupted, "Not everyone who says 'Lord, Lord,' will enter the Kingdom of Heaven, but only the one who does the will of my Father who is in Heaven. Many will say to me on that day, 'Lord, Lord, did we not prophesy in your name and in your name drive out demons and, in Your name, perform many miracles?' Then I will tell them plainly, 'I never knew you. Away from me, you evildoers!'"

"Amen," Ben replied. "When Michael put those verses together, he got up and ran out of the sanctuary. You and Carrie were right behind him. Derrick, Susan and I were on your tail, followed by Robert. Our parents didn't budge from their seats, which, at the time, I thought was a little weird." Ben resumed combing. "We found Michael in the youth group room flat on his face crying to God."

Allison reached behind her and held Ben's hand for a moment. "My heart ached when I saw that."

"We all knelt down and placed our hands on him while we listened to his prayers. Finally, he sat up and looked at all of us. He wiped away his tears and looked at peace. But his next words woke us all up to the truth about God." Ben paused the brushing again and felt a surge of emotions well up in him. Allison was doing the same. "He said, 'Don't you get it? No matter how good we think we are, if we don't spend time talking with God, getting to know Him and Him knowing us, nothing we can do will get us into the His Kingdom. People will do good works for Him without *spending time* with Him. That is why we were created. From this day forward, I will spend a lot of time talking with Him. And constantly giving praise for the salvation that comes from the birth, life, death, and resurrection of Jesus.' Michael paused for a few minutes and looked each of us in the eye. 'Will you join me?'" Ben wiped a tear from his face at the memory. "That day, in that room, with our friends, on our knees and faces on the floor, we joined him and made our walk with Jesus real."

Allison turned around to face her husband and cupped his face with her hands. "Remember where your strength comes from."

He looked her in the eye with resolve. "I am," he said. "My strength comes from the Lord. And I will continue to remember." They kissed.

It was then that they heard sniffles coming from the children's bedroom. They went to investigate and found seven of their children on their knees beside their beds praying for the very thing with God they heard their parents talking about. They went in, knelt beside their children and joined them in prayer.

The following morning, as the family had finished breakfast, Allison and her three eldest daughters, helped finish cleaning the dishes, since the boys helped make breakfast. Ben was walking back from the bedroom when a loud shriek was heard from the bathroom before the door was flung open.

"AAAAAAAAAAAAAHHHHHHHHH!", a wet Roberta came out screaming. "MICHAEL! YOU FORGOT TO PUT THE SEAT DOWN AGAIN! WHEN ARE YOU GOING TO LEARN?!"

"That is quite enough, young lady," Ben quietly but sternly said. *Man, that girl can screech!* he thought. "Michael will get reminded again, however, did you make sure the seat was down before you sat?"

"Why do I have to do that? If Michael would just put it down, I WOULDN'T HAVE TO!" Roberta argued, glaring in the direction of her younger brother.

Ben knelt down to look into his daughter's eyes. He had already noticed that her backside was wet. "Haven't I taught you to be aware of your surroundings? This is an example. You can't scream at Michael if you didn't do your job first. So, from now on, double check the seat before you sit down. Hear me?"

Roberta hung her head. "Yes, "Daddy," she said. However, she glowered at her brother, who was peeking from around the corner of the kitchen.

"Alright, then. Let's get you cleaned up." Ben led her back into the bathroom.

Allison walked up behind Michael saying, "I think we need to have a little talk, young man." Michael spun around to look into his mother's eyes and knew he was not out of trouble. "Thank you for lifting the seat. We girls appreciate that kindness." Michael was beginning to look relieved. "However, we would appreciate it more if you would put it back down again when you are finished." Then she leaned in closer to his ear and quietly said, "Because your sister can really screech. And we want to keep her screeching to a minimum." Michael looked at his mother and smiled. She continued, "Do you understand me?"

"Yes, Mama," was his immediate response. "I don't want to hear her screech either." Allison patted him on the head and went about her business.

FROM THREE AND UP

Ben continued to train. And he trained the children from ages three on up, just as his dad and his dad's friends taught him. He even taught Allison to protect herself. And remembering what Michael Roberts said that day long ago, he started to spend alone time with God. Allison's heart swelled with love for her husband as he did. *God is so good. Even in times like this! Allison thought, praising God in her heart.*

Ben and Allison were trained to memorize passages of the Bible from a very young age up until the night they were kidnapped. Now, in their apartment together, they worked through what they knew and helped each other on the passages one or the other didn't know or remember.

Having their Bible was handy. This study helped prepare Ben for his next fight. And everything he and Allison learned, they taught to their children.

When Ben went out for his next fight, Master stopped him.

"Before you speak, I have something for you," he said. Master had a pregnant woman and a very young girl brought out. He had the woman gutted and the unborn baby yanked out and both of them tossed to the crocodiles. Then he had his soldiers rape the young girl to death. The little one did not even appear to be ten years old.

Throughout all that was going on in the arena, Allison and her children, Carrie, age six, Susan, age five, Whitney, age four, Roberta, age three, Michael, age two, Derrick, age one, and baby Robert could hear everything from the bedroom where they were praying. Since there was no roof over the apartment, although they couldn't see, they heard everything.

This time, Carrie asked the question Allison didn't want to answer. "Mama, why do they hurt the children and women? And why does Daddy have to fight? It scares me when I hear the screams. I am always overjoyed when Daddy returns, but what will happen if he doesn't one day?"

Allison looked at her children with dread in her gut. "There are evil people in this world," she said. "We just happen to be dealing with some of the worst this world has to offer." She took a deep breath before she could continue, silently praying for the right words to say at this time. "God has placed us here, I believe, to rid this world of some of the evil. As to what would happen if he doesn't return," Allison paused, then looked grimly at her daughter, "there are things evil does to people that are worse than death." She raised her hand. "Please, don't ask me what those things are because I won't answer that question until you are older." The children looked at their mother and nodded. Whenever she used that phrase, she always followed through. They trusted their mother's wisdom, even in times like this. "However," Allison continued, "we must *always* be in prayer for your father." She held out her hands. "So, let's get to it." They all bowed their heads in the apartment. Not totally understanding it all, but always feeling a sense of comfort from God, they prayed.

Ben stood firm as he watched the torture. Inwardly, he was sickened but he remained stoic on the outside.

"That is what will happen to your family if you ever lose."

"I had that figured out a long time ago," Ben said. "That was absolutely unnecessary! Now may I speak?" Ben did not hold back his disgust at what had just happened.

"Oh, go ahead. As if I care." Master, outwardly, looked as if he didn't care about Ben's continued defiance. Inwardly, he was beginning to notice that Ben was not afraid of him. *What does it take to break this man?* he thought.

The men in suits behind Master nodded to each other and knew one thing. Unlike the previous fighters, Ben had no fear of Master. It gave them hope for the first time in years.

Ben looked around at everybody in the area. Then he spoke. "Jesus spoke these words, saying, 'Do not store up for yourselves treasures on earth, where moths and vermin destroy, and where thieves break in and steal. But store up for yourselves treasures in Heaven, where moths and vermin do not destroy, and where thieves do not break in and steal. For where your treasure is, there your heart is also. The eye is the lamp of the body. If your eyes are healthy, your body will be full of light. But if your eyes are unhealthy, your whole body will be full of darkness. If then the light within you is darkness, how great is that darkness! No one serves two masters,'" Ben said with emphasis. "'Either you will hate the one and love the other, or you will be devoted to the one and despise the other. You cannot serve both God and money." He noticed a little fidgeting in some of those listening. "'Therefore, I tell you, do not worry about your life, what you will eat or drink; or about your body, what you will wear. Is not life more than food, and the body more than clothes? Look at the birds of the air; they do not sow or reap or store away in barns, and yet your Heavenly Father feeds them. Are you not much more valuable than they? Can any one of you by worrying add a single hour to your life?'" Ben started to point at the people who were there, trying to make the words personal. "'And why do you worry about clothes? See how the flowers of the field grow. They do not labor or spin. Yet I tell you that not even Solomon in all his splendor was dressed like one of these. If that is how God clothes the grass of the field, which is here today and tomorrow thrown into the fire, will He not much more clothe you-you of little faith? So do not worry, saying, 'What shall we eat?' or 'What shall we drink?' or 'What shall we wear?' For pagans run after these things, and your Heavenly Father knows that you need them. BUT SEEK FIRST HIS KINGDOM AND HIS RIGHTEOUSNESS, and all these things will be given to you as well. Therefore, do not worry about tomorrow, for tomorrow will worry about itself. Each day has enough trouble of its own.' Jesus the Word, the Son, God himself spoke those words. He who has power and authority."

"Yeah, yeah," said Master. "Commence fighting." This time Ben fought three soldiers.

Before they started, Ben made a bold move. "Hold on for a minute." His audience was immediately dumbfounded that this fighter had the audacity to counterman the master. "Our apartment has no roof, and my children can hear everything. They are now realizing they have heard these words before. My wife and I read them to the children every day." While he was talking, he prepared his body for the upcoming battle by flexing and relaxing his muscles and staring at his opponents. "Their curiosity about God is a refreshing and heartwarming time for us. I hope it can be so for all of you."

Master seemed a little anxious. More of his soldiers seemed to be paying attention to Ben's words. The ninja had taken mental notes.

The three-man fight was another victory for Ben.

In the following years, Allison continued to give birth in the same month each year. Ben continued to fight a few times each year. He continued to share scripture before every fight. He told those listening of the names of Jesus in Isaiah. The beatitudes. The birth, life, death, and more importantly, the resurrection of Jesus. He spoke of their importance. Ben identified Jesus as God.

He talked of Esther, Samson, Moses, Noah, David, Paul, and John. He spoke of the salvation from Jesus. He pointed out that to understand the truth of Jesus. one had to recognize his or her guilt of sin. Although Master didn't seem to care, his soldiers were listening and starting to make some decisions on their own.

Ben's wife and children listened as well. He kept praying and trusting God to put the needed words in his mouth. From the apartment, Allison and the children quietly added their prayers to his.

Training Comes to Fruition

In the eleventh year of their captivity, Ben and Allison were preparing him for his second fight of the year. But something was bugging him before he stepped out.

He looked into his wife's eyes and with a voice loud enough for his children to hear said, "Be aware of your surroundings."

Fear flitted across Allison's face before resolve returned. *Typical of Allison Ben thought.* She nodded and placed her hand on his chest. "Noted," was all she said.

Ben walked out and saw eight men with swords; Japanese katanas to be exact. Using his peripheral vision, he also noticed movement on his right and left. With a shake of his head, he counted the adversaries. He stretched out his arms, as if bored, to his sides with three fingers showing on his right hand and two fingers on his left. Allison saw and called her daughters deeper into the apartment. She sent the smaller children into the master bedroom and gathered her four oldest daughters to the middle of the kitchen. There, they huddled down.

"Put your acting postures on and look terrified. Act when I do," she quietly said.

"Acting terrified? That won't be much of a stretch," Carrie said. She was the eldest at eleven years old, and did as instructed. So did Susan, ten, Whitney, nine, and Roberta, eight. They were not necessarily acting but they readied themselves, calling into memory what their father taught them during their many training sessions.

Ben reached his usual starting spot, looked up to Master and gave slight shake of his head. Master noticed and became curious what Ben was up to.

Without notice, Ben ran to the nearest doorway. His opponents hesitated a few seconds and then took chase as they smelled blood in the water. *Maybe he is human after all one soldier thought.* Once inside the doorway, Ben turned around and stood. The fighters hit the doorway as one and fought to see who could break free to kill Ben. However, they soon saw that he had a Katana in his hands. He had picked it up when it was dropped in the collision.

With some very quick, precise moves and without hesitation, Ben cut and killed every one of his opponents. Then he looked toward the apartment.

While Ben was finishing up his fight, five men entered the apartment. The first man to enter saw Allison and the girls huddled on the floor looking terrified. He got greedy. "Looky here, boys," he called to the others. "Our playthings are ripe for the taking, just as Master said they would be. Let the fun begin." He took a step towards the women.

Immediately, Allison spun on her arms, swinging her right leg hard into the knee of the first man. He had placed all his weight on left leg and the knee buckled as tendons and cartilage tore. Through the force of her kick, the femur and tibia broke as they separated from the knee. He went down hard and received a second kick across his nose with the ball of her foot. That ignited Carrie, Susan, and Whitney, who went into action attacking the now-surprised four men who remained.

The second man was sticking his tongue out at Carrie and making perverted gestures towards her. "I am going to have some fun with that little bitch," he called to his friends and he went for her.

Carrie jumped up and kicked the man on his lower jaw with the ball of her foot, causing him to bite off his tongue. She followed that up with a kick to his chest, sending him to the floor. Susan repeated her mother's move and connected with another man on his knee, causing him to crouch down in pain as Whitney ran up and clawed at his eyes.

The fifth man grabbed Carrie by her hair and threw her to the wall. She fell to the floor, dazed. That was the last thing he ever did. Ben entered and spun his head around one hundred eighty degrees causing him to see Ben's face just before he died. In quick succession, Ben broke the necks of two more men. Whitney was pulled off the man she was attacking, and Ben finished breaking his knee. Then he began slamming his fist into the man's face. Ben then focused on the last man and, without skipping a beat, he kicked him in the groin. As the man went down, his face collided with Ben's knee, which knocked him out. He was awakened when Ben grabbed his face by the outer eye socket and the end of his jaw. Both places are known for having sensitive nerves where, when pinched, can cause extreme pain. Ben used his other hand to do the same thing to the other man who was still alive.

He dragged them out of the apartment and threw them to the ground. He went back in and tossed the dead men on top to the first two.

Then, Ben looked directly to Master and shouted, "Remove these vermin from my house!"

Many of the people in close vicinity of Master felt a shift in power at that moment. More people felt hope returning to them. Of course, they did not let those thoughts slip out for the master to know because they all were indentured in one way or another.

Ben turned around and walked back into the apartment looking at his family. Allison was checking on Carrie. Susan and Whitney were frozen in the middle of the room. Roberta was rocking in the corner by the cabinets with her arms around her knees and her face buried between them. She was crying hard enough to shake her whole body. Ben picked her up and she immediately wrapped her arms around his neck.

"I didn't do anything, Daddy!" she cried. "I'm sorry! I didn't do anything!" She said over and

over between sobs. Ben held his free hand to
Susan and Whitney, who ran to him immediately.
They hugged him as hard as they could and
started to cry with their little sister. Allison and
Carrie came and sat beside Ben.

"Sshhhh, Berty," Ben said. "You did nothing
wrong." He was trying to calm Roberta. "Look
at me," he said. She leaned back and looked her
daddy in the eyes. "You are only eight years old.
I am not upset with you. *No one* is upset with you.
Your sisters have had at least one more year of
training than you. They did all they could do. I am
not expecting more than you can give." Her tears
slowed a little as she listened. "You will get older,"
he said gently in her ear. "You will get smarter.
You will get braver as you train to the next levels.
Your courage will shine when you absolutely need
it." He gestured to the other girls. "Look at your
sisters. They still love you and are grateful you are
their sister. There is no shame for you or on you.
We love you just the way you are."

"Thank you, "Daddy," Roberta said then
continued to cry and hold on to her daddy's neck.

"You girls," he said, pointing in the direction of Allison, Carrie, Susan, and Whitney, "I am very grateful to you for your assistance with your mother. Are any of you hurt?" The three girls said no or shook their heads. Carrie had already recovered from her collision with the wall. Allison held out her right leg, which was starting to sport a nasty bruise. "Not exactly the type of treatment your dancer's legs deserve," Ben said. He patted her leg and she leaned into him. "Let's pray."

The girls huddled around their father and bowed their heads. The other children ran out of the bedroom and joined the rest of their family.

Ben started, "Heavenly Father, I thank You that these children You have gifted me with are unhurt. I thank You that Roberta didn't have to find her courage this time. I know, Lord, You will show her when the time is right for her courage to be released. Show her there is no shame today. *No shame.* I thank You that Carrie, Susan, and Whitney were able to help their mother and sisters in defending against evil men. I thank You for the courage and ability they showed in defense as well. May any injuries be healed soon. We rebuke the evil one and ask for a hedge of protection to be around this little family as we are surrounded by evil forces bent on our destruction. I thank You for guiding my hands and mind as I am forced to fight. May I count on Your strength and wisdom to continue to protect those I love. Once again, Lord, remind Roberta that she did nothing to be ashamed of. We come and ask and give thanks in the name of Jesus, the name that has power and authority, Amen."

He hugged his daughters and kissed each one on their heads.

Carrie, Susan, and Whitney hugged Roberta and went to check on their other brothers and sisters.

"Thanks for the heads up," Allison whispered in his ear. "We need to keep an eye on the girls. Something this traumatic is going to affect them."

"True," he replied. "I know what it is doing to me. We will keep an eye out. What about you? I trained you as well. And you responded brilliantly." Ben got up and gathered some ice from the freezer then wrapped them in a towel. He came back and applied it to her bruised leg. "You hit him really hard to earn this."

She leaned her head on his and quietly said, "Yes I did." They stayed in that position for some time, only moving when the baby needed to nurse.

MASTER'S UNINTENDED CONSEQUENCE

Master was a bit surprised by the actions of the mother and daughters. *I will have to plan better for the next time,* he thought. He turned his back to the activities below as the crews deposited the defeated assailants into the croc pit.

The short ninja that was always behind Master leaned forward and quietly stated, "If I don't kill that man, you will fail." Master seemed to not hear, but a slight shiver ran down his spine imperceptibly.

A couple of hours later after Master and crew had left, the Bickles family had an unannounced visitor.

"Knock. Knock," came a quiet whispered voice. "It's Doctor Woo. I have come to see if anybody has any serious injuries from this afternoon."

Dr. Woo was an elderly man of Chinese descent. He stood approximately five-feet-eight inches tall, though he was a little stooped forward. His hair was full but showed more gray than the original black, and his face showed a hint of caring but was otherwise solemn. Ben relaxed and let the doctor in.

"Master does not know I am here," Dr. Woo said. "The guards seemed grateful to have me come here tonight," the doctor stated. "I wanted to check on you myself. Any injuries?"

"Would you look at my wife's leg? I think it will be just a bruise, but while you are here you might as well double check it for us."

Allison came into the dining room and sat down while the doctor checked out the injury.

When he finished his examination, he declared that, indeed, it would be just a bruise. "Are there any other injuries that might need my attention? Perhaps the girl who was thrown to the wall?"

"Carrie," Allison called out to her daughter, "please come out here. The doctor wants to be sure you are ok."

The doctor checked Carrie for a possible concussion and found none. There was a little bump on her forehead, but that was all. "Wonderful, Mr. Bickles. You have a very strong, very tough family. I had better go now before the guards get nervous and shoo me away. There are a lot of people hoping and praying that Master's reign of evil will end soon so we can be free. But you didn't hear that from me." Dr. Woo turned and rushed out, being sure not to make any noise.

"Well, I for one am grateful you two are not seriously injured. What say the whole family play a game of charades." Ben clapped his hands and smiled at the potential of some family play time. The rest of the family came out and enjoyed a good game of charades. Of course, Daddy always lost.[6]

SALVATION FOR THE NINJA?

As time passed, Ben's opponents became less enthusiastic about fighting him. Even though Master kept increasing the number of opponents for each fight, they lost. They lost even when Master started to give weapons to his fighters. Although some of the weapons injured Ben, he still prevailed. His scars would become a testament to the physical pain he would suffer, regardless of his victories.

---

6 It was at this moment (somewhere nearby but unbeknownst to Ben and his family), Amina, Javier, Torrance, Nelson, and Cassondra Bickles were sold to slavers and forced on a ship to begin their seven-month journey into the world of forced debauchery.

Allison's nursing skills were put to the test after each fight, as well as her psychological skills. The added noise of the children was good, but there was very little that kept him motivated. According to Ben, Allison was perfect at her task. Ben told them, as he told Master and those with him, that no weapon devised against him would stand.

Over time, they began to believe him.

A month after their fourteenth child was born, during their fifteenth year in captivity, on the night before Ben's next fight, Master got an idea. He called his trusted lieutenant, Hirohito Tachibana, the shadow ninja.

"You are ninja trained. Yes?" asked Master.

"Yes, Master," the ninja replied calmly.

"I have a special job for you," Master started to tell him as he looked at the apartment where the Bickles family were sleeping.

"Yes, Master. What is your command?"

"You are to get in the apartment without waking the Bickles, then take the infant and next youngest child. The infant is for my special friend's satanic sacrifice. The child is for the cannibal in America. Do not try to drop in from the top, even though there is no ceiling. Bickles has somehow made that way a trap. You would not be able to be silent that way. You must enter through the doorway. As you know, there is no door. Can you do it before they awaken?"

"Yes, Master. Silence is my specialty."

Master paused a while. Without looking at his lieutenant, said, "Go. Now!"

The ninja bowed and left. An hour later, dressed in his ninja attire and under the cover of total darkness, he arrived at the doorway. As he tried to enter the doorway, he ran into something very hard. *There is not supposed to be a door here.*

Suddenly, a big hand grasped his neck and lifted him off his feet. Having witnessed all the fights and the preaching, the ninja knew he was dead, one way or another. Even though he had ninja skills, his willingness to fight had left him.

Then, he heard a quiet but authoritative voice speak, "What are you doing here, little man?"

The voice belonged to Benjamin Bickles. Tachibana went limp and told Ben the whole story about the children. While Ninja spoke, Ben kept his voice quiet and calm, although his anger was ignited. Afterward, Ben asked, "Before anything else happens, I have one question. I know you have been in attendance at every fight and heard all my sermons. It is now time for you to make a decision. What do you say about the free gift of eternal life through Jesus the Christ?"

"With all I have done in my life," Ninja responded, "how can anyone forgive me? I am not worthy of forgiveness. All that I can hope for is that I will be reincarnated as nothing lower than a viper. At least they only kill for food or defense. I have done much worse," Hirohito said as he resigned himself to eternal damnation.

"It is appointed *once* for man to die and then the judgment. There is no reincarnation," Ben said, then he waited to let that sink in. "Have you blasphemed the Holy Spirit?"

Hirohito was surprised at that question. "I don't know. Aren't my evils enough to do that?"

"Those are just sinful actions. I will assume you haven't blasphemed. Since you are still alive, you can still be forgiven and serve Jesus throughout eternity."

"At this late hour of my life. How is that possible?"

Ben looked at him thoughtfully, then said, "One of the men nailed to a cross next to Jesus said, 'Jesus, remember me when you come into your Kingdom.' Jesus answered him, 'Truly I tell you, today you will be with me in paradise.' If that man can be given the free gift of life, then so can you."

Hirohito said back, "Don't you understand, I have sent thousands of children and women to slavery or death. I have done too much evil to be given such a gift."

Ben put the ninja on the floor and invited him to sit where he was. Ben took his own seat across from him and continued to talk to the man who felt defeated. Allison woke up hearing voices from the doorway. She got out of her bed, looking into the darkness, and was able to make out the silhouette of her husband sitting in the doorway. He was talking to a man opposite from him. She heard the conversation and immediately went back to her bed, kneeling down beside it. She started to pray for the salvation of the other man. Her passionate prayers woke the children, who came to her and asked what was going on. She told them what she knew, and the children joined her in prayer at the side of the bed.

No one slept the rest of the night as Ben and Hirohito argued back and forth. Hirohito constantly rebutted Ben's arguments concerned he had committed too much evil to be saved.

"Moses committed murder," Ben said, trying to reason with the ninja. "King David committed adultery and murder. Saul sought out early Christians and had them killed until he met Jesus on the road to Emmaus. His life changed from that moment." Ben spoke quietly, no longer angered but hopeful. "I think it is time you meet Jesus as well."

When he said this, the other man went silent. After a few moments of silence, Hirohito fell on his face crying. He confessed his sins to Jesus, asking to be forgiven and promising to serve Him through eternity.

Ben knelt beside him and laid his hand on the small man. There was no hostility. The sun had started to shine through the windows. Hirohito stood, looking like a man alive and smiling. "I feel a huge mass removed from my body," he said, astounded, "and I feel great joy! The greatest joy I have ever experienced." Tears flowed down his face.

Ben stood and greeted him. "This is your new birthday," he told Hirohito. "Welcome to the family, brother." Ben hugged him happily and received an equally happy hug in return. Allison and the children came out of the bedroom, expressing gladness for their new brother in Christ.

"You know," Ben said, "Master is going to kill you now. Do you want me to stand with you?"

Hirohito responded, "No. I will do this myself. Besides," he said, smiling, "I have Jesus at my side now." With that, Hirohito walked to the center of the arena and waited.

Heavenly Host and a Semi-final Fight

Master arrived shortly thereafter and saw the entire Bickles family standing in front of the apartment. He turned his sight on his lieutenant. "Why have you not done what I ordered?" he asked.

With a bold voice, Hirohito replied, "I no longer serve you or your evil. I serve Jesus the Christ!" His shout astonished the troops he once commanded.

Master stared right at his former subordinate, seething under his calm expression. Then, he held his hand out and ordered, "Give me your weapon.". The nearest soldier at his right did as ordered, handing him a loaded pistol.

Master shot his former lieutenant.

Just before Master pulled the trigger Hirohito was bathed in a bright light that went away as he died. It did not go unnoticed by Master and the men in suits that Hirohito Tachibana's face had the look of peace as he passed away. Master was a little bit unnerved. The suits were puzzled at first as well, then they began allowing themselves to have hopeful emotions. They looked at the Bickles family and saw a true miracle.

Everyone on Master's side of the arena saw the Bickles family surrounded by a great host of human-like creatures. The beings were bathed in glistening white robes, some with wings, that covered the entire space from wall to wall and floor to ceiling. Everyone who saw it felt extreme fear. Everyone, that is, except Master. He felt a movement up and down his spine and wondered what it was. *Fear?* he mused, *I refuse to allow it.* For the suits, it was a sign that gave them hope. However, from that moment on he never tried to bother the Bickles family again.

The Bickles family did not see the Heavenly Host and wondered at the reaction of the forces opposite them.

After the family returned to the apartment and the remains of Hirohito were tossed into the croc pit, Ben went out to fight his schedule battle that day. This time, there were twenty-five fighters dressed in armor and weapons.

Master spoke first, "Win this fight and the next one will be your last. Against me."

Ben acknowledged the situation and did away with his usual warm-up routine. He put on the face of love before he started to speak again. He did not want a combative mood to show as he knew this is decision day for these men.

To all in the arena, he spoke, "Today, you need to make a decision. Continue to serve Master or serve the *true* Master, Jesus the Christ. If you choose Jesus, lay down your weapons and confess that Jesus is your Lord and Savior."

One by one, eight men dropped their weapons and started to confess.

Master shot each one dead himself.

Ben calmy looked at him and said, "You have only killed the body. They are now seeing Jesus, face-to-face. They are rejoicing with Him." Ben sighed briefly, preparing to fight the remaining seventeen men. "You continue to do foolish things. Jesus is waiting for you. You do realize that there will come a time when every knee shall bow, and every tongue will confess that Jesus the Christ is Lord. You will do it willingly or under compulsion. Your choice." Ben pointed to the bodies on the floor. "These men did it willingly."

Three more men dropped their weapons and started to confess. Master shot them, too. "ENOUGH TALK!" Master bellowed. "FIGHT!"

This fight was extremely tough because of the armor. However, the soldiers' fighting spirit had fled them at the sight of the heavenly host, so they were filled with fear. Ben was injured more severely this time during the fighting. He felt the knives piercing his skin, the tip of a spear, and the smack of chains making contact with his back and legs. Somehow, the weapons never touched his head. And as before, Ben prevailed. He stumbled into the apartment and Allison went to work. This time, their four oldest daughters helped out as well.

"I praise God every day that He brought us together," Ben exhaustedly breathed. "And that we have such precious children."

The youngest one started to cry. "Time to feed that little rascal," Allison said to her elder daughters. "Girls, make sure we got all of Daddy's injuries taken care of."

"Yes, Mama." They said in unison and continued to address their Daddy's wounds. As the daughters fully took over, Allison got up to attend to the baby.

"Daddy," Carrie asked, "is what Master said about us true? About what would happen if you lose?"

Ben paused before answering. "Yes. Which is why I endeavor to not allow him to win. With God's help we will prevail."

"But—"

"No buts," Ben said, cutting her off. "How about we pray to take away your fears." So, they did. God answered their prayers and removed their fear. However, they were still a bit concerned as to who would prevail; Master, or their father.

WHO WILL BE THE VICTOR?

The family enjoyed a couple of months of peace and Ben had a couple of months to heal and recover from the last fight before Master called Ben to come out to the arena. That day, Ben hugged and kissed his family. Then they prayed and he walked out.

Master was just as naked as Ben, when he was in the arena. *An interesting twist*, Ben thought. *Definitely fit and trim. Not an ounce of fat to be seen. But some rather odd scars all over his body. He must have been in some serious fights. With man or animal?* Ben considered as he sized up his final opponent.

"This battle will determine who is fed to the crocs. No more talking. No more preaching. Just fight." Then with a boastful laugh, Master said, "I have watched you fight. You made sure to never repeat a battle. That is until the last couple of fights. You repeated your moves which tell me you have exhausted your repertoire. You know nothing about me. I know everything about you. I will be victorious!"

Allison, who was standing in the doorway of the apartment, called out to Ben. He looked and saw Allison calling him over to speak to her. Ben turned to Master and raised his finger at him. "One moment, please," he said before turning without waiting for an answer. Ben walked back to see what his wife wanted at a time like this.

"You know," she said, relishing in Ben's rebellion against the man, "I have almost never let you *have* your rage throughout our lives?"

Ben was curious where this line of questioning was going to lead. "Yes," he told her. "I know full well. Which is why I am grateful to God that you are my wife. But why do you ask?" Master started walking slowly toward the couple.

Allison saw what Master was up to but remained calm for her husband's sake. "Today, do not stop your rage. I cannot explain it. But I feel deep in my soul that you must be full on fighting this man. You are very smart. I have done everything I can to help you keep your rage under control. Today you must *release it!* Release your rage upon that most evil man!" She reached up and gave him a quick kiss, then whispered in his ear, "He is about fifteen yards away and closing."

Ben looked at his wife and winked while he let his rage boil up within him. His muscles prepared for action while adrenaline poured through his body like a flood.

Master started boasting, "I am a descendant of Idi Amin of Uganda, Pol Pot of Cambodia, and Kim il Sung of North Korea. It is my destiny to rule this world. I follow my ancestors' vision by domination. I cannot be defeated by someone as simple as you. I have been watching you these many years and have studied your techniques. I have found you repeating some, more and more. I now know you have no other surprises left. You are brave. You are strong. You are the most formidable opponent I have ever seen. But today, you will be dead. I OWN YOU!"

"Bold words," Ben replied, not turning around. "Your kind of tyranny only lasts for a short time. Today, your reign of tyranny ends." Ben's words caused fear to creep into Master's mind and this time, it was a fear he couldn't shake.

Ben remained gazing at Allison until she told him the master was within five yards. Then, he moved with a speed that surprised Master, who was no slouch in hand-to-hand combat. and planted his right foot across Master's jaw, sending him to the floor. "That was for Roberta!" Ben declared.

Master smiled and seemed completely unfazed. "Nice move. Doesn't hurt a bit." He wasn't lying.

Master was born with a congenital disease known as CIPA, Congenital Insensitivity to Pain and Anhidrosis. He could feel touch, receive pleasure, and feel everything a normal human can feel. Just not pain. Master learned at a very young age how to protect himself. That, however, never stopped him from martial arts training. He went on the attack immediately with a series of kicks and punches that put Ben on the defensive. Master even got in a lick with his foot to Ben's head. That surprised Ben. The only other person to ever land a punch or kick to his head was Michael Roberts, his childhood friend. Thankfully, Ben's training prevented him from becoming dazed at the blow. "Well now, that was a surprise," he retorted.

The two men circled each other, looking for the right time to go on the offensive. A step here. A step there. Each observing the other's response, totally aware of how dangerous the other man was.

Suddenly, Master made a small misstep and Ben pounced. Master recovered quickly and the two naked men were in close combat. They threw punches and kicks that did little damage until one punch hit Ben in the kidney. He knew he was going to feel that for a couple of weeks. Ben's counter to Master's head sent his opponent back a couple of steps. Ben finished that move with a broadside kick with his shin. His blow connected with Master's ribs, breaking five and sending three of them into his left lung.

Master knew he had been wounded badly as he felt a twinge—a slight pain. He had never felt it like this before, and he fell to his knees, coughing up blood, his breathing affected. Master looked up and decided it was the time to make a quick grab at Ben's genitals.

Ben expected the move and stepped past Master's hand. He gripped Master's arm between his legs. Spinning around, Ben turned so fast and hard with his legs that it caused a compound fracture of the humerus, radius and ulna bones. Master's shoulder separated, as well as his elbow. Ben's move had so much wrath it made the arm totally useless. "THAT WAS FOR ROSETA!" Ben announced in his rage.

Master felt another twinge and looked at his arm, mesmerized by the blood flowing where the bone protruded the skin.

Once again, Ben took advantage. He placed his opponent's foot on a nearby chair then body slammed Master's knee, tearing ligaments, cartilage, and breaking the femur. Master was totally immobilized and felt a twinge again. He realized he was bested, as he could barely breathe or move. "THAT WAS FOR TERESA!" Ben's voice was loud and clear.

Allison was watching what went on around the area, as were the three people in suits usually around Master. Each inwardly cheered for their own champion.

Ben then stepped to the side of Master and reached for his scrotum. "You were going to deprive me of mine. Now I am going to deprive you of yours." After grasping the sack and the testicles, Ben yanked with all he had and tore his testes along with the skin around the penis. "THAT WAS FOR ALL OF THE PEOPLE WHOSE LIVES YOU HAVE DESTROYED THROUHOUT YOUR LIFE!" He tossed the body parts into the pit.

Now that Master felt. It was something he had never experienced in his lifetime. *Is that what pain feels like*, Master thought. *I don't like it.*

Ben stepped back a few steps and calmed his breathing. He noticed another odd thing. There was a wash basin set up about twenty yards from his position. He walked over to wash the blood from his body.

While Ben was washing, Master recalled his life, realizing it would soon be over. *I am sorry, Father. I tried to follow everything you taught me. That my disease was a blessing and not a curse as you guided me through the years. You showed me how to fight without getting injured. You admonished me to gather dedicated friends with the same values to watch over me. You taught me that girls and women are replaceable creatures, good only for pleasure or procreation. You saw me getting pleasure by playing with my manhood.*

You showed me how to use it properly when I raped my little sister at eight years old. Then you watched as I tossed her into the river where the crocodiles were. When you saw the joy on my face as I watched her being eaten by them you celebrated my joy. That was when I learned to love those beautiful reptiles.

Master smiled as he remembered more. *When I was twelve, you encouraged me to rape my mother several times before slitting her throat. You cheered at the joy I displayed. You said I needed to outwardly be a good and decent man while secretly enjoying my perversions. After that you guided me in martial arts training, always keeping in mind my disease, schooling and business.*

I did everything you said. I have the best friends and business acquaintances. They serve me well and protect me.

You also advised me to document everything and everybody as that would be my shield from those who would try to stop me. I became that best type of businessman. I am loved, Father.

You also told me that if anybody would stop me it would be the Christians. So, I made it my goal to destroy everyone I could. I did not expect that vision of yours would come true.

My hatred of the Japanese came when you pointed out their atrocities throughout their war with China. I have put their total destruction in place, though I am sorry I will not see their ultimate demise.

Master looked at the injuries his body received at the hands of that Christian. So much blood. So much blood.

"I thought you were supposed to love your enemies," choked Master through the blood foaming out of his mouth. "Look at you now."

"I do love you," Ben said, "as a human being created by God. I hate *your sin*. If I had not loved you, I would not have shared the Word of God with you in hopes of you coming to repentance. One question," Ben said as he finished washing, "Who do you say Jesus is?"

"If I tell you what you want to hear," the defeated man choked, "will you spare me?"

"It's not about what I want to hear. It is about what God knows about the truth in your heart. So don't lie. Also, whether I spare you or not is not up to me. God will let me know what is to be done with you."

"In that case," he sneered, "Jesus was an egotistical moron that deceived others to make himself to be god."

"Wrong answer! Last chance. Will you change your life to Jesus?"

"I will see you in hell first! I hate you Christians!" He coughed out more blood.

Ben was able to evade the blood that spewed out of Master's mouth. "Wrong answer again."

Ben didn't finish him off. Instead, he put two fingers in Master's nostrils and dragged him to the pit where he tossed him in, alive. The crocs were grateful and extremely vicious. Several had risen up on their tails and grabbed Master before he landed. They were tearing him apart before he made it to the water.

Ben didn't watch the action below. He had heard it many times before. It saddened him that someone would say and do such horrendous things and, when offered hope of salvation, decides to curse God instead.

Ben noticed the big soldier who killed Teresa and called him over, asking to see the massive sword he was holding. The man was a bit confused as the one he had known as Master was dead. He knew that the rule was, whomever defeated Master was to, then and therefore, be the new master. But he was hoping to kill at least one of the children that was in the apartment. Now, however, he reluctantly handed the sword over to him. Ben made it appear as if he was looking at a finely tuned instrument. Suddenly, he smashed the butt end of the sword in the man's face, causing him to stagger back a few steps. Ben quickly repeated the blow until the man fell back into the pit. Once again the crocodiles rose up high on their tales and repeated what they did to Master.

"HER NAME WAS TERESA AND SHE... WAS... INNOCENT!" Ben screamed. He slammed the sword broadside on the edge of the pit with such force, it broke the sword. Then he tossed the pieces into the pit.

A wave of relief swept over the remaining group of Master's servants. That included everyone wearing suits. Their torment was finally over and their hope was renewed. Ben looked up to the suited personnel and saw wet faces as tears flooded down. Not what he was expecting to see.

WHO ARE YOU?

Ben turned and glared at the spectators, including the men in suits with their briefcases. They stared back, smiling and nodding their heads at him and each other. Although this activity puzzled him, Ben couldn't care at that time. He turned to head back to the apartment, a scowl dominating his face. Allison, who stood in the doorway with her feet spread and arms held across her chest, noticed Ben's mood. She retreated into the dining/kitchen area and waited for Ben to enter.

*Lord, grant me the strength to endure what is to come
next. Please!*

When he walked into the room, he saw Allison
leaning against the table. He walked up to her and
just stared into her eyes.

She reached up and cupped his head in her hands.
"Your anger and aggression are not relieved," she
quietly stated as she brushed his hair aside. All Ben
could do was just stare at her, although he normally
relished her caresses. "Give them to me," she said.
This request seemed to puzzle her husband. His
scowl darkened at her. "Don't question. Don't
think. Just give me your aggression and anger. Let
me have it so you can be fully relieved."

Ben shook his head, wanting to deny her request.
But she would not be denied. She knew what he
needed, and she was willing to do whatever it
took to bring her husband back from the abyss
of torment.

"Give them to me!" she said, getting more forceful
in her request. "Give them to me! Give them ALL
to me. Now!"

That did it.

Ben took her, right there on the table. They began to make love aggressively, but not violently. The first rounds were hard on her. *Lord, grant me your strength*, she prayed to her Lord before she told Ben, once again, "Give it to me!"

Ben knew he wasn't treating her right, but he was unable to stop himself, especially since she kept urging him on. Finally, after what seemed like eons, he seemed to be spent.

She cupped his face in her hands as she saw the change in his countenance. "*There* you are," she said, her voice soft and somewhat breathless. "There you are. Welcome back, my love." She kissed his forehead, cheeks, chin, nose, eyebrows, and finally his lips, all the while praising God because Ben's anger, frustration, and aggression was finally gone.

Ben suddenly realized what he had done to her, and horror hit him. "Are you ok?" he asked. "I never wanted to hurt you."

"I will be sore for a bit but, yes, I am ok." Tears started to fill his eyes, but she kissed them away. "Do you have one more left?"

He looked at her with concern and nodded. She wrapped her arms around his neck. "Then, let's have one more go around," she touched him gently. "But this time as loving husband and wife." He paused for a few seconds, gazing into her eyes again and slowly lowered his lips to hers. They made love again and it was indeed for love. Afterward, he rested on his back on the table, staring at the ceiling.

Ben's mind raced through memories. Roberta's violation, to Teresa's murder, to the faces of all the men he had killed, to the faces of his friends, to his children. He wondered what was going to happen now that his main antagonist was dead and gone.

Suddenly, a softly spoken question took over his mind.

"Who are you?"

The voice belonged to Allison, who was lying on the table next to him with her right leg across his. Her head rested on his shoulder as her hand caressed his. Ben massaged her ribs. *The very ribs that were hit by a rifle butt the first day they were there*, he mused. She gently touched his face, shoulder, and chest before curling her fingers in his chest hair. Allison's eyes were closed, enjoying the intimacy.

Memories of their teenage years flooded Ben's mind. Once a month, while Michael, Derrick, and himself were combing Allison, Susan, and Carrie's hair (on whichever porch was the choice of the evening), they would play a game called "Who are you?" Most of the time, the responses were on the make-believe scale. Occasionally, they made the question serious, to help them remember who they were.

One time, Ben said he was a dwarf, one that can crawl into small places.

Leave it to Michael to find fault. "You do realize that," he began, "if you are such a dwarf and you are walking on the busy sidewalk with other people, things could get rather odorous. All someone has to do is fart and your face is the immediate recipient of the pass." Ben changed his mind after that. "Sorry, Ben," while everyone snickered. "I saw an old video of a comedian making such a joke and I just couldn't resist because you seemed so serious." *Leave it to Michael to turn a good thing into something different,* Ben thought.

These thoughts continued to flood his mind as, once again, the question pierced through. "Who are you?" He turned his head so he could look at the person asking. His eyes met hers as she had opened them and tilted her head to see into his eyes. He returned to staring at the ceiling, still not answering.

She reached over, and with gentle but persistent pressure, turned his head so that their eyes met again. *"Who are you?"* Her voice was barely above a whisper.

Tears started to flood his eyes as he finally answered her question. "I am a man. Created by God to do His will. I am a husband of one wife, although I haven't performed my role as husband perfectly," Ben said, remembering the adulteries. "I am the father of many children. I pray they recognize me as Daddy and not just father. I am the son of Manfred and Jamie Bickles. I am a man."

"Yes, you are," she said, her voice barely above a whisper.

He looked at her with concern on his features. "Am I? Really? Have you seen what I have done?" He suddenly stopped and realized she had. Every bit of it. "I mean, The adulteries. The killings! How can I be a man for God with all that has happened. How can he really love *me*? Did I do right, Allison? Did I do right?"

She took a few minutes before she replied. And with her voice once again barely above a whisper and her hand continuing to caress him, she turned his face to hers. "I can't fully say," she began. "But I know this. Do you honestly think you could have defeated all of them without God's hand on you?" Then she turned his face to hers. "What is done is done. We have to lay everything at His feet continually, just as we have been doing all these years. Benjamin Manfred Bickles, for the rest of your life, never stop devoting your life to Jesus. Let Him use you for His will. And if He wants you to do this all over again, do so with all the courage He gifts you with." She kissed his eyes. "We will take each moment, each day, each week, each year, no matter the circumstance, with joy. Why? Because we know we are solely devoted to Him." Ben looked up again and said, "Thank you, Jesus the Christ. I await your orders. Use me as You will."

Allison smiled wide, knowing her husband had indeed returned. She kissed his tears away and then almost suffocated him with her kisses as she held on to him hard, rejoicing. When they finally came up for air, she reminded him of their children. "I think it is time we brought the children out. They could be bouncing the walls waiting for us."

"Good idea," he admitted. But when they were about to get up, they slid a little.

"Oops!" Allison said. "Looks like we made a mess." She had to admit the table was rather slippery. They fell back down on the table laughing.

"Young Mrs. Bickles, you get up and clean yourself off. I will start to clean up this mess. I think a shower would be ideal." Allison laughed with her husband before she got up to take a shower. Ben gave a swat on her backside as she left which caused her yelp a little. Ben got up slowly and proceeded to clean the table and the chairs. By the time he was about to tackle the floor, Allison came back and sent him to the shower, picking up where he left off. When Ben finished dressing, he checked with Allison, who had completed the cleanup. He went to the room where the children were and let them out. Wisdom told him to step back as the rush to get out would have trampled him over.

After the excitement was over and the children realized that their daddy had defeated the enemy, they hugged their parents hard enough to make everyone fall to the floor. There, Ben reached for the one-year-old, but Allison received the baby from Carrie, who immediately wanted to nurse. Ben faced Allison and took her free hand in his. He leaned in so that their foreheads touched before calling the children to join them in prayer. The children huddled with their parents, relishing the opportunity of a family prayer. Outside the doorway, the suited men heard the call for prayer and waited, listening as Ben led the prayer time.

"Heavenly Father, Lord God, and Jesus the Christ," Ben started. "Thank You for guiding me to finish the path You have designed for me. We can rejoice that I don't have to fight for the man called Master anymore. However, we don't know what will come next. Are we free? Can we go home to our families? We need Your continued guidance and protection. And, if it be Your will, may we see our families and friends again. However, not our will, but Yours be done. Amen."

The children added their Amens as they got up and started cheering their daddy's victory. Despite the celebration, Ben heard the suits making sounds at the door.

He spun around, ready to face whatever danger that may come next. His protective instincts still on high alert.

GERALDO SANCHEZ

"Mr. Bickles. I am Geraldo Sanchez," one man said. "I am Mr. Kim Chan Lee's business attorney." He noticed the 'Who is that' and 'Why should I care' attitudes as they crossed Ben's face. "'Master,' as you knew him. I guess I am no longer his attorney but yours, as you are now leader of His empire."

"What do you want?" Ben said, taking a step toward Sanchez. The man was a short and stocky, with male pattern baldness and a swarthy complexion that said he was from a South American country, Ben surmised. He also carried himself as a man of authority yet he seemed to have a caring look on his face. Ben remembered him, often sitting or standing behind Master and that he always wore a black suit with a blue tie. He wore the same outfit now. "You and the other suits were always behind Master," Bensaid to himself, "Umm, Mr. Kim. I repeat. What do you want?" He took another step. "And Mr. Bickles is what people call my father."

Sanchez held his hands high in a posture of surrender. "We, Mr. Bickles, have all been enslaved by that evil man and held in place because of the evil he would, and has, done to our families. We are extremely grateful for your victory, which frees us from his tyranny. But we are nothing more than accountants."

Ben stopped moving, much to the relief of the suited men.

"We need to get you up to date on the organization as soon as possible," Mr. Sanchez said. "That is why we are going to meet with you tomorrow morning. You can have the rest of today with your family." He turned to leave but felt a nudge from one of the other suited men. He turned back to the family. "OH!" Mr. Sanchez said, eyes widening. "Pardon me. There is one more thing. We will have clothiers here first thing tomorrow, so you and your family can be fitted with clothes. This will include undergarments, shoes and suits for you, sir." He gestured to Ben. "Also, we will bring crafts, learning books, and such for your children to keep them occupied during our briefing." He checked his thoughts to be sure he covered everything. "With that, we will see you after morning breakfast, Mr. Bickles." He turned and walked out.

"Hold on!" Ben said with an air of command. Sanchez and company stopped and turned around to face him. "Many times I hit him hard enough to hurt him. He didn't seem fazed at all. Especially when I broke his ribs. That in and of itself should have incapacitate him."

"Let me tell you what you were dealing with." Sanchez went on, in a quiet voice because he didn't think the children needed to hear. He got closer to Ben and Allison before he went on to explain the disease Master had to deal with, the guards that protected him, how only one part of his body gave him great pleasure. It was clear how he used that for his prosperity, and how he was able to fight and win. That is until now. "His guards have been ordered to not retaliate against you were you to be victorious. They are all, now, committing suicide to prevent you from dealing with them as per his orders. And, yes, they were that devoted." Sanchez gave a small head bow, turned around and left.

Ben was stunned by these events and slowly turned around to face his equally puzzled family.

Roberta was the first to speak. "Clothing? Undergarments? Does he mean shirts, pants, skirts, bras, panties, socks, and shoes like you have been telling us about?"

Allison responded, still shocked at what she learned about the now dead master. "Yes. That is exactly what that means."

Roberta crossed her arms across her chest and with an attitude of defiance, stated, "I don't need them, and I don't want them. I am happy the way we are!" She was joined by Whitney, Michael, and Derrick. The other children were confused as to which way they should go and what to think about it all.

Allison clapped her hands. "Alright. School is in session. Everybody sit down." The children obeyed immediately. So did Ben, Allison noticed. "Sweetheart. Why don't you stand next to me." Ben got up to stand next to his wife, trying to put on a serious face for his children. Some of them giggled a bit. Allison frowned at him, and he just shrugged his shoulders. When he did that, Allison just shook her head at her husband's silly behavior. *So relieved to have you back, my love,* she thought.

Roberta, with a chip on her shoulder, had plopped down on the bench by the table without uncrossing her arms or losing her attitude.

Allison began, "Clothing serves several purposes. First, because of man's sin, God made clothes for the first couple, Adam and Eve. This is because nakedness became an avenue for sin. Especially out in the world. You saw the evil that is out there," she said, indicating the arena's direction. She had her children's full attention after that. "Clothing also hides scars, sores, and other blemishes to keep people from being disgusted by looking at those things. Clothing also protects the body from scratches and other small injuries to the skin, as well as from the weather. We are light-skinned. So, if we are standing under the sun too long, our skin will burn." She waved her hands. "And that is very painful." Roberta uncrossed her arms. "Also, there is weather that will freeze your bodies. Clothing is needed to keep us warm. When the wind blows strong, it drives small items like sand, twigs, leaves and such that can bruise, cut or do worse to your bodies. But clothing can also help with accentuating your beauty."

Ben chimed in on that, "You don't know it now, but your mother wore a dress on our senior cruise that made me bug-eyed and stupid because she looked beyond gorgeous."

Allison responded, "And your Daddy wore a tuxedo." Allison saw the puzzled looks at that word. "It's a very fancy suit." The children seemed to understand that. "I thought I had died and gone to Heaven to see such a handsome man." Then she focused on Roberta. "So, you see, clothing is absolutely necessary in the outside world. Understand?" Roberta nodded, followed by the entire family. Ben exaggerated his nods and made the children laugh. Allison looked at her husband with her hands on her hips and Ben looked up to where the walls would have met the nonexistent ceiling, so as to not recognize Allison's posture.

The rest of the day the family played games and just had a good time together without the stress that had covered them for the last fifteen years.

Carrie had walked over to her dad and gave him a huge hug. "Daddy, you seem really happy now. I am so glad to see it. I love you, Daddy!" She squeezed him as hard as she could. Ben responded by returning the hug and shedding some tears. "I'm sorry, Daddy. I didn't mean to make you sad." Carrie was on the verge of crying herself because she didn't want to hurt him.

"I am not sad, my daughter," Ben replied. "I am so happy that I can be happy in spite of the years that are now over. Having you happy, for me, was just the dessert after dinner. I love you so much. Thank you for your love for me. And your prayers." They squeezed each other again. Allison saw and heard the exchange and her heart swelled with joy.

That night, everybody, slept well and peacefully. That is, except Ben. Ben's constant state of protection had not waned. He was still on alert.

PLAYING DRESS UP

The following morning's breakfast was a raucous affair. Everybody was trying to figure out what the clothes would look like and if they would like them after they were made. Ben was starting to wash the dishes when Roberta came up and helped him. Ben realized she wanted to say something and waited for her to broach the thoughts on her mind.

"Daddy?" She started as she was wiping a plate dry. "I am sorry for my attitude yesterday."

"That's ok, Berty." He handed her another plate.

"I still don't like the idea of wearing clothes, but I believe Mama is right. We need to. I want you to wear clothes to hide your scars."

Ben was a little taken aback by his daughter's straight forwardness. "Are you ashamed of my scars?"

"Oh, no, Daddy. Those scars are you. I just want them to be just for us and us alone."

"Are you saying you are proud of the scars?"

"No again, Daddy. I don't think anybody else in this world will understand the pain you went through to get those scars." She stopped drying the plate and looked at her father. "You are *our* daddy. And I don't want anybody else to say that those scars belong to anybody else."

Ben wiped his hands dry and led his daughter to the bench by the table. He wiped away her tears before he spoke. "Berty, these scars tell a story. Of how I, with God's help, battled to make things right in this world. I understand you want ownership because your daddy earned them. However, there may be other children who can claim ownership as well. I don't know if they are alive or not. And if they are alive, I don't know where they are. I am talking about the possibility that you may have twenty half brothers and sisters. I will find out about them soon. But if you want me to only expose these scars to family alone, I will be sure to do just that. Ok?" She jumped into her daddy's arms and apologized for being selfish.

Just then, a knock on the doorpost got their attention.

Ben stood up so quickly that Roberta was pulled up with him. He placed her on the floor behind him. Protection mode wasn't going away anytime soon.

"Excuse me again, Bickles family," Mr. Sanchez said from outside the apartment. "It is time. Mr. Bickles, will you bring your family out here, please." Mr. Sanchez peaked in, but backed out as Ben and Allison escorted their children out of the apartment for the third time. The children were still a little hesitant to venture out of the apartment as they had been well taught never to go past the doorway. It took some extra coaxing by their parents, but they finally decided to follow them. In front of the family were dozens of people standing in front of piles of fabric. To the right of the piles were dozens of sewing machines waiting to be turned on.

Ben now understood the noises he heard early in the morning.

Mr. Sanchez pointed to the personnel behind him. "These people are tailors and seamstresses,"

he said. "They will be measuring and making
the lion's share of the shirts, pants, and skirts
for everybody. Mrs. Bickles, you will also have
a couple of dresses and casual clothes made for
you as well. Mr. Bickles, you will need some suits,
a tuxedo, and casual wear made especially for
you. Now," Sanchez said while gesturing, "if you
all would step up to the squares on the floor, we
will get started." Ben walked over to the square
assigned to him. The rest of the family hesitated
until he had stopped on the square. Seeing all was
safe, they went to their assigned squares.

Ben held up his hand. "Any wrong moves or
inappropriate activity will be acted upon severely.
Understand?" All the tailors and seamstresses
agreed by nodding.

"Not to worry, Mr. Bickles," said Mr. Sanchez.
"They all know who you are and what you have
done. They only want to serve you, happily, for
freeing them from Mr. Kim."

Ben looked at each person, recognizing their
joy and willingness to serve him and his family.

He nodded to Allison and the kids and greeted the people.

"Thank you for helping us with making our clothes," he told them. "We are very grateful for you." All the tailors and seamstresses couldn't smile big enough and went to work.

Mr. Sanchez once again addressed Ben and Allison. "Mr. and Mrs. Bickles, undergarments will now be made. We have multiple designs and sizes available. But each child and adult must have proper fitting undergarments sized for them. It will call for test fitting. I hope you are prepared for that."

Before either parent could respond, Roberta spoke up. "I am not wearing panties or bra until I see my mama wearing them."

Mr. Sanchez was speechless. Ben helped him out. "As you can see, we have a little rebellion on our hands." Mr. Sanchez nodded, turning his head so they couldn't see him blushing at the young girl's boldness.

Ben went first and was fitted with boxer briefs. Allison went next, receiving a proper bra and panties. They turned to their children and told them to get measured. One by one the children allowed themselves to be fitted with undergarments. Roberta glared at the woman assigned to help her. The woman looked to Allison, who winked and nodded, allowing her to proceed. She smiled back at Allison, then turned to Roberta and glared at the girl.

The boys chose the same style as their father while the girls imitated their mother. Memories flooded Ben and Allison with the days before they were kidnapped and the fuss they made sometimes about how cute the underwear should be. They laughed at each other as they knew what the other was thinking. The two parents looked down the line at their children to see how they were doing. All of them were wiggling around trying to get used to wearing clothes. Some of the younger ones were in the process of removing their underpants or panties. Allison barked at them, and they stopped still wiggling and feeling odd.

The older girls were amazed at their bras. They were told a proper fitting bra was a fine thing to wear.

"I know that all this is new to you," Ben said as he tried to encourage them. "But you all look marvelous. It will take some time to get used to, but you will be fine."

Roberta wouldn't show it, but she liked her underwear too.

Mr. Sanchez called to Ben, "Now, it will take some time for the tailors and seamstresses to finish the pants, skirts, shirts, dresses, and suits. We created an area for the children to play in. It has some crafts, games, and artwork, which should keep them preoccupied while Mr. Bickles will have a preliminary consultation about the organization."

While he was talking, another group of people arrived. They escorted Allison and the children to the entertainment area. Once they were gone, Mr. Sanchez took Ben to the end of the sewing area, where six more people in suits were waiting. Ben was a little self-conscious about meeting

these folks in his underwear, but then he realized
they had been watching him for the last fifteen
years when he was naked. *Oh, well,* he thought. *It's
just for now.*

They sat down at a table and Mr. Sanchez pulled
out a huge pile of documents. "I know that that
evil man is recently dead, but we need to move
fast for the changing of the guard, so to speak.
Introductions will be made as the need arises."
Sanchez handed Ben a folder. "There are six
legitimate businesses that Mr. Kim owned to make
the world think he was an honest businessman.
The first legal business is Convair-Consolidated
Aerospace," Sanchez said, pointing to the folder in
Ben's hand. "They recently garnered the exclusive
contract to build all the new space shuttles
and starships for the Space Federation, along
with supplying several airlines with airplanes.
You now own 85 percent of the shares for that
corporation."

"In essence, Mr. Bickles, you own the company,"
said Ronaldo Esperia, a Guatemalan, the president
of Convair-Consolidated. Ben nodded again. Mr.
Sanchez made introduced them to one another.

The attorneys lined up, awaiting their own introductions.

"Oh, forgive me. This is Rosiland Kapree," Mr. Sanchez said, indicating woman of average height. She was a little on the plumpish side, with wide brimmed glasses and blonde hair tied in a severely combed, tight bun. He turned, then said, "And this is Sherp O'Hara." O'Hara was a squat, little man from Ireland, looking something like what the stories called a leprechaun. "These two are now your personal attorneys and will guide you in this process. They are here to make sure you are properly informed, and are formidable at their work."

"I am supposed to trust them immediately?" Ben asked.

Mr. Sanchez sat in his nearby chair, folding his hands across his belly. "Let me help you understand something. As you have already guessed, Mr. Kim was a brutal man. All of us were compelled to work for, that is *obey*, him. In my case, my wife is missing two fingers because I questioned him twice. We all have those types of experiences. While you were fighting Mr. Kim, we were silently rooting for you. We all feel you would be a fair leader. Someone with a heart, if you will. So, it would be in our best interest to help you be that leader."

Ben sat back and looked everyone over. There was a significant pause before he finally agreed to continue. But then, Ben's tailor came to inform him that his suit was ready. Ben excused himself and accompanied the tailor to the square he was originally standing on. The tailors helped him with his shirt and made sure it fit well, which it did. Next came the pants, which fit perfectly as well. Then came the jacket. Ben was floored at how well everything fit and looked on him. A moment of emotions struck as he remembered the night of their senior class cruise dance. He shook the hands of his tailors and thanked them warmly. They were pleased to do such good work for him. Ben returned to the legal team while the tailors finished the rest of the clothing he would need.

"Looking quite the businessman, Mr. Bickles." Mr. Sanchez said when Ben walked back into the meeting. He glanced behind Ben and smiled.

"First, I believe someone has a surprise for you."
He pointed, making Ben turn around. When he
did, Ben caught his breath.

There stood his wife in a properly fitting, lavender
casual dress with four-inch heels.

"Absolutely gorgeous," Ben finally said. She
beamed. Then he noticed their children and his
tears flowed. He got up, walked over to them, and
embraced each one of them. The children were
new to the clothes concept, but they loved their
father's response. The girls each wore dresses
to match their mother's and the boys wore dress
slacks and shirts.

Unfortunately, none of the children liked the
shoes or the underwear.

The girls were arrayed on Allison's left while
the boys lined up on her right. Ben caressed the
cheeks of all his daughters and gushed at how
beautiful they were in their new clothes. He took
the hands of each of the four eldest daughters,
one at a time, and had them twirl around as they
had seen him do with their mother when they had

a chance to dance. This caused the girls to smile radiantly at their father while the younger girls twisted their skirts around.

After that, he went to the boys and praised each one for being the strong, handsome young men he knew them to be. The older boys were quite pleased with the comment while some of the younger ones weren't so sure that clothes were necessary.

Then he approached his wife. Ben reached out his hand to Allison. "M'lady," he said, "may I have this dance?"

Allison absolutely glowed at the request and responded, "It would be my pleasure, sir." She took his hand and let him guide her to the center of the room that used to be his combat area.

"Since you haven't worn shoes for years, are you going to be ok with this?" he said, concerned.

"True, they feel foreign for now, but I will endeavor to dance to my heart's content for the next moments. Then I will change to the flats they have for me."

Though there was no music, Ben led his bride in a Viennese waltz. Only a couple of steps were needed for their bodies to remember the motions. They focused on each other and ignored the rest of the world. Their children watched, enthralled at their parents' motions. The boys watched their steps and the girls focused on the love radiating from their parents' eyes. When Ben and Allison stopped, the room was silent, but the two continued staring into each other's eyes.

Beginning with the seamstresses, the room exploded into applause. And with that, the death room was changed into a dance hall.

Allison caressed her husband's face. "Sweetheart. I will dance with you the rest of our lives, even to old age when we can only bump wheelchairs and wiggle without breaking bones. I know how much you have adored my legs," she said smiling. "Well, to be truthful, you adored Carrie and Susan's legs as well when we wore the heels. But it has been fifteen years barefoot and my feet and legs are no longer used to them. They are hurting bad right now and need to get them changed immediately." She suddenly reached down and removed her heeled shoes. She breathed a small sigh of relief."

"Not to worry, my love. I will retrain these feet and legs so we can dance well again, and you can appreciate them at your leisure."

Ben kissed his bride passionately before he sent her back to the children while he dealt with the business at hand. Once with the children, Allison immediately put on her new flats. Once there, she admitted to the clothiers that it had been a long time since she wore such heels and would need some time to get used to them again.

Ben reconsidered letting his wife go. Smiling, he went to his wife, and took Allison's arm in his. He motioned to the children to walk over to the table where Mr. Sanchez and the other suits stood.

"Ladies and gentlemen, I present to you Allison Bickles, my wife, and our children."

The attorneys and businessmen happily greeted
the family, commenting how good they looked.
Allison was gracious while the children were
nervous. A minute or so later, some people
showed up and gestured for the children to return
to the tables at the far end of the open area. On
those tables were new craft items. With excited
glances at their parents, who nodded for them
to go, they headed over to see what all stuff was
about. They saw crayons, watercolor paints, paper,
tongue compressors, glue, and glitter. The last
item was to their parent's horror. They knew the
glitter was hard to get rid of. But they shrugged off
the impending mess.

"Now, Mr. and Mrs. Bickles. Let's get down to
business," said Mr. Sanchez.

Mr. and Mrs. Bickles spent the rest of the day
getting acquainted with the legal businesses.
Even though they hadn't graduated from high
school, the two grasped things rather quickly.
Their children were well-entertained with crafts.
A few paper airplanes made their way to the
business table, disrupting the meeting so they
could be thrown back to their makers. But the

meeting continued, only pausing long enough for bathroom breaks and a light dinner meal, and when the baby demanded some nourishment from mama.

The tailors and seamstresses finished all the clothing, and the entire wardrobe was closeted in the apartment. When all the business of the day had been completed, the businessmen took their leave. Mr. Sanchez and the two attorneys stayed for some additional conversation.

That night, Roberta slept with her new clothes. That included the undergarments.

THE NEW BOSS

Mr. Sanchez started the meeting with one bombshell they had not expected. "Tomorrow," he stated, "you will meet the other business leaders. There are thirty in all; each and every one of them are illegal, unethical, and immoral.

In a nutshell, as you Americans like to say, totally evil. Be prepared. All but one head of each will be here tomorrow. They are not friendly. There is one leader who is laying low for now, a Mr. Darrin Johnson. I think you may already know him. He was a classmate of yours."

That name caused great agitation, drawing major scowls from both Ben and Allison.

"What is he up to?" Ben said with a snarl, not hiding his disgust.

"Mr. Johnson and his righthand man, a Mr. Marc Richards, head up a major prostitution ring. They have a special way of blackmailing the wives of sailors and Marines when they are deployed. Johnson has quite the network built up over the years. He's personally responsible for the 'accidental' deaths of ten wives who refused his blackmail."

Ben turned to his wife. "Now I am certain they are responsible for Michael and Carrie's disappearance," he said. "Dead certain." Allison agreed, tears flowing down her face at the memory of their dear friends. Ben turned back to Mr. Sanchez "How do you know this?"

Mr. Sanchez folded his hands and leaned on the table. "One of Mr. Kim's odd quirks was that he demanded full accounting of everything in his organization. There are accountants like us all over Mr. Kim's organization, always keeping track of everything and everyone. Every girl that had been kidnapped, raped, killed, or distributed has been meticulously accounted for. *Everything* was recorded. When they were first seen. When they were kidnapped. By whom were they purchased. How they fared, including if, how, when and by whom they were killed. Buried, burned, or dropped into the sea. Everything!" He let that all sink in. "Now, pertaining to Johnson and Richards, the thing is, they hide in plain sight. They are both serving in the United States Navy and currently deployed."

Ben stood up so hard his chair flew back several yards. He put up a finger, and walked away for a few minutes, calming his temper with prayer. When he returned, he looked at the attorneys and Mr. Sanchez hard before he spoke.

"We need to destroy those evil businesses," Ben said resolutely. "Will you help me?"

Everyone at the meeting smiled. "Absolutely!" Sanchez replied. "We know of many who would love to see them gone. Just say the word. It will take some serious planning, but we are more than willing to get it done. I have some ideas on how to implement the plan."

At that moment a commotion occurred with some of the children. Allison excused herself and left to find the cause. When she arrived, she immediately noticed some of the children had taken their clothes off and the older girls and boys were trying to get them to put their clothes back on. A few sharp words from Mom quelled the rebellion and all were soon dressed again. She returned to the meeting with a happy face as if she never left.

Ben leaned over, placing his fists on the table. "First, the meeting tomorrow. Then we plan." Ben changed the subject. "How are we getting away from here.?"

Mr. Sanchez searched for and found a file, which he plopped open on the table. Several pictures of airplanes slid loose. He said, "You now own a few restored military aircraft from between 1940 and 1970, plus one converted Lockheed Constellation passenger plane. I understand you are a multiengine rated pilot."

"I was. Our dads had us train in operating several different aircraft. Contrary to official regulations," Ben admitted and then looked a little curious. "Converted?"

"Turboprop as opposed to radial engines."

"Nice!" Ben nodded and smiled at the thought of proper improvements of the old airliner.

"Oh, one other thing." Once again, Mr. Sanchez placed a file on the table. "I think you will find this most interesting. All of the boys who were kidnapped with you were sent home via different cities around the states. Also, all the girls arrived safely in different cities as well. They were all pregnant, and ordered to give birth or they and their families would suffer. All the babies but one were born. The one was a miscarriage, therefore, there was no penalty for the young lady."

"All alive?" Ben said, incredulous. "We didn't know." He sat down and reached for Allison's hand. "They are alive! God be praised!" Then, they remembered. "Roberta and Teresa," Ben said, quietly.

"Excuse me?"

"All the girls are alive except Roberta and Teresa. Roberta was brutalized and murdered and Teresa was murdered."

"Oh," Mr. Sanchez said. "I misspoke. Sorry." He lowered his head as did the other accountants and attorneys.

"At least everybody else is now safe," Ben replied. "That's a tremendous relief." He looked at Allison. "I guess I have more children to look after." Shaking his head, Ben let out a quick chuckle. "Mr. Kim wanted me to have it difficult, should I win. He got his wish." He became serious and looked at Sanchez. "You said 'no penalty.' What did you mean by that?"

"The girls were warned that aborting the babies was not an option for them. If they did, Mr. Kim said he would have their parents murdered, their sisters raped then placed into his sex slavery situations, and their brothers would be sent off to the slave camps. Mr. Johnson's crew were placed in charge of overseeing the girls to make sure they gave birth to the babies."

"He didn't skip a beat," Ben said as he realized he had nineteen more children out there. *Lord, bless them and keep them safe*, he prayed in his heart. *Mothers and children. Please.*

Mr. Sanchez stood up. "We will leave for now and return before sunrise tomorrow," he said. "Get some good rest tonight. Tomorrow will be a trying day."

As Ben was about to walk back to his family, a thought occurred to him. "Just one more question, if you please. Are we going to have any problems with his other business associates?"

"Such as?" Sanchez asked.

Ben paused and scratched the back of his head, "The other rich businesspeople Mr. Kim may have associated with as a power broker group?"

Kapree and O'Hara glanced at each other. Sanchez lowered his head. "Yes," replied Mr. Sanchez, "he had a few friendships with some powerful men around the world. What you, sorry, *we* are trying to do will affect them. Mr. Kim supplied them with whatever they requested to satisfy their perversions." Sanchez shook his head. "They may be a problem. However, they all hated Kim. So, they may leave you alone if you continue Kim's services. Since we know you are not going to do that, they may have issues with you. They can be," he paused, "formidable. But be assured, you and your family will be surrounded by security."

"What about possible attempts at hostile business take overs"?" Ben asked.

"You are secure there as well with the help from Kapree's work to protect your assets and position."

Ben looked at Kapree, who responded, "We have been, how should I say, informing them that it will not be business as usual." She then smiled at her new boss and said, "Be wary, but you can always rely on us. We are being vigilant about everything that concerns your businesses. Plus we are, now, always in prayer. It's the most secure thing we can do."

Ben nodded in appreciation. "Please, keep me apprised."

They shook hands and went their separate ways. Once they were gone, Ben and Allison cried into each other's shoulders. The children came out and joined the huddle, happy their daddy was no longer required to kill anyone whenever he left them. Conversation grew to an excited pitch as they shared about their crafts, their clothes and the excellent food they ate while Mom and Dad were away. They went on and on. But the energy died down quickly enough. For it had been a long, interesting, and exhausting day. Everybody was tired from all the excitement and went to bed early. Even the baby slept through the night. *Thank you, Jesus!* Ben thought as he put her down.

CRACKDOWN ON MR. KIM'S EMPIRE

Ben awakened early, showered, and put on a new suit. He tried to be as quiet as possible so Allison and the children would get some extra sleep. However, as soon as he got back to the bedroom to dress, Allison was already up and she wasn't alone. With the help of their eldest two daughters, Allison began the process of making breakfast. She made hamburger steak topped with three sunny side eggs and a side of sweet potato hashbrowns. Everything was slathered in butter, just the way she knew he liked it.

"Thanks to Mr. Sanchez," Allison told him, "we have the ingredients for your meal. I hope the children will like it, too." She seemed quite proud of herself and spoke to her husband's unasked question. "I made the request just before he left yesterday and all of the food came in after you went to sleep. For once, you slept soundly."

Ben just smiled and took a bite. Immediately, euphoria spread across his face. With each chew, the look he gave her told her he would show his appreciation that evening. His last bite completed, Ben stood up and kissed each daughter on the forehead, thanking them for a wonderful meal. Then he went to Allison and performed a dip while kissing her, much to the delight of the children present.

There was a knock on the doorway. Ben looked saw Mr. Sanchez standing there with a smile on his face. "I hope I am not intruding," he said and gave a short bow to Allison. "I need to update you on those you are meeting this morning." He gestured out of the apartment. "Shall we get started?"

Ben added one last peck on Allison's lips and started to head out. However, he turned around and said he wanted seconds. Allison knew he wasn't talking about food. Ben gave her a solid lip lock before he finally walked out. *I will never tire of the taste of that woman!* he thought as he walked away.

Allison stood there smiling before she heard Carrie ask, "What are we going to do today, Mama.

"We, young lady, are going to clean up after we feed the rest of the family. Then we will spend the rest of the time praying for your father. Let's get moving." She ushered her daughters to the kitchen area to finish making breakfast for the rest of the family.

Lord, guide his thoughts and actions, she prayed silently. Grant him Your wisdom in handling these evil people. Thank You, Jesus.

* * * *

Upon entering the death-room-turned-dancehall, Ben noticed it had, once again, changed. There was a lone table in the center with a couple of rifles and several pistols laid neatly upon it. All had appropriate ammunition. Standing on the opposite side of the table were the same suited personnel he met yesterday.

Ben was greeted with smiles and hearty handshakes. He noticed his attorney, Rosiland Kapree, wore her dirty blonde hair down in a low ponytail, with makeup was on the sparse side. Sherp O'Hara, the other attorney, couldn't wipe the smile off his face.

"Today is going to be a glorious day, Mr. Bickles!" O'Hara said, almost bouncing with enthusiasm.

Ben smiled back. He replied, "We will see, Mr. O'Hara. We will see." Turning to Sanchez, he asked, "What is all this?" He pointed to the table and mostly vacant building.

Sanchez wiped his forehead. "As I mentioned yesterday, there are thirty illegal, unethical, and immoral businesses that Mr. Kim had in his operation. You will be meeting all but one today." His tone grew serious. "They are a vicious group and only care about their own skins and wallets. Add to that, they know about each other, and hatred abounds within them. Many think the others were crossing into their territory. Squabbles have broken out from time to time. The only thing they all agreed upon was their fear of Mr. Kim, whose brutality kept them in line. He also helped line their wallets and fed their perversions. Anyone who got too far out of line would have chosen to be eaten by the crocs instead of the punishment they received." Mr. Sanchez paused to let Ben's imagination run for a bit. "Now that they know Mr. Kim is dead and gone, they are starting to feel a little bold. However, they may be less leery of you as it has been made known to them about your preaching. They have no fear of God."

"This feeding their perversions seems to be a recurring theme," Ben said casually. "That is going to be a problem for them. Who are these spawns of Satan?"

Kapree handed him a folder containing the information he asked for. "Their backgrounds come from all over the world. However, another idiosyncrasy Mr. Kim had was that they all were supposed to speak English as fluently as if they grew up in America. That was because, before the nations had their civil wars[7], English was still the language of business around the world despite China's attempt to change it to Mandarin. These people will try to fool you by saying they don't understand English. They will try to stonewall you. You must be on your toes with this group. If they smell blood in the water, they will kill you, kill us, and enslave your children after getting their jollies with your wife."

---

7 Many countries had civil wars and major disruptions at the same time as America's second Civil War.

Inwardly, Ben fumed. Outwardly, he looked cool and calm. "How much time before they all arrive?"

Mr. Sanchez checked his watch. "You have about thirty minutes."

"Thirty minutes." Ben smiled. "Really giving me more than enough time to prepare," he said in a somewhat mocking tone.

"My apologies," Mr. Sanchez replied. "When they found out about Mr. Kim's death. They contacted each other and decided to come as a group as soon as possible—"

"—to see if they can catch me off my guard."

"To be truthful? Yes, sir."

Ben sat back in his chair and tapped the table. "Well, then. Let's not have them be disappointed." Sweat began beading on Sanchez's bald pate. "At first," Ben added. That drew a few nods from the suits and the attorneys. Mr. Sanchez looked at Ben as if to say, "be on your toes."

LITTLE BUNNY

"I assume this is not for show?" Ben pointed to the weapons.

"Actually, Mr. Bickles," broke in O'Hara. "We are hoping that is all they are. But we are certain you are proficient with their operation."

Ben looked more closely and realized he was very familiar with all the weapons, despite the years that had passed. "Someone has done their homework," he said looking over the people in front of him.

"That would be me, sir," came a soft voice from one of the suits. Mr. Kim ordered me to investigate your life. I hope I was thorough."

Ben looked at him hard. "Exactly how thorough?"

Sanchez stood between the two men. "He is our most thorough investigator, and I guarantee he knows how often you had your diapers changed when you were a baby. Please don't get cross with him. He was doing his job, albeit reluctantly."

Ben continued to stare hard at the man for a few more seconds before he relaxed. "I am sorry for still having my senses on high." He shook the hand of the man, giving reassurance that his life was not forfeit. "I understand."

Sanchez looked briefly at his phone. "Ah," he said. "Your guests are outside of the fence. I will go greet them." He moved as if to go but stopped suddenly, turning around to face Ben. "There is one whom all of them hate but fear as well. Heinrich Hasenpfeffer. He is about as brutal as Mr. Kim and thinks he should take over the empire. That man is merciless and doesn't care one wit who he hurts or kills to get his way. Also, he's loud and boisterous. That would be the one to break first. Oh, and he is in charge of acquisitions. Human acquisitions."

"Noted," Ben said as he reclined in his chair at the table and looked bored. *Hasenpfeffer, huh?* He thought.

Several minutes passed before the entourage entered the building. Ben could hear an argument in full bloom. He glanced over to the noise and took note of a big blond-haired man. He was face-to-face with an equally large Asian. The blond man wore American western-style blue jeans with a stained white, long-sleeved shirt, American western boots, and a tattered straw hat. His skin was darkened by many years in the sun, Ben assumed. The Asian, on the other hand, wore a standard business suit, belying his dirty business situations.

"I DON'T CARE WHAT KIM WANTED. THOSE FIVE CHILDREN BELONGED TO ME. I HAD JOHNSON PROCURE THEM AND BRING THEM TO MY BOAT." The blond-haired man was spitting as he spoke. "I HAD ME QUITE SOME FUN WITH THAT BLACK GIRL. MY CAPTAIN WAS TO BRING THEM HERE SO WE COULD SHOW THEIR DADDY HOW MUCH FUN THEY WERE! BUT NO! YOUR PIRATE GOES AND RAMS MY BOAT AND NOW EVERYBODY IS DEAD! AND THAT IS ON *YOU* SINCE YOU CAN'T SEEM TO CONTROL YOUR PIRATES!" Spittle flew from his mouth during the last sentence.

The big Asian spit back, "I HAVE HAD ORDERS
TO SUPPLY THAT ISLAND WITH VALUABLE
THINGS FROM THE EXPENSIVE YACHTS AND
BOATS SO KIM COULD HAVE HIS HIDEY HOLE
FOR RETIREMENT. THE ISLAND WAS
SUPPOSED TO BE A SECRET! YOUR BOAT
WOUND UP THERE. MY CAPTAIN ONLY
DID HIS JOB!"

The two men stood toe-to-toe, and it looked
like they were going to add physicality to
their argument.

That is when Sanchez stepped in between them.
"Now gentlemen, this will have to wait. You are
here to meet the new boss!"

The blond man was unfazed. "*I* AM THE NEW
BOSS. NO PANTYWASTE IS GOING TO TAKE IT
FROM ME! WHERE IS THIS SO-CALLED BOSS?"
That caused the Asian man to look around. They
both settled their eyes on Ben, sitting casually by
the table. "Surely it's not this idiot!" the blond
said, still loud, but no longer shouting.

Sanchez didn't reply but continued to lead the group to the table. Behind the blond and the Asian walked four women, looking like they robbed a leather boutique. The first, a tall, long black hair, fair skin, blue eyed, Finnish woman around thirty years old, wore a full black leather body suit. The next, a Tibetan, was in a full-length red dress with waist-high slits on both sides of her legs, more commonly known as a *zansae* or Mandarin gown. The third, a very dark-skinned, slender Ethiopian, wore a white leather halter top with a short white skirt and thigh-high white leather boots. The fourth woman looked like she had just walked out of the Mongolian steppes. Although they were currently in the tropics, she still wore her native furs. They all had looks of disgust after hearing the argument from the two loudmouths.

Behind them came the remaining twenty-three bosses. They were from different nationalities, and all were wore stylish and expensive, though relatively standard business suits. They remained silent but seemed angry. By what, Ben was about to find out.

The entourage finally arrived at the table where he sat. As if he owned it, the blond reached for one of the weapons. He stopped when he saw a.50 caliber pistol pointed at his head.

Ben saw the big blond move for one of the guns and instantly grabbed the pistol. Without looking, he aimed it at the head of the man. The blond-haired man took offense and stood as tall as he could, trying to be as intimidating as possible, assuming Ben was a simpleton. With a calm controlled voice, Ben asked, "Black girl? Did you keep track of her name?" He still hadn't looked up at any of the newcomers.

The blond man responded, his bravado returning "Who are you to ask me anything?"

Sanchez stepped up and introduced the man to the group. "Ladies and gentlemen, this is the man who defeated Mr. Kim and is now the chairman of the empire."

"He will be chairman when *I* say he is chairman, and not a moment before," the blond man boasted.

Ben slowly turned in his chair to face the man. In a quiet voice, he asked Sanchez, "Would you care to introduce this fool to me so I may have a name to write down?"

"Ah, yes. This is Heinrich Hasenpfeffer." Sanchez went to stand by the other suited men, ready for anything to start.

"Hasenpfeffer? Like a little bunny?" Ben said, starting to toy with the big man.

The big blond started to charge the table and once again stopped when he found himself staring down the barrel of the pistol. "I'll show you little bunny!"

"Not now," Ben said in a nonchalant manner. "Maybe later."

That enraged the blond-haired man, but he didn't take another step. This became quite the curiosity to the remaining group. A showdown was in the making. They were sure the man with the pistol couldn't be the man who defeated Mr. Kim.

"Now that I have your complete and undivided attention," Ben said, "answer my question. What was the Black girl's name, and the names of the other children kidnapped with her?! Now!" To emphasize his point, Ben cocked the pistol because there was no cartridge in the chamber before. *At least he abides by the rule to assume all firearms are loaded.*

This bluff caused the lady in black and the one in white to have a little admiration for Ben. Both noted that he would not be an easy pushover. Hasenpfeffer may have bitten off more than he could chew. A few members of the group started to move around, trying to circle behind Ben to ambush him.

Quicker than a flash, Ben spun around and shot the first two in the head. He followed that up by ordering the rest to remain as one group. They obeyed without hesitation, except for Hasenpfeffer, who glowered at the man he still considered the impostor.

Ben pointed the pistol back at the blond man.

"I believe I asked for the names of those children," he said. "Answer me, now." Ben's voice was still well controlled and soft but it had gained an edge that said an answer had better be forthcoming.

Hasenpfeffer took out a small notebook and flipped a couple of pages. Finally, he spat, "I don't know why you care about the names, but the Black girl was named Amina Bickles. The boys were Nelson Bickles, Torrance Bickles, and Javier Bickles. The little girl with the freckles was Cassondra Bickles. Who is going to care about them. They are dead because of the pirates that destroyed MY BOAT!" He roared at the Asian man.

Kapree and O'Hara moved behind Ben while Sanchez stepped up and confidently declared, "This man that defeated Mr. Kim is Benjamin Bickles." Then he said, with deliberate emphasis, "The father of those children." He stepped back to let that sink in. Most of the group started to take steps back.

Not Hasenpfeffer, who puffed up himself and decided to double down on his claim. He leaned in toward Ben and said with a sneer, "That little Black was the sweetest and tastiest treat I had ever played with." Then pointing to Ben. "What do think about that, sir?" The last word, he said in disgust.

Ben slowly lifted his right leg, removing his shoes and socks. He repeated this action with the left leg before standing up to remove his jacket and neatly place it over the back of the chair. Then he removed his tie. Ben looked around the building and started a history lesson.

"I have spent the last fifteen years here," he said. "I was naked for all of that time, forced to fight to the death to protect my family and friends. I defeated every opponent. I finally defeated Kim. My family and friends are safe." He pointed to the big blond. "Or so I thought. Now I see that my days of defending my family are not over. Not with the likes of you around. Now that I know my other children are alive and I find out you are responsible for their kidnapping and rape, I will not abide having such as you in MY," Ben pounded his chest, "organization." Once again, he pointed to the blond man. "Come here, Little Bunny, and we shall see whether it is you or I who is the chairman." Ben moved to the center of the floor he knew so well. With hands on hips, he waited for the big man to make his move.

Hasenpfeffer looked back at the group then and at Ben. He puffed out his chest and strode over to where Ben was standing. Hasenpfeffer wasn't planning on stopping in hopes of catching the "impostor" off guard. The suits and Sanchez just smiled in anticipation of Ben's inevitable victory. The other group was not sure who they wanted to win, the big boisterous blond, or the calm but highly dangerous Bickles.

Hasenpfeffer tried to circle around and get to Ben's blind side. That was his undoing. As he closed in on his prey, his face was met with a quick succession of kicks and slaps that forced him to the floor in a fog. Hasenpfeffer felt his last sensation as a heel slammed onto his neck, breaking it in several places. He went completely numb. Unable to move or breathe, he felt his hair being pulled and then a sense of falling as he was thrown into the croc pit.

The remaining members of the group swallowed hard as they had never seen anybody move so fast and effectively. The men grew fearful. The women grew fearful, but also excited. Some considered enticing him with their charms.

Ben quietly walked back to the chair, put on his socks and shoes followed by his tie and jacket. Then he sat down, looked at the group and smiled. "Now," Ben said, "how about we get acquainted." Pointing to the man Hasenpfeffer was arguing with when they entered building, he said, "I will start with you. Come forward, tell me your name and the business you have been offering the previous owner."

The big Asian man stepped forward, stood by the table, placed his hand over his heart and bowed. "I am Mohammed Fassi. Leader of the pirates of the South Pacific and Indian oceans. I—"

"Pirates? How many ships? How many personnel?" Ben interrupted.

"Currently one hundred thirty-two ships and two thousand fifty-one crew members and office workers."

"Ok. Thank you. Step aside." Ben was deliberately terse with him and the rest of the group. Fassi was dumbfounded and annoyed at being dismissed so quickly, but he walked away. The introductions and clipped responses by Ben continued until it was the women's turn. Each woman thought to use their seductive attributes to get in with the new boss.

The first to step up was the woman in white leather. Ben took note of how the white contrasted with the woman's very dark, almost black, skin. She seductively walked up to the desk and placed her hands on the desk, causing her to lean toward Ben and show off her, what she considered best, assets. Ben looked into her eyes and motioned for O'Hara. He spoke into O'Hara's ear and the little Irishman ran off to the apartment. Shortly, Allison walked out and proceeded to stand by Ben. She wore a white blouse and blue shorts. She placed her hand on her husband's shoulder and looked at the other woman with an air of ownership. O'Hara remained stationed at the entrance of the apartment.

"This is my wife. Any other acts of seduction by any of you will be met with severe punishment,"

Ben declared making sure all the women understood.

The woman in white stood up and with an annoyed face declared, "I am Vega Vishan of Yemen. I am the trainer of all girls for sex slavery. I—"

"Child sex slavery? How young are the girls?" Ben interrupted.

"We start with girls as young as three years old. Our customers dictate the desired ages."

Allison stepped up. "Three years old?" she asked. "Disgusting!"

This outburst from Allison did not go unchallenged. The woman in white drew out a dagger and charged at Allison. But Ben's wife was ready for the attack. Allison instantly squatted down and swept her leg into the other woman's knee, breaking the joint and causing Vishan to land on the floor. When she landed, she began crying in anger and pain, cursing Allison in her native Arabic.

Ben stood up, kissed his wife and sent her back to the apartment. O'Hara returned to Ben when Allison had reached her children.

Ben turned to the group and with fists on the table, ordered two men to retrieve Vishan. It was amazing how quickly they obeyed his orders. "Anybody else willing to try seduction to get your way?" The other women shook their heads and stepped back. "Alright. Now, let's get this interview session over with. Who's next?" He sat down with his hand next to the pistol he used before.

No more incidents occurred after that. All interviews were brief, and Ben was clipped with everyone. Nobody was happy, but at least they showed proper respect. Ben had already known about everyone because of the briefing Sanchez and the suits gave him prior to the meeting.

"That concludes today's meeting," he finally said. "You all may leave. Now! And if anyone wants to challenge me, feel free to try." No one took him up on that offer. "Now get out!" he commanded. They turned as one and practically ran out of the building, cursing as they went. Vishan had to be carried.

When the last person in that group had left, Ben addressed Sanchez. "I need to see the list of all the compromised law enforcement and military personnel in the territories where they operate. I want it by tomorrow. After that, I want you to compile a list of military and law enforcement we can count on to act and destroy those operations and the people involved." Ben paused with his hand on his forehead. "Hopefully we can rescue a large number of people and children from their enslavement. I will need Kapree and O'Hara to stay for a bit to talk over some legalities."

"Very, well, sir," Sanchez replied. "And if I may say, very well done today, sir. They may not like you, but you have their respect. And again, if I may, their fear." He bowed. "I will see you in the morning, sir." Sanchez and the suits departed from the building, understanding the daunting task Ben had just given them.

Ben addressed the attorneys next.

TAKING ON AN EMPIRE OF EVIL

Ben found two more chairs, brought them to the table, and asked Kapree and O'Hara to sit with him for a few minutes. "I want to know something," he began. "I fully intend to destroy all the evil businesses Mr. Kim owned. In your opinion, am I starting on the right foot by having Sanchez bring me the lists tomorrow?" He looked both of them in the eye, waiting for their response.

"Mr. Bickles," started Attorney Kapree, "after watching you these last few years, frankly, I am amazed you didn't kill all of them on the spot today." She nervously brushed a loose hair behind her ear. "But yes. Having Sanchez bring you those lists is very important. It will take some time, but they will try to overthrow you at any perceived neglect on your part."

"Neglect?" Ben asked.

O'Hara jumped in, "If they do not get their bonusses and little pets, they will revolt. Mr. Kim kept them on a leash by making sure they were well paid and protected from any prosecution by the authorities."

"You mentioned 'little pets.' Can you be more specific?" Ben was feeling a little uneasy about that.

Kapree was ill at ease to continue. But she did. "Mr. Hasenpfeffer required very young girls to satisfy his appetites," she said. "Thank God *that* evil need not to be fulfilled. Miss Vishan desires to make a beautiful woman her slave. I will not go into any details, but rest assured, the slave never survived beyond six months."

O'Hara added, "There is a pirate captain that loves hunting down yachts every three years. He does it for the sole purpose of looting, raping and murdering. He is allowed to do this to keep Mr. Kim's secret island hidden from the world while supplying goats for his planned retirement plantation. You get the picture?"

Ben sat back in his chair, deep in thought. "What legal issues will I need to be made aware of?

Surely there are authorities looking for and watching it all?"

"Having the lists of military and law enforcement personnel firmly in Mr. Kim's employ will be invaluable for you when you launch your cleansing action." Kapree noted Ben's slight surprise. She deduced his strategy. "Oh, yes, Mr. Bickles, it doesn't take an experienced inquisitor to know what you are planning." You must understand. We have been doing Kim's will for many years. And both of us have been appalled and disgusted at what was asked of us. I rebelled once, and my baby daughter was taken from me. Mr. Kim allowed her to be fed to a cannibal in America. He made me watch the video." She couldn't proceed as the memory resurfaced. Ben reached out his hand and covered hers. Kapree was surprised by the comforting touch, but did not remove her hand from his.

"What she is trying to say," O'Hara continued for his co-counsel, "is that we, as well as Sanchez, know the ins and outs of every person, place, or thing in this organization. And we would love nothing better than to destroy it. All you need to do is ask and we will protect you and your family." Then he added, "By the way, that was a brilliant move, having your wife participate in the meeting. It solidified your place as boss. Vishan has never been beaten by another woman. Until today." Then with a pointing of his finger, O'Hara said, "That will make her more dangerous and more than likely to do something royally stupid, which is what she does when she loses her temper. You have been warned."

Kapree brightened. "Your wife can take care of herself from my point of view," she said.

Ben glowed with pride, saying, "My wife would fight to the death to protect her babies, even from me, if it ever came down to that." With a wink of his eye, he added, "I am sure that will never be the case." He stood up. "I will need more information, but that is enough for now. The two of you need to go home and put together a plan, as I will be doing. Tomorrow we will see what we can agree on. With Sanchez's lists, we should be successful in freeing many people and ridding this world of Kim's empire of evil." They stood up with him and shook his hands. Kapree, however, couldn't hold herself back and gave Ben a hug and a thank you. After that, they left the building with what looked like a skip in their steps.

It was then Ben realized he hadn't been in prayer since his morning time with God. He walked into the apartment and was swarmed by his family. Allison waited until the last child got her hugs and kisses. Before she could move to him, Ben was holding her tight saying, "Thank God! Thank God!" over and over. She waited until he was finished and then received the kisses she coveted.

"I hope I did well for you by dealing with *that* woman!" She looked into his eyes to see the truth.

"I am more than pleased," Ben replied. "However, I am sorry you had to get involved at all. But you performed brilliantly. The message was understood loud and clear," Ben assured her. "Unfortunately, that woman is going to hold a grudge. But I assure you, she and her minions will be among the first to be purged."

"That's a relief," Allison replied. Then with great concern in her voice, she told him, "I noticed you haven't prayed since this morning. Have no fear, we," She pointed to their children, "have been praying almost nonstop for you." She brushed some hair off his face. "We have your back, now and forever." She looked at the children. "Don't we, kids?" All the children cheered and danced around their parents. Soon, Ben and Allison joined them in whooping, hollering and dancing.

That evening, after the children and baby were tucked in bed, Ben got to combing Allison's hair, as was their ritual. They enjoyed the calming silence for several minutes.

Ben finally spoke. "It is not going to be an easy road ahead of us," he said. "We are going to dismantle Kim's evil empire. I am afraid there will be more bloodshed, anger, and destruction. In the end, I pray hundreds, if not thousands, will become free again. I am going to get out of here and to Hawaii as soon as possible so we can get under friendly protection. May take a couple of weeks to a couple of months." He paused to straighten a rather stubborn lock of hair. "We have the vehicle to transport us out, but I will need to get acclimated to how it handles."

"However long it takes is in God's hands," she said and placed her hand on his. "We will do whatever you need. You do have some brilliant children that you can train to help you." Allison lowered her head, looking down. "I heard all that the attorneys said. They seem hopeful, and so do I. But I am sorry you had to kill again so soon." She turned around and held his face in her hands, drawing her face closer to his. "Tonight, relax, refresh, and release your tension. Sleep peacefully after your prayers. Deal with tomorrow's issues tomorrow. Please." She kissed him.

He wrapped her up in his arms and returned the kiss. "Thank you, my love. *My Princess!* I will endeavor to follow your orders to the letter. I am so, SO grateful God made you for me. Let's finish and go to bed." He gave her one more kiss and a few more strokes of the comb before they did just that.

Different Boss. Different Company Standards.

In the morning, Mr. Sanchez, Miss Kapree, and Mr. O'Hara arrived bright and early. Allison greeted them. "I am afraid I let Ben sleep in this morning. It was the most peaceful sleep he has had in years. I just pray his PTSD will not be too overwhelming." They said they understood and went to prepare for the day's work.

They were taken aback when Ben finally showed up, but he apologized for being late. After a moment, Ben noticed their faces when he apologized and questioned why they were startled.

"We are not used to the boss apologizing for anything," O'Hara explained. "It was unexpected."

Ben put his hand on the Irishman's shoulder to reassure everybody. "Different boss. Different company standards." His broad smile was genuine, and the others relaxed for a bit. Then they got down to business. The first thing was to peruse the lists Mr. Sanchez brought. One thing stood out and caught Ben's attention.

"There is a scripture that says, 'Those that are with you are greater than those that are in the world,'" Ben began. "What I am seeing here is that the good military, the good law enforcement, and the good politicians vastly outnumber the evil." Ben looked up at the ceiling, then back down to his associates. "I don't think the good people of this world recognize that." He stood up with enthusiasm, his arms stretched out with realization. Then he placed them firmly back on the table. Addressing Sanchez, he asked, "With your connections, how soon can we get a force around the world to take out the evil side of this empire?"

Sanchez was beginning to catch Ben's thinking. "Give me half an hour, and I will answer that question fully." He stood up and walked a few yards from the group to make a few phone calls. Kapree, O'Hara, and Ben started discussing the legal loops Ben's companies would have to go through to make everything totally legitimate. Ben then knew he had earned their respect and devotion. *Light will shine through the darkness. Lord, Jesus. Let there be Your Light! he prayed silently.*

Sanchez let out a whoop and almost sprinted back to the table. "I have the assurances," he said. "There are enough of the forces we need to make an assault on all thirty bosses and their minions within two weeks. They understand that the utmost secrecy must be adhered to for success. They are already, as you Americans say, 'chomping at the bit' to end the evil!" Sanchez raised his hands to the ceiling. "God be praised!" That brought applause from the others and from the apartment as Allison and the eldest children joined in the celebration.

Ben had to be sure about one thing. "What about Vishan?" he asked. "She is going to want to seek revenge against Allison for her defeat."

"Vishan is going to wait until her leg heals before she acts on any revenge motion. By that time, she will, more than likely, be killed defending her territory." Then with a shrug Sanchez said, "Or she will be executed after a very swift trial. Either way, I can assure you, you and your family will be safe." When the reverie settled down, Sanchez had a sober expression on his face. "I am old enough to remember what the world was like before all those civil wars," he said. "Before hostilities broke out evil, vastly outnumbered good. At least that is how it looked." He shook his bald head. "It's sad. So much humanity had to die to make things right." Sanchez sat back, remembering those days. "Now it looks like more death is to come. But this time I am going to rejoice when the evil is eradicated." He fell silent.

The rest of the morning belonged to planning and making contacts. Suddenly a voice echoed from the apartment.

"Lunch is ready," Carrie, the eldest child called out. "Mr. Sanchez, Miss Kapree, Mr. O'Hara, you are invited to join us."

O'Hara called back, "What's cooking?"

Carrie responded, "Hamburger steak and eggs with sweet potato hashbrowns."

At that, O'Hara got up and trotted to the apartment.

Ben chuckled. "I think he likes what is on the menu!" Sanchez laughed and Kapree got up amid her own giggles. Everyone walked to join the family for the meal.

Ben slapped Sanchez on the back, "Time for some old-fashioned home cooking, Sanchez." It took him a minute, but then Sanchez laughed at the change of pace from what he had endured the last thirty years under Mr. Kim's domination.

As they arrived, Ben heard Susan chastising O'Hara. "We must wait until we have given thanks to God for this meal before we eat, Mr. O'Hara."

O'Hara laughed as Ben and Sanchez entered the room. "I have been caught. What do you suppose the punishment will be?" Allison enjoyed the mood as she finished placing the food on the table.

"Well, my friend, that depends on who caught you," Ben remarked. "Carrie, Susan, Whitney, or Roberta?" O'Hara pointed at the girl who called him out. "Ah, Susan." Ben patted him on the shoulder. "You are in luck," he confided. "She is the more forgiving of the girls." Then he nodded to Roberta. "Your life would have been forfeit with that one." Roberta put on a fake scowl at O'Hara which caused all in the room to have a good laugh. "However," Ben said, "it *is* time we give thanks." The family all held hands. Kapree sat between Michael and Carrie, Sanchez between Derrick and

Ben, O'Hara between Susan and Roberta. Roberta gave him an extra strong squeeze with a sly smile.

They all bowed as Ben started the prayer, "Heavenly Father, Lord God, and Jesus the Christ, one in essence, three persons. We give You belated thanks for the victories here and ask forgiveness as we have started work to destroy the evil without consulting You first. May the work we do be guided by Your hand and may we accept Your chastisements when we try to go it on our own. Thank You for the new friends we have with us today and may You bless them with Your Spirit and forgiveness for what they have done in the past. And may that past be forgiven by those affected by the work placed upon them by Mr. Kim. Thank You, Lord Jesus, for Your sacrifice to gift us with Your Salvation. Now, we humbly ask for Your blessing on this meal and fellowship for which we give great thanks. We come to You in the name that has power and authority, Jesus! Amen!" All the family members called out their own Amens. Miss Kapree started to cry. Mr. O'Hara held a lump in his throat and Mr. Sanchez was quite sober for a few minutes.

Roberta noticed Mr. O'Hara and wrapped her arms around him. She laid her head on his shoulder, "You are loved, Mr. O'Hara," Roberta said. Tears began to flow down his cheeks. "You are loved with an everlasting love, and underneath are the everlasting arms." O'Hara patted her arm and rested his head on hers.

Kapree openly cried at Roberta's words. Michael and Carrie, on her right and left, hugged her, laying their heads on each of her shoulders. "I don't deserve all this," she said, hanging her head.

"You are right, you don't." Kapree snapped up to look at Ben as he said this. "Just as we don't deserve the free gift of salvation and love that Jesus has for us. But He gives it anyway because of His love. Please receive His free gift of love. And ours." With that, Michael and Carrie gave her an extra squeeze.

She laid her head on Carrie's and patted Michael's arm while looking at Allison and Ben. She mouthed the words, "Thank you," to them.

A tear trailed down Sanchez's cheek. That was the only sign that he was touched as well.

Allison decided that was enough with the sad tears. "Now that we all have that understanding, let's enjoy this meal God has granted to us." The children let out a whoop and the guests were given first choice. At first, the three guests were hesitant to act. But when Sanchez finally smiled, they acted as one and started digging into the food before them. Each guest was amazed at how the family still had joy in their lives. This joy rubbed off on them, who enjoyed a robust family meal for the first time in a very long while.

PREPARATIONS

The meal eventually finished, and Sanchez, Kapree, and O'Hara offered to help with cleaning the dishes. At first Allison said they didn't have to help. But Kapree countered, "We haven't had the pleasure of just being human for quite a while. Please, let us repay you for freeing us from the evil we have had to do." Allison relented and the three guests shared the duties with the four eldest daughters, enjoying the good-natured teasing they received from the girls.

Ben's heart leaped for joy as he heard such laughter in the kitchen. Allison wrapped her arms around Ben's arm, laying her head on his shoulder. "Sure would be nice if we could get the children some outside time. Whaddyathink?" she said with a sweet tone.

Ben looked at her, pondering how to facilitate that when Sanchez suddenly spoke. "If you give me an hour, Mrs. Bickles, I can have those people who were here earlier, the one with the crafts, come back. They can help you entertain the children while Mr. Bickles works with us to dismantle the empire."

Ben's eyebrows raised and Allison responded, "That would be wonderful, Mr. Sanchez. When do think we can get the children outside of this building?"

"Hard to say," Sanchez answered. "We have to wait and see how complete the dismantling will be. Right now, it is still too dangerous for them to go anywhere because this place is being watched. The first time a child steps outside, they will attack. I am sorry for the delay."

Allison waved it off. "It's alright, Mr. Sanchez," she told him. "We can wait a little longer to be free. Thank you for your concern and assistance for our family." She walked up and gave the man a kiss on the cheek. Ben had never seen anyone blush such a deep red as he saw on Sanchez's face that moment.

At that, Sanchez, Kapree, and O'Hara walked to the opposite side of the facility and started to set up a command post. Ben stayed with Allison and the children until the people arrived to entertain the children.

Allison was grateful that the projects were age appropriate. There were simple items for the younger ones, and more complicated games for the older children. Ben suspected that his time with his children and wife would diminish for a time as the organization was dismantled.

As Ben was about to join Sanchez and company, Allison gathered the children around their father asked him to kneel. When he did, his children surrounded him, putting their hands on him. Allison laid her free hand on his head, and the baby she was holding copied her mother.

Allison led the prayer. "Heavenly Father, Lord God, and Jesus the Christ. We ask for your wisdom to overflow Ben and the others as they work to end the evil side of this organization. Be their guide. Be their strength. Shower them with your Holy Spirit, flood them with Your wisdom, and keep them from harm. In the name that has power and authority, Jesus the Christ, we pray these things. Amen." The children followed with their Amens and showered their father with hugs and kisses. Ben was overwhelmed with love and peace as Allison guided their children back to the crafts area. Once the kids were with their crafts, she returned and gave Ben her own round of hugs and kisses.

Ben didn't want to leave. *If that woman keeps kissing me like that,* he thought, *I won't ever want to be out of her sight.* Eventually, Ben went to the area designated as his office. It was basically a table, chairs and computers at one end of the open area.

Sanchez, Kapree, and O'Hara and the rest of the team went right to work, showing him all the workings of the empire, both good and evil.

"Where have we started the demolishing?" Ben asked when they got to the African operations.

Sanchez responded. "Vishan and company are already gone. She put up a little fight, although her injury prevented her from fighting full force." He looked over his reading glasses to check Ben's demeanor. Seeing him engaged, Sanchez continued, "Over 2000 young girls have been freed from slavery."

This admission caught Ben by surprise. "Eliminated? How? And so soon?"

Sanchez called to one of the other information keepers for the file regarding the raid on Vishan's organization. When it was placed in his hands, he looked at his new boss, "Do you want to read it for yourself?"

After a few moments of thought, Ben answered. "No. Take me through it."

Sanchez commenced to read the file. "Just so you know, the timeline starts as soon as she leaves Pago Pago." Ben nodded. "Our information about the friendly forces in the area was put together within a day." Sanchez looked at Ben, "Remember, Kim had us keep complete documents for his business and for the opposition, so this is pretty reliable information. We already had what we needed just waiting there, so we had to just activate the plan." Once again Ben nodded in acknowledgment. "The mission required a silent assault on four different compounds, plus the head office. Like Kim, Vishan was cruel to those who worked against her. And since your wife injured her, she had to be immobile for a couple of weeks. That timing worked to our advantage."

"Four compounds?" Ben was beginning to appreciate the enormity of the organization.

"Oh, forgive me, those were only the ones in Ethiopia. She had ten others throughout the world."

"What?" Ben asked, astonished "Where else?"

"Brazil, Argentina, Saudi Arabia, China, Japan, and Colorado, within the United States."

Ben sat back in his chair as if stung. "Are you saying you were able to eliminate her entire operation? What about *her*?"

"Patience. Patience. May I read on?"

"Yes, please. Sorry." Ben leaned back.

"The forces were contacted and informed. Absolute secrecy had to be maintained, so all military personnel went on absolute lockdown until everything was finished. Only certain law enforcement personnel that could be trusted were involved in the planning. Silence was key. The victims needed to be secured. Hopefully with no losses. The coordinated assault on all compounds and the head office took place three days ago. As we hoped, complete surprise was on our side. Over two thousand girls were freed and taken to nearby medical facilities for examination. All her forces were captured or killed in the assaults. Vishan, herself, was in her office violating an eight-year-old girl when her door burst open."

Sanchez raised his eyebrows and smirked. "She didn't have time to shit or go blind. They took her out to the main office area where all the desks and furniture had been moved to the outer walls. The troops didn't care about her screams of pain or vile threats. They knew who she was, and she received her comeuppance. Some of the children she had violated herself were armed with knives and clubs. Once she was incapacitated, those same victims then beat and carved her to pieces within minutes."

Again, Ben sat back in his chair. He wasn't expecting that much.

Before he could speak, Sanchez added, "Shortly after that, all of the people left with the troops. Jackals were ushered into the office and the doors were closed behind them. You can guess what happened next."

Ben realized he had stopped breathing at that news and finally breathed again. "What about the other facilities?"

"Almost identical situations." With a bit of mischief in his eye, Sanchez continued, "The news spread fast and soon enough, the whole organization is in an uproar. It will be far more difficult to close out the other evil businesses of Kim's empire, but I assure you, we will not stop until they are all gone and their assets destroyed. I *do* have a note of concern. Miss Heikkinen, the woman in the black leather body suit is thrilled at the loss of Vishan. They hated each other. And Miss Heikkinen wanted to expand her business by adding Vishan's organization to hers. Now she thinks she has carte blanche to take over."

"That means—"

"She will be next." Sanchez finished Ben's sentence. "Do you see now? This will be a long war against those people."

Ben had to admit he really didn't have much of an idea about the full scope of what lay ahead of them. "Looks like I now know what my life's work is going to be." Ben sighed, still shocked by the number of girls enslaved at that time. He immediately thought of his wife and daughters. Mentally, he checked out of the discussion, sighing as the long-held questions arose in his mind.

Sanchez caught the disconnect and put down his glasses. He turned off his monitors, folded his hands, and placed his elbows on the table.

"Is something amiss, Mr. Bickles?" he asked. O'Hara, Kapree, and the others stopped what they were doing and followed Sanchez's lead.

Ben slowly looked into the eyes opposite him. After several seconds, he quietly said, "I have so many questions that need to be answered before we can proceed. Will you answer them for me?"

All looked at Sanchez, waiting for his response. He answered thoughtfully, assuming he knew what the questions would be. "Ask away."

Everyone turned their eyes to Ben.

"Why were we always naked?" They could see the earnestness in his face.

Sanchez let out a long breath and leaned back into his chair. "As you have already been made aware," he began, "you are the thirteenth group to be kidnapped for the very purpose you fought these last fifteen years." Ben nodded. "The parameters were the same for everyone. One boy was chosen to be the potential champion. When he won his first fight, six girls were chosen from his group. From the six, the chosen champion was ordered to choose a wife. Also, they had to be naked. We questioned Mr. Kim about that because we thought it was unnecessary. He said that it was what he wanted and did not feel the need to share his plans with us. Two groups ago, the attorneys kept questioning the situation." He pointed to the two lawyers, "Mr. O'Hara and Miss Kapree are their replacements."

Ben leaned back and nodded again. "So, nobody, save Mr. Kim, had any idea why."

Sanchez leaned forward with his elbows on the table and hands clasped again. "Mr. Kim had a lot of idiosyncrasies he never told anyone about. He did not take kindly to anyone questioning him. I know that's not the answer you were hoping for." Leaving his elbows on the table, Sanchez raised his hands and rested his chin on them. "Let me guess the rest of your questions. Why were all of you fed so well? Why were your children allowed to be schooled? Why was your request for a Bible granted? Why the constant increase of difficulty with each fight? Why was your family required to remain in the apartment? Why were your classmates required to watch you and your wife's intimate moments? Why were you required to impregnate your classmates?" He paused, looked at Ben. "Am I getting warm?"

Ben chuckled a bit. "Smoking hot!" he replied. Everybody laughed at that.

"The only answer I have been privy to was the question regarding impregnation. He planned on all the groups to be impregnated to help resupply his business. As the champion he chose continued to win, more children would potentially be born. If, or should I say, *when* the said champion lost and was killed, all his children became the property of Mr. Kim." He raised his eyebrows. "You can guess what happened to them." Ben nodded. "However, no champion, got past the second fight, except for you. As you progressed, it became noticeable to me that Mr. Kim grew afraid of you," Sanchez said, pointing to Ben. "You were the only one who was not afraid of him."

Ben straightened up and said, "Of course I wasn't afraid of him. I am afraid of the One who can destroy my soul, not the one who can destroy my body."

O'Hara was the first to reply. "Much to our chagrin, we *all* were afraid of the man who could destroy our bodies. I, for one, am deeply ashamed." Several others nodded their heads in agreement. "But then, why did you fight so fiercely?"

"I fought to protect my friends and family. I recognized early on that I was a tool for God to destroy the evil here. I just prayed I didn't become the evil I fought against." Then a thought occurred to him. "You say there were twelve other groups? Where were they from?"

Kapree answered that with a matter-of-fact tone. "Russia, South Africa, China, Japan, Argentina, Germany, Sweden, Iran, Israel, Spain, Morocco, Australia," she said. "And finally, your group from the United States."

Ben let all that sink in. "What a tragedy. So many lives destroyed for money and evil pleasures." He slapped both of his hands on the table. "Let's get back to work. It is long past time for the destroyers to be destroyed." At that, the monitors were turned back on and the discussions restarted, getting quite animated.

"If I may," Kapree started a bit later, "I believe I have an idea as to why all the nudity." Everyone present turned to her, anticipating her conclusions on that subject. "Humiliation is a stumbling block for people trying to successfully defend one another. All the other chosen champions couldn't get past the humiliation of being naked in this arena. It made them easy prey." She paused to let the thought sink in. "Since you showed no such humiliation, you were able to focus on the task at hand," she leaned closer to accentuate the next thought, "which caused, first, Mr. Kim to be puzzled at your indifference. Then as you progressed, he became fearful of you, especially once you started to preach." Sanchez and O'Hara nodded in agreement. "You must have been naked many times with your friends for you to be so unconcerned."

At that, Ben had to reply. "Actually, not since we were babies being bathed by our mothers in the same place had we ever been naked in front of our friends, especially the girls. That was a conditional promise we made with God."

"Then, why weren't you ever humiliated?" Sanchez asked.

"I had to protect my friends and family, something I would sacrifice my dignity for." Ben had one more question. "Why were all the girls, my wife, and my kids kept naked? More humiliation?"

Kapree answered, "That was to make them a liability to you and to prepare them for the onslaught that was to come should you have lost." That caused the rest of the group to nod in agreement.

"Well, I was humiliated at first, but I wasn't going to let anybody see it," Ben clarified.

After acknowledging Ben's response, the group got back to work.

Sometime later, At the point where Japan was the center of topic, something caught Ben's attention. "Hold! Hold! Hold! Are you saying that the deprivation of Japan escalated when Mr. Kim's forces infiltrated the country?"

THE FALL OF JAPAN

O'Hara was taken aback with Ben's outburst. "That is true," he said. Kim sent a large force into Japan because that country was one of the few that did not suffer a civil war. Their population was still high but the government had been weak for quite some time. Also, none of Japan's allies could lend a hand since each country suffered their own civil war. During this time of weakness, some of Kim's operatives became judges, prosecutors, law makers, law enforcers, and military commanders. Due to the high population, it was easy to send the people into self-preservation mode. They stopped caring for one another and let the deprivation take over. Japan's pride plummeted. Politeness was destroyed. Kim called it his crowning achievement to subjugate an entire nation."

Ben chewed on that information for a few minutes. Sanchez and company halted what they were doing, waiting for him to respond. "How did the mafia types surrender?" he asked. "With their egos and little armies, shouldn't they have put up some sort of fight as their territories were invaded?"

Sanchez looked toward the ceiling for a couple of minutes, frustrated because he didn't want to have to discuss this part. However, Ben had asked the question, and he deserved an explanation. He blew out a breath before he spoke, grateful Ben was willing to wait for an answer. "They prefer to be called *Yakuza.* They definitely frown on the term mafia, although between you and me there is little difference. They also prefer to be called clans. Ah, thank you," he said to Carrie as she passed around some snacks and water. Susan brought the coffee for those who preferred that. The two quickly hugged their dad and ran back to the apartment. Sanchez continued. "The clans put up a fight at first, mostly against each other because of the goading by Kim's personnel. There were a few clans that caught on early. But by that time there were sufficient forces from Kim's side to wipe them out within a couple of days. Thirteen clans to be exact. Kim had the undivided attention of the remaining clans and has lorded it over them since." Sanchez made sure Ben was keeping up. "In other words, the clans became virtually null and void. They were allowed to keep their businesses. But that was it. Because they ceased to, for lack of a better word, patrol and protect their territories, the local degenerates became emboldened. And before you ask, yes, some of the clans' businesses were on the immoral side."

Ben closed his mouth as he was about to ask that very question. *Clan leaders with such high egos and pride must be chomping at the bit to get their power back*, he thought. *Even though they are not necessarily godly in nature, maybe I can help.* He said to the group, "I wonder what they would think if they got their power back. Would they be more moral in their dealings with others? Would their feuds with each other be lessened? Also, what is this chicken thing"?" Ben asked, pointing to a brief mention in the report they were looking at.

Kapree piped up with a hint of anger in her tone. "That is not chicken. It is *chikan*. The term refers to the public molestation or rape of women traveling on public transportation, from young girls to business age. This happens on trains and buses, and recently, on the streets and sidewalks all around the country. There is no fear of prosecution of the assailants."

Ben became openly angered but also confused. "Why is such a thing in this report, given Kim's other evil doings?"

Kapree continued. "Prior to Kim's invasion, the percentage of young girls, from middle school age to their mid-twenties, being molested or raped was as high as 30 percent. After Kim's influence, those percentages are as high as 95 percent. Adding insult to injury, the police and prosecutors usually blamed the girl for enticement. They still do. Such are the rulings from Kim's prosecutors and implanted policemen."

Ben stood up so fast that his chair went sliding away from him. "95 PERCENT!" He shouted, then covered his face. He turned around and took a few steps to regain control. He eventually put his arms at his sides and turned to look at his crew.

"That is absolutely unacceptable. And the clans are doing nothing?"

"Let me give you some more background on the whole situation." Sanchez continued. Kapree and O'Hara looked very nervous at this point. "Kim hated the Japanese. We don't know why, but his hatred was strong. He was able to meet up with some men from China who also had a severe case of hatred for them as well. Most of them were descendants of the Nanking regional areas devastated during World War II. The incident was historically known as the Rape of Nanking. The Japanese deny it of course, but it is amazing there are still people who hold that grudge, especially after the civil war China suffered. "

Ben rubbed his jaw, remembering the history of World War II.

"It was when the United States was at war that Kim hatched the idea of destroying Japan. With his penchant for abusing women and girls, he decided that having control over the government and law enforcement would guarantee his success." Sanchez was ill at ease telling his new boss this information because of his personal involvement, having been responsible for keeping the records and unable to stop the plan. "Mr. Kim had so many millions of people sent to infiltrate the Japanese society. They were able to speak, read and write fluent Japanese, and at his command, they executed the plan."

"Let me guess, *chikan* was involved?" Ben surmised.

"That was a very small part," Sanchez continued. "The entire military was sent to Guam. All of the Air Force, Army, and Navy were sent away. The military personnel were uneasy about the move, because Kim's generals were now in charge, but they obeyed and left for Guam."

"Wait a minute," Ben said, a little confused. "I thought the U. S. had control of the bases there."

O'Hara answered, "That was true until the United States had its own civil war. All land troops were placed at the borders and the Navy was patrolling the shores. That meant all other bases around the world were vacated in order to protect America's mainland."

Ben didn't like that bit of history.

Sanchez leaned back, wiping the sweat from his face. He really didn't like this part of his job. "Once the military was gone, things happened rapidly, including a total blackout of communications with the military. Once the blackout was complete, the order was given and the Constitution was annulled. Japan's Prime Minister signed into place the law that legalized rape. Females of any age, at any time, in any place, were under attack in Japan, and no one was to protect them. Anybody trying to was immediately sentenced to death." Sanchez leaned forward, wagging his forefinger in front of Ben. "Nothing happened at first, except demonstrations around the country. Those were quelled by drones spreading cyanide gas over the demonstrators." Sanchez waited to let that tidbit hit home, and it did. Ben was speechless as his anger was reaching a boiling point. "No messages ever escaped the country to inform the world of what was happening per Kim's communication blackout. And because of the weaknesses of her allies, Japan was alone. Multiple millions of people were killed that day, and worse, they were left to rot. The streets are still filled with the rotting bodies. Not one person who tried to defend the women and were killed were given a proper burial. The stench is sickening beyond belief. Many women and girls started fleeing to the countryside, but most never made it out of the cities. No rapes occurred for the first couple of months and the people started to think they were duped, relaxing their security. They were terribly wrong." Sanchez paused and shook his head. "Do you need me to say more?"

Ben was still in disbelief but he answered, "You have come this far, now finish it."

"Very well. About a year and a half ago, it started. Multitudes of men were sent to Kyoto and Osaka. After classes had begun, the men entered all of the schools and colleges and commenced the "rape campaign." Any boy or teacher that tried to save the girls was immediately killed by those thought to be classmates or teachers. The police were called, and a few tried to do what was right. But the honest law enforcers were assassinated by policemen who were Kim's associates. After that, the entire country was under attack. Most fathers, husbands, and sons perished in defense of their families. Again, to add insult to injury, most girls and women were raped by multiple men all day long that day."

Ben stood up and walked away. He went into deep prayer to ask for God's strength to handle this information. He was also becoming very grateful he had terminated Kim.

Sanchez continued when he returned, though Ben remained standing. "Women and very young girls were constantly under attack on the streets, in the alleys. If they tried to hide in their homes, the homes were broken into. You can guess the rest. Even the perverts of society caught the fever and joined in the devastation. Those young girls and women who made it to the forests and mountains were safe only for a short time." Sanchez could only shake his head. "As you can imagine, although Japan did not suffer a civil war, that did not mean they escaped devastation. From then until now, suicides skyrocketed among the women and girls. Many women became pregnant. Most terminated their pregnancies or killed the babies when they were born." Sanchez then reached with both hands towards Ben. "Truth be known," he said, "it was more humane for Nagasaki and Hiroshima than for the Japanese people who have lived through Mr. Kim's devastation." Ben was quite taken aback by that admission. To think that the nuclear bombings of those two cities and that aftermath was more humane was still inconceivable. "That is why we are *beyond* grateful for your victory. Now we can eliminate the evil from Japan by destroying all of Kim's followers. Even to this day, bodies are rotting around the country." Sanchez paused to take a deep breath. "Because of Kim's desire for total accountability, we can, with the help of the clans, and the military, wipe them out quickly."

"How?" Ben asked, still pacing. "This is pointing to the spirit of Antichrist. Not the Antichrist, but the spirit of."

"Antichrist?" O'Hara exclaimed.

"In the time of the end, a man will rise up and be the world leader and force a devastation that makes the last forty years pale in comparison. He and those times are prophesied in the Bible." Ben explained.

Sanchez continued, "At this time, the clans are doing nothing. That, however, doesn't mean they don't *want* to something about it."

Ben collected his chair and brought it back to the table. "Since we are in the business of dismantling the evil side of the empire," he said as he sat back down, "do you think the clans would be willing to become allies, along with the return of the military, in mopping up and setting the moral compass of Japan on proper footing?"

Sanchez, O'Hara, Kapree, and everyone else looked at each other. Some shrugged their shoulders. After a moment, O'Hara answered, "We haven't thought about it that way." He rubbed his stubble on his chin. "Do you have any ideas?"

Ben smiled, then said, "Actually, I do, though I know it will be playing with the devil a bit." He paused for a few minutes before he stood back up. "I need to bring my thinking to God to make sure we are doing the thing He wants us to do. Adjourn for today. I have a conversation with God I must attend. Good night, everybody." He started to walk away, then turned to face the others. "If,

however, you want to keep working, be my guest."
He turned to walk back to the apartment where
his family was waiting.

Yakuza Helps or Hinders

"Orange and black, Mom?" Roberta was
protesting the day's clothing colors. "You know my
favorite colors are purple and gold, and Michaels
is green and yellow. And why do all of us have to
wear the same colors?"

On this particular day, Allison wanted to celebrate
her high school's colors by having everybody wear
an orange t-shirt with black shorts. To include the
baby and toddlers. "They are your dad and my
high school colors. And I wanted something to
remember about those days." She said sternly with
a hint of sadness.

That explanation did not pass muster with most
of the children as Ben, who was also dressed on

orange shirt and black pants, looked over the sea of orange and black. Roberta started a protest that ended when Mom put her foot down.

"We will be doing these types of things with the other colors in coming days. So today will be orange and black. And that is final!" Allison pointed to floor with a stern look that brokered no disobedience. Ben did all he could do to maintain a straight face.

Roberta stomped her foot as a last sign of disagreement. Several of the children thought it was fun to be all dressed alike.

Outside of the apartment the ladies, who made it their mission to serve the family that freed them from servitude to Kim, giggled to themselves as they listened to the disagreement. They came to take out the laundry and clean the clothes for the family. They waited patiently until the family marched out of the apartment. As soon as the last child passed through the door, all of the children ran over to the games and crafts areas. The ladies went in, put away the clean laundry where Allison had designated, and found the dirty laundry piled up beside the doorway.

Even though there was a bit of an odor they were still smiling because of their freedom.

Ben just marveled that Allison was able to corral their herd of children. After the ladies gathered the laundry, he finished dressing for work and went out to the office where he met with his crew. He had to smile at the joyous noise coming from his family. And orange and black were perfect colors as far as he was concerned.

"They will be arriving tomorrow morning, Mr. Bickles," Kapree informed her boss, holding her nervousness in check. She along with Sanchez and O'Hara were also in the spirit of things as they wore orange shirts, black pants, and black ties. Kapree's hair was tied up into a pony tail. This was a week after Ben was first informed about the situation in Japan.

"Tomorrow morning?" Ben responded. "Excellent. How many clans are we expecting?"

"All of them, sir."

"ALL?"

"Yes, sir," Kapree said. "Apparently, they *all* want their dominion back."

Mr. Sanchez answered. "And they are abiding by the truce you recommended. Quite the feat, if I do say so myself. Your argument must have been very persuasive."

You have quite the connections, Sanchez," Ben said, smiling at his new friend.

"Accurate record keeping has its perks, Mr. Bickles."

 "That it does," Ben acknowledged. "By the way. I never asked you what your official title is."

Sanchez chuckled a bit. "I guess, if you must be official, I could be considered to be the chief operating officer, COO for short."

Ben cocked his head, "Works for me. Now returning to the topic at hand, ridding a nation from such tyranny benefits everybody, except for the tyrants wishing to pass on those *blessings*." Ben used air quotes to emphasize the last word.

"Unfortunately," he said, "Japan's perceived peace will need to be broken for a short spell. Given the information from all of you, 80 percent of Japan's judges, prosecutors, defense attorneys, law enforcement, and military leadership personnel will need to be removed or killed before good can take over. And while all that is going on, the citizens will need protection. Maybe this will be a time for the clans to do the right thing."

"I am not keen on this one, Mr. Bickles," O'Hara piped in. "But I will trust you anyway."

With a pat on the back of his new friend O'Hara, Ben continued, "Let us finish preparations and get some rest, then." He smiled at the group. "We will deal with tomorrow when tomorrow comes." With a raised finger, he admonished, "Make sure you are all in prayer. We are definitely going to need God's guidance and wisdom."

The group felt more reassured and went about their work. And pray they did.

Early the next morning, after breakfast and multiple hugs and kisses from his family, Ben walked out with peace in his mind that he attributed to God. He was greeted at the office area by Sanchez and friends. "All is ready?" he asked.

"As ready as we can be, sir," Kapree stated with more confidence than she felt.

"Excellent," Ben said, noting her tension. "Miss Kapree, relax. Lord willing, God will prevail today." He turned to Sanchez, "How soon?"

"Within the hour, sir."

"Also excellent." Ben perused the group. "Alright, what is up?" he asked, putting his hands on hips.

After some foot shuffling and hanging of heads, O'Hara finally spoke. "This truce between the clans is sketchy at best. There is a great possibility that violence will happen without notice."

"Do we have the perceived feuding clans separated while they are here, as I requested?"

"Yes, sir. But we are not you, so we are a bit fearful."

"Good. Fear will keep you on your toes, looking out for trouble. However, I firmly believe an additional time of prayer to calm your souls is needed. Let's take care of that now." They all bowed their heads as Ben called on the name of the Lord to bring calm and wisdom to the hearts of all present. He asked the Lord to make everyone aware of God's voice when He speaks this day. When the prayer was finished, Ben recognized the divine calm that had come over everyone. He knew it well. "Now," he stated, "let us greet our guests."

With that, the waiting *Yakuza* clans entered the building. They were escorted to their staging areas, making sure the feuding clans were separated as best as possible. Ben identified the leaders and subordinates, noticing there was one thing clearly missing.

"Gentleman and ladies," Ben called out while standing behind the tables, facing the clans, "isn't it a Japanese custom to bow to your host when you enter their home or place of business?" He was met with stares, so Ben changed tactics. "If I were invited by one of you and entered your place of business, would you not expect me to bow to you? What I am asking for is no different," Ben said, putting his hands on his hips and staring them down. "Show respect."

It took a few minutes, but eventually, each of the leaders and clan members bowed and apologized for their lack of respect. Ben lightly bowed back as he declared that no offense was taken. He invited the leaders to sit at the appointed desks and began his speech.

"First of all," Ben began, "I don't want to know anybody's names. Unless you feel compelled to offer it. I am Benjamin Bickles—"

One younger leader interrupted, "I don't care who you are. I want to speak to Mr. Kim."

"You can if you feel the need," Ben replied. "You will find what's left of him in the crocodile poop." He pointed to the pit opening in the floor. Given the responses to his statement, he knew he had their attention. "I am the one who put him there. And in so doing, by his decree beforehand, I have become the chairman of the organization." That drew serious anger from some of the clan leaders. "However, I am in the process of dismantling and destroying the evil branches of the organization. Do you have any idea what that entails?" Again, the overall response was surprise.

Just what Ben was hoping for.

One of the women who, at this point, was the leader of a clan asked the question all the others were contemplating. "Why are we here then? More demands?"

Ben sat down and leaned back in his chair and smiled. "Quite the contrary," he stated. "I have a plan for you to return your country to what it was before Mr. Kim's group showed up." With a slower pace, he said, "Or make it better. More livable. More friendly. More loving." He reached out, indicating the entire group with an open palm, "Your choice."

Some of the leaders looked like they heard nothing while a few had their curiosity piqued. Ben knew that those who weren't showing any emotion were actually quite interested. He was sure that their relationship with Mr. Kim's organization left them less than hopeful.

"However," Ben said, "first things first. In front of each clan's leader are several copies of the Christian Bible. It has been translated into Japanese. They are for you to read. Or not. Your choice." He saw several scowls but chose to ignore them. "All I ask is that you *consider* reading them. My first priority is to share the Gospel of Jesus the Christ and the salvation He offers to all mankind. The choice is yours." A few of the leaders fingered the books and flipped through a few pages then closed them, waiting for what was to come.

Ben stood up, walked around the table and sat on it. "I understand that rape has been legalized and allowed to run rampant throughout your country. Throughout the entire nation. Women and girls are being raped at any time and any place. And I understand that anyone who interferes are legally mandated to be killed on the spot. Am I mistaken?"

That brought a response from each member and leader, except for a couple of young men who stood stoic. Ben noticed, making sure to memorize these men's faces and position. *Those two are likely participants in those actions*, he surmised.

One of the leaders decided to challenge Ben on this issue. "What do I care if girls are groped on the trains," the man said. "My daughter doesn't ride the trains."

Ben noticed the instant hurt expression from the young woman behind the man who spoke. Pointing to her he asked the leader. "Is that young lady your daughter?"

The man didn't change his position, though he nodded.

Ben addressed her. "Have you ever been groped or raped since Mr. Kim's group arrived in Japan?" As he suspected she flinched as if slapped. The woman quickly composed herself, though a murmur went around the room. Clearly, Ben was not the only one who saw her reaction.

Her father immediately turned to face her. Locking eyes with the woman, he realized the truth. "You have?" All she could do was nod and lower her head in shame.

Ben stood and addressed her. "I don't know about Japanese culture, but as a Christian, you have nothing to be ashamed of. Only the person," he paused, "or persons..." Her head snapped up to stare at him. Ben softened his tone. "I see. You have my deepest apologies. It is my understanding that over 95 percent of the girls in Japan have been assaulted in this manner before they graduate from high school." Some of the other women started to show shame. A few cried. Fathers hung their heads in shame. Ben spread his arms wide. "Are you now willing to listen to my suggestions so you can reclaim your country?" A few heads looked at him, curious. "Yes, I said *suggestions*. They will not be demands." He sat back, waiting for them to respond. However, he kept his eyes on the two men he had noticed before. They started to show some nervousness and anger. Ben pointed to the two men. "Maybe you two would rather keep the status quo and continue raping young girls. Perhaps you attacked one or more of the young women and girls here and want to continue your perversions?"

The clan leader in charge of the two men spun his chair around, glaring at his underlings. They immediately started talking at the same time, trying to defend themselves. A quick order barked at them by their leader brought them under control. That leader stood up and addressed the women. "Have these two ever assaulted any of you? Please be truthful."

Three women nearby raised their hands. All three were from a clan that had been feuding with. He addressed the women's leaders.

Ben looked at the two men, murder in his eyes. "Is this why you all are feuding?"

Those three leaders stood and, in Japanese, admitted the truth. The clan leader looked at the two men and ordered them to be detained. He apologized to the other leaders in Japanese and then, in English, he said, "You may have these two to do as you wish. They have brought shame to my clan."

Ben was happy to see the clans still had a sense of chivalry left. He disagreed with Mr. Kim's intervention upon their territories and country. As Ben spoke, his strong, calm voice penetrated the tension. "I am glad to see that all of you agree on *something*. Will you now hear me out?"

It took a moment, but eventually each clan leader nodded in agreement and focused on Ben. "Thank you," Ben said when he had their attention. "Frankly, I will not be checking on you after today, so please hear me." Motioning to Sanchez, several large monitors were turned on, showing videos of Japan from surveillance drones supplied by your military. "As we speak, multitudes of Mr. Kim's forces are being rounded up or killed." With a slight nod, Ben continued. "Mostly killed." *That definitely got their attention*, he thought. "That includes some prosecutors, judges, attorneys, law enforcement, and politicians. Anyone who has sent Japan into a moral and deadly cesspool is getting justice today. Your very own military has quietly returned and are executing the plan to reclaim Japan. They have to get past the revulsion of the rotting corpses until their job is done. Here is where you come in." Ben looked at the men and women, ready to hear his ideas. *Now comes the 'gotcha.'* "I understand most of you want to keep authority over your territories but you also want a better reputation with the local people. Am I wrong?" Looking around, he noticed no dissent. "Excellent," Ben said. "Now here is my proposal. Continue your truce, but eliminate your immoral businesses," *That caused a stir.* "Keep your status as Yakuza, but make it more of a protection agency," Raising his finger for emphasis, "but not by forcing payments from the businesses. In other words, no more extortion!" *That ruffled a few more feathers,* Ben was almost smiling internally. "Be willing to stand up for the women of your territories. Actually, for your whole country."

Some of the men listened intently. Some seemed opposed to the proposal. The women leaders were on the edge of their seats waiting for what came next, each liking what they are hearing.

One of the leaders who wasn't particularly fond of the idea decided now was the time to speak up. "What do you mean 'stand up for our territories?'" he asked.

"Exactly what I said," Ben stated with a flat tone. "First, assign some of your more conscientious men to ride the trains, buses, and patrol the streets in your territories. Let the people know you are there for their protection. Do not ask for compensation. Do it for the benefit of the people, not yourselves." Ben looked around, then said, "I understand that sometimes the train stops overlap each other's territory. When your men are about to enter the trains, they must let the other men off so they can get on the next train heading back into their own territory. Therefore, the truce must stand. No one clan can harass the other since you are all performing the same public service."

"You won't interfere with our business in these matters?" asked the same man.

"No. As a matter of fact, you all have the option to follow the plan or not once you leave here. I will not interfere. However, I can see that all of you want a less immoral Japan. More joy for the children. Women shopping without fear of being assaulted," Ben took a brief pause. "Just so you understand what I am ultimately recommending, when your men catch a rapist or molester, those men must be willing to provide evidence and appear in front of a judge and testify for the girls. Let the rapist rot in prison. Once we have eliminated Kim's people, all you will have left will be Japanese perverts. Along with the military, clean up your country. Work together." Ben sat down and waited for their response.

They looked at each other. Even the clans at conflict with each other began to talk over the plan. They became so engrossed in their discussions that they didn't notice the tables, chairs, tablecloths and place settings, with both chopsticks and silverware, being set up behind Ben by his family and some local caterers.

A Meal to Show Cooperation

After about an hour of discussion, one that never rose into an argument, they all settled down and stood from their tables, facing Ben. One of the younger leaders was chosen to speak. Ben was all ears.

"Mr. Bickles," the young clan leader began, "normally, such suggestions would fall on deaf ears. But given the current circumstances, we have agreed to continue the truce and work to implement your plan." They all bowed to him.

Ben bowed back, a little taken aback that they had all agreed. When he finally recovered, he was jubilant. "Excellent!" he said. "Excellent indeed. Just so you know, it will take many years for the women to trust anyone or anything. Be patient. Japan will not be healed overnight." Ben clapped his hands and waved to Allison, who was standing by the tables with their children. She waved back. "Ladies and gentlemen," Ben announced as he turned back to the clans, "I request that you join us for lunch. My wife, along with some local caterers have made a feast for you. Some of the food is typical Japanese fare while some is American. There is plenty, so you can eat to your hearts' content. The tables are set up for each individual clan, but if you are willing, you may sit with members of other clans. Come and eat." Ben said with a wave of his arm, inviting them to follow him to the tables.

After a few moments, they all followed him, sitting at the tables without squabbling. The leaders sat at one table together, much to Sanchez's amazement. Mostly, the clans stayed by themselves, but a couple of tables had a mix of clan members.

Ben called for quiet. "As a Christian," he began, "I can't allow the food to brought to you without giving thanks. If you are willing, please join me in prayer." Most held their hands together and bowed their heads. Ben didn't know which god they were praying to. Still, he gave thanks and asked for a wonderful time of fellowship as they ate their meal. "By the way, my family and I will be serving you."

One of the leaders stood and objected. "No leader serves anyone," they called out. "Leaders are to be served."

Ben responded, "Jesus, the God I serve, stripped down to just a loin cloth and washed the feet of the disciples who worshipped Him. He taught that we should all have the mentality of servants, especially leaders. Who am I to not do otherwise?"

The man sat down, a little confused about these Christians. But he accepted the service. Each leader did, and contemplated Ben's words in their own hearts.

As young Susan was serving, Ben caught the leering look of one of the men. He immediately walked over, drew his fifty-caliber pistol and aimed it right at the man's head. "Look at my daughter like that again," Ben warned, "and you will be tossed into the crocodile pit with a hole in your head and a mess for your friends to clean up! Have I got your attention?"

The man looked to his leader for permission and then stood up. He bowed deeply and apologized for his inappropriate behavior. Ben put his pistol back in its holster, smiled, and moved on. It took several minutes before the people resumed their reverie. But the inappropriate man was scared to the point of not being able to eat.

When the meal was finished and all ate their fill, Ben invited everyone back to the conference area. After assembling, Ben pointed to the different colored folders in front of each leader.

"In the red folder are the names, addresses, and photos of any remaining Kim personnel in your territories. I have gathered it for you, to help you finish the cleanup. I think you should have some satisfaction by helping with that. Not only that, your actions should help the populace start to trust you, while making the punks and rapists begin to fear you." The clan leaders opened the folders and recognized some of the faces. Ben continued, "The Blue folders contain information on the political offices that need attention as well. However," he paused, raising his finger again, "I abhor bullying. Do everything for the good of the people. Understand?" Again, they all agreed. "The white folders are the lists of the good law officers, prosecutors, politicians, and military personnel. I recommend you work with them and develop an effective rapport with them. Help them so they will not be overwhelmed with the work of restoring Japan."

One of the lady clan leaders stood, addressing Ben. "What you are asking of us will be difficult. We," she said and waved her arm to the other clans, "have a lot of historical animosity between us to wipe away. And then there is the long road ahead. I, for one, will implement this plan immediately. But only after I settle with the clans that, before today, were in a feud with us." She bowed to Ben and the other leaders stood and bowed as well.

Ben returned the bow, as before. "Let the people praise you and come to trust you. Let the punks and perverts fear you. May there be joy in all of Japan because of you. Work hard to be servants to the people." He bowed again. They returned the bow.

Not long after the meal, all the clans left, but not before each leader shook his hand and thanked him again for his hospitality.

Ben stood with Sanchez, Kapree, O'Hara, and the others, watching them leave. Allison joined them and was the first to speak. "That went far better than planned."

"Far better indeed," Ben agreed. In fact, everyone in the office area agreed. "I was serious when I said I will not be watching over them. However, I will appreciate a report or two from time to time. I pray God calls Japan to Him."

"You got it, Boss!" O'Hara answered.

Ben looked out the door the clans had left through. "Is it time to leave this place, Sanchez?" Ben asked.

"Yes, sir."

"Well then. Time for me to focus on the Constellation then, since I will be flying her out of here."

"Tomorrow a good time to start?"

"That's perfect."

"There is one thing that still bothers me," Ben said. "Darrin has yet to answer the summons."

"Once his deployment is over, I am sure we will be able to deal with him, Sir," Kapree answered.

"Looking forward to that day," Sanchez added. Ben patted him on the back and agreed.

READYING TO LEAVE

In the morning, the entire family finally exited the building that had been their home for fifteen plus years.

The children were wearing their shoes, but not without many initial protestations. Mama prevailed. Because of the fear and exhilaration of going outside for the first time, there were no squabbles about what they were wearing, except for the shoes. Some of the children wanted to dash out the door while others had to be gently coaxed by the adults. Once out, and after taking in the view of Pago Pago from their home, they group collected the small ones and guided to the airfield. The airfield housed Mr. Kim's vintage and functional aircraft. Ben recognized the fighters, bombers and commercial aircraft, which were mostly from World War Two. Amid some of them were a P-51 Mustang, a P-38 Lightning, an F4U Corsair, a B-17 Flying Fortress, a B-29 Super fortress, a P-47 Thunderbolt, a B-36 Peacemaker, and when Ben saw the Lockheed Constellation, his mouth dropped for a moment.

The Lockheed Constellation was a dolphin shaped, three tailed airliner, originally built in the nineteen forties, was used by the military and civilian passenger and cargo companies. Ben noticed it had been given updated powerplants, such as the Constellation, which now had four turboprop engines instead of the original radials.

"Turbo props?" Ben asked, impressed by the efficiency and power. "When were they installed and are they functional. I assume everything was done safely?"

"That craft, my fine furry friend, is a work of art," O'Hara's said, pointing at the Constellation. His excitement got the best of him. "It took approximately two years of engineering and metalwork, with about a hundred and thirty people, to make everything functional and safe. It works like it is supposed to." He breathed a sigh of admiration with the last word.

"That is wonderful information," Ben said, "but it doesn't answer my question." He emphasized the next word. "*When* did they install the engines? *When* was the last time it has flown? And one

more thing. *When* was the last inspection and
or service?" Ben looked at O'Hara, waiting for
the answer.

"Sorry, Boss," he said, fidgeting a few seconds
before responding with a list of answers. "Installed
four years ago. Last flown, Ten days ago. Last
service, three weeks ago. Last inspection?" He
shrugged and looked back at Ben. "I haven't
the slightest idea. I don't believe he ever had it
properly inspected."

"Ever?" Ben was not happy about that last item.
"Since that is to be our get out of here plane, A
full inspection is the first thing we need done. I
will not fly it until then. However," he said with
smiling at O'Hara, "while that happens, I will
acclimate myself to this marvel of engineering."
His admiration showed in the way he looked at the
plane. It was truly a marvel to behold. He squeezed
his wife's hand.

"You fly, Boss?" O'Hara asked in amazement.

Ben smiled, "My friends and I were trained to
pilot aircraft when we were young—single and

multiengine and jets. I am rated for multi engine and turboprop. Truth be known; I am a little giddy at the thought of being on the controls of this beauty."

Remembering how much her husband loved to fly, Allison got excited for him, and for the fact that they would soon be going home. She had to admit, she also admired the big airliner. She fondly remembered the many times Ben took her up in the small airplane at home. She just adored watching him exuding confidence as he masterfully handled the controls.

Ben's excitement went up a few notches as he looked over the other aircraft. With great enthusiasm, he pointed to the aircraft and declared to Allison, "Michael would just salivate for the opportunity to fly the P-38." His tone turned sad, "that is if he is still alive."

Allison was also a bit sad at that thought, so she placed her hand on his shoulder. "Carrie would love to be right there, flying with him. We'll continue to pray that they are still alive and waiting for us to return."

Ben touched her hand before moving to the next fighter, "Robert would give his right kidney to fly that Red Tail P-51, the one representing the Tuskegee airmen," he pointed to another craft. "And Derrick's heart would skip a beat if he had the chance to be at the controls of that old B-36 over there." After a few moments of thought he said, "Another work of engineering genius."

While Ben and Allison were walking around, impressed with the planes, their children were taking in the great outside world. A few were a bit fearful of their first steps through the door. Carrie, Roberta, Michael and Derrick, on the other hand, wanted to run around seeing, touching, and smelling everything. They were all amazed at the brightness of the sun, and their parents immediately warned them about looking directly into it. Not only that, the smells of the sea and vegetation were almost overwhelming for them. The insects flying around them were most definitely a bother.

They still managed to catch their father's enthusiasm about all of the airplanes.

"Daddy, what are we going to do with those?" Susan asked, pointing to the planes.

"Well, most of them will just stay here," he said. "But that one," he pointed to the Constellation, "is our ride out of here. It will take us back to where your mother and I were raised. Your mom and I call it home." Before Susan could ask her next question, Ben turned to Sanchez. "Please tell me that a fully qualified crew is available."

"I am so sorry, sir," Sanchez said, "but Mr. Kim left orders that the crews had to be eliminated when he died. All of them." He put up his hand. "And before you ask, no, those orders were not given to us. Hasenpfeffer got those orders and he fulfilled them with relish. I just found out late last night when I tried to get in contact with the crews. I knew you didn't need to know precisely at that moment, so I waited to tell you today."

"Are there any crews around the world available to fly this thing?" Ben had become a little concerned that their departure would have to be delayed even more.

"I have an inquiry going on right now," Sanchez replied. "But I am not too hopeful."

Ben looked down for a few minutes, then up at Allison. Next he looked at Sanchez, O'Hara, Kapree, and finally back at the aircraft. He started pacing between the Constellation and Allison. From time to time, he would look at his daughters. It was obvious he was trying to come up with a plan. He finally stopped pacing, right in front of Allison. He shook his head a few times before he spoke. "I have a plan and you," he said, pointing to his wife, "are not going to like it."

Learning to Fly

Allison remained stoic when she replied, "And why would I not like it? This wonderful plan of yours?" Her hands went immediately to her hips.

Ben glanced at his four eldest daughters, then back to Allison. "I will teach the second officer's job and the engineer's job, fundamentally, to the girls. That way, they can help me fly this behemoth."

Allison looked into her husband's eyes to make sure he hadn't lost all his marbles. "*Our* daughters?"

"Yes. Carrie, Susan, Whitney, and Roberta." Then he said, with a little bit of pride. "They're plenty smart."

Having heard their names mentioned, the four girls perked up to hear some more.

"Yes, dear," Allison uttered, not overly convinced. "They are very smart, but that is quite a lot for them to learn in such a short time." The girls looked from one parent to another, like they were watching a tennis match, heads and eyes moving in the same direction and at the same time.

"They only need to know the basics, and they can relay the information to me. I can tell them what they need to do if changes are needed," Ben said, trying to be optimistic. "Piece of cake."

Allison still wasn't sold. "Aren't you going to be busy enough just trying to fly that thing?" she asked.

"True, but I will be training them as I train myself on the operations." Pointing to the Constellation he said, "These are some of the most pilot-friendly airliners to fly. We just need to leave here and land in Hawaii. From there, we can find a proper crew to finish getting us home."

The girls focused on their mother, waiting for her response. She looked from Ben, to the airliner, to her daughters, then back to Ben. "I have no fears about your abilities in piloting this thing," she said, "but to include the girls?"

"Mama, we can do it," exploded Roberta. "Trust us. We won't let Daddy down." With a little impish look she added, "Much." Then she giggled.

"You are not helping your cause," Allison jokingly replied. Then, all seriousness, she looked at Ben. "Promise this will work," she said. "And what am I supposed to be doing while you train the girls?"

Ben sheepishly responded, "Watch over the rest of the children."

Sanchez immediately exclaimed, "Just so both of you understand, Kapree, O'Hara, and I will be traveling with you. We are, after all, your officers in the organization. We would be delighted to help the missus with the children."

Allison surrendered. "Thank you. I will greatly appreciate it. You, sir," she said, pointing to Ben, "had better keep your promise about the girls."

Ben threw up his hands, "I haven't promised anything yet."

"Yet!? Well, get to promising."

"Yes, dear. In as much as it is in my power, I promise to properly train and trust our daughters to complete the task ahead of us and make sure they are ready to fulfill their assigned duties."

Allison nodded. "Very well then," she declared. "Get to work. I want out of this place as soon as possible." She winked, letting him know he was on her list if he failed to follow through. At least that was his interpretation.

"Yes, dear."

Ben bowed to his wife and the girls jumped up and down, cheering as they did so. It was clear to Ben that they didn't really care or understand what lay ahead.

"First," Ben said, "I need to get acquainted with the plane, then I will start teaching. So, until that time, everybody needs to stay clear of all the aircraft here." Ben pointed to all the children, some of whom pouted a little. "I know there is a whole world out there to be discovered," he told them, "but we are going to have to take things a step at a time. I need to make sure this big bird is airworthy." He turned to Allison, "Sorry sweetheart," he said, "this is going to take several days for me to inspect the entire plane and make sure all is functional. Then comes training. Then comes flight training." After a brief moment, he uttered, with great aplomb, "Then we will fly home! Any questions?"

"Are we there yet?" Allison quipped, smiling.

"Yes, dear, we are there." They both laughed at the old joke. The children giggled because their parents laughed but none of them got the joke. Ben noticed some of their puzzlement. "Don't worry children. You will get the joke soon enough."

They were not convinced.

"So, boss," chimed in O'Hara, "I am ready to join you with your inspections. I oversaw that engine's updating, so I am somewhat knowledgeable about the Constellation."

"Excellent!" Ben said. "Let us get with the program. The sooner we certify the old bird, the sooner we are gone." Ben patted him on the back, and they strode off to do just that.

Allison was a little sad because she felt he assumed she would do little else besides looking after the children. Miss Kapree noticed the emotion and stepped close to Allison. "Don't worry, Mrs. Bickles, all men do that when a highly specific task enters their sphere of influence." She placed her hand on Allison's shoulder. "C'mon," Kapree said, "Sanchez and I will help you corral your little herd and show them around." She reached for the baby. "First, let me help by taking this one off your shoulders so you can have a break."

Allison gratefully passed the child to the other woman and the baby was excited because Miss Kapree loved to play.

As Kapree held the little one, her emotions were mixed. She couldn't help but recognize how much this little cherub resembled her lost baby. Holding her was great healing.

Sanchez then led the party to a grassy area and pointed toward the sea on the horizon. The children were immediately mesmerized by the view. A couple of the younger children tried to wander away, but they were soon called back by their mama. Obedience was easy this time as the children were all a little anxious about the outdoors. Over the next few days, however, that changed completely. Their more adventuresome natures took hold and Allison had to ask Ben for more help keeping them in line. Ben was more than willing to help and was quite apologetic that he had left her with the little rascals that first day.

After about a week, Ben invited Carrie, Susan, Whitney, and Roberta to enter the Constellation's flight deck. All the switches, gauges, and displays seemed overwhelming for them, but Ben quietly pointed out that they would be quite knowledgeable about it soon enough. He assured them that, in a few weeks, they would know enough to help him keep track of the systems so he could fly confidently. Ben then started to point out the more important gauges and switches for the second officer's seat. From there, he moved to the engineer's seat and pointed out more of them, focusing especially on gauges pertaining to engine operating parameters.

"Now girls," Ben said, wanting to calm their minds. "I have shown all of you a lot today. Don't worry about not being able to understand it all now. That will come as we start the training." He placed his hands briefly on each of their heads, "I have no doubt you all will do excellently because you are so smart. Once you have grasped what you need to know and are a bit more trained, we will take a few test flights before we leave. So, please, be calm." He smiled. "We have time. We will be fine. You are not going to get it at first. But you *will.* Also, add this whole endeavor to your prayers. Ask God to grant you peace and wisdom, and we will be just fine." The girls nodded, still quite uncertain their father knew what he was talking about.

Minute by minute. Hour by hour. Day by day. The girls were drilled about the two stations on the Constellation. They were progressing faster than Ben could have imagined.

From time to time, Sanchez would provide a report on the operations to dismantle the evil side of the organization. One evening, at supper, Ben made an announcement. "Tomorrow morning, after first inspection and training, I am going to start up those engines for the purpose of taxiing the plane. I want to get used to the sounds and the gauges in actual operations. If all goes well, I plan to take our first flight in the afternoon. So, girls," He looked at his 'crew' and said, "sleep well. Let tomorrow's situations be for tomorrow. Tonight, we rest." That caused quite a clamor among the children and it took some time to quiet down.

Later that evening, after the children were put to bed and the baby nursed, Ben and Allison did their nightly ritual. Ben noticed Allison was uncommonly quiet, so he asked what was bothering her.

"Oh, nothing," she said.

"Don't give me that garbage," he said as he combed her hair, "something is bugging you. Now spit it out." He found a rather snarled lock of hair.

"As you wish," Allison said as she turned to face him, stopping him. "Do you think it was wise to announce your plans for tomorrow at supper tonight?"

"Yeah. Why?"

"You expect them to have a good night's sleep?"

"Well, yeah."

"You saw how the girls were. Each one is excited about it. If they sleep at all, I will be the most surprised."

Ben thought about that for a few seconds. "Oh, I didn't think about that," he said. I will check up on them before we go to bed."

"Are you even sure *you* will sleep tonight?"

He thought about that a little longer. "Now that you mention it, I am not sure. There is so much at stake. I see your point. I should have waited until after breakfast tomorrow. I am sorry."

"Let's pray that God will grant us all perfect peace tonight." Ben agreed and they prayed. Unbeknownst to them, their children were listening and prayed right along with their parents.

As Ben and Allison were going to bed, they checked on the children and were greatly relieved to see they were all sleeping well. Then they went to bed. It was a couple of hours before Ben finally fell asleep. Allison was relieved. Shortly after him, she slept as well.

The following morning, Allison woke up as the children were starting to wake up. She instantly noticed that Ben was not there. She laid her head back on the pillow for a few moments. *He is probably getting the children ready for their exciting day*, she thought. *Wait a minute! I only hear the girls talking about what to expect today. And they are all in the bathroom together.* Then she realized something. *Why weren't they arguing about who should be in the bathroom first?* That did it. Out of the bed she flew, wanting to see what was going on. Or, what was *not* going on.

She opened the door to the bathroom and was amazed to see four happy dancing girls nicely taking turns at the sink. "Alright girls," she asked. "What's up?"

Carrie turned to her mother and mumbled, "What do you mean 'what's up?'" She turned to spit out the toothpaste preventing proper speech. "We are so excited about the plane that we don't have time to argue. Besides, Dad said if we argued like we always do, we wouldn't be allowed to help him fly the plane." The other three girls animatedly nodded their agreement.

"Oh," said Allison, a little surprised that that was all it took to stop the arguing. "And where is your dad?"

After taking her turn to spit out her toothpaste, Susan replied, "Oh, he is already performing the preflight inspection. He said that as soon as we are done getting ready and have finished our breakfast, we were to meet him there. But, and I quote, 'You had better eat a full meal because we may not be able to stop until tonight.'"

It was then that Allison finally heard some motion in the kitchen. *Odd.* Upon entering the kitchen, she found Michael and Derrick preparing breakfast for everyone.

Michael saw her first and smiled at her, "Oh, hi, Mama!" he declared. "Dad wanted us to make sure our sisters were well fed and that you were to be left alone to sleep." Then with an exaggerated grin he said, "Good morning, Mama!" Derrick repeated the greeting with equal enthusiasm.

Allison returned the greeting and decided to check on the younger children, who were just starting to wriggle around their beds as they were waking up. The baby was wide awake and got excited to see Mama, ready for the morning feeding.

His day is going to be different, Allison surmised.

After the premeal prayer, the girls' excitement bled onto their siblings, so breakfast was a noisy affair. Once everyone was fed, Michael and Derrick told their sisters that they would take care of the cleanup, so they could get out there with their dad.

Allison piped up, "Alright, who are you and what have you done with my children?"

Initially, the children were a little puzzled by that question coming from their mother, but noticing the smile on her face, they soon realized she had said a funny. Then they all laughed. The four eldest daughters got up, hugged their mama and kissed her on the cheek. Then the four sisters kissed the baby on the forehead, hugged their brothers, and scampered out to catch up with their father.

Allison was stunned. *They hugged their brothers!? That's a switch.*

Out at the airplane, Ben and Mr. O'Hara were performing the preflight inspection around the outside of the Constellation.

"You hear that?" Ben said suddenly.

Caught by surprise at the change of topic, O'Hara was a little slow to respond. "Hear what?"

"That cacophony."

"Oh," O'Hara made as if to hear for the first time. "Yeah."

"Not your normal noise around the airfield."

"I guess not."

"Sounds like music to the soul, huh?"

O'Hara smiled, nodding. "Yeah."

"Where do you suppose it is coming from?"

"Your children, perhaps?"

Ben looked down to his friend. "Yeah," he said. They both laughed at that and turned to face the girls running and giggling towards them.

When the girls finally arrived, they couldn't contain their enthusiasm and kept jumping up and down while laughing and squealing. Ben joined in their reverie and jumped with them.

O'Hara thought, *Insanity has finally taken over.*

Suddenly, Roberta stopped and glared at her father, "Daddy, are you mocking us?" she accused

Ben stopped jumping and composed himself, then smirked. "Why, yes I am," he stated. Roberta and her sisters once again started laughing. Ben and O'Hara joined them. Eventually, everybody calmed down as the importance of the next few hours finally took hold of them.

Carrie offered up a question, albeit a little fearfully, "Daddy, are we really going to start up the engines today?" she asked. "And are we really going to fly this thing?"

FIRST FLIGHT

Ben placed his hand on her head, saying, "Yes. That is exactly what we are going to do. Don't worry, you will have to lean on your training. Trust it." He looked at each girl, "And I know you are all afraid right now," he told them. "Good, because if you weren't, I would send you back home. You need to have a healthy respect for the value of the work you are about to perform." Once again, he looked each daughter in the eye, "I have the utmost of confidence in each one of you. You are smart, brave, strong and most important, Mine!" That last statement caught them by surprise and raised their confidence levels several notches. "Shall we go and get it done?"

They looked at the airplane and then back at their dad. Carrie answered for her sisters, "Yes, Daddy! We are ready."

With that, they boarded the Constellation and prepared for the day's work.

Once inside the flight deck, all was business. Ben took his seat at the captain's chair. Carrie was the first to sit in the second officer's chair, and Susan sat at the engineer's station. Whitney sat behind Carrie and Roberta sat beside Susan. Once they put their headgear on, they went through all of the preflight check lists as they had done a hundred times before.

Ben turned to his daughter and asked, "Are you ready?"

At that, Susan started to shake a little bit. Carrie looked at her dad with the expression that said, "Are we really doing this?"

Ben knew the fear and uncertainty flowing through each one because he remembered the first time he flew his first solo. He had the same apprehensions then. "I was scared, too, when I first had to start up an engine by myself. So, believe me when I say I know what you are going through. But also believe me when I say you will do very well." They looked back at him, only a little convinced. "Alright, Susan, you know what to do. Start engine number one."

Susan nodded, swallowing hard as she reached for the appropriate switch and turned it on. They all heard the slow winding up of a turbine engine as she called out the appropriate information until the engine reached the assigned rpm. Remembering her training, she called out that all was working "normal and proper." Glancing over her shoulder, Ben verified that she was correct. Susan started to calm down as everything they trained for was coming to fruition. She smiled with a sense of accomplishment.

Ben switched from looking out to engine number one as the propeller started to rotate so he could keep an eye on Susan. He made sure the propeller was in the position where there was no thrust. The other engines were started in the same manner and completed with success.

Roberta was amazed that all went as planned and found the engine noise a bit disconcerting, but not terrible. O'Hara was out on the apron in front, signaling to Ben that all was well. Ben signaled back and O'Hara ran around the aircraft to remove the chocks from the wheels.

Ben looked at Carrie, telling her they were going to start to move after one more check with Susan to make sure all parameters were a go. Susan confirmed. Moving the prop controls forward on the panel caused the Constellation to begin to roll forward on the ground. Carrie was all eyes as she followed her father's motions to make sure she could do the same. Whitney shivered as she first felt, then saw the plane in motion.

Ben taxied the plane up and down the taxiway several times, increasingly assured his daughters were going to perform excellently. Then he lined up on the runway. "This is just going to be a test run," he said to his daughters. "We will accelerate

to just before takeoff velocity and shut her down.
I want to get a feeling from the controls before we
actually take off."

The girls were now totally focused on their jobs,
losing any nervousness they originally had. When
Ben called for takeoff power, Susan called out
all was ready, and Ben moved the throttle to full
power. The plane started to roll along the runway
with startling quickness, setting everyone hard
into the back of their seats. After a few seconds,
he drew back on the throttle. The airplane slowed
down to a safe speed and reentered the taxiway.
Once there, they parked the plane in its original
spot. O'Hara replaced the chocks on the wheels
before positioning himself in front and signaling
for the engines to shut down. Ben so ordered and
Susan went through the proper procedures to shut
them down.

Once all was silent, nobody moved for a
few moments.

Suddenly, Roberta let out a whoop that startled
Whitney. Everyone then laughed. Upon exiting
the airplane, Ben told O'Hara and his daughters,

"After lunch, we will do that again except this time we will fly. Let's go tell the rest of the family what happened and have some lunch. What do you say?" Surprisingly, it was O'Hara that led the cheers as they walked back into the building they currently called home.

When they entered the building, all the other brothers and sisters clamored around their older sisters who were a little bit subdued. Allison saw their faces and called the other children to help set the table and let their sisters rest until lunch. The younger siblings were disappointed that their sisters wouldn't share their experiences with the plane.

Roberta answered their disappointment, "That thing is so powerful. It's actually terrifying." Looking around at her siblings faces, she added, "But don't be afraid. We will help Daddy get us to our new home. God will guide us and cover our fears." She held her arms out to them and they joined her, Susan, Whitney, and Carrie in for a group hug.

Michael then grabbed Roberta by the hand and said, "Then all of you need to eat a good lunch.

You need to fly. Therefore, you need your energy," he said before looking at their mother. "At least that's what Mama said."

"That's right, Michael," Allison said. "Let's eat." She turned to her husband and, after greeting him with a great kiss, she said, "Sanchez and Kapree are joining us." She took his hand and led him to the table. "How did our daughters perform?"

Ben watched over his children as they prepared for prayer and answered her. "Beyond my wildest imagination." He took ahold of Susan's hand. "Yes," he pronounced, "beyond my wildest imagination. Let us pray and give thanks." All held hands and bowed their heads.

After the meal, as the crew was heading back to the Constellation, Sanchez caught up with Ben with some serious news. "I must warn you that you must stay below one thousand feet as you are not officially licensed for the Constellation. If Air traffic control somehow catches you, tell them you are part of the maintenance crew finishing an annual inspection." Ben looked puzzled. "There are still some elements of Kim's group active in the area, and they will be looking for you. We are working hard to eliminate them, but it is taking more time than originally thought. One of those elements," Sanchez said, "is Mohammed Fassi's pirate ship, The Pearls of Pleasure. It is currently unaccounted for."

Ben acknowledged the warning and advice by placing his hand on Sanchez's shoulder. "Understood. And will comply."

"Yes. Well then. I had better get back and help your missus with the little ones." With a chuckle, Sanchez added, "They are a lively bunch."

"That they are. They take after their mother."

"Oh, really?" the men turned around to find Allison and the children had been following them. They had been quiet, but Allison spoke up "I thought everybody should see their father and sisters at work. Plus, I want to see that thing in the air."

Ben walked over to her and planted a great kiss on her before he said, "Then you have come to

the right place. We will see you when we return."
She returned his kiss and waved at the girls as they
entered the plane.

All checks were completed and the engines were
running. The Constellation was at the end of the
runway facing the wind. Ben got the full thumbs
up from his second officers and engineers. It was
time. At full throttle, the airplane rolled down the
runway and finally, it lifted off the ground. On the
ground, Allison and the children cheered. O'Hara
and Kapree got caught up in reverie, too.

Only Sanchez was subdued.

In the aircraft, the girls concentrated on their
tasks but were also feeling a little giddy as they
realized the ground below them grew smaller. Ben
leveled off at nine hundred fifty feet of altitude.
He wasn't fully comfortable flying so low, but
he understood the caution. Ben put the plane
through its paces and was elated at how well it
worked. After about two hours, he returned,
landing the plane with ease, much to the relief of
his crew. After he parked the plane and O'Hara
placed the chocks, he made his decision.

We are going home!

This time his daughters, as they departed the plane, were in very high spirits and couldn't stop talking and laughing if their lives depended on it.

"I thought my tummy was going to come out my mouth when we took off!" laughed Roberta.

"Same here!" declared Susan. "That was the most amazing thing."

Allison ran up and jumped on Ben, crushing him with a hug when he came to here. "Are we going home?" she asked between kisses.

"Yes, dear sweet wife." Lifting his head to the sky, Ben shouted, "LORD WILLING! WE ARE GOING HOME!" He twirled her around and danced.

"When?" she asked. At that question all suddenly got quiet waiting for his response.

Ben paused, taking the time to look everyone in the eye before he spoke. "Tomorrow."

At that, all the children started singing and dancing. Allison looked into her husband's eyes to be sure he wasn't joking. When she saw the truth there, she broke down and cried. Susan suddenly ran over to find out why her mother was crying.

"Your father and I have been here a long time," she told her daughter. "It hardly seems real that we are finally going home." Allison fell to her knees and praised God for their deliverance. Ben joined her, both in tears of joy and in prayer. All of their children surrounded them with hugs, surprised to see their valiant father crying as well.

"These are tears of relief and happiness, my children," he said as he hugged each one with such love. "Everybody, join me in prayer giving thanks." They all knelt and held hands. Even Sanchez shed a few tears in the emotion of the moment.

That night, it took some work to get everybody calmed down enough to sleep. While Ben was combing Allison's hair, he admitted his relief. "We have been here long enough. This will be the last time I comb your hair in this pit of hell. Hopefully, we have turned it into a den of righteousness."

He paused his combing. "Lord willing, that is."
Allison patted him on the hand and rested her
head on his chest. Several minutes passed before
he resumed combing. Upon finishing, they went to
bed and slept soundly. Once again, the baby slept
the whole night through, much to the joy and
relief of her parents.

THE REDHEAD AND THE BLOND

Before the sun started its rise on the horizon,
Ben and Mr. O'Hara had finished their preflight
inspections and topped off the fuel. They returned
to the apartment to have breakfast with the family,
Mr. Sanchez, and Miss Kapree. Although there was
a note of joy during the meal, there was also a hint
of anxiety as the children grasped the fact that the
home they knew would be no more.

After making sure everything was clean and in
place, they left the building for the last time.

"Daddy, "Whitney asked, "if we aren't coming back, why did we clean the place?" She was curious about that. "No one will see that place again."

Ben turned around, facing his children. "We don't know when or if anybody will ever live there again," he said. "But we are responsible to make sure it is in better condition for the next person. It is called 'Loving your neighbor,' and we need to do that, especially those neighbors we will never meet in this world."

"Loving your neighbor," Whitney quietly repeated. "You read that from the Bible the other day." Then her face lit up like a Christmas tree. "Now I get it! Thank you, Daddy! Thank you, Mama!"

"Why are you thanking me?" she asked her daughter, wondering why she had been included.

"Because, you have been saying those words for a long time," answered Whitney. "Now I understand."

Ben smiled, walking with his family toward the Constellation carrying the baby who sensed the excitement growing and had become a little wiggly.

"Michael and Roberta! Put your shoes back on!" commanded Allison as they walked. Several other children were about to take their shoes off as well until their mama ordered otherwise. "The pavement here is very hot. We don't want burned feet to start our journey."

"Yes, Mama," Michael said, obeying meekly.

"Yes, Mama," Roberta replied with a little more defiance in her tone. However, one cross look from her mother wiped her attitude away immediately.

As they came within a few feet of the steps leading to the inside of the aircraft, Ben stopped and addressed the group. "Before we board the airplane for our journey, we need to have God bless this plane and this flight. This plane belongs to Him. So, let's kneel and pray." The warmth of the concrete seemed to have no effect as everyone knelt.

"Heavenly Father, Lord God, and Jesus the
Christ," Ben started, "thank You for the
opportunity to leave this place and start a journey
towards our new home. Bless this airplane and
guide us as we fly. Calm any fears that may arise.
May we have a mechanically uneventful ride. We
claim this airplane in the name of Jesus. The name
that has power and authority. Amen."

Everybody stood up, about to start the climb
to the deck of the plane. Ben stood in front,
blocking everybody. He noticed anticipation and
apprehension flitting across everybody's faces.
"First things first. Carrie, go ahead and sit in
the second officer's chair. Roberta, you are the
first to sit in the engineer's station. Susan and
Whitney will start by helping Mama, Mr. Sanchez,
Mr. O'Hara, and Miss Kapree to make sure your
brothers and sisters are seated properly. You
will take over for your sisters in the flight deck,
relieving your posts every two hours. The rest
of you," he waved his right index finger at the
other children, "Obey your mother, sisters, and
our other guests so no one will get hurt. Are you
hearing me?" There followed a chorus of "Yes,
Daddy," from the rest of the children. Ben hugged

his wife and whispered in her ear, "Good luck. Sorry I have leave you to this duty without me."

"Mr. Bickles," Allison said lovingly, "you have nothing to be sorry for. You will be getting us home." She kissed his cheek. "Safely, please." At that, the rest of the family walked up the steps and entered the airplane. The younger children became bug-eyed as they entered. They walked slowly through the aisle, fingering the cloth covered seats. Allison guided each one to their prearranged rows, an older child sitting next to a younger in hopes of alleviating some fears. It was obvious all of them were a bit fearful for this new experience. She and made sure they were all buckled in. A couple of the smaller ones didn't like the belts and removed them. Upon making that choice, they received a stern command from their mother, whose tone ended any attempt at a revolt.

Allison finally sat down and received the baby from her husband. She planned on nursing the child during takeoff, hoping to keep the child calm and quiet. Mr. Sanchez sat in the back while Miss Kapree sat in the seat opposite Allison.

Ben kissed each child on the head as they entered the aircraft, saw that they were settled in, and went up to the flight deck, took his seat, and went through the preflight checklist. Then, with a sign from Mr. O'Hara, he started the engines. Mr. O'Hara waited until the engines were running before he entered the plane and closed the door. Mr. Sanchez had procured a man to stay behind and remove the chocks and stairs from the departing aircraft.

Before the plane started rolling, the children heard a voice speaking over the intercom. "This is your captain, or Daddy, whichever you prefer. I think we need to rename this airplane since we own it. So please, talk amongst yourselves and come up with a name that will be appropriate for it. Now sit back. We are going to start moving." With that, the plane started to roll heading toward the runway. The level of excitement jumped a few more notches. There was also a little fear and holding of hands at the new situation, as well as the sensation of rolling towards the runway. Almost every passenger tried to look out of the windows as the landscape changed.

Michael pondered a few minutes about his father's request about the name on the airplane. "Mama,"

"Yes Michael." Alison answered.

"I have a suggestion for this airplane."

"What is it?" Allison turned up her attention to her son.

"I think we should call it 'Miss Adventure,'" he said, pleased with himself.

"Miss Adventure?" Allison mused. "I like it. What does everyone else think?" Those that were able to hear their brother agreed with him. "When we get a chance, son, you can tell your father the decision."

Michael beamed. "Thank you, Mama!"

Once on the runway, Ben called for full power and the plane accelerated at a rapid rate, forcing the passengers into the backs of their seats. The noise was also something new to them and the younger children held on to the older siblings assigned to them. Once the plane left the earth, the children observed something new. They all giggled as they felt tummy tickles and saw the land and buildings getting smaller with each moment. They were also amazed at all of the water around them.

Ben leveled the aircraft at nine hundred fifty feet above sea level as Mr. Sanchez recommended. He turned to the heading that set them towards a halfway point between Guam and Hawaii. He didn't want to turn towards Hawaii until they were well away from any potential areas where other aircraft were operating. Apparently, according to Sanchez, secrecy was important for the first few hours. He never completely divulged why, but Ben was in complete comfort, trusting that Sanchez had their best interests in mind.

They stayed below a thousand feet above the ocean for a long time. After two hours, Susan replaced Carrie in the second officer's seat and Roberta replaced Whitney at the engineer's station.

Allison came up to check on Ben, asking, "How are you doing, sweetheart?"

Ben smiled as he turned to look at his precious wife. "I am doing fantabulous! Surprisingly well, considering I haven't flown since the weekend before we were kidnapped. This is still amazingly fun!"

Allison was relieved. "How is our progress?"

"Well, as I told you before," he said, "we have to fly northwest for about two and half hours, so we don't run into any commercial flights. Then we will turn north heading directly to Hawaii in about," he checked the clock, "fifteen minutes."

"Thank God!" she declared. "Does the airplane feel right to you? I think it is running quite smooth."

"It most definitely feels right," Ben said. He smiled and caressed the controls. "Yes, ma'am, she feels right indeed. Looking forward to the faces of the folks at Hawaii when this old relic lands."

Allison giggled as she saw the little boy in Ben shining through. She looked out of the windshield and saw something on the water. "What is that?" she asked, pointing.

Ben looked, and saw two ships on the horizon. He realized they would be flying directly over the ships. As they got closer, they saw that the first one looked as if it were a pirate ship. The other looked like a yacht that seemed to be getting towed by the pirate ship. They seemed to be heading toward the distant island.

Ben asked Allison to have Sanchez come up to the flight deck. She turned around and motioned to the COO and main bookkeeper, who immediately came forward.

"Sanchez," Ben began, "do you remember the name of the one pirate ship that is unaccounted for?"

Sanchez recalled for a couple of seconds. "Yes, I believe it is called The Pearls of Pleasure. Why?"

Ben pointed to the ships that were fast approaching. "What does that look like to you?"

Sanchez looked and couldn't believe his eyes. "Yes, sir, that is The Pearls of Pleasure! And it looks like they are towing a large yacht to that island on the horizon. If I am not mistaken, that island is the one Mr. Kim was having prepared for his retirement."

Immediately, Ben told Susan to mark the position and heading so they could report the information to the authorities as he flew the plane right over the two ships. The crew of the pirate ship didn't expect any aircraft in the area and were surprised that an airliner suddenly flew over them. They tried to shoot the airplane down, but it had moved out of range too quickly. No bullets hit the Constellation, much to the relief of the crew on the flight deck of the plane.

Having been distracted by the ships, the airliner flew very close to the island the ships were heading to.

As they passed by the island, Allison looked out to see the beautiful place. She noticed people on the beach who seemed to stop moving as the plane neared. Then she gasped.

"BEN!" she shouted "TURN AROUND AND GET CLOSER TO THAT BEACH. I THOUGHT I SAW A RED HEADED WOMAN AND A BLOND MAN."

When he heard what Allison said, he gasped. *Those aren't butterflies in my stomach*, Ben thought. *They were gymnasts performing routines.* Ben needed no more information. He turned around to make a second pass, staying well away from the ships.

With a slight bank to the left, Ben piloted the airplane as close as he dared and looked at the people on the beach. Everybody on the plane looked out the port side windows to see what Allison was so excited about. Allison maneuvered herself to look over Ben's left shoulder, pointing when she saw the people again. They were fairly certain who the two main persons were on the beach—Their long lost childhood friends, Michael Roberts and Carrie Samuels! Ben went around again, moving the plane slowly to get as close as they dared for one more pass. That sealed it.

Michael and Carrie were alive!

However, the pirate ship was still aiming for the island, which raised alarm bells in Ben's mind.

"No more flying safe. We need to go higher and get someone's attention." Ben called for full power and pulled back slightly on the wheel to gain altitude. Allison, in her elation, went back to the children and put them through their paces to regulate their ear pressure as they began climbing to around twenty thousand feet above sea level.

They got someone's attention alright. The Constellation was noticed by the United States Navy aircraft carrier, The Geronimo and her escort ships. The carrier was named after the president that served right after the Second American Civilian War, Placido Geronimo. Geronimo was the leader of the defense of Kansas City, the battle that started the civil war. He went on to command all of the National Populists that eventually won the war. As president, he reinstalled the original Constitution and the country's adherence to it. Putting his money where his mouth was, he served only two terms although there was a great call out for him to remain the president. The aircraft carrier that bore his name was keeled midway through his second term. The fighter jets that were on patrol were immediately dispatched to the intruder. Just what Ben was hoping for.

"November Whiskey Five-Niner-Niner-Niner, you are flying over unauthorized airspace. You need to turn right ninety degrees immediately! Over."

"Navy fighter, this is November Whiskey Five-Niner-Niner-Niner. We are declaring an emergency. I will give you the coordinates of an island that is about to be attacked by a pirate ship called 'The Pearls of Pleasure.' On the island are Michael Roberts and Carrie Samuels who went missing over fifteen years ago. Do you need me to repeat? Over."

"Did you say Michael Roberts and Carrie Samuels?"

"Yes. With 98 percent certainty."

"Your voice sounds familiar. Are you Benjamin Bickles?"

"Yes!" Ben said. He tried to look at the fighters on both sides to determine who had identified them.

"Ben, this is Charlie Roberts. Michael's younger brother! I am on your left." Ben looked to his left and saw the pilot wave at him. Charlie continued, "I am going to give you the radio frequency to contact the carrier and present them with the coordinates. I have been ordered back to the carrier, effective immediately. What is your heading?"

"Hickam Air Force Base Honolulu, Hawaii."

"They will be apprised of your arrival. God speed and glad to see you are alive. Here is the frequency..."

Charlie and one of the fighter jets turned away while the remaining two escorted the Constellation out of military airspace.

The children were in awe of the fighter jets that could be seen on both sides of the airliner.

Hickam/Pearl Harbor Joint Base

Ben received the frequency information and contacted the carrier, giving them the island coordinates. Once received, the captain of the Geronimo dispatched two destroyers, one American, one Japanese, as they were involved in joint operations, to the island coordinates.

Allison went back to the children and made sure all was well.

None of them had their shoes on.

Whitney suddenly spoke up, "Mama! I gotta pee!"

Knowing more about the airliner than anybody, O'Hara chimed in, "My apologies. I should have shown everybody where the toilet is. Follow me young lady, I will show you now." He led the young girl to the area behind the seats where a makeshift bathroom was built. Whitney went in, closed the door and did her business.

Once the door closed, O'Hara returned to attending to the other children, all this time missing his own.

Several hours later, they landed at Hickam Air Force Base. Upon landing, they were immediately surrounded by security forces as they sat on the plane. Air Force security moved them to an area secluded from other active aircraft. The children were beside themselves with curiosity and wonder at all the buildings, cars, trucks, aircraft and people that were outside. They were glued to the windows and repeatedly called out to each other about what they saw. Allison, Mr. O'Hara, Miss Kapree had their work cut out for them trying to calm the children down. The adults knew things were about to get quite serious and needed the small ones to be on their best behavior.

Mr. Sanchez was busy on his phone.

After Ben shut down the engines, he was greeted on the radio by the officer in charge, General Malcom White of the United States Army. He was standing beside the Constellation within eyesight of the flight deck.

"Mr. Benjamin Bickles, I am General Malcom White. I am your liaison while you are here. A medical crew will be arriving shortly to send up some hazmat suits for you and your family. You will wear them until you get established in the quarantine facility. We have a crew that will secure your aircraft for you. Do you understand what I have just told you?"

"Yes, sir," Ben said. "We will comply."

"Welcome home Bickles family."

"Thank you. Are the security forces necessary?"

"I am afraid so, Mr. Bickles," General White replied. "Until we are certain of who you are, you will be under tight security. You understand."

"I do. Just don't frighten our children in the process."

"Understood. I will pass on the word." With that, General White moved away so the appropriate personnel could approach the doors of the airplane.

The steps were put in place and a sealed passageway was attached around the door.

The medical team, wearing hazmat suits, arrived by bus and waited until the sealed passageway could connect the bus to the door of the Constellation. When that was completed, they walked up the stairs toward the door. Ben opened the plane door, and the team passed hazmat suits to Ben. The children were a little nonplussed about having to put their shoes back on, but their parents stood firm. Soon enough, everybody was suited up, and they climbed down from the plane through the passageway, and onto the bus That was waiting for them.

The children thought this was a fun day.

"Riding in an airplane and a bus! YEAH!!!!! What a whole new world there is out here." Michael's enthusiasm was running high. "Tall buildings. Small buildings. People everywhere. And those things called cars." The variety in the people they saw were of most significance to the children; sizes, shapes, skin color, short hair, long hair, no hair. The variety of clothes also caught their attention. One group of people caused them a little distress as they were dressed like Mr. Kim's soldiers. Ben tried to ease their anxiety by telling them how those men and women were the security forces protecting the military base. The children acknowledged their father's words, but were still a little anxious.

The cars and trucks traveling along the highway were something to behold. Allison assured her sons and daughters that those vehicles were just the same as the bus they were riding in. During the ride to the hospital, one or more of the children complained about the suits they were required to wear. Soon more children were complaining. Allison had to constantly remind them that their discomfort would last for only a little while and it was important for the health and safety of both them and the other people they would meet. "We don't want to get sick," she cautioned, "and we don't want others to get sick because of us. We may have brought some sort of disease with us. We will soon be in a place where we can be free from these suits. Have patience."

QUARANTINE

They were taken to the base hospital and guided to the fifth floor, which was on a separate wing that had been secured for their time in quarantine. They were told to remove their suits and pile them by the door. The children couldn't get the suits off fast enough, and they ran around the area in relief as the adults looked on. A couple of people, also wearing hazmat suits, entered and removed the pile of discarded items. After that, two other people in suits walked in. They went directly to the table near the center of the room and put down some folders, gesturing for Ben and Allison to join them. The children followed closely, their nervousness quite evident.

"Mr. and Mrs. Bickles," the man said, "I am Dr. Hugh McBean, and this is Nurse Heather Morse. We will be administering the physical examinations. This will include drawing blood, urine and fecal samples, and an overall checkup on everybody's health. If you, sir, would go first, I think the children would be less afraid of the situation."

The children were wide-eyed and open-eared
as their dad was checked over. The doctor
commented on the multitude of scars on Ben's
body, but Ben offered no explanation. Then it was
Allison's turn. All went smoothly. Even the sample
taking. However, it was obvious that the fecal
samples would have to be acquired later.

Then it was the children's turn.

Given what they had seen during the past years,
they initially balked at sample taking. The poking
and prodding of the physical exam were not
well received, either. Mom and Dad assured the
children that the doctor and nurse were not out to
hurt them.

When Susan was first poked with the needle,
she glared at her parents letting them know she
felt betrayed. She then glared at the nurse and
declared, "That wasn't a pinch. THAT WAS A
POKE! THAT HURT!"

Allison responded firmly but quietly, "You know
how your sister Teresa is a little anxious right
now. Calm down so she won't have a panic attack."

She got closer and in her ear she whispered, "We know it is a little painful, but you need to learn to endure it." She held her daughter's face into her hands and looked eye to eye. Please understand." Susan nodded and apologized for her response. The nurse nodded in understanding while Ben and Allison looked towards their eight-year-old daughter with concern hoping and praying that she wouldn't panic. The expression on her face was not promising.

Whitney, Roberta, Michael, Derrick, and Robert all took their shots in stride, although they didn't like it. When it came to Teresa's turn, however, her parents' fears were confirmed. She went into a full blown panic, kicking, screaming, and clawing to protect herself. For being eight years old, she was more than a handful for one parent, including her father. Eventually they teamed up and held her tight with Ben holding her arms and upper body hard to his chest and Allison clamping her legs tight to herself. In this fashion, Teresa was totally immobilized. Or so they thought. She tried to turn her head around so that she could bite her captor, which was something she was trained to do at an earlier age. Ben was a little caught off guard but reacted just before her teeth caught flesh.

"NOW! DO IT NOW!" Allison yelled at the nurse who instantly responded.

As soon as the needle was removed, Teresa calmed down and chuckled a little bit, "That didn't hurt."

Ben and Allison immediately released her and she ran to be with her brother and sisters, purposely to be held by Roberta, her strongest sister in her opinion. Roberta's love and protection for her little sister had always been strong and Teresa was the calmest when she was around her. Ben and Allison just looked at each other and shook their heads knowingly as they knew it was their daughter's way of thinking about things. Panic at first, then act as if everything was alright after. The rest of the children, although they cried, held still and didn't create a fuss.

By the time their evening meal arrived everyone had settled down, realizing they were not in any danger from the new people in their lives. Ben noted how they were, once again, forced to live in a small, confined space. *Oh, well,* he thought. *We have done it before. No big issues.*

After the meal, the family gathered and held a long prayer session. When it was bedtime, there wasn't much dissent. Everyone slept well, except the baby, who needed to be nursed along with a diaper change in the middle of the night. With the exception that they knew they were in a different place, on a different island, in a different country, life was a lot like it was before. The children were, at this time, not as impatient as their parents were about staying there.

A few days later, the doctor and nurse returned with more files, so the family gathered around.

"I am pleased to announce that all of you are strong and healthy. However, Mother, Dr. McBean said, not thinking it was necessary to look up from his reports, "you need a little more iron, as you are nursing. Father, those scars can be reopened and closed so that they can barely be seen. If you like, we can take care of them this afternoon."

"That won't be necessary," Ben replied. "These scars will remind me of what has been sacrificed for others."

The doctor looked up into the eyes the man across the table from him to read his face. After a few seconds he said, "Ok," still not looking up. "Just offering. Also, there are no abnormal parasites in anybody. You are good and healthy. I understand your friends, Michael, Carrie, and their family are two floors above you. However, you are not to have any contact with them until their quarantine is over as well. Understood?"

"We don't like it, but we understand," Ben replied.

"Excellent," the doctor said, finally looking at Ben. "Now, we must go and check on the Roberts family. We will be in touch with you often to make sure all of you are appropriately vaccinated. See you then." With a wave they were gone.

Looking the children over, Allison remarked to her husband, "Vaccinations! Oh, that will be a joyful time." Ben noted the sarcasm. And agreed. "Oh, by the way," she said quietly, "I am pregnant again."

It didn't matter how many times she told him that, Ben always got excited. "At least this one won't know the horrors the other children did." Also, the news that their childhood friends were alive and two floors above them caused Ben and Allison to hold each other with great joy.

Since the family was used to being secluded in a small area, they were able to pass the time as they did the past several years; playing games, schooling, and sometimes annoying each other. The quarantine went quickly, but they had to wait a few more days for the Roberts family quarantine to be over.

JUST A GENERAL VISIT

General White and his attaché arrived at the room where the Bickles family were about to be released from their quarantine. The news he shared was not welcome to the family. "Mr. Bickles, I am sorry to have to tell you this but your stay in quarantine will need to be extended. Due to your relationship with Mr. Geraldo Sanchez, Rosiland Kapree, and Sherp O'Hara, the Immigration and Naturalization Service are asking for your patience. They are almost through with their investigation, so hopefully it won't be long." Before Ben could ask, General White said, "I am not privy to their reasonings. It frustrates me as well, as we are trying to schedule your trip home. We were hoping that next week you would be on your way. Hopefully, I have some good news for you though. The Army has taken over some of the old Dole and Ewa plantation land just outside of the city. We have housing there, and you will be reunited with your friends on that land once you leave here."

Ben had to ask, "Are my friends and employees being treated well?"

General White chuckled a bit. "One would think that, since I hold the rank of general, I would be briefed on all things involving this base. Sadly, that is not so. However, I have been informed that your three friends are being treated well based on their help in righting the many wrongs done by Mr. Kim and his associates. They will be released into your custody soon and will finish their interrogation at Sioux Falls."

"Do you have any estimate as to when we will be released from this quarantine?" Allison was a little perturbed at the delay of their release.

General White faced her, "My understanding is that it should be no longer than two weeks. I pray it will be even less. Anything else?" Ben and Allison looked at each other, and then shook their heads at the general. "Good." General White turned to leave. He stopped and faced the couple again. "By the way, do you know a Robert Jefferson from Sioux Falls?"

That name surprised them. "Yes, we do," Ben proudly replied. "He was a Musketeer with Michael, Derrick, and me in our youth. Extremely smart. He was a couple of years younger than us, but he was most definitely an outstanding Musketeer."

"Well, good. Just for your information, he is my son-in-law. My daughter's little sister got them together."

Allison's faced lit up at the thought of meeting Robert's wife. "Tell us about them."

"Once again, though I am a general, I have not been allowed to discuss their business due to his current occupation. Just know they have been informed about your return, and they are most elated at the potential meeting. Why am I always the last to know?" He raised his hands and let them drop to his sides, saluted the family and walked out.

Allison's mood went up at the name of Robert Jefferson. "I hope she is good princess material. Oh, rats. We should have asked him about Derrick and Susan. They could have children by now, if they got married."

Ben rubbed his chin. "Funny, if he knows Robert, he should know about Derrick. I am certain they both made into West Point. And Robert would have definitely talked about Derrick."

"Maybe he just forgot to mention him or, as the general kept saying, he 'is not privy to that information.'"

"Since we are stuck here a little longer, we will have to pray for our new friends. And besides," Ben said, hugging his wife, "my anticipation of meeting Michael and Carrie is sky rocketing." Ben went over to report the new information to their children.

The day finally came when they were allowed to visit the Roberts family.

LOST MUSKETEERS AND PRINCESSES REUNITED

Ben, Allison, and their family were guided to the stairs, climbing four flights to the floor where the Roberts had been staying. Ben and Allison could hardly contain themselves, they were so filled with anticipation. At the door, they held hands and looked into each other's eyes. Their guide, a large orderly with a broken arm that was in a cast and sling, He used his other hand to enter a code and open the door. He went in to let the family on the other side of the door know they had some other guests. Then he opened the door wider and let the Bickles family enter.

Inside the main front room, Michael and Carrie were informed that they had more guests. When Michael and Carrie saw who were walking in the room they fell to their knees and cried. Then they rushed up to hug their longtime friends. Michael and Ben cried on each other's shoulders while Carrie and Allison did the same The tight hugs the men gave each other would have crushed lesser folks. Tears flowed without embarrassment as the friends looked each other over. Eventually, they released each other, then Michael hugged Allison and Ben hugged Carrie.

Noticing the plethora of children in the room, Allison was amazed at how Carrie looked. "Girl! Fifteen years and all those children haven't changed you a bit."

"I can say the same for you, young lady," Carrie responded. Waving her arm, she said, "With this herd, you have been just as busy."

"I think we each have quite the story to tell." Allison admitted and locked arms with her fellow Princess.

The children of both families just stood and looked at the other kids across the room. Carrie, Susan, Whitney, and Roberta Bickles caught sight of Benjamin, Derrick, Robert, and Troy Roberts, noting the red hair of Troy, the blond hair of Derrick, the strawberry blond hair of Robert, and the flaming red hair of Benjamin, and the pale skin they all had. Their hearts fluttered a bit. The young ladies each decided they would talk to their mom about that later.

Derrick, Robert, and Troy Roberts couldn't take their eyes off the beautiful, dark-haired girls from the other family. Carrie's huge waves and darker skin made her look the most like her mother. Susan's hair was black, straight, and long, ending just below her butt. Whitney's hair was the same brown as her father's and her skin had his

Mediterranean tone, although her facial features resembled her mother. Roberta's hair was brown, with strong waves which complimented her skin tone, which was lighter than any else in the family. She shared her father's nose and her mother's eyes. According to the Roberts boys, those girls were beauty personified. They each decided, without saying anything, that they would talk to their dad about it.

Ben Roberts had one arm around a young girl while another young woman held his unoccupied arm. The room was largely divided by contrasting coloration of the families. The mostly light brown-skinned, dark brown to black haired gang of Bickles with Asian facial features like their mother or Mediterranean like their father. On the other side were the pale-skinned, blonde to red haired Roberts group.

On the Roberts side there were five that stood out due to their darker tan, brown, or almost black skin. Before complete family introductions were made, Ben Bickles was curious about the dark-haired teenagers mingling with the Roberts family. Michael saw where his friend's eyes were focusing and rounded up the Bickles children, who had just spent the last three years on the island with the Roberts. He brought them over to be introduced to Ben.

"Benjamin Bickles," Michael said, "I would like to introduce you to Amina Bickles (the young woman holding on to Ben Robert's arm), Nelson Bickles, Javier Bickles, Torrance Bickles, and Cassondra Bickles. They are your children, I believe." He turned. "And children, this is Benjamin Bickles, the man your mothers told you about. This is your father."

Allison Bickles sucked in her breath as the names were mentioned. Ben walked up to the children who were looking at him with hope in their eyes. *My children? Then the girls survived!?* His heart almost skipped a beat at the pronouncement. Allison stayed back and was equally astonished at the news.

"He is just like the picture our moms have!" exclaimed Cassondra. Amina's face showed joyous wonder that she could finally look into her father's eyes. The boys were also somewhat stoic at first, then with agreement they beamed with recognition. First Torrance, then Javier, shortly followed by Nelson came to him. Each wanted to jump into his arms, but they waited for Ben's response. Ben looked each one in the eye. Then he pointed to Amina. "Are you Miriam Deng's daughter?"

Her face lit up even brighter with a grin as she nodded. "Yes," she answered. He smiled back and she hugged him. "Hello Daddy!" He returned her embrace and couldn't speak for a few minutes. Ben kissed her on her forehead, and they released each other.

He looked at the young man next to her. What he noticed choked himself up a bit. "Are you Michaela Salazar's son?" Javier nodded and smiled.

"Michaela was a twin," Ben said. "Did she tell you about her sister, Roberta?" Again, with sadness, Javier nodded. "Were you told what happened to her?" Javier looked down and his shoulders shook as he remembered what his mother said about his aunt's death. Ben hugged him. "I am sorry," he told him. "I ruined such a good moment. But I am so happy to finally meet you, my son."

At that Javier wrapped his arms around his father and cried. "I'm sorry, Father!" The entire Roberts family were amazed, as those were the first words Javier had spoken since he came to the island. Javier fell to his knees and Ben went down with him. The Bickles children gave the father and son space and went to stand by their mother. As the moments passed, all who were in the room were caught in the moment. The Roberts family huddled together, realizing something wonderful was about to happen.

Ben responded, "Sorry for what, Javier? I am the one who is sorry it took me so long to meet you."

"I am sorry I am not strong like you," Javier cried. "You must be disappointed with me!" Ben could barely understand his son through the sobs. He looked up to Michael, questions in his eyes.

"They were kidnapped by Darrin and Marc and sold to the owner of a sailing ship. They were raped repeatedly for seven months before they landed on the island. The boys haven't spoken a word since," Michael smiled a bit. "Until now." That was the information Ben needed at that moment.

Ben stood up and lent a hand to his son. "Stand up, Javier Bickles."

Javier looked up and saw something he had not expected. Love! He slowly stood up with a sense of hope.

"Javier Bickles," Ben said with authority and care, "I am Benjamin Bickles. Your father. Javier Bickles, YOU are MY SON!" Ben paused to let that sink in for a few seconds. "Today, you will not receive condemnation. You will receive the start of full redemption. I repeat," Ben held out his arms. "YOU are MY son, and I love you!" At that, Javier began crying again. He went to his father and hugged him, hard. Ben looked at the other boys. "Do you feel the same?" he asked. When both boys nodded, Ben stated, "Then come here my sons!"

Three teenage boys hugging their father for the first time is not a normal sight, but these were abnormal circumstances. Ben wiped the tears from their eyes as Nelson and Torrance each cried out, "DADDY!" Since all three boys had been violated by men, they were ashamed to be called boys or men—let alone sons. This confusion and fear had kept them silent. Until now. When they finally met their father, the way he showed them what true love was all about overcame the hurt in their hearts and they overflowed with emotions they were finally safe enough to feel.

"Let's have a look at you," Ben said, putting them at arm's length. He looked them over and smiled. "I bet *your* mom is Florence Thornberry," he said, pointing to Nelson, who beamed at the recognition of his mother. "And *your* mother would be China Huisen."

To that Torrance responded, "Ye-Ye-Yes sir!" He was equally elated that his mother was remembered. "B-b-but aren't you ashamed of us?" he said, taking a while to get the words out. "They d-did b-b-bad things to us. I feel ashamed."

Ben tried to reassure his son. "For you," he replied, "there is no shame. You didn't do *anything* wrong. *They* are the ones who are to be ashamed. *They* were the ones violating God's will. *They* are the ones who should be punished. And if they died in their sins, *they* will be punished for eternity. Again, my son, you did nothing wrong. As I said before, you are *my* son and I love you dearly."

"As much as them?" Torrance asked, pointing to the children huddling by Allison.

Ben placed his hand on the young lad's shoulder. "I love you as my son, equally as much as them." Nelson, Javier, and Torrance once again hugged their father, crying hard with the realization that they were not going to be hated for what happened to them. The knowledge of the fact that their father loved them made them cry all the more, and Ben cried with them for a long while.

Eventually, he looked at Michael Roberts. "Brother, I am so grateful they landed in your hands. Thank you for watching out for my children."

Michael nodded. "Give thanks to God for guiding them to us."

"Yes, you are right. Thank you."

Allison, still holding Carrie's arm, was starting
to shake with so many emotions flowing through
her. She looked at her husband, letting her love
flow to him from where she stood. Carrie noticed
what her long lost friend was going through and
hugged her closer.

"Now this little lady," Ben motioned to Cassondra,
who was standing by herself", "must be Heather
McClusky's little girl." Cassondra cried out.
"Daddy!" she exclaimed before jumping into
her father's arms and wrapping her small self
around him.

Amina retrieved her daughter from Ben Roberts.
She waited until Ben and Cassondra were
finished and brought the little girl to her father.
"Daddy, I would like to introduce you to your
granddaughter, Blessing Roberts." Blessing wasn't
so sure about him, but her mother still said,
"Blessing, this your grandpa Bickles."

Ben's eyebrows raised at being called grandpa,
but he accepted the little girl, who didn't resist,

though she was curious about the big man. She paid close attention to the color of his eyes, skin, and hair and the shape of his patrician nose.

"Grandpa?" Blessing said, looking from her mother to the man and back to her mother.

"Yes, sweety," Amina said, "your grandpa." She smiled to reassure her daughter.

Blessing finally looked long and hard at the man holding her and finally reached around to hug him. Then she smiled. "Grandpa. My grandpa!" was all she said.

Ben looked at Michael and exclaimed, "I'm not old enough to be a grandpa!"

Michael laughed and replied, "In this case, yes you are."

Ben held his granddaughter at arm's length and looked at her face. He immediately noticed the blue eyes against her darker skin. The eyes looked a lot like a man he had killed. *Hasenpfeffer!* To be certain he looked straight at Ben Roberts, asking, "Are you the father?"

Amina stepped in front of her father. "No, Daddy," she corrected. "A rapist is the father. I have no idea who. However, 'Red Beard' is indeed her daddy. We intend to be married once we are eighteen years old. He hasn't touched me in that way yet." She looked at Ben. "We want to honor God and wait until marriage." Then with deliberate emphasis she said, "But he is Daddy to Blessing."

Ben carried his granddaughter to the younger man with his name. "Is there something you need to say to me, Benjamin Roberts?" Amina interlocked her fingers, pointing her index fingers to her nose as she waited for Ben's reply. She was a little fearful for her Red Beard. The rest of the Roberts and Bickles families looked on in wonderment.

Ben Roberts remembered what his father told him in case this should happen. "Mr. Bickles, sir," he began. "I request permission to court your daughter Amina with the intention of leading to eventual marriage, sir. When we are eighteen. Sir."

Ben Bickles chuckled and handed Blessing over to him. "There is no way I am coming between you two. You not only have my permission but also my blessing. I believe you have already been taking care of her for her to have such a smile after all she has been through." Ben Bickles had to look up to look into the eyes of Ben Roberts. He was amazed at the strength he felt when he shook the teenager's hands.

Amina walked over to stand beside her Red Beard, wrapping her arms around her fiancé's free arm. "Thank you, "Daddy," she said before stepping up and planted a kiss on his cheek.

"However," Ben asked, "how, in the wide world of sports, did you trust this, what did you call him? Oh, yeah, Red Beard?" Ben Bickles curiosity was getting the better of him as he thought Amina would have some serious reservations about men, given the assaults she received at their hands.

Allison quietly spoke into Carrie's ear. "This should be interesting." Carrie just winked at her fellow Princess with a smile that said something was about to erupt.

Amina responded to her father's question. "Do you *really* want to know?" Her face started to show that mischief was afoot.

"Yes," said Ben B. "I don't understand the situation. How can you be so attached to this guy?" Pointing to "Red Beard."

"Well, you see, Daddy," Amina began. Michael and Carrie covered the mouths knowing that Amina's personality was about to shine. "I was relieved that we were rescued by Papa Michael and Mama Carrie, and family, on the day we landed on the island. I am grateful that Allison Roberts was willing to sleep with me to calm the nightmares I was having that first night." Amina looked a little downcast and reflective for a moment. "The next day, I found myself standing on the edge of the rock. It overlooked the ocean and I could see quite a number of sharks swimming close by. I thought that, if just fed myself to the sharks, I wouldn't be a target for those type of men anymore." She paused as if to catch her thoughts. "It was then that I heard someone coming up behind me. I told him to stop, or I was going to jump." She looked up into her father's eyes. "Wouldn't you know it?" she said. "He took three more steps and sat down. As you can see, I didn't jump."

Ben glanced at Red Beard. "How did you know she wouldn't jump after you took those extra three steps?"

Ben Roberts shrugged his shoulders. "I didn't know," he replied. "Those extra steps got me closer should she decide to jump. I was hoping I could catch her before she got too far from me."

Ben Bickles looked at his soon-to-be son-in-law. He asked, "You think you are that quick?"

"Yes."

Ben Bickles looked over to his fellow Musketeer, for confirmation. Michael just nodded, still covering his mouth. Ben noticed the mirth in his friend's eyes before he returned his gaze to his daughter.

Amina continued, "It was then he asked me if I could turn around so he could talk to my face. He told me that, since I was still naked, if my butt started talking, he would jump to the other rock." Ben raised an eyebrow at Red Beard, who had a sheepish grin growing on his reddening face. "That made me smile. And I was brought out of my depression for a few moments."

"What did you do?" Carrie Bickles asked. She couldn't contain herself.

Amina smiled at her half-sister. "I turned around and walked to stand right in front of him, watching his eyes at every step. When I stood right in front of him, he was only looking at my legs. He then asked me to sit down so he can talk to my face as he didn't think my legs had much to say." Her father was beginning to see why his friends were covering their mouths. Something was yet to be said. Amina continued, "So, I sat down, noticing how he changed his gaze from my legs to my face. He never looked at my body. It was then that I started to think I could trust this brute." That brought a few giggles from the Roberts children.

"She called him a brute!" Allison Roberts said with a little giggle to her sisters, Susan and Kathy.

Amina continued, "The first thing he said after that was that I needed a skirt and bra!" She raised her hands at her sides. "I mean, he had a naked girl standing in front of him and he wanted her covered up!? That's what caused me to start to trust him." Then with a raised finger, she said, "*Start* to. I told him how I was called Black trash and he immediately told me 'God doesn't create trash. Man trashes what God has created.'" She put her hands on her hips. "That is what truly endeared me to him." Her father looked at Red Beard again with great admiration for his restraint. "But, you know," Amina said, definitely with a look of mischief on her face, "Had I farted at that moment, I would have lost him forever!"

That did it.

Allison started laughing into Carrie's shoulder. Red Beard could only smirk. Allison, Susan, and Kathy Roberts fell into a girl-giggle huddle. The rest of the Roberts family began laughing as well. The Bickles children smiled, unsure what to do.

Ben stood frozen to the floor, not believing his daughter said what she did. Then he started laughing.

Michael regained his composure and explained, "It took two years for these children, your children, to cease having nightmares. And this little lady," he said, pointing to Amina, "started showing her personality. As you can see, she has an interesting sense of humor."

Allison Bickles looked at her friend, "No doubt she will fit well in your family," she said.

Carrie Roberts admitted, "That she already does."

Michael broached another topic. "By the way," he began, "I think it is time I introduce you to our little gaggle of gigglings." He went down the line introducing each of his children to their friends, each child waving happily as he did so. That included the, mostly, stubborn Kathy.

Allison noticed Richard Robert's artificial leg. "Oh, my goodness," she said, "what happened to you?"

Without skipping a beat, he retorted, "God saw that my leg was a little stuck up and decided it had to go." More rounds of laughter came from the Roberts family. Ben, Allison, and their children didn't understand the humor.

Carrie Bickles interpreted, "A stick got stuck in his leg. We pulled it out, thinking we had it all. However, a small piece remained and caused gangrene to set in." Remembering the emotional pain she had at the time, grew a little melancholy. "We had to chop his leg off in order for him to survive," she said with a darker tone in her voice.

Allison held on to her friend hard, thinking to herself how hard that would have been to have to do that to her own child.

Ben took the time to compose himself and then he introduced the Bickles gang. Just as all of the introductions were completed, an orderly entered the room.

MORTIMER HITCHBACK

The orderly walked up to Michael, informing him that they had some important people needing to talk to them.

"Go ahead," said Allison Bickles said. "We will help watch the children." She took them over to mingle with the Roberts children. They mostly just looked at each other's' features that were so different from what they were used to. The darker tan, dark hair, and dark eyes of the Bickles clan contrasted with the fair skinned, blond to red hair, blue to green eyes of the Roberts group.

Carrie hugged her friend and, with Michael, walked over to greet their "guests."

In came a corpulent man, just shy of six feet tall, with perfect male pattern baldness and a mustache so long, it covered his mouth as he spoke. He wore a gray business suit, complete with matching vest and a red tie adorning his white shirt. He was followed by an almost sickeningly thin woman who wore a gray female business suit, with a black shirt and no tie.

The third person to enter was shorter man with a full head of gray hair. He wore a black suit with blue pin stripes, a blue shirt and black tie. Last to come in was a mid-sized woman with her brown hair tied up in a bun wearing a gray business suit with skirt.

"Good morning," said the first man. "I am Mortimer Hitchback. I represent Lloyds of London. This is Mr. Jackson Brown. He is the representative of the First National Bank of Hawaii. I will introduce the others as needed. I understand that I am in the presence of Michael and Carrie Roberts. Will you, please, have a seat?"

The Roberts sat at the table opposite Mr. Hitchback. *Direct and to the point*, Ben thought. *No nonsense.* Ben and Allison stood with the two groups of children, watching the following proceedings with interest.

Are they in some kind of trouble? Why a banker? These thoughts rolled through Ben's mind as he observed the situation of his beloved friends.

"First thing we need to do," said Mr. Hitchback, is open an account for you with the bank here." He

held up his hand as Michael was about to speak.
"Your account in Sioux Falls has been closed due
to inactivity. The funds you had in your account
were recovered by your parents, and they are
holding those funds in trust for when you return.
Now, Mr. Brown will guide you through the
process and then we can continue. Mr. Brown,"
he said, indicating the man with the black and
blue suit.

Carrie was surprised by that information.
"Holding for us until we return? That is what I call
optimism!"

Ben and Allison agreed with her.

Mr. Brown had a handheld device that he tapped
on. To the children this looked a little silly.
However, their curiosity was piqued as it took
only a few minutes to set up the accounts and,
soon enough, Mr. Brown declared that it was all
finished. *Electronics can be a wonderful thing*, Ben
had to admit to himself.

"Now we can proceed," said Hitchback. "We had
a submersible check on the wrecks just offshore

of your island. There are thirty-five yachts and
one pirate ship. All of the yachts have been
identified. They were all insured by us. We have
since discovered the mole in our organization and
got rid of him. Permanently, He will be in solitary
prison the rest of his life." He let that thought sink
in. "Every three years, one of the yachts would
go missing. and our investigations turned up
no answers. Until now. Since you have occupied
the island for so many years and have, basically,
homesteaded the place, the island is yours. And,
since you are the people that pointed us to the
wrecks, you are to receive finder's fees."

The baby inside of Carrie decided at that moment
to shift position. "OH!" she said as she moved.
"Sorry. This little rascal has rotten timing." She
chuckled. Everyone around her smiled.

Hitchback nodded. "these yachts were some of
the most expensive ever built. So, the finder's
fees come to one hundred eighty million dollars.
The money will be deposited into your account.
Mr. Brown?"

"Done!" Mr. Brown said a few seconds later.

"Now," Mr. Hitchback pointed to his left, toward the skinny woman, "This is Mrs. Florence Hitchback. My wife. She represents the families of those lost souls on the yachts. Mrs. Hitchback."

The woman leaned forward on the table, with her hands clasped together and resting on her elbows. "As Mr. Hitchback stated, I represent the families that perished at the hands of the pirates. Rewards were offered, and not rescinded, for finding the whereabouts of their friends and families. I have been authorized to distribute those funds to you for giving so many families closure. The rewards total eighty million dollars. Thank you. Mr. Brown."

Once again funds were transferred.

"Last," Mr. Hitchback said, "this is Ms. Hillary Stein. She represents the group that evaluated the pirate booty you pointed out to your rescuers. All-in-all, the valuation is ninety-five million, three hundred sixty-two thousand dollars. You have the choice of keeping any of the treasure or taking the lump sum. Again, the choice is yours." She waited for Michael to answer.

"Whoever is faithful with very little will also be faithful with much," Michael said quietly. After a long moment, he looked up. "We have no need of the treasure. We will accept the money." He looked at Carrie. "This is all so much to take in!"

Mr. Brown said, "Done. Whenever you are ready, we can facilitate transferring to a different account. Thank you for your time."

My guess that they were in some sort of trouble was way off. Good for them. Ben smiled inwardly at what he and Allison just witnessed.

At that moment, the orderly rushed in and pointed to the monitor.

OUR HOME

"You must see this!" the orderly exclaimed as he turned on the large television monitor and raised the volume.

A reporter was saying, "As you can see, the volcano on the island that has been reported as the home of Michael Roberts and his wife Carrie Samuels, has erupted. They were stranded there with their children for over a decade. You can see the ash cloud ascending miles above ocean. Upon closer inspection, it looks like only the two rock outcroppings and a sliver of beach are what is left of the island. This appears to be an identical eruption as the Hunga Tonga eruption of 2022."

"Daddy!" cried Susan Roberts. "Our home! Our Home!" The other Roberts children began crying. Some just stood, stunned. The Bickles children felt a sudden pang of sadness for their newfound friends. Ben and Allison Bickles felt just as stunned as their fellow Musketeer and Princess, remembering the beautiful island they flew by when they discovered the Roberts family on the beach.

Michael composed himself quickly and called his children to him. The visitors watched on.

Michael looked up and said a quick prayer for wisdom. "The island was indeed, our home," he

told them. "But it was only going to be temporary.
This whole earth is only a temporary place to live.
We will find another place, with God's guidance,"
he said, remaining calm. "And we will continue
to grow and learn and love. We had a wonderful
life on the island. But we will continue to have
a wonderful life wherever God puts us." He
motioned for Ben. "My fellow Musketeers Ben,
Derrick, Robert and I would sing together in
church. One of the songs goes like this:

> *This world is not my home*
> *I'm only passing through.*
> *My treasures are laid out*
> *Somewhere beyond the blue."*

At this point, Allison and Carrie joined in. As
did the sergeant, Mr. Brown, and Ms. Stein. The
Hitchbacks had never heard the lyrics.

> *The angels beckon me*
> *From Heaven's open door*
> *And I can't feel at home*
> *In this world anymore.*
> *Oh, Lord, you know*
> *I have no friend like you*

If Heaven's not my home
Oh, Lord, what should I do?
The angels beckon me
From Heaven's open door
And I can't feel at home
In this world anymore.

When they finished singing, Ben stepped back. His children were smiling because they loved to hear Daddy sing. "Mama and I wanted to return to the island ourselves and live out our days," Michael said. "But God says, 'No.' Apparently, he has another adventure for us. We must remember, the Word of God, says:

He has shown you, O mortal, what is good.
And what does the Lord require of you?
To act justly and to love mercy
And to walk humbly with your God.

Michael held up a finger to emphasize a point. "That last part is very important. If we only do the first part, we have no place in God's Kingdom. That last part tells us that He wants us to talk to Him. To walk with Him, so that both of you will get to know each other. That is why we were created," he said, looking at his children. "To be children of and friends with God. Let's pray together." His children gathered close. The Bickles children huddled around their parents.

"Lord," he prayed, "open our hearts, our minds, our eyes, our ears to you. May we grow to love you more. To talk to You more. May we come to know You more and for You to know us more. And," Michael added, "may we enjoy the next place You will put us. In Jesus's powerful name, Amen."

"Amen!" The children shouted.

"Amen!" said Ben and Allison.

"Amen!" said Mr. Brown and Mrs. Hitchback.

"Yes, well." Mr. Hitchback felt out of place at that moment as he never set foot in a church nor cared for the message of Jesus when he came across a believer spreading the Good News. He and his associates shook hands with Michael and Carrie and then had these words, "Your lives are drastically changing from this time forward. We will be at your beck and call if you need any other assistance in these matters. So long for now." He bowed and immediately left.

Michael sat back and looked at Carrie. "Did they say hundreds of millions?" he asked.

"That's what I heard," she replied.

"Not what I was expecting when I woke up this morning. What other surprises are in store for today?"

"Is this a big enough surprise for you?" said a voice. Everybody turned to see who was at the door.

"CHARLIE!" the Musketeers and Princesses said in unison. Michael ran to latch on to his younger brother. They embraced for a long time, crying in each other's arms. When Michael released him, everybody took turns smothering the man with love. Ben and Allison could just wonder at the joyous reunion that had just exploded in front of them. They, both, were hoping silently that they would also enjoy that type of homecoming when they finally returned to their home in Sioux Falls.

When he had time to breathe, Charlie took out his phone and made a call. Another device that interested the children. Ben and Allison greeted him warmly and thanked him for his part in recovering their treasured friends. It took a couple of minutes for Charlie to compose himself and remember why he was there.

"Now, everybody," he stated. "Look at the monitor."

On the screen were faces very familiar to Ben, Allison, Michael, and Carrie. It was all their parents, brothers and sisters crowding onto the phone screen. What immediately followed was a cacophony of voices:

"MY SON! MY SON!"

"MY BEAUTIFUL DAUGHTER!"

"MY CHILD!"

"DAD!"

"MOM!"

"I KNEW YOU WERE ALIVE!"

As things started to quiet down and tissues passed
around, somehow, a question was heard.

"Who are those beautiful little urchins behind
you?" Ben and Allison introduced their children
to their grandparents, aunts, uncles, and,
yes, cousins.

Michael and Carrie followed suit. The joy was
almost too much for Carrie's mom to contain.

"Charlie," Carrie Roberts's mother said, "we
couldn't believe what you told us. But now I see
my beautiful daughter and her husband and the
whole gaggle of grandkids. We have been waiting
for news about you for forever."

"What a joy to see and talk to you, too, Mom.
Is that Candace behind you?" Carrie's elation
was almost more than she thought she could
possibly survive.

"Yes, your sister never gave up on you. Has Charlie
told you that she is his wife?"

"What? No. not yet." Carrie turned around to hug
Charlie again.

Candace spoke up, "We were together a lot when
you two disappeared. We eventually started seeing
each other for real, and then we got married.
Can't wait to hug you in person when you
get home."

"Same here. So much to tell you." Carrie could say
no more as she sobbed out her joy.

"You make sure you get here safely," Ben's dad
chimed in.

"In as much as it is within our power, we should
be seeing you in about three weeks." Ben
assured them.

"There is more," Charlie said. He nodded his head
and five women with their entire heads covered
entered the screen. They were placed in front
of the grandparents. Then he waved to Amina,
Nelson, Javier, Torrance, and Cassondra to stand
front and center.

The teenagers anticipated what was coming
next as they looked at the covered women. They
began clapping and jumping up and down,
about to burst.

"Now, ladies, remove your head coverings,"
Charlie said. He was enjoying his part in the
festivities.

The women were revealed to be Miriam Deng,
Michaela Salazar, Florence Thornberry, China
Huisen, and Heather McClusky.

"MAMA!" the children cried in unison. The
women were shocked to silence at first and then
burst out in joy seeing their children for the first
time in four years. Three of the ladies were so
surprised that they couldn't remain standing and
fell to the floor. They were so surprised none of
them could speak for several minutes. Then things
got really loud as the children and mothers cried
out their joy at seeing one another. Once more,
things calmed down and Amina went to her Red
Beard. She retrieved her daughter again, this time,
to present her to her grandmother.

"Mama, this is Blessing Roberts. Your granddaughter." Florence was speechless. "Before you say anything, let me explain. She doesn't know her father. That person was one of my rapists. But she *does* know her daddy, Benjamin Roberts. My Red Beard. We are engaged to be married when we reach the age of eighteen years old." She motioned for Ben to join her. Florence was aghast at the size of Ben.

"That giant of a man is to be my son-in-law?" Florence asked, astounded.

"Yes, Mama."

Florence blew a kiss to Ben. "Welcome to the family, my daughter's Red Beard." Everybody laughed at that.

"Oh, and Mama? We have one more surprise for all of you." She waved over her father. Joyous sounds resounded again when Ben Bickles entered the frame. Their love for the man obvious.

"Is Allison there, too." Michaela asked.

"Right here, ladies." Allison moved to be next to her husband.

"God be praised!" Michaela cried. "You made it!"

"We will see all of you soon," Ben said as all waved goodbye for now. Air kisses were thrown all over by both parties.

"Gotta go, folks. See you all soon." Charlie said, ending the call. He turned to see the tears of joy flooded the room. "Oh, by the way, Charlie said to the adults, "Darrin Johnson and Marc Richards have been found to be operating a prostitution ring. Darrin had a vile blackmail scheme that he used on the wives of deployed sailors and Marines. Being in the Navy was just a cover. It is believed that he is directly responsible for the deaths of ten sailors' wives assumed to have refused his scheme. Unfortunately, thousands of wives were affected. Ben," he said, looking around, "your heads up was crucial. And Michael capturing them set the investigation into high gear. Carrie, what you confessed to the Admiral did not fall on deaf ears. My wife was included. I am on my way home to reconcile with her."

"You are not going to divorce her,"
Carrie declared.

"No," said Michael firmly. "The blackmail scheme,
from an evil standpoint of view, was brilliant. But
like Hosea, I will redeem my wife. Michael and Ben
brought light on the darkness," he said.

"What did Darrin do to you, Carrie?" Allison
asked, worried.

"How about I catch you up on that at a later time?"
Carrie replied. Allison nodded.

Ben Bickles suddenly spoke up, and, pointing to
the orderly, who was still in the room, "Put that
report of the island exploding back up on the
screen, please."

Puzzled, the orderly eventually did as asked. *Or
was it an order?* he thought. Part way through, Ben
called out and pointed to the screen, "Stop there!
Can you zoom in on that spot?"

"Yes, "sir," The orderly said. As the picture started
to zoom in on what was once Michael's altar, he

could see two people standing behind it, flipping the middle finger to the drone sharing the video.

"There!" shouted Ben, once again pointing to the screen, "There! Pause it! Right there! Michael, is that who I think it is? Darrin Johnson and Marc Richards?"

Michael stepped up to have a closer look. After a little scrutiny, Michael declared, "You are right! How on earth did they escape from the Navy?"

Charlie piped in as he hung up his phone. He had made a call to his home base and found out some interesting information. "They were helped to escape by some Navy SEALs. But they were recaptured," he interjected, "and then they were brought by boat to the island by some of the sailors and Marines whose wives were abused by Darrin and his cronies. Despite warnings from international authorities to stay away because they were certain that the island's volcano was about to erupt, they went to that island. As you can see, Darrin and Marc seemed to think they were free and safe."

"Please continue the video." Nelson said quietly as he, Amina, Torrance, Javier, and Cassondra stepped closer. "And if you can, zoom in more," please?"

The orderly looked at Ben and received confirmation to proceed. They noticed an expression of defiance on the two men's faces. Then the volcano erupted, obliterating the two men.

"YEAH! YEAH! TAKE THAT! BURN IN HELL!" It was Cassondra's voice that broke the silence. "BURN...IN...HELL!" She broke down in tears, then rushed to Carrie Robert's arms. Amina headed to Ben Roberts's arms while the three boys sought solace in the arms of their father. Michael Roberts walked over to his fellow Musketeer and joined him in consoling the three boys. All else was quiet as the five children sobbed out their anguish and relief. Finally, their tormentors were no more.

The orderly stopped the video and turned off the monitor. Solemnly, Charlie turned towards the door, his visit ending. "See you when you all get home," he said

Ben, Michael, Allison, Carrie, and all of the children hugged him. He was overjoyed with the situation that he couldn't move until the sergeant, who had a tear of his own, tapped him on the shoulder and escorted him out.

After several minutes, Ben released his sons and asked, "What was that about?" He turned to his friend in hopes he could shed some light on the situation. "What did those two demoniacs do?"

Michael answered, "Darrin and Marc were the ones who kidnapped your children and sold them into sex slavery. But," he said proudly, "they received a beating from these children when they arrived on the island with the Navy. I captured the two of them, stripped them, and tied them to a tree. When your children saw the two there, they immediately began assaulting them with rocks and sticks." Michael shook his head. "Darrin and Marc received a beating second only to Jesus himself. The difference is that Jesus didn't deserve His beatings."

Allison walked over to Ben's left and wrapped her arms around his arm. Then, in a soft motherly voice, she said, "Children, come here." The Bickle's children knew she was talking only to the five, and they walked over to their father and his wife. Once there, they received a crushing hug from Allison and Ben, together. The Roberts children felt happy for their adopted brothers and sisters. And the Bickles children stood there, trying to process the information they had just heard. Soon, everybody in the room became part of a huge hugging situation. After several more minutes, Ben kissed his five children, wiping the tears from their eyes when he noticed them. Ben was happy to see how they were starting to feel relieved.

There was still something in Cassondra's demeanor that dictated not everything was quite alright. Ben signaled to his wife and friends. Subtly indicating his daughter, he mouthed, "We need to keep an eye on this one." His friends nodded in agreement.

When all had settled down, Ben had a message for everybody. "Children, we have to see this as both a triumph and a tragedy."

Amina responded. "Tragedy? How are those two deaths a tragedy? I thought it was a complete victory."

Looking at Cassondra, Ben answered Amina. "Triumph," he began, "because of the evil those two handed out. Tragedy, because they decided to choose death over life."

This puzzled Javier. "Death over life?" he asked.

"Yes," Ben said. "I don't want anybody to go to hell after God's judgment. Not even those two. However, they chose to do evil that leads to the second death."

"Second death?" Kathy Roberts said, entering the conversation. Her parents were glad for that, as that was when they knew their daughter was listening.

Ben acknowledged her. "Yes. Kathy, is it?" Kathy nodded. Ben then looked at all the children. "We will all die in this life. Most of us in old age. Some will be gone when they are younger. But we all have a decision to make—a second death or eternal life. Eternal life comes from a personal relationship with God through Jesus the Christ. The second death comes from deciding to not have that relationship." Ben looked around at the children. "Many will choose to do evil, others will try to be good enough to enter God's Kingdom. But without Jesus, getting into the Kingdom for eternity is impossible, because God's standard is perfection. Because of our sins, we can never be perfect in this life. But here is the thing," he began pointing to all of the children. "There will come a day when each one of you will be called to make that decision for yourself. As I said before, choosing life or death. Those two men chose death. That is a tragedy." The children started to murmur among themselves. "That is also why we parents teach you about God. And about what Jesus did to help us enter His Kingdom."

"I understand," Amina said. "But I can't be anything but joyful that they are no more. That they can't hurt anyone anymore."

"Can you, at least, forgive them?" Michael Roberts asked.

It took a few moments before Amina could respond. "To be truthful? I don't know. At least, not now."

"I appreciate your honesty," he said, acknowledging her heart. "But we need to remember to pray for our enemies," Ben added. "Jesus told us to do that much. Take it day by day and see what you may think about it in the future." Amina nodded and buried her head in Red Beards chest.

"Let's all hold hands and ask God for the strength to forgive our enemies." Michael said. He reached out to hold hands with the children closest to him. "I need to find it in me to forgive as well. Let us pray."

Amina, Nelson, Torrance, and Javier prayed fervently with Papa Michael.

Cassondra quietly seethed. *I will never forgive them*, she thought. *NEVER!* When the prayer was finished, Carrie Roberts looked into Cassondra's face, as she was still clinging to her. The young girl still had rage in her facial features. "Cassie," Carrie said softly, "may I tell you something?"

"About what?" came an angered, terse response.

"Now, young lady, you know better than to talk to me like that," Carrie chided.

Startled, Cassondra looked up to her other mama. "I'm sorry, Mama Carrie." The voice was quiet and repentant.

"That's better. Now I am going to tell you about what those two did to me." Cassondra raised her head to look into Carrie's eyes with a questioning look. "No, you five are not the only ones they hurt." She now had the attention of Amina, Javier, Nelson, and Torrence. "They forced me to," she put up air quotes, "date Marc. Darrin and Marc both blackmailed me by threatening to use my sister in their schemes if I didn't agree, and showed me the vile ways some girls were treated by terrible men." She paused to gather herself. "I saw girls being raped, tortured, and even murdered for the men's personal pleasures." Ben and Allison Bickles were shocked at what they were hearing having never known the details. Their hearts broke to think their beloved friend and sister had been treated that way. Allison started to cry. The children were frozen in place, their own fear rising. "In fact, they were so determined to destroy me, they tried to kill me that night on the ship," she said, looking at her husband. "Thankfully, as I went over the rear railing, Michael caught me and saved me." Then with a little chuckle, "Although, I thought we were going to die in that storm." Then she reached down, cupping Cassondra's face, "If anyone deserves to hate those two, I do. But to be truthful, I pity them. Like Ben said, they chose death over life. I would have preferred that they chose life. Their eternity would have been much brighter."

"But how can you forgive them? They were monsters!" Cassondra asked with a tone of bitterness.

"I can forgive them," she said, "not because it will do them any good, Forgiveness is not for the ones who did you wrong." Carrie placed her hand on the young girl's heart and said, "It is for *you*. It's so that bitterness doesn't rule your life. And so that revenge doesn't destroy you. Revenge belongs to God. And believe me, God's revenge on those two will not be pleasant."

"That's an understatement," Michael Roberts chimed in.

Carrie continued, "Cassie, please let the spirit of forgiveness take control before bitterness rears its ugly head." Cassondra couldn't respond at that moment, but she nodded and hugged her second mother's neck. After a long moment, she began to cry. Amina, Nelson, Javier, and Torrance walked over to hug their little sister. They stood for a while, hugging and crying with her.

Allison buried her face in Ben's chest, soaking it with her tears. "I had no idea," she bawled. "I had no idea." The other children were caught up in the emotions of the moment and most of the younger ones from both families cried as well.

Carrie patted the head of Cassondra. "It's ok," she told her. "You forgive when you are ready. Papa Michael, me, your Daddy Ben, and Allison will be there when you need us. And I am sure your mother will be there for you as well." Once again, she held the young girl's face in her hands. "Please believe me." Cassondra just nodded and clung to her second mama.

When all had calmed down, Allison walked over to her fellow Princess and hugged her hard. "I didn't know." She sobbed onto her shoulder. "I didn't know." Carrie reassured her friend that she had indeed forgiven Darrin and Marc, even though she was truly relieved that their reign of terror was over.

I RECOMMEND A BATTLE

The days passed with joy and a lot of noise after that. At mealtime, both families ate together in the dining area of the housing on the land. One day, by odd coincidence, the four eldest Bickles sisters sat across from the four eldest Roberts sons. There was tension and some noticeable attraction between them, and the parents noticed it all.

Amina sat to Ben Roberts's right, as expected. But there was more to the tension in that section of the table.

There appeared to be lighthearted banter between the families, however, there was also a little bite in some of the comments from the Bickles sisters toward their counterparts on the other side of the table. Carrie Bickles was a little put out that her half-sister, Amina, was laying claim on the big Ben by the way she was wrapping her arm around his. Also, even though Roberta Bickles seemed attracted to Troy Roberts, her comments seemed to have the most venom attached to them. Her facial features also seemed a little combative throughout the meal.

Ben Bickles knew something had to be done to eliminate aggression from his daughters.

The next morning, the families came together again. Ben pulled Michael aside.

"Did you see that last night?" pointing to young couples.

"You mean the *three* lightning strikes?"

"Yes."

"Couldn't miss them," Michael said. "However, something seems a little off. Do you have a clue about it?"

"Yes," Ben started. "My daughters only saw hate and violence towards women and girls from men. Except, initially, for me," Ben explained." I am the only reference of how a man should love a woman. More recently, they've received different treatment from Mr. Sanchez and Mr. O'Hara. I believe they want to trust your sons, but their fears are strong. So, I recommend a battle. I have been training them since each one was three years old. I bet you have done the same."

"'Train up a child in the way he should go and when he is old, he will not depart from it,'" Michael quoted. "It definitely paid off for us when the time came."

"It sure did. Little did we know."

"You mentioned a battle."

"Yes," Ben replied. "My daughters against your sons. They have a lot of aggression to get rid of. Roberta will be the most aggressive as she is still dealing with shame when she wasn't able to get past her fear a few years ago. Think you can you help?"

Michael knew his friend but wanted to be sure what he was suggesting. "I am fully aware what we were taught. I don't want your sons to get injured. My daughters are very good at defending themselves."

"Is that a boast or truth?" Michael asked.

Ben raised his hands in submission. "Definitely not boasting. I am sure you trained your children as well. Even though the threats you dealt with weren't as present as what mine dealt with every day."

"You know I can see right through you, brother. You have always been the better fighter out of us Musketeers, but don't think for a second I have been slack in teaching my kids. The pirates may not have always been around on daily rounds but trust me when I say the threats we dealt with were very real. I understand what you went through was far more stressful. You also had Allison there to keep you balanced. Frankly, even with Carrie beside me, I don't think I could have performed as well as you." Michael paused for a few seconds. "I have an idea for your suggestion to work. Are you willing to hear it?"

Ben remembered their youth when only Michael was willing to challenge him when he got a little too ahead of himself. "Michael, my Musketeer brother. I would be the greatest of fools to not hear your suggestions. Let me have it."

"First off, my sons will not fight your daughters," Michael said. This caught Ben by surprise. "Second, my boys will only take a defensive stance. Not to retreat, but also not to attack."

Ben thought for a few minutes. Eventually he understood Michael's reasoning. "I, actually like that idea. Your sons are big and strong, and the way you spoke about their life on the island, I firmly believe they can take the assaults of my daughters." Ben slapped his knees and stood up. "I will trust you to plan." He placed his hands on Michael's shoulders. "I am so grateful to God for bringing us together again, my brother."

"'A iron sharpens iron, so one man sharpens another.' As much as we need Jesus, we still need one another, too. We are stronger together."

"Allison is not going to like this."

"Neither will Carrie. But I understand what you are trying to do and I will fully help you with the healing of your daughters. Set it up for this afternoon. I will prepare my sons." They affectionately bumped shoulders and went their separate ways.

Michael called his sons Ben, Derrick, Robert, and Troy over. When they arrived, Michael set his plan in motion.

"Do you boys like the Bickles sisters?" When they all nodded, Michael said, "Good. I bet they are a little skittish around you?" Again, they nodded.

"Seems like they don't trust us." Ben mentioned.

"They don't." Michael said. He went straight to the point, explaining what the girls went through.

"How can we help?" Troy asked.

"Here is what is about to happen," he said. "They are going to fight you." That raised some eyebrows. "However, you are *not* going to fight them." Puzzled looks took over his sons' faces. "You are to face them with your hands behind your backs. Never go on attack, just dodge and weave," Michael said, demonstrating as he spoke. "Do not back down. Deflect any blows that might get past your defenses. Never retreat. Let them wear themselves out attacking. They will be angry and very aggressive. Do not attack, but again, never retreat. As they wear themselves down, they will need to rest. That is when you go to them, grab their wrists, put their arms behind them, draw them to you and hold them, looking into their eyes with lovingkindness, for about four seconds." This caused the boys to be a bit surprised at the recommendation. Michael continued, "Then release them and back up a few steps. Put your hands behind you again. And wait. They will have one of two responses. One is they will be stunned and confused. On the other hand, they will become enraged and attack you again." He looked at his sons. "Pray for the stunned response, but wait a couple of minutes. Then walk up to them, slowly wrap your arms around them, and just," he paused, "hold them. Don't squeeze them. Just hold them. Let them vent. If what I think will happen *does* happen, you will have wives for the future. Good ones. Except for you, Ben. You are already spoken for. But Carrie Bickles needs to know there are good men out there. Understand?" They nodded. "Now, repeat the instructions back to me." They did.

That afternoon, everyone met in the gym. The girls were dressed in white T-shirts with the bottom of the shirts tied in a knot on the side. They also wore black shorts. But, of course, no shoes.

Carrie Bickles was talking to Amina, getting her permission for the coming battle. "I know what my dad is doing," Carrie told her.

"And what is that?" Amina had her suspicions but wanted her to say it out loud.

"He knows my sisters and I have the heart flutters for those Roberts boys." Carrie looked a little sad. "But given what we went through, trusting men is a struggle. Susan has her eye on Derrick. Whitney has her eyes on Robert. And Roberta won't admit it, but she is drawn to Troy." She paused before she finally had to admit, "And I have been watching Ben, but have no fear, I know you two are glued to each other. What are your thoughts about this?"

Amina agreed, as she was confident Ben was only trying to help Carrie get over her distrust of men. "I will be honest. I don't know what the final outcome will be, but I trust Red Beard's intentions with you. You can trust him. Just remember, Carrie," she said. "*My* Red Beard." Carrie winked, hugged her new found sister, patted Blessing on the head and went off to the battle.

The boys wore khaki shorts and black sleeveless shirts. Also, no shoes. Carrie stood opposite Ben, Susan opposite Derrick, Whitney opposite Robert, and Roberta opposite Troy. Redheaded, pale-skinned boys faced darker tanned, black haired girls. *Opposites all the way around*, Ben thought.

There was an understanding that there would be no holding back. The boys looked at their dad and winked before putting their hands behind their backs. This puzzled the girls a bit, but they went into their fighting stance.

Allison and Carrie were unsure about their husbands' strategies but held silent. Ben blew the whistle, and the girls launched. The boys were prepared and did as their father recommended. The strategy was effective. Eventually the girls started to show signs of fatigue. Their rage kept them going longer than expected but the boys did not waver nor retreat.

Roberta's rage was more an expression of the shame she felt for not fighting those years ago when her mom and siblings were attacked while her dad was fighting. She gave Troy all her rage and shame, but Troy was up to the task. Finally, the girls stopped to catch their breath. That's when the boys moved in. Each one grabbed their assigned girls' wrists, put

their arms behind and drew them in. Although it was
a little awkward, each boy was able to hold them snug
while looking into the girls' eyes with lovingkindness.
As discussed, they held them there for roughly four
seconds. The girls went wide-eyed as they stared at
their "opponents." Then the boys released them and
backed away, returning their hands to behind their
backs. Then they waited.

As Michael had predicted, the girls were stunned,
not knowing what happened.

The boys moved in then. They did it slowly, with
their arms at their sides. When they reached
the girls, they carefully wrapped their arms
around them and held them. Initially, the girls
tried to fuss, but soon started to cry and latched
themselves on to the boys.

Troy quietly said to Roberta, "You are loved
with an everlasting love. And underneath the
everlasting arms."

He repeated these words over and over until
Robert's anger and shame fled and she held on to
Troy hard.

The other boys repeated the same phrases. With the same results.

Ben looked at Michael and said, "Interesting strategy. I'm glad it worked." Allison and Carrie were equally astonished at the outcome. Allison was especially grateful because her daughters now knew that there were other men like their father; kind, loving, and, above all, dedicated to Jesus.

The young "couples" walked back to the parents, holding hands, the girls leaning their heads on the boys' upper arms. Allison ran to them and smothered her daughters with hugs and kisses.

"Mama, do you feel comfort, protected, and cherished when Daddy holds you like that?" Whitney asked.

"Yes," Allison answered. "Just like that."

Then she hugged and kissed the boys, who blushed. The other parents joined them. As did all the other children.

"Dad, we held them just like you hold Mom,"
Robert said. "It was nice. Better than hugging
our sisters."

Michael turned to Ben, "Training them also means
showing them by example."

"You are right, my friend." Ben smiled at the
Roberts boys.

Ben Roberts left Carrie to stand with Amina
and Blessing. Carrie just grinned at Amina and
mouthed her thanks to her.

Michael admonished the couples, "Although this
healing started with a hug of lovingkindness,
don't be in any hurry to advance the pace of your
relationships. You are all still quite young. Don't
rush physical things and never, I repeat, never be
together alone, not until you are married. Pray
with each other and for each other. May Jesus
be the glue in your relationships. And you must
understand, you will be tempted by other girls or
boys. It is important to be aware."

Ben joined in, "Took the words right out of my mouth. Just remember boys, do no harm to my daughters. Understand?"

"Yes, sir!" they said in unison. From that point on the young couples seemed inseparable, especially Roberta and Troy. Roberta vowed to never let Troy out of her sight, ever.

THE HUNT

One day, as the parents were relaxing on the patio on the back side of the mansion and the children explored the vast inner lawn of the plantation, something caught their eyes.

In unison the Allison, Carrie, Ben and Michael all hollered, "CHILDREN! FREEZE!"

The tone and volume that the children heard broke no disobedience. That included the youngest toddlers. Everyone immediately froze where they were, knowing to wait for their parents to tell them what to do next.

What the parents had all seen was a large boar hog standing on the edge of the lawn. It was inside the fence.

Ben quietly asked, "Now what?"

Suddenly, he felt something zoom by his head. Right after that, an arrow entered the boar's neck, severing its spine. With a slight squeal, it dropped right where it stood.

Ben spun around and saw his namesake, Ben Roberts, with another arrow. It was nocked and ready to launch if needed. Michael, Ben, Carrie, Allison, Ben Roberts, and Amina hollered at the children to run into the house immediately.

With no delay, Derrick Roberts, Robert Roberts, Troy Roberts, Carrie Bickles, Susan Bickles, Whitney Bickles, and Roberta Bickles scoured the yard for all of the toddlers. Each sibling grabbed and held one of the smaller kids under their arm as they ran back to the house. Derrick Bickles was last and made sure all were accounted for.

"Where did you find that bow and the arrows?" Ben Bickles asked of Ben Roberts.

"When we arrived here, I looked around and discovered the armory. There are some firearms there as well."

"Ben, Derrick, Robert, Troy, Allison, and Susan," called Michael,". "Go, grab a bow and several arrows. Meet me on the back patio again. That boar's family may come here to find out what happened. Since there is an open season on the wild pigs in Hawaii, we need to be ready to finish the job."

"What about me?" Ben Bickles asked.

"No offense, my friend, but I think you might be a little rusty with the bows."

Several minutes later, Ben returned with a semi-automatic rifle and two thirty-round magazines taped together. "I am not rusty with this!" he said when he saw Michael.

Michael was impressed. It felt good to have his friend stand beside him. To Michael's right, his children were in line with their arrows at the ready. Everyone stood, silent and waiting. They didn't have long to wait. From the fence line came seven sows and a multitude of piglets of various ages. They approached the dead boar and raised an alarm. But it was too late for them. Each sow had their spine severed by arrows, and before the piglets could run too far, rifle shots rang out and seven piglets dropped where they were.

In the house, Carrie Roberts stood by the window, praying that all the arrows would fly straight and true. Later, she was grateful to God for saying "Yes" to her prayer.

Michael came in with a stern look on his face. "Children," he called out. "Load up on as many arrows as you can carry. Ben," he said, point to his friend, "load up on some more ammunition. We are going to hunt the rest of those piglets down." Everybody did as ordered.

"Daddy, let us go with you," Carrie Bickles cried out, pointing to her sisters Susan, Whitney, Roberta, Michael, and Derrick. Teresa stuck to Roberta as if she had been glued to her. She was definitely going along as well." We can carry the piglets back here." Ben was unsure about allowing his children to go along because they were not trained in hunting.

"Not a bad idea, my friend," Michael Roberts said. "If we don't have to carry them back here, we can continue to pursue the rest."

Ben looked over his expectant children, shook his head and agreed. "Alright. You may come. But do exactly as you are told so you won't get hurt. Hear me?" They all nodded and promised to do just that.

"In the meantime, sweetheart," Michael said, "call the Army and explain what is happening. Stack the boar and the sows in a pile and burn them. Then gather the piglets and place them over by that tree about twenty yards from the right of the patio. I am sure the Army is going to like the pig feed we are about to give them."

Without saying a word, Carrie Roberts had Michael and Derrick Bickles help her with the boars and sows, while Allison Bickles gathered Allison Roberts and her sister Susan to round up the lifeless piglets.

The hunting party trotted into the foliage, following the way the piglets went. It didn't take long for the group to realize Derrick Bickles had an uncanny knack for tracking. With his seeming sixth sense, they found and killed over sixty piglets. After an hour of nothing happening, Derrick declared that they had found all the piglets, so the hunt was called off. With the Bickles girls hard at work dragging two piglets at a time back to the mound after the hunt was over, it didn't take long for all of their carcasses to be added to the others by the tree. By the time everyone was finished, the Army personnel had arrived to haul away the piglets for butchering.

"A feast indeed," declared the lieutenant. "Our soldiers will be greatly pleased for this." He saluted the families and left to finish his detail.

Michael Roberts turned to Derrick Bickles. "Young man," he said with pride, "we have a friend that can track and hunt like no one on this planet. After today, I do believe you can give him a run for his money. And if my hunch is correct, you are named after him." Without looking away he asked Derrick's father, "What do you say, brother?"

Ben walked up to his son. "I wholeheartedly agree. I think our fellow Musketeer, Derrick Henderson would love to take this young man under his wing. Frankly, I am impressed as well." He grinned and rubbed his son's head. "By the way, I just remembered young Ben. That arrow was a little close to my head."

Ben Roberts replied, "I missed you by three inches. I didn't have time to consider the closeness. I knew I was only going to hit the boar."

Michael placed his hand on his fellow Musketeer's shoulder. "Just so you know. My children never miss their targets." He repeated himself with emphasis. "Never."

Three piglets were left behind, so they were butchered and roasted. Both families fed well that night.

MILE HIGH TEACHING

Three weeks later, they were all given approval to leave Hawaii and head home to Sioux Falls. Their parents, grandparents and other family members were elated to hear the news.

They all said goodbye to their temporary home, the former plantation mansion. Excitement and concern flitted across the children's faces as they boarded the bus that was to take them to Pearl/Hickam's airport field where the large Constellation air liner awaited them.

"Are you going to fly that big airplane again, Daddy?" Asked Teresa Bickles.

"I don't know Terry. We will find out when we get there. But here is what I do know. Uncle Michael will sit second seat if I am." Ben patted her on the head.

"Well, if Uncle Michael doesn't know what to do, we can teach him." Boasted Whitney with a giggle.

"And I would be very grateful for your guidance."
Michael replied, chuckling.

Suddenly a great cacophony of noise erupted as
the Bickles girls started explaining what to do at
the second seat and the engineer's station. Michael
made it look like he was taking it all in and asked
questions all the way to the air field. It made for
quite the entertaining ride for both families.

The Roberts children were a little apprehensive
about leaving the confines of the ground as the
plane took off however, the Bickles children told
them that all was going to be ok. After all, they
were experienced in flying, of course. These voices
were added the other conversation and made for
a rather noisy bus ride. Allison and Carrie quite
enjoyed the racket. At least the children were
occupied well.

Upon arrival at the airfield's terminal, Ben and
Allison, and the rest of the Bickles gang were
joined by three other people they haven't seen
in about two months. Geraldo Sanchez, Sherp
O'Hara, and Rosiland Kapree. A round of hugs,
pats on the back, a in general, a joyous reunion.

Roberta almost crushed O'Hara when they met. Something he cherished immensely. Then introductions were made to the Roberts family. Carrie expressing her immense gratitude for their care of her friends.

After the short celebration, they were led into the building where they were Greeted by General White. He couldn't hold back his joy at seeing these families finally on their last leg towards home.

"Benjamin and Michael," General White said, "I have some news that might interest you. We have hired two retired airline pilots and an engineer who are familiar with the Constellation. Unfortunately, they were unavailable when you left Pago Pago to come here." He motioned to Ben. "You two are to ride with your families and help with the young'uns. I wish all of you safe travels. And please give my regards to my son-in-law, Robert Jefferson, when you see him."

"That we most assuredly will do, General. And thank you and all the men and women who helped us these past two months. We are eternally grateful." Ben said as he shook the general's hand.

Michael turned the Bickles girls, "Although I am grateful for your tutelage, girls. It looks like I won't need it after all."

"Oh, yes you will, Uncle Michael." Roberta immediately corrected. "You and Daddy will be flying this huge plane when we get home. So, you had better remember everything."

Michael smiled, "I guess you are right. I misspoke."

"Of course I am right." Roberta winked. "That should never be a question."

Her mother walked up behind her and whispered in her ear. "Don't push it, young lady."

Roberta blushed, "Yes, Mama."

"Safe travels, Bickles and Roberts families. I have been to Sioux Falls several times in the last few years. The culture has changed a bit, so you now

have fair warning. Goodbye and Godspeed."
General White then saluted, receiving hearty
goodbyes from the families as they were guided
out to the plane. After they were all on board, he
quietly said to himself, "I will see you again soon."

General White stood there until the Constellation
was airborne.

* * * *

Carrie's pregnancy was progressing well. It was
recommended they wait until she had given birth,
but Carrie was adamant that her child be born in
Sioux Falls. She won that argument because she
had her family and friends' support, and everyone
was pleased to be allowed to leave. They gathered
the families together for one last teaching session.
Michael, especially diligent, looked over his
children. They grew up on an island, separated
from humanity. Separated from civilization. *They
will be in for some severe culture shock*, he thought. *I
need to prepare them as best I can.*

"Children," Michael began, as he spoke to both
Roberts and Bickles children. "You have grown

up away from humanity and civilization, albeit in different ways. You all need to understand that there are so many people that will love and cherish you. You have families and friends waiting to meet you. That is when you make new friends." He took a long breath and let half of it out. "However, there will also be people, children included, who will not like you. Some will not like the fact that you put your trust and love in Jesus the Christ. Some will hate you for that because they hate Jesus. They will try to make you turn away from Him. They will sound nice and friendly, but they are evil. The reason why I say that is because they are trying to get you to turn from Him." The children became quite somber when they heard these comments. "You still need to love them as Jesus loves them—"

Ben interrupted, "However, you are not to accept their sin. As I have told my children countless times, 'Love the sinner but hate the sin.'"

"Exactly," Michael continued. "Now we understand that is not going to be an easy thing to do. Some of them will want to be your friends. Be friends with them. But when they want to only be friends if you accept their sin, that's when it is time to say 'no.'" He looked around to see if the message was getting through.

Allison Bickles piped in, "If you ever have any questions about that, all you have to do is ask us." She pointed to herself, then to Ben, Carrie, and Michael. "And you can also ask your aunts, uncles, and grandparents, whom you will meet very soon."

Carrie Roberts added, "And remember, you can always pray for God's wisdom and be prepared for His response., too. He operates on *His* schedule, so sometimes you may wait for His answer. But He will *always* answer. You know His voice," she reminded them. "Rely on Him for guidance." The younger children did not completely understand what was being said. But they were comforted, knowing that they could ask their parents for help. And they could ask God, too.

The day finally came, and it was time to board the plane heading home.

THE GYMNASIUM

They took the time to gather for prayer with the pilots. Mr. Sanchez, Miss Kapree, and Mr. O'Hara, temporarily released from immigration, and the revamped FBI accompanied the families. Ben's assistants were told they would have to meet separately with immigration authorities once they arrived in Sioux Falls. They enjoyed helping with the children, especially the babies.

Things started off nice and peaceful on the flight as the plane took off. The journey was rather unadventurous after the initial fear of leaving the confines of earth. There was excitement and fear among the children as the plane took off. However, the Bickles children told them that all was going to be ok. Eventually, the excitement turned to boredom as they flew over the ocean. The parents taught the children how to yawn or swallow or just move their jaw around to help with the changes in pressure in their ears.

Ben and Allison stood at the front of the passenger cabin. They observed Red Beard sitting with Blessing, who alternated sitting in the seat next to him or on his lap. She entertained him with wild stories about the island. Red Beard smiled from time to time as he listened in.

Behind him sat Amina and their eldest daughter, Carrie, enjoying quite the animated conversation.

The next three rows were occupied by the Roberts brothers Derrick, Robert and Troy. Sitting next to them were the Bickles sisters Susan, Whitney, and Roberta. In that order. They sat rather peacefully with the girls resting their heads on their newfound boyfriends. They, too, listened to the chatter of Amina and Carrie, giggling from time to time.

To their left, the front row was occupied by Teresa Bickles and Kathy Roberts. They became fast friends at the plantation and were quietly animated in their descriptions of their lives so far. Behind them sat Carrie Roberts, who was quietly nursing her, almost one-year-old, toddler. O'Hara was in the next row, holding the youngest Bickles child. Everything remained relatively calm as she slept. O'Hara had a complete look of peace.

Ben was happy for him because of the years of servitude to the evil tyrant, Mr. Kim.

In the far rear seats, Miss Kapree and Geraldo Sanchez were busy going over some notes that would continue the assault on Mr. Kim's empire. Walking between the rows from the rear was Michael, assisting the children when there was need. Near the rear in the same rows, Richard Roberts had Michael and Derrick Bickles in stitches with his wild ways of storytelling. The rest of the children sat throughout the cabin. Some watched the waves below. It wasn't long before most of the younger kids fell asleep, much to the relief of the adults. The seats behind O'Hara were empty and that is where Ben and Allison finally rested, Allison receiving her child from O'Hara because it was time for his feeding.

They landed in San Diego to refuel and then the excitement grew as they all knew the next time they stopped, it would be home. No one slept this last leg of their flight. The landscape was too new to them and the chatter rose enough to give the adults assurance they will be alright.

When they felt the Constellation starting its final descent, an initial wave of excitement followed by silence as the reality set in that they were almost home. That silence remained as they were landing at the airport in Sioux Falls it was midmorning and everybody was tired. Still, a roar of voices exploded with clapping followed by everybody trying to see out the windows at the airport.

The pilot was ordered to follow the Air National Gurd mobile control vehicle to park on the east end of the tarmac that the Air Guard operated from. Once the plane parked on the tarmac,, it was surrounded by security forces.

Ben looked at Michael, "They seem to be serious about this."

Michael agreed, "I looked around and I don't see any of our family members out there. Curious."

A stairway was placed just outside of the door. Ben opened the door, and an Air Force colonel stepped in.

Good afternoon, Bickles and Roberts families and friends. I am Colonel Washrack, the base commander. I am here to welcome you home and to help you out of here. Upon disembarking from the plane, immigration officials will separate Mr. Sanchez, Miss Kapree, and Mr. O'Hara from the group. The flight crew will remain to help with securing the aircraft. Now if you would follow me, I will take you to the bus that has been assigned for you. It will take you to your families. He turned and walked down the steps, followed by Ben's associates. They said their goodbyes and that they would see each other as soon as the authorities were finished with them. And that they would be bringing their families. All was to fulfill promises the immigration services had made in Hawaii.

After first shaking hands and giving hugs to the flight crew, Benjamin and Allison Bickles lead the children down the steps onto firm ground. Michael and Carrie brought up the rear, making sure all were accounted for. They stood at the top of the steps as emotions suddenly struck them with the realization that they were finally home. Michael had to hold on to his wife as her legs were a little wobbly because of the emotions rushing through her body. Once they were finally on the ground, Ben, who had waited until all were safe on terra firma, started to follow the colonel again.

Suddenly, Teresa Bickles ran up to her father in distress. "Daddy, stop! We have to pray and give thanks to God for getting us here safely! It's like Roberta says, 'If we stop praying, God will think we have forgotten Him!'"

Ben froze in place with the realization that his little daughter was right. He picked her up, hugging her while thanking her and apologizing for forgetting Who comes first. He turned to face the families. Everybody. I have been informed that we are not right with God at this moment. We need to thank God for getting us here." He then knelt down, followed by Allison, Michael, Carrie, and all of the children.

Ben then prayed, "Heavenly Father, Lord God, and Jesus the Christ, thank you for watching over us these past years and bringing us home again. Thank you for the knowledgeable flight crew and the sturdy Constellation as our ride. Thank you, Father, for Teresa's reminder. Out of the mouth of babes. We give thanks in the name of Jesus the Christ. Amen."

The children joined in with their own Amens. Ben looked around and noticed the colonel and some of the security personnel had their heads bowed.

The two large families were loaded onto a bus and driven to the high school, Washington High School to be exact. The children were wide-eyed, except the really young ones. But that was because they were napping. The Bickles children were explaining to the Roberts children that the school colors were orange and black.

"At least that's what my mama said," Teresa Bickles was telling Kathy Roberts.

Michael, Carrie, Ben, and Allison paused at the front door of the school. It had been a long time since they had crossed that threshold. They also realized that, technically, they had not finished their schooling. The emotions they were feeling paled in comparison to what they were about to see.

The families were guided to the gymnasium by the principal. The Bickles family had been sent to the north door while the Roberts family went to the south. The anticipation of meeting their parents and siblings after so many years was almost overwhelming for Ben, Allison, Michael, and Carrie. Even the children felt the emotion of the situation as both families entered at the same time.

The room exploded with cries and screams from all around. The Roberts and Samuels families were on one end of the gymnasium with the Bickles and Ver Hoeven families on the other end. Moms hugged daughters. Moms hugged their sons. Dads did the same. Brothers and sisters tried their best to get their hugs in as well.

Then the grandparents saw their grandchildren.

The Roberts children enjoyed the love from their grandparents, aunts and uncles. The Bickles children got scared and scattered. It took quite a while for Ben and Allison to calm their children down so they could make introductions

In the middle of the gym stood four women with their spouses, and Miriam Deng, who stood alone. Her husband said he was too busy to attend and would see his "daughter" Amina later. When the children saw their mothers, the reunions were equally as loud as the previous ones, and the children received crushing hugs.

When things had calmed down a little, Amina brought Blessing to meet her grandmother face-to-face. Both grandparent and grandchild rejoiced in each other from the first moment they saw one another. After that introduction, Amina brought over her Red Beard. Miriam was absolutely floored at the size of Ben Roberts, but she regained her composure enough to give him a loving, motherly hug. Ben received it with pleasure and kissed the top of her head. Miriam cooed and snuggled her future son-in-law a little. She winked at her daughter and quietly said, "I see what you like about this man." Red Beard blushed.

As the day progressed, their trust grew a bit. Some of them even began sitting on their grandpas' and grandmas' laps. The children began to see how love for one another is where family is. Finally, both families' children began playing with their new cousins.

It was a good day indeed.

MANSIONS

Towards the end of the day, the families were taken to their new homes by the same bus that brought them from the airplane. They were brought to two mansions that had been left unoccupied since the war. Both properties were located in the south of Sioux Falls in the Lincoln High school district. Their parents told them that the church members and many classmates helped clean and fix up the homes for their arrival. The families offered thanks for their church brothers and sisters and their classmates as well.

The former residences were the first to be attacked during the Second American Civilian War when the Triple-As (Americans Against America) struck the city. The two properties were left in disarray until the news of the Bickles and Roberts families being found alive and well.

"Our children are going to attend Lincoln?" Allison Bickles grimaced. "With all the red, white, and blue of their patriot mascot?" she groaned. "You realize how that is going to grate on my Washington Warrior sympathies?"

Upon that realization, Carrie put her hands over her mouth in mock horror while Michael played as being sick to the point of vomiting.

"Well, I guess, FOR NOW, it can't be helped. We did have a few friends from Lincoln, Roosevelt, Jefferson, O'Gorman, and Sioux Falls Christian. Although I do shutter at the thought those other schools' colors potentially adorning our home," Michael said with exaggerated resignation of the obvious. "First, our children need to be caught up on their education so they can be accepted into the high school. Or any other schools as well." Carrie nodded in agreement as they waved good night to the Bickles family. Then, with the guidance of their parents, Michael and Carrie led their children into their new home.

When Ben and Allison brought their family to the mansion assigned to them, which was approximately fifty yards south from the Roberts domicile, they were amazed that it was bigger than the one Michael and Carrie received. Both properties were registered as to being four acres in size, a quarter of which were the expansive domiciles. At the request of Manfred Bickles, Ben's father, they all entered the five-stall garage where a big item was hidden behind a curtain. Manfred and Jamie, Ben's mother, stood in front of the curtain and waited or everybody to get settled in the garage.

Manfred then addressed his son. "Ben, I had prepared your graduation present for you before you were taken. I never got the privilege to give it to you on the day you were to receive your diploma." He choked back a few sobs. "However, today is a more perfect time to give I to you." He reached around with his wife's help and started to remove the curtain. "So, here it is."

Ben was wide-eyed with anticipation. Allison was clinging to his left arm in great anticipation as well. When the item was revealed, Ben fell to his knees. In front of him was a fully restored 1996 Ford F-350 crew cab long bed pickup truck that his father and friends drove during and after the war to come to Sioux Falls to meet their intended brides. Ben knew about the truck because it remained in the barn on the farm where the Musketeers and Princesses grew up. Manfred had promised him to restore it for his son. Upon research, he decided to paint it with the forest camouflage the Army had the 1980s.

When Ben could finally speak, he said with a quivering voice. "That's one of the most beautiful things I have ever seen." Allison was also in tears because she knew she would have been riding in the truck with her man.

The children couldn't understand what all the fuss was about. "I don't see what you are excited about," Roberta piped in. "It looks like two shades of green and a shade of black that don't make a pattern. It's ugly," she said, wrinkled her nose.

Manfred Bickles suddenly grew solemn, as did Christian Ver Hoeven, Allison's father. Jamie Bickles, Ben's mother, and Binh Ver Hoeven, Allison's mother, also fell silent and somber. Manfred addressed the group, "Listen closely, children. What I am about to tell you is something I haven't told my own children. I was part of a sniper squad during the second civil war. Your grandfather Christian, the Roberts grandfathers, and two others, whom you will eventually meet, made up that squad. We were more than good at what we did. We were assigned to eliminate the instigators that fired up the Triple A's." The children didn't understand who their grandfather was talking about but did understand that now was not the time to interrupt. "Somehow we got together around Fort Smith Arkansas and stayed together until the end of the war." Christian moved to stand behind his buddy and placed his hand on Manfred's shoulder as he saw that his best friend was about to crack at the remembrance. Manfred acknowledged the hand and stood a little taller with the added strength. "We were told to move to Memphis and join the battle there. It was in Memphis that we found this old truck. We looked it over and saw that it was still operational.

Finally, we had a vehicle that could haul our gear plus the six of us. We moved on to Nashville, Tennessee next. There we found six of the most beautiful nurses this world has ever seen."

"The most beautiful, indeed!" Christian added. Jamie and Binh blushed a little with pride that their husbands still thought of them that way.

Manfred continued, "Some Triple A's had surrounded the women with the intent to kill them, but we six were not having that. God made such beauty, and we had to protect God's creation. The enemy was easily done away with and the relief on those women's faces was worth all the struggles we were going through because of that damnable war. So, we six took those nurses with us through Chattanooga, Tennessee and then to Atlanta. We received some injuries at Chattanooga and were very grateful to have nurses with us to tend to our wounds. Atlanta was the most vicious battle of the war. We lost a lot of good men and women on our side. Some five thousand Triple A's had to be killed before Atlanta was ours. Then for some God-forsaken reason, somebody who thought he was in charge of the war told our nurses to go home. They had no choice. We six felt an emptiness that was indescribable after that." A tear trailed down his left cheek. Then he inhaled a strong breath and continued. "From there we went to help with the final battle at Washington, DC. We were present when the surrender happened. Thank God that awful war was finally over." Manfred seemed to not be able to speak anymore.

"Don't stop now!" exclaimed Whitney. "What happened to the truck and the nurses? Did you ever see them again?" The other children added their versions of the same questions.

That seemed to have brought Manfred out of his doldrums. He looked up and smiled a sad smile "Well," he said, "the nurses were from Sioux Falls. So we, now veterans, decided we needed to see if we can fill the holes in our hearts. We drove that old pick up all the way here." Then he raised a finger, and his smile brightened, lighting up his face. "We found those nurses, and they agreed to marry us." The children were in awe of that claim. "Yes, my grandchildren. Your grandmothers were two of those nurses." Manfred looked at his wife. "And my wife is the most beautiful women God ever created." At that he fell silent. Jamie and Binh walked up to their respective husbands and hugged hard as they shed some tears.

Some of the children were impressed. However, after several minutes, Roberta broke the silence, "Still looks ugly to me." As the room chuckled, she smiled and winked at her father. Ben returned the smile and wink. Manfred and Christian looked up at the girl and started to laugh harder.

"Camouflage was never meant to be beautiful." Manfred admitted.

"Dad, how is it you claimed sole ownership since you and your friends found it and used it together?" Ben was curious how he could receive such a gift.

Manfred rubbed his chin and chuckled. "We used a very sophisticated method to decide ownership." He paused for effect. It was very silent as everybody waited for him to continue. "We drew straws. Shortest straw declared the owner." He tapped his chest. "And that was me."

Ben laughed. "Dad! Shortest straw? Sophisticated?" Manfred could only shrug, grin, and nod. Ben shook his head and smiled. "Thanks, Dad." He hugged his father hard. "It will be used properly."

"Alright everyone, time to enter your new home." Christian Ver Hoeven, Allison's father, said. He stood by the door to the garage entrance, and everybody started moving towards the door.

Ben took one last glance at the truck.

The children waited for their parents to enter first. Christian opened the door that led into a combination pantry and mud room. Binh, Allison's Mother, stood by the next door and opened it when most of the family was well into the pantry.

Ben led the way while holding Allison's hand as they entered the kitchen area. Allison was in absolute awe at the woodwork that was displayed in front of her. And the amazing amount of storage that was available in the cabinet. She covered her mouth with both hands and was speechless for several minutes.

"I remembered how you described your perfect
kitchen when you were starting high school."
Twirling around, Allison's mom asked, "Does this
fit your dreams?"

All Allison could do was nod. She ran to her
mother and cried as they held each other.

"It's perfect, Mama!" Allison cried. The children
walked around opening drawers and doors
and were amazed at the number of dishes,
silverware, pots, pans, the size of the sink, oven,
and refrigerator. Ben just stood and watched
the commotion and Allison's response to her
new kitchen.

After opening and closing a few cabinet doors,
Whitney made an observation, "Mama," she said,
"the cabinets are quiet. No noise. And they open
so easily! Not like the cabinets at our apartment."
The children still had a sense that the apartment
they were born into was theirs.

Derrick chimed in, "And everything is so clean!"
The other children agreed with their siblings.

Christian placed his hand on Ben's shoulder, "Just so you know, the rest of the furnishings are not new. However, they should be good enough until you two decide how to furnish the place." Ben looked at his father-in-law and nodded with understanding.

"What about security measures?" Ben asked.

"Waiting for your decision on what to use." Ben nodded at that.

Manfred Bickles, Ben's father, called from the living room, "Ok, everybody, now that you have dissected the kitchen. Time to come to the living room before we head to the bedrooms." The children reluctantly stopped with the drawer and door opening and entered the living room and stopped at the doorway. Ben and Allison were bringing up the rear and were wondering what would stop their horde in their tracks. When they investigated the living room, they understood why. A huge banner over the large fireplace, with bright red, white, and blue letters with stars interspersed said, "Welcome home, Bickles. Time for you to stay put. We have missed you, dearly." It was signed by all the church members that worked on the two mansions for the past two and a half months. Under the banner stood Ben and Allison's siblings, their spouses, nieces and nephews.

"Wow, Dad! The whole shebang!" was all Ben could say. More hugs and giggles and chatter ensued. After about an hour, Manfred called the room to order and stated they had better explore the bedroom wing so the family might get some rest tonight. Before anybody moved, Christian called for a time of prayer. They all bowed their heads and folded their hands, waiting for him to start. He gave thanks that Ben and Allison were alive and well and fruitful in their repopulation efforts. He thanked God for the availability of the mansion. He also asked that, given the excitement of this day, everybody would be able to sleep well. With the Amen and some pouting, waving, and hugs, the siblings took their families and went home. Finally, Binh and Ben's mother, Jamie, stood by the doorway of a hallway leading to the bedroom wing.

Ben and Allison were asked to stay in the living room while the grandparents guided the children to their rooms. Since they had never been separated from them, Allison was a little apprehensive about being left behind. But Ben wrapped his arms around her and turned her towards the living room, knowing full well her "Mom's ears" were on full alert. The laughter and screams of delight told them that all was well.

The living room was huge with a vaulted ceiling with the same woodwork throughout that matched the kitchen. And as they were already informed, the couch, chairs, and tables were definitely mismatched and on the "well used" side.

Allison wrinkled her nose. "Definitely has that lived in look."

Ben agreed with a little mirth in his voice. "Lived in for sure. If you would like, would you want the responsibility to, how should I say, *modernize* the place?"

"Ah, geez, I don't think we will have the money. It is a rather large place." She said sarcastically as she swept her arms around the room.

Picking up on her humor, "Let me take a look at the checkbook and see what we can afford." They looked at each other and burst out laughing.

"Checkbook? Do they actually use them anymore?" Allison asked, still laughing.

Ben shrugged. "I don't know. It was just the thing to say at the moment."

They paused for a few minutes and just stared into each other's eyes. Then, as if on cue, they started to sway together and, with a little more momentum, they started to dance a waltz around the large living room. They were so lost into each other that they didn't hear Binh, Allison's mother, enter the archway leading into the living room.

"Oh, Allison," Binh called and immediately quieted herself as she beheld her daughter and son-in-law waltzing around the room. She was amazed that they never touched any of the furniture. She turned to look down the hallway and caught her husband's eye. With hand gestured she was able to convey that the children and the other grandparents need to join her, but quietly.

In a couple of minutes, all the children and their grandparents stood beside Binh and just enjoyed the moment. Ben and Allison had no idea they were being watched. Carrie and Susan held each other's arms and rested their heads together in contentment. Roberta encircled Manfred's, her grandfather, arm and just smiled. The rest of the children just watched on with joy as did Christian and Jamie.

When Ben and Allison finally stopped dancing, they didn't lose eye contact and kissed. "Children," Christian said. All the children looked up to their grandfather as he started to speak. "What you are seeing is the second greatest gift any man can give to his children. The first is a permanent relationship with Jesus. The second most important gift is how he loves his children's mother." The children looked at their parents and smiled. Ben and Allison finally realized they were being watched and just enjoyed the family moment.

"Grandpa," Roberta answered. "That is something Daddy has given to us all our lives. I pray my future husband acts the same." The rest of the children agreed and went to join their parents in a group hug. Eleven-year-old Michael and his sister, Susan, extended their arms to have their grandparents join.

Eventually, they all made their way back to the bedrooms. Ben and Allison took note of the placement of the bedrooms in relationship to the bathrooms worried about the potential issue. But she needn't have bothered. In this mansion, each of the children's rooms had their own bathrooms. The furniture was in used condition. The children were elated that, although they would be sharing their room with another sibling, they would not be sleeping stacked on one another as they had been at their apartment.

When Ben reached his Master bedroom, he was relieved when he saw that the beds were oversized. He smiled, content with the idea of not having his feet hanging over the edges.

Jamie tapped Allison on the shoulder, "Just so you know, Michael and Carrie's place are furnished the same way. Since you and the other Musketeers are six-foot-six inches tall and the princesses are six feet tall, we knew you would like some comfort in your sleep. The children have the same size beds, since, as we have seen with Michael's boys, size is an issue. The beds are the only things new in the houses. Like you two, the Roberts will have to go shopping for new furnishings. May all of you sleep well in your new beds." Christian, Binh, Manfred and Jamie told their children that they would be staying the night and helping if the children had issues so that Ben and Allison could get some good rest. Everybody slept well that night, since it had been a long day, having flown in that morning, meeting the rest of the family, and then coming to this mansion that would be their new home.

* * * *

Michael and Carrie's new home was a huge two story, from the outside, brick surrounded mansion with a five-car attached garage. The brick was tan in color, with some showing old age while others were obviously new replacements. The wooden front doors were obviously new and surrounded by glass on the top and sides. They were made of heavy, solid three-inch oak. The family entered the front entryway through an enormous archway.

"Michael!" exclaimed Carrie. "Our living room at the farm wasn't this big. I am very curious about the rest of the place." Michael just stood with his mouth agape, looking at the size of the interior.

In front of them was what they eventually turned into the family room, with a massive fireplace separating the entryway from that area. To the right was the immense kitchen and dining room which had already been outfitted with a large table and chairs. Since all of the original furnishings were destroyed in the attack, and due to the lack of time to acquire items appropriate for a mansion, the new furnishings were on the more inexpensive side.

Carrie was beside herself at the size of the kitchen and all the appliances. The amount of storage space almost overwhelmed her. "Oh, Michael," she uttered in awe, "this kitchen is absolutely heavenly." Michael just smiled at his wife's enthusiasm. Most of the children were in awe of the whole place. Some of the younger children were a little scared while others were absolutely wide-eyed with amazement. Just short of three months ago, they were living happily on the island.

figured Michael's and Carrie's parents positioned themselves to the left of the entryway. They stood by the stairs leading to the second story master bedroom. On that floor were eight additional bedrooms divided by five bathrooms. Each contained a bathtub with shower, toilet, and at least two sinks. The master bedroom contained its own full bathroom with two toilets and two sinks. When the family finally made their way upstairs, Carrie was so dumbstruck that she couldn't move once she saw where she would be sleeping. Tears started flowing down her cheeks as she took in the whole area. The children had scattered to look at the bedrooms and bathrooms, becoming a screaming mass of humanity as they darted from room to room. Each one declared that a certain bedroom was theirs. Michael just held onto Carrie, feeling the same emotions. *How can this be our home*, he thought. *It's so big!*

In the master bedroom, Michael made note of the oversized mattress. He was happy he wouldn't have to go back to having his feet dangle over the edge of the bed due to his height.

Michael's father, Troy, came and patted his son on the shoulder. "Since we know our children and our grandchildren will follow suit, we made sure you two can sleep in comfort," he said

Kristy Roberts softly broke into Michael's thoughts when she spoke. "Son, if you two are amenable, we," pointing to Carrie's parents and his father, "would be willing to help settle the children into their rooms," Her face showed an expectant, hopeful expression. "If you would like," she added.

Michael quickly glanced at his wife and nodded to his mother. The children's grandparents then turned, leaving the Master bedroom and calling the children to them. The grandparents told their grandkids that they were going to help them get acquainted with their new rooms.

Not all the children were happy with their new home. Kathy seemed a bit scared. Her grandfather saw her standing alone and went to her, kneeling down beside her.

"What is wrong, Kathy?" he asked.

Kathy looked at the room and then at her grandfather, then shrugged. Troy waved to his son to have him join them. Carrie caught the signal as well, noticing a rather somber Kathy. She was normally an extremely active and happy girl. Cathy followed her husband and stood behind her daughter, placing her hands on the girl's shoulders.

Kathy looked up. "Daddy," she asked, "is this really our new home?"

Michael nodded as he replied, "Yes, Kathy, it is."

"I don't like the noises."

"What noises?"

"The noises outside," she replied, "and the way everything sounds in here." Some of the other children heard her statement and walked over, nodding their agreement with her.

Michael sat back on his heels and looked up. "Of course." He looked at Carrie and his dad with recognition. Then he called out to the family to meet with him in the dining room. In a few minutes, all were assembled, sitting in the chairs around the table. He had Kathy stand beside him with Carrie still laying her hands on the girl's shoulders.

"Children," Michael began. "It has just occurred to me that you might be a little uneasy about living here and sleeping in these rooms. It has only been about three months since we were removed from the island." With his palms facing the children, he began waving them at each one, "There are going to be different noises that you are not accustomed to." Then he waved to the outside, "The cars and trucks drive by at all hours of the day and night along the interstate highway, which is just about three-quarters of a mile away. Cars will drive by on the street out in front of this property. Although this house is quite tight and quiet, some noises will get past the walls. These sounds are still new to you," he said. "And the beds are not what you are used to either."

"That's right," Carrie said.

He reached for Carrie's hand, "However, this is what your mom and I were used to when we were kids." He noticed a slightly raised hand, "And

Amina as well. You will eventually get used to it all as time moves on, but just know that longing for the island will never go away. Truth be told, I miss the island as well. It was a very good place to live, and we had an excellent life there." He paused for a few seconds watching his children's expressions as they considered what he said. Most were getting the idea. A few were still a little skittish about the move. "Tonight will be our first night here," he stated. "Your grandparents have offered to stay and help with some of you who may get nervous about the new sleeping arrangements." Michael folded his hands. "With all the excitement of our return to our home, we haven't taken the time to give God thanks and to ask Him to watch over us. Let's bow our heads and do that now."

Everybody bowed their heads and held each other's hands. Kathy was a little happier when her dad mentioned praying to God. She realized that it had been a long time since they did that. Prayer was her comfort zone. Michael prayed, asking God to watch over the family as everybody was trying to get used to a new home. He also prayed for his family and friends to tap him on the shoulder if he had neglected his time with Him. Micheal continued the prayer, thanking God for their safe travel. For reuniting with their extended families. For the people who renovated the house and for his and Carrie's parents in helping to get settled. He asked for God's calming presence during the first night so everyone would get a good night's sleep. When Michael finished, there was a rousing Amen from the children.

"Now it is getting late," he admonished. "We traveled a lot today. You finally met your grandparents, aunts, uncles, and cousins. And now we are here. My guess is that all of you will fall asleep rather quickly because of how tired you actually are. So, let's all get settled in your rooms and we will be there to tuck you in. Now, off you go."

The children got up and walked over their daddy, giving him some big hugs, thanking him for remembering to pray. Then they slowly made their way back upstairs to their bedrooms.

Ben and Amina stayed behind, laying out their case as to why they should be together in their own room, reminding Michael and Carie about the vow they made before God about remaining celibate until marriage. The couple reiterated that they fully intend to keep that vow. Ben and Carrie's side of that debate was that they wanted to make sure there was no area of temptation that would have caused them to violate their oath.

Michael summed it up this way, "You two are at the most dangerous ages for temptation to rear its ugly head despite your good intentions. On the island we all slept together in the one room. Keeping your vow was easier then because of the potential audience that would be watching. Here with the two of you in one room by yourselves, the temptation would be almost too much."

Ben had to acknowledge the truth of that. "So, what are you suggesting?"

Michael breathed deeply to calm himself before he spoke. "Ben will have his own room. Amina will share a room with Kathy and Blessing. However, she will be able to have some time for privacy away from those two. This way, Blessing is not separated from her mother. Sharing a room with Kathy will be good for Blessing, since they seem to get along very well. During the day, in front of everybody, you two can stay glued to each other. On the day you will be married, Amina will move in with her husband. You are going to have to wait until Amina is eighteen, in four years. Do you see that is a long time to remain celibate given how high the temptations would be?"

Ben and Amina looked at each other and knew they had no further argument. They walked away a little sad but reassured each other their love and commitment to their vows are still strong. Blessing was happy to stay with Kathy, who had strongly attached herself to the little girl on the island and wanted to continue that relationship.[8]

Michael and Carrie, along with their parents, made the rounds to be sure all was well with each child. The children still had a little excitement left in them, given the recent hours. However, once the adrenaline finally left their bodies, most showed signs of weariness.

When they had completed the tucking in process, Carrie held on to her husband for several minutes

---

8 Despite her love for Kathy, Blessing would leave her bed and go to sleep with her mother for the first few months.

as they stood in the hallway. "I sure hope they all sleep well tonight. I could use the break." She kissed her husband and declared that she had to pee because the little one in her belly was parked on her bladder. Michael got out of her way and thanked both his and Carrie's parents before he walked to the master bedroom. When he got there, the baby and the next youngest were waiting for him. He tucked them into their cribs and settled on his bed, waiting for his wife.

When she arrived, he asked, "Want me to brush your hair tonight?"

"I'd love that," she replied. And they set about the room, creating the space for their nightly ritual. However, instead of the usual conversation, she fell fast asleep after a few strokes. He laid her down gently on the bed and settled behind her, wrapping his arms around her. Before he, too, fell asleep. Even with all the excitement of the day, sleep came easily for everybody.

The next morning, both families walked out to their respective driveways and started praying around the perimeter of the properties. They dedicated all that was within said perimeters to Jesus the Christ. As they met at the back of the properties, both families continued on to the other families' property. Finally, they met at the front and together, they declared their Amens.

"Have you heard from Derrick and Susan lately?" Michael asked his fellow Musketeer.

"To be honest, I haven't. I wonder what they are up to."

It was then that Ben received a phone call from the FBI.

TROUBLE WITH IMMIGRANTS

Ben was going to put on one of his suits when his mother, Jamie, stopped him and told him to wait a few minutes. She reached into the master bedroom closet and returned with the tuxedo he wore on the cruise sixteen years ago. "Wear this," she said.

Ben looked a little puzzled. She continued, "It will bring you closure to the events of that year. They need to see you looking at your greatest. Sanchez, Kapree, and O'Hara need to see it as well." Ben still didn't understand the sentiment. But knew better than to argue with his mother.

He dressed, kissed his wife, hugged each of his children, and left with his dad in the old pickup. His dad had to drive, as he didn't have a current license, which was something Ben knew he had to rectify as soon as possible.

Arriving at the federal building, which was still in reconstruction after the war, Ben was escorted to the FBI office. There his friends and subordinates were guarded by the federal marshals and immigration agents. As soon as Ben entered the room, his three friends were taken to three different rooms, and they were not allowed to speak to each other.

Ben was escorted to a fourth room with three windows so that each person in that particular room could observe any of the interrogations in the other three. Ben surmised that his friend's windows were one way, but they couldn't see the fourth room, only mirrors. However, all three friends knew where Ben would be.

Then the interrogation commenced.

In Room 1: Two agents were in the room with Sanchez. Sanchez had been cuffed to the table and was dressed in an orange jump suit. He had a look of confidence that belied his nervousness regarding the situation. Both agents wore tailored suits. One wore a full suit with a white shirt and black tie. He sat across from Sanchez while the other stood with his back to the door. That agent left his jacket at his desk and sported a blue shirt with blue tie and black trousers. Neither was carrying a firearm but still had tasers

"State your name, please," said the seated agent.

Without hesitation, Sanchez answered. "I am Geraldo Dela Vega Sanchez."

"Where are you from, Mr. Sanchez?"

"Originally, Venezuela. Lately, my family reside in Brazil."

"I didn't ask about your family. Right now, I couldn't care less about them," said the agent.

This last statement drew ire from Sanchez, and from Ben, who looked at the agents with him. His facial expression let them know that he was a little perturbed at the attitude of the interrogating agent.

"If you know about them, please," Sanchez asked, "are they safe?" He leaned forward in his chair, hoping to hear some word about them.

"I just told you," replied the agent, "they mean nothing to me at this time."

Sanchez sat back in his seat with resolute determination. He was not going to answer any more questions.

"So, Mr. Sanchez, what was your relationship with Mr. Kim Chan Lee?"

Mr. Sanchez gave no response, just a dead stare.

After a few minutes of waiting, the agent continued, "What was your job in the organization?"

Once again, Sanchez was silent.

The agent sat back in his chair, realizing he had committed a faux pas. "Alright, Mr. Sanchez, Your family is alive and well. They are right here, in Sioux Falls."

That perked up Sanchez. But he was puzzled as to why they would be in the United States, let alone Sioux Falls. He decided to remain silent to be sure the information was, indeed, fact.

The agent continued, "Ah! You don't believe me." He pointed to the door. "Maybe you will believe me now." The standing agent opened the door and there stood Sanchez's wife and children. All with noticeable deformities of the hands.

"*Mi Corazón,*"[9], cried Sanchez. His wife stood in surprise and covered her mouth. As she was trying to speak, the agent closed the door.

Ben looked over at Room 2, where agents were interviewing Kapree. "As you can see, we know about your foster family, Miss Kapree." The female agent across from her looked a little triumphant. "So, now are you going to be straight with us?"

Anger flitted across Kapree's face. "Trying to get to me through my family will only make me angry."

"Angry, huh?" The agent paused for a few seconds. "Were you angry with Mr. Kim when he used your family for leverage to attain your obedience?"

Without hesitation, and with venom spewing from her mouth, "You're damn right I was! Rather, I am *still* livid with him."

"Then why didn't you fight back or refuse to cooperate with his demands?"

---

9 *Mi Corazón* means "my sweetheart."

Tears started to fall down her cheeks. She took a
deep breath and answered, "I did. And every time
I disobeyed or argued back, I was given a video
of my mom, my baby brother, my little sister,
someone in my family having either their fingers
sawed off with a dull knife or a foot chopped off."
Kapree stopped and wept for a few minutes. The
agent waited, a cold expression on her face. "I
finally realized that I was going nowhere, and my
family would suffer if I continued to be defiant."
With that, Kapree fully broke down in tears and
answered no more questions.

"Do you think a little crying is going to get
sympathy from us?" the other agent, a male,
said while the lawyer continued to sob and look
down. The agent looked at his female partner
and shrugged his shoulders. After that, they went
outside into the hallway.

She looked back at the door and asked her
partner, "Do you think I went too far? Or is she
putting on a show? One would think she would
be a lot tougher after serving that madman
for so long."

"I think she is telling the truth," said the man. "Maybe she isn't so tough and is relieved that her servitude is finally over."

Once again, Ben turned to glare at the agents accompanying him. This time they registered his concern over the proceedings. "What would you do when faced with that level of tyranny?" Ben asked. "Your families being tortured like that to gain your obedience. What would *you* do?" The agents registered their discomfort at the thoughts.

One tried to be valiant and answered, "I sure wouldn't be a part of an organization that enslaves children and women."

Ben took one step toward the man and said, "Liar!"

At that, the agent said no more. Ben turned away from the agent towards O'Hara's room.

Room 3 was more of the same.

"My wife had her fingers cut off every time I even flinched a second in obeying Mr. Kim. My son had his right hand cut off with a *butter knife*," O'Hara said sadly, his eyes pleading with the interrogating agent to understand. "They made me watch the livestream because they knew how to push the right buttons for me." O'Hara paused to compose himself. "That is another reason why we kept meticulous records of everything and everybody that participated with Mr. Kim, including the victims. Mr. Kim told us to do it, but it was also our way of fighting. We knew that, when the time came, we would have all the evidence to destroy his empire. And, by God, with Mr. Bickles victory, we are doing just that!" He sat back in his seat with an attitude of satisfaction. O'Hara knew he had made his point.

The agent understood and stepped out with his partner, conferring with the other interrogating agents in the hallway. They all came to the same conclusion that, if they were being honest with themselves, they would also have done the bidding of such a tyrant if their families were treated the way Mr. Kim had done.

The lead agent decided to switch things up. "it's time for Mr. Bickles to answer some questions," he said. "Put him in Room 1 and take the three aliens to the viewing room." The other agents didn't understand why, but obeyed, shrugging their shoulders and making the switch. The lead FBI agent and the lead immigration agent went into the room with Ben. Sanchez, Kapree, and O'Hara looked on with some apprehension as they saw Ben. They knew he was about to face interrogation because of them.

The agent who interrogated Sanchez then told them, "Now we are going to see if you are to be charged for your crimes or receive your citizenship and be free." Pointing to Ben behind the glass he said, "It is all up to him."

In Room 1, Ben was annoyed on the inside, but he showed complete calm on the outside. He knew Allison was not there to help him remain calm so he had to do it himself. *That level of self-control is going to be difficult*, he thought. *But I need to gain some now. Lord, guide my tongue.*

"Now, Mr. Bickles, please state your full name," the lead FBI agent began.

"Benjamin Manfred Bickles."

"What do you do, Mr. Bickles?"

"Do?"

"I am sorry. Let me rephrase. What is your occupation?"

"Currently, I am CEO of Mr. Kim's empire."

"How did you attain that position?" the agent asked, chuckling. "Mr. Kim promote you?"

"In a sense, yes," Ben replied. "I killed him to attain that position." He looked to see if that admission struck a chord. It did.

"So, you are admitting to committing murder to become CEO?" The agent acted as if victory was his to claim.

"Nope," Ben corrected. "I defeated him in battle. He lost."

"Why did you fight each other?"

Ben leaned back in his chair and recited, in condensed form, what happened to him and his family over the last sixteen years. When he finished, he glared at the agent.

The agent was amazed at the whole story and decided to challenge some parts by declaring, "I think I should have twenty of my agents to attack you and see if you are telling the truth or not." Ben smiled. As did His friends behind the window. The agents with them were not so confident as their boss.

Ben responded, "Today? Or tomorrow?"

His confidence was a little disconcerting to the lead agent. "We don't need to go that far," he said.

Sanchez chuckled. "Damn right!"

Ben leaned forward, "Let's cut through the mud. This whole thing today is just about whether to charge my friends with crimes or grant them legal immigrant status. Their families are already here," Ben said. He changed the subject, poking the table top with his index finger. "Without their meticulous documentation, the destruction of the evil side of the empire will not be thwarted. I need my team, their contacts, and the information they have to finish the job. With their help, we have eliminated a child sex training ring, removed all of the associated pirate vessels and crews, and set forth the means for Japan to recover from the destruction Mr. Kim set in place there." Then he stood up and leaned on the table. "So, just release them, restore them with their families, grant them citizenship, and let us finish the work we need to do." After his statement, Ben just looked back and forth at the FBI agent and the immigration agent, waiting for their decision. He remained on his feet and, putting his hands on his hips, he paced the room over and over.

The lead agent took the immigration agent out of the room and conferred with those waiting in the hall. After about an hour, they came to a conclusion. The lead agent entered the room and walked Ben out into the main entrance of the building. There, Ben and the three families waited for what came next.

Soon, Kapree, O'Hara and Sanchez walked around the corner in their own clothes. They were free people. Ben understood the great weeping joy he heard as the three were reunited with their families for the first time in years. All three apologized to their family members for the injuries they suffered at the hands of Mr. Kim's men. After what seemed like an eternity, they finally noticed Ben standing alone with a smile on his face. Sanchez and O'Hara went to him, patting him on his back because his front had been taken over by a jubilant hug from Kapree.

The lead agent walked up to Ben, offering his hand. Ben took it, and, while they shook hands, the agent said, "Finish the job." Ben nodded and the agent walked back to his office.

As the group of friends walked down the steps to the sidewalk, Manfred Bickles stepped out of a bus at the curb. "Time for these folks to see their new homes," he said. "You are going to have to wait a couple of days to continue your work."

"Thanks, "Dad," Ben said as his friends and their families stepped into the bus.

"Mr. Bickles!" Sanchez said, beaming. "We be Americans!" A great cheer rang out as the bus rolled down the road.

PROVERBS 31 WOMAN

A couple of weeks passed as the families settled into their new homes. Michael Roberts and Benjamin Bickles decided, after conferring with their wives, that this particular Saturday, they would take all of their sons, including the babies, and head into the trees out of sight of the houses for some exploration and training. The mothers had their daughters for the rest of the day.

Kathy Roberts stood in front of her mother with hands on her hips looking rather perturbed.
"I want to go with Daddy and my brothers," she insisted.

Carrie controlled her mirth and replied, "Sorry, dear, but today is for the boys. Your father said that next Saturday, you girls will go with them into the trees and the boys will stay here with Mrs. Bickles and me."

Kathy stomped her foot and immediately regretted it as her mother's face showed her annoyance. "Tough, young lady. You will stay here with your sisters and the Bickles daughters today." Then with a shake of her index finger" Carrie said, "Now, you had better behave. You hear me?"

"Yes, Mama." Kathy said. She pouted and walked over to be with her sisters.

Carrie looked at her daughters, "Roberts girls, let us thank Mrs. Bickles and her daughters for allowing us to join them on their back patio for today's get together." All of the girls immediately thanked Allison, who graciously accepted their thanks before offering some lemonade for refreshment. "Now girls," Carrie said, "gather around and sit down as I read from the Book of Proverbs, Chapter thirty-one, beginning with verse ten." Some of the girls were excited to hear the words from the Bible. Others were not as enthusiastic. But all settled at Carrie's feet.

Allison Roberts had Kathy sit between her legs. She hugged her, usually delightful, little sister. "I told you we will get a chance to go to the woods next Saturday." Kathy tried to wiggle out of her sister's hug but soon stopped when she saw her mother looking right at her.

Roberta Bickles looked a little sullen but inwardly she was bouncing with joy. She relished hearing and reading the scriptures. However, she, for some reason, felt it necessary to act a little contrary. Nobody but Troy Roberts could figure her out. She loved that about him, but today he was with his father in the woods.

Carrie opened her Bible but first prayed, "Father God, open our hearts, minds, eyes, and ears to what You want us to know about You. Amen." She looked at the Bible and started reading verse ten.

> *[10] An excellent wife, who can find her?*
> *For her worth is far above jewels.*
> *[11] The heart of her husband trusts in her,*
> *And he will have no lack of gain.*
> *[12] She does him good and not evil*
> *All the days of her life.*

¹³ She looks for wool and linen,
And works with her hands in delight.
¹⁴ She is like merchant ships;
She brings her food from afar.
¹⁵ And she rises while it is still night
And gives food to her household,
And portions to her attendants.
¹⁶ She considers a field and buys it;
From her earnings she plants a vineyard.

At this point, Kathy, turned around to look at the woods where the boys went. Blessing, who had a hold of Kathy's arm, gently tugged on that arm to get her to face forward again. As always, Blessing's gentle nature won over the more exuberant Kathy.

¹⁷ She surrounds her waist with strength
And makes her arms strong.
¹⁸ She senses that her profit is good;
Her lamp does not go out at night.
¹⁹ She stretches out her hands to the distaff,
And her [NJ] *hands grasp the spindle.*
²⁰ She extends her hand to the poor,
And she stretches out her hands to the needy.
²¹ She is not afraid of the snow for her household,
For all her household are clothed with scarlet.

22 She makes coverings for herself;
Her clothing is fine linen and purple.
23 Her husband is known in the gates,
When he sits among the elders of the land.
24 She makes linen garments and sells them,
And [n]supplies belts to the tradesmen.
25 Strength and dignity are her clothing,
And she smiles at the future.
26 She opens her mouth in wisdom,
And the teaching of kindness is on her tongue.
27 She watches over the activities of her household,
And does not eat the bread of idleness.
28 Her children rise up and bless her;
Her husband also, *and he praises her,* saying:
29 "Many daughters have done nobly,
But you excel them all.
30 Charm is deceitful and beauty is vain,
But *a woman who fears the* LORD, *she shall*
be praised.
31 Give her the product of her hands,
And let her works praise her in the gates.

She laid her open Bible on her lap and looked at
the faces of the girls. "Our mothers used to read
these words to us every time the boys would go on
their survival outings. And I am so glad they did."

"How are we supposed to remember all of that?" Susan Roberts asked.

Allison Bickles, who stood behind them answered. "Only by repeating these moments and your own personal reading as you memorize the Word of God. That is how you will learn and remember."

"So, what does all of this mean?" Carrie Bickles asked.

"Glad you asked that. We will tell you." Looking around Carrie suddenly realized that all of the young faces were expectantly waiting for the answer. "First, let me say this. All of you are years away from being someone's wife. However, it will be better for you to know and understand your role as a wife while you are still young. What you may not know is that the boys are getting the same instruction from their fathers about how to behave as a husband. God gave different roles and rules for each one's behavior. What we are looking at today is for you, not the boys. Understand?" Most of the girls nodded, although the much younger ones didn't really understand. But they didn't want to be separated from the group.

"Before I answer the unasked question, I want
to shift our seating positions for the rest of this
time together. So, I would like all Roberts girls to
sit with their backs to their next older sister. The
oldest, which would be Allison, will sit between
my legs. That is, when I get down on the ground."
Because she was quite pregnant, Carrie took
some time to sit down and settle in. "Not the most
comfortable but we will manage."

Then, one by one, the Roberts girls sat between
the legs of their older sister. "Now, Bickles family,
you set up the same with your mother." Alison also
took a little time to sit as she was also pregnant.
Soon enough, all of her daughters were settled in
their places, just like the Roberts.

Carrie continued, "You will see that brushes and
combs were placed next to you. Now each of you,
pick up a brush and, with nice smooth strokes,
brush the hair of the girl in front of you." There
was some initial giggling when all of the girls
started to brush each other's hair. But soon they
all calmed down and started to quietly enjoy the
situation. "Let me take this a little bit further.
You older girls will understand what I am about

to say, but you little ones need to listen anyway. You are going to hear this many times as you grow older. God made Adam out of the ground. He then made Eve from Adam's rib. I believe that all girls are born with a rib that belongs to some boy out there. For example, I have my husband's missing rib." Pointing to her friend at the back, "And Allison has her husband's missing rib. So it is with all of you. You just have to trust God to get you two together in the future." Roberta shivered at the thought that she has Troy's missing rib. She, then, smiled at the idea.

Susan Bickles asked the question that was on several of their minds. "Why did God make us boys and girls?"

Carrie took a few seconds to respond. "I don't have the exact answer," she began, "but this is what I understand. God made Adam incomplete, which is why he made Eve. It is said that woman is the completion of man. That when a man and a woman come together in marriage, they complete a part of God's creation, forming a bond that represents of a part of God, Himself. However, each couple has a distinctly different bond and

reflects a different part of God. For example,"
She points to the other Princess, "My relationship
with my husband is glued together by God, just as
Allison's is with her husband. Those relationships
are different in certain ways, but we still reflect
an image of some part of God. We complete His
creation. That is only if we seek His guidance in
our respective marriages." She looked to Allison
for some acknowledgment that she was on the
right trail. Allison just smiled and nodded.

Amina spoke up next. "So, Red Beard and I had
better seek God's ok first before we get married?
I just assumed that since we connected as tight as
we have it was a done deal."

"If you haven't talked to God about that," Carrie
said, "then you had better start now." With a wink,
she added, "I have a feeling He has already given
His blessing. But you two had better guarantee it
first." Amina nodded. There was a little murmuring
from the young ladies because everybody assumed
Amina and Ben Roberts were a given.

The question-and-answer session continued as
the girls enjoyed having their hair brushed. Many

times, both Carrie and Allison had to answer certain questions with, "I don't know."

* * * * *

As the boys entered the wooded area behind the houses, the Roberts gang ran and started climbing the trees as they used to on the island barely three months ago. The Bickles boys were quite hesitant to follow the other boys. Everything was still so new. This world was scary as they were still conditioned to the small apartment. They wanted to do more but were still hesitant.

"Dad," Michael Bickles, the eldest son, had what he believed to be a serious question. "Is this ok?"

"Yes, Michael," Ben replied, "but not right now. Right now, we need to sit over here in this little clearing."

"That's right," Michael Roberts. "BOYS!" he called out. "Climb on down and come here. Time for a lesson." The Roberts boys were a little disappointed that their fun was cut off and reluctantly climbed down as ordered. One by one, they came to stand beside their father.

When everyone was gathered, Michael declared, "Today will start new lessons for you. Sometimes we will have those lessons together with your sisters. Sometimes it'll be just the boys. Like today. Sometimes there will be small groups that are closer in age. We may do things individually. Sometimes with just us men. Or with your mothers. And, sometimes, with your grandparents." He looked around to make sure he had their attention. For the most part, he did. Only the very youngest ones seemed inattentive. But that was expected. "Now, the Bickles family had the benefit of having the Bible read to them." Michael and Derrick Bickles nodded in agreement. "However, my Roberts clan didn't have the Bible available. They were only able to understand what God has in store for them by the lessons their mother and I could remember from what we memorized in our youth. So, Bickles," he pointed to the appropriate faces, "have patience with us as we read from the Bible for the first time since coming here." He placed his hand on his fellow Musketeer's shoulder. "Ready?"

"Ready as we will ever be," Ben admitted. "One more thing, when we are in a group like this, we will only be looking at what God wants us men to be. We won't be looking at anything that would be for the girls only. And we will answer any questions to the best of our ability. Ok?"

Only nods were given. Some did it enthusiastically, others were not quite so sure.

Ben wanted to begin with a word of prayer. "Boys, we should never read or speak God's word without first seeking Him in prayer." Everybody clasped their hands together and bowed their heads. The younger ones looked around to see if everybody else was doing the same thing.

"Lord God, Heavenly Father, and Jesus the Christ," Ben prayed, "around us are young ears that are willing to hear Your Word. Open our hearts, minds, eyes, and ears to the understanding of what You want us to know about You. We thank You for having blessed us with the written Word. May we recognize Your blessings in it. Thank You. We come in the name that has all power and authority, Jesus. Amen." When Ben looked up, he saw he had their complete and undivided attention. He began speaking. "From the Book of Proverbs, I will be reading from chapter three:

My son, do not forget my teaching,

but keep my commands in your heart,

2 for they will prolong your life many years

and bring you peace and prosperity.

3 Let love and faithfulness never leave you;

bind them around your neck,

write them on the tablet of your heart.

4 Then you will win favor and a good name

in the sight of God and man.

5 Trust in the Lord with all your heart

and lean not on your own understanding;

6 in all your ways submit to him,

and he will make your paths straight. [a]

7 Do not be wise in your own eyes;

fear the Lord and shun evil.

8 This will bring health to your body

and nourishment to your bones.

9 Honor the Lord with your wealth,

with the first fruits of all your crops;

10 then your barns will be filled to overflowing,

and your vats will brim over with new wine.

11 My son, do not despise the Lord's discipline,

and do not resent his rebuke,
[12] because the Lord disciplines those he loves,
as a father the son he delights in."

This brought a little frown from most of the boys. Discipline was not what they wanted to hear. Ben looked up from his reading and understood their reactions. He had the same when he was a boy. He continued,

> *[13] Blessed are those who find wisdom,*
> *those who gain understanding,*
> *[14] for she is more profitable than silver*
> *and yields better returns than gold.*
> *[15] She is more precious than rubies;*
> *nothing you desire can compare with her.*
> *[16] Long life is in her right hand;*
> *in her left hand are riches and honor.*
> *[17] Her ways are pleasant ways,*
> *and all her paths are peace.*
> *[18] She is a tree of life to those who take hold of her;*
> *those who hold her fast will be blessed.*

Some of the boys started to squirm and get a little restless. One snap from Michael's fingers and all had settled down. Ben continued,

¹⁹*By wisdom the* LORD *laid the earth's
foundations,
by understanding he set the heavens in place;*
²⁰ *by his knowledge the watery depths
were divided,
and the clouds let drop the dew.*
²¹ *My son, do not let wisdom and understanding
out of your sight,
preserve sound judgment and discretion;*
²² *they will be life for you,
an ornament to grace your neck.*
²³ *Then you will go on your way in safety,
and your foot will not stumble.*
²⁴ *When you lie down, you will not be afraid;
when you lie down, your sleep will be sweet.*
²⁵ *Have no fear of sudden disaster
or of the ruin that overtakes the wicked,*
²⁶ *for the* LORD *will be at your side
and will keep your foot from being snared.*
²⁷ *Do not withhold good from those to whom
it is due,
when it is in your power to act.*
²⁸ *Do not say to your neighbor,
'Come back tomorrow and I'll give it to you'—
when you already have it with you.*
²⁹ *Do not plot harm against your neighbor,*

who lives trustfully near you.
[30] Do not accuse anyone for no reason—
when they have done you no harm.
[31] Do not envy the violent
or choose any of their ways.

This caused a little stirring with the Bickles boys because of the life they had in the apartment so far away.

[32] For the LORD detests the perverse
but takes the upright into his confidence.
[33] The LORD's curse is on the house of the wicked,
but he blesses the home of the righteous.
[34] He mocks proud mockers
but shows favor to the humble and oppressed.
[35] The wise inherit honor,
but fools get only shame.

Ben looked up and saw confusion written across several faces. Some were looking down, trying to digest everything they had just heard.

Ben Roberts was the first to speak. "Those are interesting words," he said, "but how are we to understand all of that?" The Roberts boys all agreed with their older brother. The Bickles boys had heard those words before, but they were also a little overwhelmed, too.

Ben Bickles responded, "Truth be known, reading God's word like this is just to get them into your heads. We fully expect that you will have questions. And we will endeavor to help you understand. Just be aware, we are learning right along with you."

"How are we supposed to trust you if you are learning as well?" Troy Roberts asked.

"The only things we have on you are our life experiences and all the years we studied God's word," his father replied. "The one thing all of you need to know is that we are *always* learning about God's new things every day. And that will go on until the day we die. Once we get to Heaven, our learning will increase all the more, as it will take an eternity for God to reveal Himself! For now, your parents and grandparents will share what we know."

Ben added, "Someday, when you are older, you may teach us something new about God. So, let's have a discussion about what was read today."

At first, only Troy asked questions. Both Michael and Ben were amazed at his enthusiasm. But slowly, others chimed in. Eventually, it became a lively affair as both children and parents loved and learned.

Finally, Richard Roberts chimed in. "Why are the girls on the porch with our moms and we boys are here? Wouldn't all that we learned today be good for them as well?"

Michael was prepared for this question. "There are some things that are meant for men," he answered, "and some things meant for women. We don't want you to be concerned about what the women are supposed to do. You are to be concerned what you men are supposed to do according to God's word. Likewise, the girls are to be concerned about being godly women. Separate courses. Same goal. Now," Ben said, "all of you will be taught by your mothers next week, and the girls will be here with us."

"Why?" Derrick Bickles blurted out.

"Your mothers will teach you how girls are to be treated and we will be teaching the girls what to expect from the boys," Ben explained.

"Why?" Derrick asked, clearly unsatisfied. "Girls are just girls. Why do they have to be treated so special?" That caused a bit of a murmur among the other boys.

Michael answered that one. "Your mother was a girl once," he told him. That quieted the boys down. "Does your father treat your mother like you treat your sisters? Or does he treat her different?"

Derrick Roberts thought about it for a few seconds. "More like his wife. Not like a sister."

"Exactly. That is why you will have those lessons next week. However, to give you all a jump start on that, let's sneak up to the edge of the tree line and observe the girls. Quietly, now." With that, the Roberts boys walked to the tree line that overlooked the back yards of the Bickles Mansion. The Bickles boys, with their lack of training, made quite the noise following their new, much quieter friends. Luckily, they didn't get caught. As they peered through the branches, they noticed the girls were happily having their hair brushed as they talked and sang songs.

"Girls are weird," Michael Bickles stated.

"Yeah. But I wouldn't want them any other way," Ben Roberts said with a smile as he watched Amina singing with the other girls. She was brushing Allison Roberts hair while her future mother-in-law brushed hers. His answer quieted the other boys as they watched.

Switch it Up

The following Saturday, the girls traipsed off into the woods with their dads. As soon as they crossed the tree line, the Roberts girls were off, running and climbing the trees, just like their brothers did the week before. The Bickles girls were quite reticent to join the fray, just as their brothers had been.

That day, the boys crowded into the Bickles kitchen. Allison and Carrie had prepared a special treat for them. "Boys," Allison said, "let's start with prayer." She waited for the boys to fold their hands and bow their heads before she started. "Heavenly Father, wash us with Your love within Your loving arms. Overflow us with Your understanding for today's lesson. May these boys grow to be kind, loving, caring, protective men. May they reflect You in their relationships with the girls they meet in their lives. We pray this in the saving grace of the name of Jesus the Christ. Amen." The boys followed with their own Amens. "Now, we have a little surprise for all of you." She motioned to the living room. "Ok, moms, come on out."

Into the crowded kitchen came Kristy Roberts, Jamie Bickles, Petra Samuels, and Binh Ver Hoeven. The children's grandmothers had the biggest smiles any grandmother was legally allowed to have. (There are no such legal restrictions).

The children clamored to get a hug from their respective grandmothers.

Once the commotion settled down, Carrie spoke, "Ok, now. Boys who are seven years old or younger will go with your grandmothers over to the Roberts house. There, they have some fun things for you to do while we talk with your older brothers."

The younger boys were ecstatic to join their grandmothers, whom they had only recently met and fell in love with. Each grandmother held a baby or a yearling as they ushered the rest out the front door, enjoying the controlled chaos as they left the Bickles house.

"I'll make sure they get there in good shape, Mama." Ben Roberts stated as he opened the door and watched the parade move towards his house some fifty yards away. He closed the front door after he saw them enter the other house. "All accounted for are safe at home." He reported to his mother.

"Thank, you, Son." Carrie smiled and then turned to the other boys in the less crowded kitchen. "Today you are going to learn a few things on how girls should be treated. And being girls, Allison and I are offering some tips and advice that will help along as you grow up and meet girls."

"Mom," blurted William Roberts, "You are not a girl. You're a *mom*." This caused a little chuckle from the other boys.

Carrie feigned insult and placed her hands on her hips. "We are *so* girls! We were just like your sisters when we were younger." Allison couldn't help but giggle.

Richard Roberts chimed in, "No, Mom." He couldn't hold his mirth, "That was when you were little. Now you are just Mom."

"Just Mom, huh? I'll show you—"

Allison interrupted, "We were younger girls back then. Sure. But we are still girls at heart. We just added being wives and mothers to our list." There was a moment of laughter and soon all had settled down. Richard had a glint in his eye, ready to pounce on anything to add to the argument.

"Now then," Carrie said, wagging her index finger at her character of a son, "let's start with some scripture to get a foundation for today's teaching time. Just so you know," she stated, "all of you will eventually be attending the local schools once you are caught up on the curriculum." That sent a little murmur among the boys. Allison winked. "You will be meeting other boys and girls who were raised in the city, not on an island or a simple apartment. You will need to know, from a girl's perspective, how to properly treat her. We are only going to offer a bit of that information here. Your fathers will get into greater detail as you grow up. Now, let's read from the book of Genesis, chapter three, verse sixteen: 'I will make your pains in childbearing very severe; Your desire will be for your husband, and he will rule over you.'"

Derrick Bickles caught the last words, "Rule over them? That doesn't sound like what Dad does with Mom." All eyes went directly to his mother.

"Well, to be truthful, he does rule over me. But not like a king, who rules over a territory," she said, pausing to gather her thoughts and then looked at Carrie. "Do you have that other scripture that will help us explain this?"

"Yes," Answered her fellow Princess, "it is in Ephesians, chapter five verses twenty-two through thirty-three." She began to read,

> [22] *Wives, be subject to your own husbands, as to the Lord.* [23] *For the husband is the head of the wife, as Christ also is the head of the church, He Himself being the Savior of the body.* [24] *But as the church is subject to Christ, so also the wives ought to be to their husbands in everything.* [25] *Husbands, love your wives, just as Christ also loved the church and gave Himself up for her,* [26] *so that He might sanctify her, having cleansed her by the washing of water with the word,* [27] *that He might present to Himself the church in all her glory, having no spot or wrinkle or any such thing; but that she would be holy and blameless.* [28] *So husbands ought also to love their own wives as their own bodies. He who loves his own wife loves himself;* [29] *for no one ever hated his own flesh, but nourishes and cherishes it, just as Christ also does the church,* [30] *because we are members of His body.* [31] *For this reason a man shall leave his father and mother and shall be joined to his wife, and the two shall become one flesh.* [32] *This mystery is great; but I am speaking with reference*

to Christ and the church. [33] Nevertheless, each individual among you also is to love his own wife even as himself, and the wife must see to it that she respects her husband.

Allison looked at the boys, "Does that clear it up for you?" A bunch of nodding followed. "Note, the husband is commanded to love his wife, but the wife is only commanded to respect her husband."

Michael Bickles spoke up, "Why is that? Shouldn't the wife be required to love her husband?"

Allison smiled, as she was expecting this question. "If you remember, back in Genesis that God said that the woman's heart would be for her husband?" She saw some lights turn on over a few of their heads. "That is automatic for a girl, which is where we mothers are going to tell you this." Both mothers planted a serious look on their faces. "You boys are to never, and I MEAN NEVER take advantage of that love with girls you are not married to! Is that clear?" she asked.

A series of, "Yes, Mama," "echoed around the room.

"Good. Now how are you to treat a girl that is not your sister?"

William immediately answered with enthusiasm, "I know! Just like Ben treats Amina. Am I right?"

His mother responded, "That is true. Ben has been a shining example in that category but," she waved her hand around the room, "the Bickles boys haven't seen how Ben treats her. So, how about you explain it to them?"

William suddenly grew shy and struggled to answer. Richard helped him along. "He protects her," Richard said. "He laughs with her. He talks to her." A little under his breath, he added, "a little too much if you ask me." He quickly regained his composure and said, "He treats her like she is the most precious thing on earth."

This caused Ben to blush crimson but to also respond, "She absolutely is."

"There," Carrie called out, "That is exactly the way you should look at girls. Precious. They are a God given gift to be cherished."

"That's how Daddy is with Mama." Robert Bickles
said quietly. "Daddy always talks to Mama lots."
He giggled. "Sometimes they laugh a lot, too.
And every night he would brush her hair in the
other room."

"That is something our friends had been doing
since we were twelve years old," Carrie said. "We
talked a lot during those times, though we were
never together alone. And our parents always
knew where we were. Sometimes they would
sit on the porch with us and just listen to our
conversations." She raised her finger for emphasis.
"That was the type of intimacy we girls really
loved. And still do. Watch your fathers. They are
the best examples for you for how to treat girls."
After a short pause she stated, "Now that you are
catching on, there are other ways to properly treat
a girl. All girls love to be told they are beautiful.
And they also want some help with daily chores to
show them that they are loved. That is where we
mothers are going to teach you. With us, you're
going to learn how to do just that." She pointed
to the stove. "First, some of you will learn how
to cook and the rest will learn how to help keep
the house clean. Now," she said looking around,

"boys eleven and under will go with me and we will learn to make the beds, do some laundry and clean up the rooms. The rest will stay here and learn how to make a meal that we will all enjoy later this evening. Let's split up." Carrie turned to her friend. "Allison, happy cooking," she said with a wink and lead the younger boys off to the bedroom wing of the house.

After Carrie's group had left, Allison waved her hands around the kitchen. "Well boys," she declared, "let's begin."

* * * * *

While the boys were gathered in the kitchen, their sisters were busy exploring the woods until they were called by their fathers to gather in the small clearing. From behind some of the larger trees came four men: Manfred Bickles, Troy Roberts, Bradley Samuels, and Christian Ver Hoeven, the children's grandfathers. The noise that followed was the girls running to them. Ben loved it, though he had to admit, it was deafening. Like their brothers did with the grandmothers, they'd fallen in love with them already, despite only knowing them a short while. Once all the hugs were passed around, the fathers called their daughters back to them.

"All girls seven years and younger," Michael Roberts called out. The little girls all perked up at being recognized. "You are going to go with your grandfathers. They will take you to the Roberts house for some wonderful fun. The rest of you, stay with us."

After they all had left, Ben started the meeting. "Girls, today's lesson is about what to expect from the boys you are about to meet when you get to the schools in the area."

"We know what to expect," stated Roberta Bickles. "We have seen how you treat Mama, and we want that, too. It is obvious how much you love her, especially when you comb her hair."

Ben was speechless.

Susan Roberts spoke up, "We love you too Daddy!"

Before Michael could respond Carrie Bickles asked Susan Roberts, "Your dad combs your mom's hair, too?"

"Oh, yeah," she replied. "They thought we were sleeping but we saw everything."

"That is what happened with us, too," Susan Bickles added.

"Did they talk all the time?" Kathy Roberts asked.

"It was almost nonstop!" added Roberta Bickles. Both Ben and Michael tried to regain control. But it was all for naught.

"I want my boyfriend to do that to me." That was from Whitney Bickles.

"I do too," Allison Roberts declared. "But I don't want just any boy. He had better be strong."

"Do you really think there are boys like that here?" Roberta asked. "Because other than Troy, I haven't seen any."

"In your case," Amina chimed in, "no one will ever take the place of Troy. Just like my Red Beard."

"Red Beard. Red Beard. That's all you think about. Nobody stacks up to him," Carrie Bickles said, mocking.

"Well, *I* can say that Derrick Roberts is one fine man as far as I am concerned," Susan Bickles admitted.

"That goes the same for my Robert," Whitney's declared.

"All I care is that the boy for me can brush my hair like Roberta did last week." Teresa Bickles said, finally finding her chance to speak up. At that, all of the girls started talking at the same time. Michael and Ben gave up trying to figure out who was talking about who.

Finally, after several minutes Ben heard, "Ain't that right, Daddy?" Dead silence followed as all of the girls looked at him for an answer.

"I am sorry. What was the question?" Ben asked. He didn't know who asked what about what. As the young ladies talked, he remembered when the princesses would just jabber on. But this was something else.

"I said, our dads will make sure we don't get involved with the wrong boy. Right?" Roberta announced.

It took a few seconds for Ben to recover but he finally answered, "That, all of you can count on. Just make sure you are always on your best behavior."

"And be careful how you dress," Michael stated. "You Bickles spent almost all your life naked, and you Roberts only had a skirt and bra. Around here, you will need to be covered up more than you are used to. Remember what we said about Genesis three. That is the foundation for why we have to wear clothes. So, be feminine but be covered. Some of those boys around here will know what you went through. They will try to act good, only to eventually cause you to sin. So," he clapped his hands, "the rest of the time we will continue your self-defense training. Get up and prepare yourselves." Michael wasn't going to give them a chance to jabber on again.

Ben was also relieved that the situation was back to some semblance of order.

That evening, while both men were brushing their wives' hair in their own homes, the ladies couldn't help but have a serious giggle fit as their husbands relayed the day's activities.

YOUR OTHER CHILDREN

A couple of months later, after settling into their new environment, Ben and Allison were taken back to the high school gym. Their parents, brothers and sisters stayed to watch over the children who were unhappy at first but soon enjoyed playing with their cousins again since they had free rein over the two extra-large properties.

At the gym, Ben found himself among most of the women with whom he was forced to commit adultery. They had brought their families, much to his delight. It took some time to get them all together as he wanted to meet them all at the same time. The women were wholeheartedly glad to see him and Allison alive, although some had a bit of trepidation about this meeting. A few of the men who came seemed a little surly. But Ben was prepared for this meeting. He was grateful to see Amina, Javier, Torrance, Nelson, and Cassondra there, along with their families. Blessing was there with her mother and grandmother.

"Ladies and gentlemen," Ben started to speak. One man snorted but Ben didn't stop. "This meeting is not ideal. Our circumstances weren't ideal." The same man snorted again. Silence then prevailed. "Please allow me to fill in some details the ladies don't know.'" He gestured about the room. "As you can see, Teresa is not here. She was the last girl. She cried as she told us that she was unable to get pregnant. She had been scheduled to have surgery a month after we were kidnapped because she knew what was in store for her."

A murmur started throughout the room, speculating what she might have known. Most were right. "I tried to convince Mr. Kim, "'Master,'" as you knew him to let her go or something. I was hoping he would have mercy on her. Teresa went out, fully expecting the same treatment that Roberta got. When she was in position, a huge man came up behind her and killed her." He paused while the reactions subsided. "I lost it. It took some time before Allison could straighten me out. But after that, I started to recite scripture and preach. It had little effect at first. But then the battle got to the final twenty-five men, the ones that participated in Roberta's death were there. I asked them, 'Who do you say Jesus is?' Eight of the men dropped their weapons and were about to confess when Master killed them. I know they are with Jesus now. Master failed." There was another round of murmurs, but he continued. "Three more dropped their weapons and were about to confess. Master killed them as well. The rest lost their will to fight but they tried. I didn't have mercy on them. After that, my fight with Master lasted maybe fifteen minutes. It was a tough fight, but I did not personally kill him. I gave him an opportunity to repent and receive Jesus, but he held onto his evil. The crocs in that pit took care of that. The huge man who killed Teresa followed him shortly thereafter." Ben had to wipe away some tears.

"Men, those of you who the children lovingly call Daddy, I will not take them from you. I am just their biological father." To Ben, a good number of the men and women seemed to sag with an immediate sense of relief when he said that. "I'd like to discuss options for me to have time with my children. So, with that being said, we will start the individual meetings."

The first one up was Donna. She had no husband. However, she had five children. She walked up and hugged Ben. Allison silently approved as she understood Donna's feelings.

Donna then sat in the chair at the table and started to tell Ben what happened to her. "I suffered a miscarriage." Ben sat quietly and just listened. "Master's men came to verify that I didn't abort the child. Thankfully, they were satisfied and left me alone. Five of the girls heard about my situation and offered to let me adopt their children, and I said 'yes.' These five are your children." She swept her arm toward the five teenagers standing behind her. "I never married because I wanted these children to call you Daddy." This surprised Ben. "I was hoping that I could live with you and Allison." She immediately raised her hands in defense. "Not to be your mistress or anything! I was hoping to help take care of your children, too, Allison. I don't want Ben for me. I just want him to be called Daddy by his children."

"Donna, we need to talk," said Allison as she led Donna away for a more private discussion. Ben greeted each child and received hugs from them all. As Donna hoped, each one called him "Daddy." Ben's heart swelled with a love he didn't know he had. And the relief he felt was a little surprising for him.

Next up came Sharon and her husband, who shook hands with Ben. "Sharon explained everything about the kidnapping and the killings. Thank you for protecting her."

Ben nodded. And then pointing to the teenager beside them, "Is this her?"

"Yes. This is Nancy. She knows about you," the man said nervously.

Ben noticed the girl tightly hugging his arm. "She calls you Daddy?"

"Yes."

"Excellent. Then it shall stay that way. However, I would like to arrange one weekend a month when she will stay with us and get to know her other brothers and sisters. Also, we will come up with a plan for financial compensation for her upbringing. Are you amenable to that?"

All three nodded in agreement. Nancy walked up and hugged Ben. "Thank you for protecting my mom, Father." Tears rolled down Ben's face as she kissed him on the cheek and went back to her parents. Ben hugged Sharon and her husband and thanked them for taking excellent care of his daughter. Allison returned in time to thank them as well.

Sharon decided now was the best time. "Ben, we," she waved around the room towards the other women, "got together to decide who will speak for the group. It was decided that the first one to speak with you would share some news about our lives. Donna should have done it," she said, indicating her, "but she told me she couldn't because she didn't think she would be able to get through it. So, since I was next, it fell upon me to speak." She paused while gathering her courage. It was clear she did not like speaking in public. "We returned home young pregnant teenagers with an umbrella of uncertainty always hanging over us. We were told that, should you lose, we would be reclaimed by Master and our children would be his as well." She swallowed the emotions trying to well up inside her. "We tried to live our lives as best as possible, knowing we were watched. We found good men who love our children as their own." She smiled at her husband, who squeezed her hand. "That umbrella of uncertainty remained until able six months ago when we all felt a heavy burden lift from us. We all got in touch with each other immediately. After talking about it, we agreed that you must have been victorious. That day, we praised God for it. You have no idea the elation we felt when heard you'd come home. Our husbands rejoiced with us but were concerned

about what you would do with your children. All
of us feel great relief about your attitude today.
Thank you, Ben. Thank you!"

She walked up and hugged him for all she was
worth, stepped back and rejoined her family.
There was an immediate explosion of applause
from the group.

Ben was at a loss for words for a long moment.
But then he said, "I did not know until the day I
defeated Mr. Kim that any of you were even alive.
I thank God for each and every one of you being
here today. Thank *you*." Allison returned in time to
thank them as well.

"Donna will be staying with us from now on as
a nanny," Allison told Ben. "She just wants the
children to have their real daddy. Are you ok with
that?" Ben thought for a bit, then he nodded and
hugged his wife.

Next up was Cathy. She was a mousey looking
woman with horribly unkempt brown hair and,
dirty, torn clothing. She was sporting a bruise on
her left cheek and eye. Her posture was totally

submissive. Next to her was what appeared to be her husband. His black hair was neatly combed, his clothing properly ironed, and he wore polished shoes. *Something wasn't right*, Ben thought.

"Hello Cathy. Where is the child?"

"*The child* is at home," growled the man. "Now are we going to get money or not?"

Ben was instantly annoyed. "The deal was I would meet the children today. Why isn't the child here?"

"None of your business," the man said as he grabbed Cathy by the back of her neck. Let's go

The man soon felt a powerful hand on his wrist as he was thrown to the ground. He howled in pain and started to throw curses at Ben. Wrong thing to do! Most of the people were amazed at the speed and ferocity of Ben's response.

"I spent years killing men protecting these women and children," Ben said. "I can see I am not finished. Cathy, what is your child's name?"

"Don't you dare tell him!" The man spat. Ben moved, and he howled again as he felt his shoulder separate from the socket.

"Allison, talk to Cathy. If the police need to go to their house, then send them. I have a feeling he is abusing that child."

As Allison was about to take Cathy away for a private talk, Cathy said, "Henry. His name is Henry. And my husband has been beating both me and Henry. I'm sorry. I'm so sorry." Allison wrapped her arms around Cathy as they separated themselves from the situation with Ben and Cathy's husband, who was spewing curses at everybody. The vilest curses were meant for Ben and Cathy. The other parents nearby moved, protecting their children from the noise.

The police arrived in about fifteen minutes and, after hearing Cathy's story, they immediately dispatched deputies who found Henry. Ben was right. He had been badly beaten and chained to a pole in the basement.

Ben told the police, "You get this piece of garbage away from me before I throw him to the crocs!"

The police removed the man instantly. Ben calmed himself down enough to not appear threatening. Soon after the man was taken away, the other parents and children slowly began settling down. The men in the gym realized how much Ben truly cared for the women and children, even now.

"When all is well, Cathy, you and Henry are welcome to stay with us," Allison said. "There he can grow up with his brothers and sisters. You can work for us and we will make sure have a lot of time with your son. Are you ok with that?" Allison calmly asked. Cathy cried with relief and embarrassment. She nodded and hugged Allison and Ben, then left with the police.

Ben took a few minutes to calm himself a bit more. "Any other man abusing my children had better leave NOW!"

No one left.

"I don't want you to fear me because of this situation," Ben said. "All I want is for my children to be happy and content. So, can we move on to the next child?"

The rest of the interviews went like Sharon's. Four other women refused to marry for the same reason as Donna. They were hired by Allison, too. Ben was mostly pleased with each of the men the women married. But Miriam's husband was setting off alarms. His posture suggested that he wasn't any too happy about the situation. He would not look Ben in the eye, but aside from that, Ben couldn't pin down the reason.

One couple surprised Ben. As they sat down with their daughter, the man introduced himself. "Hi, Ben. Do you remember me?"

Ben nodded. "I sure do. Alexander Reef. I do believe we have some unfinished business."

The man grinned. "We sure do. As you may have remembered, our last meeting caused quite the stir in the classroom the day before all of you went missing." Ben was uncertain why his classmate would be smiling at that remembrance. "That was the day you caught me trying to be a bit forceful with Corral here," He pointed to the woman next to him. "You thought I was trying to bully her and, as was your way, tried to stop the bullying by grabbing my hair and forcing my head back." Ben grimaced at the memory. "That was when Corral finally spoke up and told you that you had the situation all wrong."

"I do remember." Ben admitted.

"Do you remember her words? She told you that I was just trying to get her to talk to me." He held Corral's hand. "She knew how I felt about her, and I knew how she felt about me. But she was so shy that she wouldn't say anything. I just wanted to talk with her and not just to her." Corral squeezed his hand. "It was at that moment she started to talk, and I am so grateful that you were instrumental for getting her out of her shell." Alexander gathered his thoughts as the emotions of the next words hit him. "The next day, all of you went missing. I couldn't tell her that I wanted to marry her because of that." His daughter placed her hands on her daddy's shoulder. "It wasn't until she returned that I could share my relief with her. That is, until she cried and said she was pregnant with *your* child." Ben saw no anger in the man's face. "She explained the situation and I told her that I would love her anyway. And I would love the child in her belly. It didn't matter to me who the father was. I was going to accept that child and love her as my own flesh." Alex shed a tear at that moment. "And look at our little one. She is beautiful, smart, strong, and she is my daughter."

Ben stood and had Alex stand. "I never had the chance to tell you how sorry I was for my actions that day." He put out his hand and the men shook hands. "I am truly sorry."

Corral spoke up. "Truth be known, Ben, we consider you to be our cupid. If you hadn't reacted as you did, I might still be silent in my shyness. I was finally able to express myself from the bottom of my heart." Then she giggled. "Do you remember my maiden name?"

Ben had to think for a few seconds. "Gables? Right? Corral Gables."

"Yes!" Her giggling rose a few notches, "So I was once known as Corral Gables and now I am Corral Reef."

Ben was a couple of seconds slow, but he finally caught on and roared out his laughter. The girl behind Alex walked around and hugged Ben. "I am so glad to you for helping my mom and dad get together. Thank you, Father." She kissed him on the cheek and returned to Alex's side.

"May I give you a suggestion?" Ben asked with a smile.

Alex was caught off guard with the request but recovered quickly and answered, "Sure."

Ben leaned toward him a little and said, "Brush your wife's hair every night before you go to bed. And have a conversation with her as you do. I guarantee, you won't regret it."

Alex sat for a few minutes, considering the strange request. Then his face lit up the whole room. "Hair brushing. Conversation. Why didn't I think of that?" Then he said to his wife, "We will start tonight." Corral giggled at the thought, instantly loving the idea.

As the mood had lightened, everybody had a better feeling about the situation. Ben was amazed that all the children were given the last name Bickles. Through the interviews, he found out just how much he was loved and appreciated by the women for protecting them even though he was forced to impregnate them. They were alive and well and their children were, too.

In the coming months visitation went smoothly. Ben visited Henry in the hospital and the boy had started warming up to him. However, he had to have his leg amputated because of the beatings.

Ben told Allison one night, "This boy needs to see love. True love. Maybe Richard Roberts could befriend him. And be an example for him. I will have to bring that up to Michael and Carrie. By the way Carrie is getting close to delivering the next Roberts into the world. Getting exciting."

Michael and Carrie did agree that Richard would be an excellent example and friend for Henry.

When asked about his feelings on the matter, Richard was as exuberant as ever. "Really? How soon can I see him?"

The next day, Richard was introduced to a new friend. Henry was not yet open to new relationships because of his torment but was soon enjoying the laughter and jokes Richard tossed out.

"Just think, Henry," Richard told him, "between the two of us we can still run a two-legged race together!"

"Maybe we can when I get out of the hospital." Henry said dryly.

"Oh, don't worry about the new leg they will make for you." Richard came in close to talk softly in Henry's ear, "They make the craziest sounds." After that, Richard winked. Henry looked into his new friend's eyes and finally laughed.

Ben spoke quietly to his friends standing beside him, "All is going to be well." Allison hugged her man, laying her head on his chest.

*The day after that meeting Ben, Allison, Michael, and Carrie got a message to meet at the high school gym yet again. The gym was getting to be their home away from home lately. They were also asked to bring their kids, which they did. They were grateful for the bus, but realized they would need another.

After being at the gym for about an hour, they heard some rustling behind the north door. All four sucked in their breath when they saw who walked in.

Derrick Henderson and Susan Schulte-Dodge walked in with three children. After much hugging and screaming, introductions were made to the children of all families.

Carrie Roberts made the declaration, "Finally! The original Musketeers and Princesses are together again."

Michael considered the small number of children Derrick and Susan had with them. "Is this all you have for children? One would think that in all these years, you two would have quite a gaggle of kids."

Derrick held Susan's hand. "We aren't married yet," he said feeling a pang of guilt when he admitted it. "Let me tell you what happened after Ben and Allison went missing," he began. "I am ashamed of my part of that story. But just so you know, I am extremely grateful for God's guidance through the years to get us to this point."

The Bickles and the Roberts were all ears.

ABOUT THE AUTHOR

I was born in Texas when my dad was in flight school for the Air Force. We moved to Sioux Falls, South Dakota, when I was only six months old and stayed there since. I graduated from Washington High School in 1975 and married my first and only wife in 1979. We moved to Brandon, South Dakota, where we raised our three children, Jeremy, Heather, and Daniel. Two of my children have blessed me with seven grandchildren, who have blessed me with my three great-grandchildren.

I worked several different jobs until I settled on being a truck driver in 1987. Given the millions of miles of windshield time, several stories came to my mind. This is the second book of many more to come.